Rise of the Storm

The Desolate Empire
Book One

Christina Ochs

First Edition

Cover design by Amygdaladesign.net

Lujin Press
Nashville, Tennessee

DEDICATION

To Ben

Thank you for making my dreams come true.
I love you.

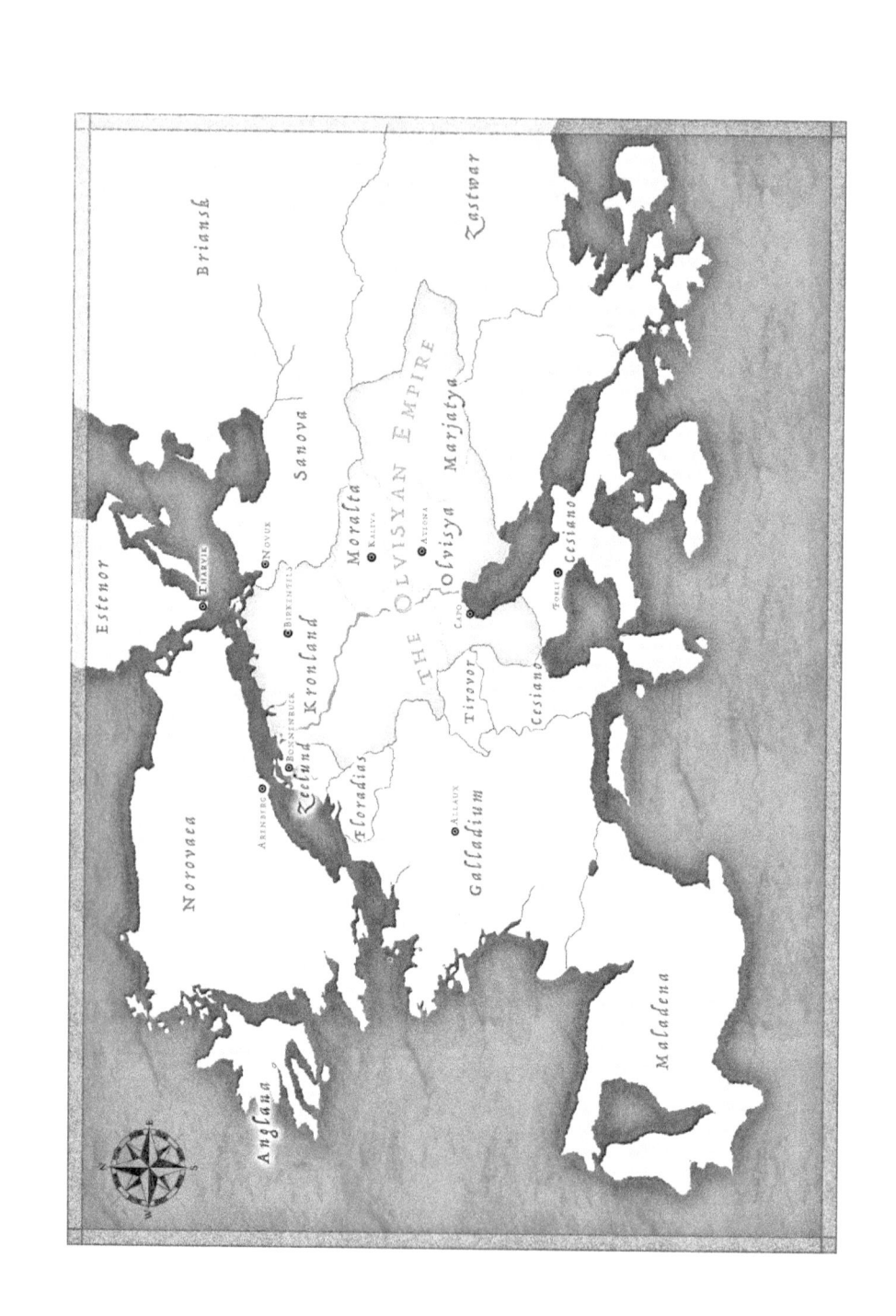

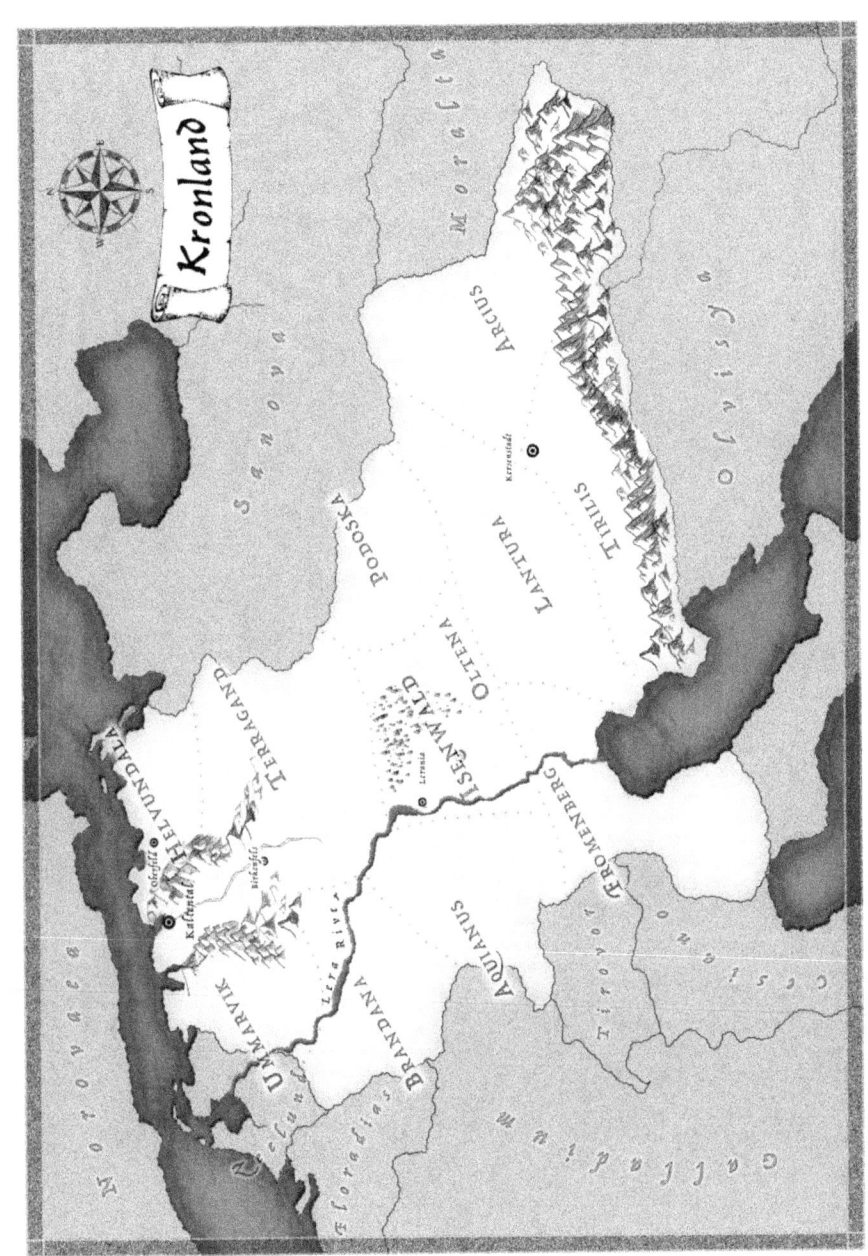

ACKNOWLEDGMENTS

Writing is for the most part, a solitary process, but I was fortunate to receive so much support on this journey.

First, I'd like to thank my husband Ben, who works hard so I can write as much as I want to, and encouraging me to follow my dream. Without him, I would never have had the courage to take on a project of this size.

I also want to thank my beta readers, Clarissa N. Goenawan, Patricia Heinrich Bailey, Cheryl Carter and Natalie Keating. Their feedback and suggestions were invaluable and I know this book is better because of their help.

I also benefited from the support of two different groups of writers. The monthly writing challenge group on Twitter (writingchallenge.org) helped keep me on track and writing on many days when I might otherwise not have. Its members have been a constant source of encouragement and inspiration. Weekend Writing Warriors (www.wewriwa.com) was instrumental in giving me the courage to put my work up for public consumption, a few sentences at a time. The talented and professional writers in that group also inspired me to finish this and get it published.

KENDRYK

Runewald, Terragand

Kendryk had come this far without being recognized; he hoped his luck would hold. Since he didn't know how long he might be in town, he'd taken his horse to the stable of an inn he'd heard of but never visited. By the time he returned to the street, it was deserted; dark cobbles shining between the tall half-timbered houses. It appeared everyone had gone to the temple square.

Kendryk was too late to find a good spot, so he stood where the street ended at the square's edge. From the top of a small rise, he could see the temple's front. He smiled at three boys jostling for position on an upturned barrel in front of a tavern, then joined a small knot of men standing on the street; local merchants from the looks of them. In his black hat and coat with its modest white collar, Kendryk thought he fit in well enough.

The men met his courteous nod with smiles and nods of their own. The priest had yet to appear, so one of them asked him, "Have you ever heard Father Landrus speak?"

Kendryk shook his head. "Have you?"

"Oh yes," the man replied. "I've been in this congregation my whole life. But of late, as you see," he nodded toward the crowded square, "Father Landrus speaks in the open so more can learn the truth. The people hunger for it."

"Rumor has it that Father Landrus has interesting things to say." Kendryk felt it was best not to mention he had only been made aware of the priest through his uncle's enraged letters.

"Interesting and true. He is making powerful enemies, but the quality of those enemies assures me that what he is saying must be made known to all."

"Rumor is that the Duke of Emberg doesn't approve." Kendryk hoped he sounded casual.

The man chuckled. "Yes, the old man has been noisy about his displeasure. Do you suppose he can silence him?"

"I think not," Kendryk said. "In the end, it's a matter for The High Temple, but the prince will have to decide if it goes that far."

"Ah yes, the prince." The man looked at Kendryk sideways. "I wonder what he'll do if it comes to it."

"Hard to say." Kendryk scratched his nose and pretended to ponder. "But I reckon he'll want to give Landrus a fair hearing before packing him off to the Imperata."

"We can only hope," the man said.

A buzz swept through the crowd as one of the temple's enormous front doors opened. A man in the plainest priest's robes came out holding a crate, which he placed on the ground. He climbed onto it and bowed his head until the crowd fell silent.

Kendryk smiled. He'd never seen a Temple official carrying his own pulpit, or indeed leaving the high altar for any reason.

Landrus raised his head. At first glance he looked rather ordinary, but even at a distance, Kendryk could see that his eyes were uncommonly intense and piercing. Unlike most priests, he wore his light hair cropped close.

"Greetings, children." His deep voice carried across the square. "It's raining, so I will be brief today."

"We're happy to hear you in the rain, Father!" someone shouted, and the crowd cheered in agreement.

"Thank you, brother." The priest smiled, then said, "Still, I will keep my words plain and to the point. Over the past weeks, I've explained the differences in worship between what is written in the Holy Scrolls and what the High Temple teaches. The Scrolls make clear that each member of the Holy Family is of equal importance and must be honored in equal measure. For centuries now the High Temple has told us that Vica, the Holy Daughter, should be lifted above the others. Perhaps you are wondering why this matters. It is in truth of the highest importance and I will tell you why.

"The Scrolls speak of a great battle that the Holy Family will fight with the forces of evil. When that time comes, our gods will lose this battle because they are weakened through our neglect. And if they lose, darkness will cover the world until the end of days. The Scrolls, however, tell us how the Holy Family may be strengthened. It is something each of us can do although we are not doing it now. Worst of all, we are not doing it because of the orders of the High Temple and the Imperata herself."

The crowd buzzed, and the men next to Kendryk muttered with it. Kendryk schooled his face into blank neutrality. This was heresy.

"These orders are evil!" The priest's voice rang out across the square. "And the truth found within the Scrolls requires us to disobey them. If Ercos the Brother and the Holy Parents continue to be weakened because of our neglect, the gods will fall in that last battle. And that battle, my children, is closer than we think."

The crowd roared its approval.

As the crowd quieted again, another clamor arose. From a street on Kendryk's right were shouts of "Make way!" along with the clatter of hooves and the clang of armor. When the mounted party appeared in the square, the close-packed crowd parted.

Kendryk's throat tightened when he saw the lead horseman. As he had guessed, it was his uncle, the Duke of Emberg, accompanied by his eldest son Balduin. The duke's progress slowed as the crowd closer to Landrus drew into a protective huddle around him.

"Stop speaking this instant!" The duke shouted, even though Landrus was silent, standing calmly on his crate. Kendryk wondered if he'd expected something like this.

The duke waved a paper. "I represent Prince Kendryk of Terragand and have come to arrest you as a rebel and a heretic. You will accompany me to Emberg Castle and await the Imperata's justice."

Kendryk couldn't believe his uncle's nerve, misrepresenting him in such a blatant fashion. He opened his mouth to protest, then realized he was without an escort of any kind. No one would recognize him from this distance and he had no way to reach his uncle or the priest.

A few angry shouts rose from the crowd and the knot around Father Landrus tightened. Kendryk's heart hammered in his chest. If he didn't intervene right now, Landrus could be on his way to the Imperata within hours. He knew his uncle wouldn't bother to consult him first though he was happy enough to use his name. And with the priest turned over to Temple authority, Kendryk's hands would be tied. He at least wanted a chance to speak with him before letting him go.

Kendryk understood his people well enough to know that if he allowed Landrus to continue teaching heresy, the situation could slip from his control in a heartbeat. And yet, something niggled at him, egging him on. He told himself he was content with his life as it was, but failed to quash a vague unease, a strong sense he had yet so much to learn and do. Perhaps the gods had sent this priest to show him what he still needed to know and light the way to some great undertaking. The part of him that always held back, that always took care to consider the consequences was defeated, at least for a moment.

He offered a silent prayer to Vica, asking for wisdom, and to give it without delay. Then he turned to the men standing near him. "Gentlemen," he said, "I need your help."

JANNA

Kaleva, Moralta

"Have you finished that lesson, Anton?" Janna asked, doing her best to pretend this was just a normal morning in the schoolroom.

Nodding, Anton handed her his slate. His equations were a mess, although he was normally good at sums. She smiled at him and put the slate aside. "Why don't we try again tomorrow?"

Janna hoped the worry didn't show on her face. The strange silence that morning had been unnerving, but now there were faint sounds of gunfire and shouting. Dimir had told her the battlefield would be leagues away; far outside the city walls. He was so convinced they'd win they never talked of what to do should the fight come to them.

"Where's Papa?" Anyezka asked.

"He's fighting in the war," Anton said, even though he'd promised Janna not to mention it in front of his little sister.

Janna sighed. "Anton, remember?"

He made a face and clapped his hand over his mouth.

"What's a war, Mama?" Anyezka asked.

"It's a big, um, meeting of soldiers," Janna said, then broke off when she heard the front door open.

"Papa!" Anton shouted, and the two children raced to the front of the house ahead of her.

Janna stopped when she saw Dimir. His face was black with soot, his clothing torn, and there was blood on his hands. Both children had also stopped short, staring up at him.

Janna swallowed. "Anton, please take your sister to the kitchen for a minute. There are two apple cakes on the table," she whispered as he tugged Anyezka down the corridor.

The children gone, she turned to Dimir. "You're back so soon. Is the battle over? Did we win?"

"Oh, it's over," he said, breathing hard, and slumping against the door. "Don't look so horrified. Most of the blood isn't mine. You and the children must go right now. We're trying to hold them off at the gates, but they are too many. They'll be inside the city within the hour."

An icy wave washed over her as her hands flew to her mouth. "Go? Go where? How? You're coming with us, aren't you?" she choked out.

"No," he said, taking her hands in his bloody ones. "You must take the kitchen wagon and the donkey. The neighbor boy will help you hitch it up. Take as much food as you can carry, and blankets."

He fumbled in a pocket and pressed a key into her hand. "There's money in the strongbox in our bedroom. Take it all. It should be enough."

"Enough for what?"

"Enough to get you to my uncle's farm. You remember my uncle and aunt, Dusek and Irina? They were at our wedding?"

"I think so," Janna murmured, though she had no idea who he meant.

"Anyway, take the cart, and go now. People are already leaving and the roads are crowded. Go as quickly as you can. You must not be here when the empress's troops break into the city."

"I can lock the door," Janna said. She tried to think, but her mind wasn't working. "We can hide until it's over."

"No you can't. I'm sorry sweetheart, but you do not understand what it's like when a city is sacked, and I'd rather you not find out."

She nodded. "All right, I'll get ready to go. But you must come with us. I don't know the way."

"It's simple. Follow the main road east for a day, then turn north at the big crossroads for Sanova. Another half-day of travel and you'll reach the town of Nitrany, and from there you ask for the Kronek farm. People will know."

"But why can't you come?"

Dimir sighed. "I helped start this. I can't run away."

"Of course you can," Janna said. "You're already gone; no one will notice if you don't come back."

"I'll notice. Besides, the more of us there are holding the gate, the more time our families have to get away. We can't win, but we can give you that. Now don't waste it. Go!" He gave her a gentle push.

"All right," The blood roared in Janna's ears and she couldn't speak until it stopped. "We'll go. And we'll wait for you at your uncle's farm."

He attempted a smile. "That's a good girl. Now come here." He pulled her into his arms and held her close for a moment, then kissed her while she fought to keep the tears back. "Tell the children goodbye for me. It's better if I just go now."

Janna nodded and forced a smile onto her face as he went out. She stood in the doorway and watched him go down the street toward the western gate. When he was out of sight, she closed the door and locked it. She looked around, saw a small chest standing in the hallway and pushed that against the door. If they ran out of time, she didn't want enemy troops strolling into the house.

Next, she went to the kitchen, trying to slow her breathing before she got there. She couldn't fall apart in front of the children.

"Where's Papa?" Anyezka asked.

"Papa had to go," Janna said. "He wants us to go on a trip and wait for him in the country."

"A trip?" Anton frowned. "What about the war?"

"He has to finish fighting in the war. He wants us to go to his aunt and uncle until it's over."

"I don't want to go to the country," Anton said. "It's boring there."

"Oh, I don't think so." Janna tried to sound brisk and cheerful all while pushing down the terror that threatened to overwhelm her. "There will be all kinds of animals. We'll be on a farm. But I'll tell you about it on the way. Can you both help me get ready?"

Anton jumped up. He always liked to help.

"Run next door and get Karel. Ask him to help you hitch the donkey to the wagon." He was out the door before she could say anything else.

"I want to help, too," Anyezka said in a small voice.

"Good," Janna said. "Do you know Papa's box up in our bedroom?"

The little girl nodded. The box was a forbidden object that the children loved to look at and guess what was inside. Sometimes Dimir would let them touch its flower carvings and bright brass latches.

"Can you bring it to me as fast as you can?"

Anyezka nodded again and ran off.

Janna turned to the larder. She emptied a few large baskets and refilled them with anything that would travel well. There was bread and cheese, sausage, and a few sacks of nuts and dried fruit. She also took a small sack of flour. If the journey ended up taking longer than a few days, she might have to learn how to bake or cook something. She hoped there would be people on the road who could help her.

Anyezka returned with the box, and when Janna opened it, she saw a few folded papers and what looked like a small fortune in coin. She would probably need the papers if she came back, so she put them in her pocket without reading them. She laid the coins out on the table and tried to smile as she said, "If I had time, I'd sew these into our clothes."

"Why?"

"My old nurse told me a story about how she ran away from Sanovan raiders when she was little, but kept tripping because the coins sewed into her skirt hem were so heavy."

"That's a funny story."

"Yes, I used to think so too." She put the copper coins in her pocket, then sent Anyezka back to her bedroom to get a purse for the rest.

Janna walked out the back door to the courtyard. Anton was telling Karel, a dull-looking boy of thirteen, that they were going on an adventure to Sanova. "Thank you for helping, Karel." She tucked a copper into his hand. "Go tell your mother you should leave the city now. Enemy soldiers will be here soon."

Karel scurried off and Anton tugged at her sleeve. "I thought Papa and the army would stop the enemy." His face was white.

"Not yet," Janna said, hoping her voice sounded strong. "He wants us to be safe, just in case. Finish tying up the donkey and then come with me. We have a lot to carry out." She sent him upstairs to pull all the blankets off the beds and put them in the cart then went to see how Anyezka was faring. She was back in the kitchen with Janna's purse.

Janna took it, filled it with the remaining coins, then tied it around her waist and under her apron.

They weren't as quick as she would have liked, but in less than an hour since Dimir had gone, the cart trundled out onto the street. They joined a flood of people and wagons streaming to the east. The shouts and explosions seemed much closer now. Janna hoped they weren't too late.

BRAEDEN

Kaleva, Moralta

The line of muskets crumpled and Braeden found himself behind the enemy. He pulled Kazmir up hard, turned around, then herded the defeated troops toward his men at arms.

"Round them up," he said. "We're going to the gates." It had taken just a few ugly casualties to shake the inexperienced troops, and once they saw the Sanova Hussars thundering down on them, wings shrieking, they broke and ran.

Franca Dura, his youngest trooper, rode up next to him. "You could hardly call that a battle." It was her first big engagement and he couldn't blame her for being disappointed.

"You could hardly call them soldiers. Townspeople and farmers with a few weeks of training. The nobility didn't bring enough to matter. What were they thinking?"

"They thought we wouldn't come." Franca looked at the bodies strewn on the field. "I wonder if they left the best to defend the gates."

"I doubt it." Braeden nodded at the men and horses disappearing into the distant woods. "Their best troops came with their nobles and ran away with them."

"Should we chase them?"

"No, our orders are to take the city. We'll get to the rest later."

By now they were behind the imperial troops gathered at Kaleva's western gate. The city walls were stout enough, but there wasn't much left of the gate. It had taken a few shots from one small gun to turn it to splinters. Men on the walls fired into the troops gathered below, but their aim was poor and most of the attackers wore helmets.

"What happens when we get in?" Franca hadn't yet been party to a sacking.

"We round up what rebels who still live," Braeden said. "Then we restore order. The foot-soldiers have a few hours to get what they can, but the general doesn't want the city destroyed. We might have to break a few heads if they get into the liquor."

The gate's last timbers separated with a crash and soldiers flooded into the city. More hussars had gathered behind Braeden, and he gave the order to go ahead. The rebels hadn't stopped fighting but now they were exposed and badly outnumbered. By the time Braeden came inside the walls it was over. Most of the defenders were dead and the few who had surrendered were wounded.

Braeden pushed through the clustered soldiers. "Make way," he bellowed. "By order of the empress, these people are to be taken prisoner." The soldiers moved aside, eager to get into the city with its promised rich shops and homes.

Braeden dismounted and walked to the small group of rebels that remained."Who is the leader here?" he asked in Moraltan, pulling off his helmet.

"It seems I am." A tall, lanky fellow with graying dark hair and red-rimmed eyes in a blackened face stepped forward. Blood streamed from a wound in his arm.

"Your name?"

"Dimir Kronek. Do you want me to surrender?"

"You don't have to." Braeden looked around and beckoned a young trooper forward. "Bind up Master Kronek's arm. I don't want him bleeding to death."

Kronek barked a laugh. "So you can kill me later?"

"Won't be me," Braeden said, "For now, we'll take you to the city jail. Your wounds will be seen to and you'll stay there until you can receive a trial."

"A trial?" Kronek winced as the soldier bandaged his arm. "Sham justice from a sham empress is no justice at all."

"You'll receive it anyway." Braeden gave Kronek a gentle shove to get him moving, then told his men to gather up the other wounded.

Kaleva had a grand city hall built of gray stone, with a roof of red slate and many fussy flourishes. Most importantly for Braeden's purpose, it had a spacious dungeon. A few pale, well-dressed, but dirty men stood blinking in the light of the corridor as they entered the building.

"Who're these fellows?" Franca asked, walking at his elbow. The clank of her armor echoed off the stone walls.

"Likely the imperial governors. The rebels captured them when they overthrew the government last month."

"They don't look hurt." Franca stared at one of them as she walked past and the man shrank back.

"No, though I wouldn't want to stand in their boots when it comes time to account for themselves before Empress Teodora. I'm sure she'll want to know why they surrendered instead of dying at their posts."

Franca snorted.

The rebels were put into cells and arrangements made for a doctor to see to the wounded.

"When's the trial?" Franca asked as they walked back to their horses.

"On the morrow, most like." Braeden swung back into the saddle. "General Ensden will call them guilty and they'll hang for treason. Counts and princes will go to Atlona to face the empress."

Franca shook her head. "I'd rather just have it over quickly."

"Me too," Braeden said. "Now let's get these looters under control. Our orders are to give them a bit of time to pick up what they can, but they're not to set fires or kill anyone."

They rode down a side street away from the town hall. A shriek came from an open window above them, followed by prolonged screaming.

"Sir, they're killing someone right now." Franca pulled out a pistol.

"I don't think so." Braeden took care not to look her in the eye. "Rape's allowed, but only for as long as the looting goes on."

Franca stared at him, her lips pressed together and her face pale under her freckles.

"It's a sacking, girl. I don't make the rules. It's how the people are punished for rebellion."

"You know that poor woman had nothing to do with the rebellion." The color rose in Franca's cheeks. "As usual, it's the men who are idiots, starting fights they can't win, and it's the women who pay."

"You're right. But it's not up to us. And you're in luck because we get to stop them now. It'll all be over soon."

Franca turned her pistol around. "Where do I start, sir?"

"With this lot."

A cluster of soldiers were coming out of a large building carrying clothing, food, jewelry and a few small pieces of furniture.

"All right fellows," Braeden shouted. "Time to head back to camp. Take what you can carry and go find your unit outside the city." He pointed his saber at a skinny young musketeer trying to hoist a plump, shrieking maid over his shoulder, "Not the girl."

The boy hesitated and paid for it with a smack from the butt of Franca's pistol, delivered with more gusto than was strictly needed.

KENDRYK

The men stared at Kendryk, surprised. The one who'd spoken with him earlier glanced toward the priest and said, "It seems you're not the only one who needs assistance."

"You must help me help Father Landrus, this moment, before my uncle further incites this crowd." Kendryk watched recognition dawn on several faces.

"But of course, Your Grace," the man standing next to him said. "Gentlemen, I'm sure you recognize Prince Kendryk, our ruler." There was a flurry of nods and awkward bows.

"I need to stop the duke before he starts breaking heads." Kendryk was relieved that the duke's party had stalled in the square for at least a moment. "Any ideas?"

"Perhaps Brande should use his voice," one man said. "It's uncommon loud."

"Excellent. Please shout my name and order the duke to stop." Kendryk looked for something to stand on. For the thousandth time he wished he were just two inches taller. Then he remembered the boys on the barrel and turned to them. "I'm afraid I need to borrow this for a moment."

The smallest of them started to protest, but one of the older boys said, "Hurry now; it's the prince himself!" And all three jumped down. Before Kendryk could think again, someone had boosted him up and suddenly he looked across a sea of hats.

The man named Brande stepped forward and bellowed, "His Grace Prince Kendryk bids the Duke of Emberg attend him at once."

The rumbling crowd quieted while the duke and his entourage swung as one in Kendryk's direction.

"By the Mother, it's Kendryk!" His cousin Balduin's stupid face was more puzzled than usual. "Say, cuz, did you come to arrest the preacher, too?"

"Don't be ridiculous," the duke said. "His Grace is clearly here on personal business."

Kendryk fought back a sudden urge to smile. It was a strange way to describe the prince of the land dressed as a merchant and standing on a barrel like an urchin at a tournament.

"You are correct, duke." Kendryk stayed up high for the moment. "Nevertheless, I must ask you in my official capacity to please stop. I don't recall issuing an arrest warrant. Oh, and Balduin, please refrain from taking the Mother's name in vain."

Balduin opened his mouth to protest, but closed it again upon a glance from the duke.

The same man who'd helped Kendryk onto the barrel handed him down. Now the entire crowd turned in his direction and parted like a miracle from the Scrolls as he walked into the square.

Kendryk had almost reached his uncle before he realized that he was not alone. Most of the men he'd been standing with were following close on his heels. He threw his shoulders back and lifted his chin a little higher.

Once he stood before the duke he put on his haughtiest expression. "The warrant, please." Kendryk made no move to reach for it, forcing the duke to dismount. It would have been a severe breach of etiquette for him to lean over his sovereign.

The duke handed him the document with the barest hint of a bow.

"This bears neither my seal nor my signature." Kendryk scarcely glanced at it before handing it back.

"I planned to get your signature later." The duke's left eyelid quivered. "I knew you would approve."

"If you had first presented me with the facts surrounding Father Landrus, I might have." Kendryk felt the need to sound as stern as possible. "As it is, I will conduct my own investigation before any further action is taken."

"If you wish. Although I'm sure this rabble-rouser is not worth your time. His guilt is beyond question. Dozens of people witnessed him accusing the Imperata of deception. How dare a common priest think he knows the truth of such matters?" The duke's voice rose to a shout. "We must stop this sort of insolence now and make an example of him."

Heat flooded Kendryk's face. Perhaps his uncle needed to be reminded once again that he hadn't been regent for over five years. He decided to save that for a more private occasion, but didn't bother hiding his impatience. "As yet, I am not convinced of his guilt. I will look into this myself and decide based on what I learn. You are free to go."

The duke slowly turned purple, but seemed to realize he couldn't lose his temper with Kendryk in public. He bit his lip hard, turned away and re-mounted his horse. Balduin snickered.

Kendryk didn't wait for his uncle's party to leave. He turned on his heel and walked toward Father Landrus, who had come down off his box, and stood waiting, a slight smile on his face.

GWYNNETH

Birkenhof Palace, Terragand

There was a soft knock on the library door as it opened.

"What is it, Edson?" Gwynneth put down her quill. She was writing a lengthy letter to a Galladian duke of her acquaintance, explaining the reasons for Terragand's dissatisfaction with Empress Teodora.

"I am very sorry to interrupt you, Your Grace," the footman said. "But it's the Duke of Emberg. He insists on seeing Count Faris at once. I told him the count was busy, but he won't be put off."

"Count Faris is always too busy to see the duke. Show him into the drawing room and I'll meet him there." The door closed again.

"You may as well copy what I have so far." Gwynneth handed the letter to her secretary, a slim bespectacled young man seated at a small desk in the corner. "I'll send the same thing to Sanova and Cesiano."

She turned to the window and watched the rain run down the glass and dull the bright green of the gardens. Then she looked at herself in a long, gilt-edged mirror, pushed a stray hair into place, smoothed her skirts, and turned to her ladies, waiting by the door. "Shall we go?"

Her heels tapped on the polished parquet of the long hallway as they made their way to the front of the palace. She glanced up at one of the portraits of Kendryk's ancestors hanging high on the walls. "I wonder if the duke is so ill-tempered because he and his son both got old Princess Lyonet's dreadful chin and ears?"

Linette giggled, but Avaron, who at thirty, fancied herself senior and more mature said, "The poor man. It's not nice to laugh. Bad enough about the looks, but that Kendryk got those and everything else must be terrible for him."

"Hush now," Gwynneth said at the drawing room door. She swept through as Avaron opened it and fixed an insincere smile on her face. "Uncle!" She put out both hands, forcing him to take them.

"Princess." He touched the tips of her fingers and bowed as briefly as protocol required.

"I'm so sorry to keep you waiting. I'm afraid you caught me quite unaware."

The duke straightened. "I only wished to speak to Count Faris for a moment."

"Oh, the count is out on business," Gwynneth said, although he was just down the corridor, toiling away in Kendryk's study. "Please, sit while I send for refreshments. Would you like a hot drink? Or maybe something stronger? Or both?" She nodded at Linette, who pulled the ornate bell rope before taking her place in the corner with Avaron.

"Nothing for me, thank you." The duke looked around, snorted, then sat on a tiny embroidered chair.

A maid bustled in.

"Tea, and those little honey cakes, if we still have them," Gwynneth ordered, then sank onto a dainty velvet settee, her skirts billowing around her. "I'm afraid Uncle, that Prince Kendryk is out as well. With the weather so dreadful though, I'm sure he'll be back soon."

"Hmph." The duke scowled at the rain streaming down the windows. "I'd prefer to wait until Count Faris returns."

"It might be hours." Gwynneth pushed back her irritation. It could be impossible to get rid of the duke. "He told us not to wait for him for dinner, but of course, you're welcome to join us." She hoped the duke understood this was a polite lie. He was often oblivious to the niceties and far too literal.

The duke grunted something negative, and then the maid returned with tea. He waved her away, but Gwynneth took a cup and a tiny cake on a delicate little plate. She stabbed at it a few times with a dainty silver fork, then leaned back.

She smiled over her teacup. "Perhaps I can help you somehow?"

"I doubt it. Your husband has been making a mess of things. I was hoping to speak with a person of sense."

Gwynneth's smile disappeared. "You forget yourself, Uncle. Prince Kendryk is the final authority on all matters concerning Terragand." She smiled again, but less broadly. "I'm afraid I'm the only one here, so you might as well tell me your problem."

"The problem is that a dangerous revolutionary is at large, and Prince Kendryk refuses to stop him."

"Goodness! That's quite a story."

"It's no story," the duke snapped. "I saw him with my own eyes. He defended this man and refused to let me do my duty."

"He must have had good reason."

"What reason could he have? This man spoke openly against the Imperata and the Temple."

"Shocking."

"It certainly is." The duke was as immune to irony as ever. "Worse, this fellow is preaching heresy at the Runewald Temple, and the people are swallowing it like the fools they are."

"I am surprised. I think we both know how Kendryk feels about heretics."

The duke nodded. "Yet here was this man, spewing his poison without shame, while Prince Kendryk refused to let me arrest him."

Gwynneth shrugged. "You may not approve, but he had the right to act as he did."

"I shall require an explanation!" A vein pulsed in his temple.

Gwynneth raised an eyebrow. "He does not need to explain himself to anyone, and especially not to you."

"The Temple is clear about how these types should be dealt with. The maxima will hear of this."

"I'm sure she will. You know as well as I do that she has no authority over Kendryk. I'm afraid you must take this up with the empress." She stood, so the duke had to stand as well. "And I suggest you take no action in that direction." She looked straight at him, unsmiling. "You may not like it, but Prince Kendryk is your sovereign lord and you must obey him. Your agreement isn't necessary."

The door opened and Edson appeared. "Edson, please show the duke out. Good day Uncle, I'll tell Count Faris you wished to speak with him."

The duke, too angry to speak, turned on his heel and stormed out. A second later, the front door slammed.

JANNA

People and wagons clogged the east-bound streets leaving Kaleva. Janna wondered if she would ever reach the gate. Her cart at last passed under the first arch when she heard several great cannon blasts followed by popping noises that might be musket fire. She heard more screaming and shouting coming from inside the city and shuddered at the thought of Dimir in the middle of that.

The noise prompted the crowd to move faster and finally Janna and her little wagon reached the outskirts of the city. That did nothing to slow the pounding of her heart. If soldiers decided to give chase, no one could stop them. She had to believe they'd be distracted by the wealth of the city and not bother with those trying to flee, or she'd be unable to hide her terror from the children.

Outside the city, the road was wider and the going somewhat faster. There were many wagons, most of them much larger and heavier-laden than Janna's. A few people rode horses but most were on foot, carrying what they could.

"Look, Mama." Anyezka tugged at her sleeve and pointed at an old woman bent double, pushing an even older man in a wheelbarrow. Janna wondered if she should stop and pick them up, but there was no room in the cart. Janna normally used it to pick up vegetables and hams in the Kaleva market; it was too small to carry three people and their belongings. It only worked now because the children were small. Besides, it was impossible to stop and help everyone who needed it. Janna forced herself to look away and distracted Anyezka by pointing out a girl her age sitting on the back of a cart that was passing them.

Once they'd been on the road for an hour, the children's excitement melted with the afternoon warmth. "Why didn't we wait for Papa?" Anyezka wondered.

Anton asked, "If Papa and his friends are winning the battle, why is everyone leaving the city?"

"The empress's soldiers were better than they expected and got all the way to the gates," Janna admitted. "Papa wanted us to be safe in case they broke through."

"But if they get in, what will they do to Papa and the other patriots?" Like his father, Anton considered himself a Moraltan patriot, not a rebel.

Janna didn't want to tell them they'd never see their father again even though she couldn't imagine how it would be otherwise. "I don't know," she confessed in answer to most of their questions.

As the sun sank beyond the low hills, the children complained of hunger, and Janna saw many people stopping by the side of the road. They'd been traveling for hours now with no sign of pursuit, so it might be safe to stop. As Janna drove the cart off the road, she noticed they were near a stream. That was doubtless why others had stopped. She and Anton struggled to unhitch the donkey, so Janna could take him to get a drink.

"Anton, can you guard the wagon?" she asked. "I'll be back in a moment."

He nodded and took up a position next to the cart, looking fierce. Janna hid her smile and took Anyezka's hand as they walked to the stream. The donkey drank for a long time and Janna felt bad. She should have stopped for water sooner. At least there was plenty of good grass around them.

Back at the cart, she saw that Anton had made a friend. He and another boy had found sticks and were playing at war.

"This is Franz," Anton said. "He's a Moraltan patriot too. We're practicing so we can fight the empress when we're bigger."

"I'm so glad." Janna forced a smile, though she hated to think of Anton going to war, ever. "Can you stop and help me hitch the donkey up again?" She wanted to be able to leave at once if there was danger.

Anton took over the job. By now he considered himself an expert in donkeys and carts and Janna saw he enjoyed explaining the details to Franz, whose family had stopped nearby.

They were on foot, pulling a barrow and carrying baskets. Franz was the oldest, and his four small sisters sprawled exhausted on the grass. Their father filled a pipe while the mother rummaged in bags. With that many children whatever food they had would go fast.

Janna walked toward them, her heart in her mouth. She was afraid of strangers, and of men in particular. So she looked at the woman. "Good evening," she said, "It seems our boys have made friends. Would you like to share supper with us? It will be cold, but there's plenty."

The woman looked as frightened as Janna, but her face became friendly soon enough. Perhaps because her efforts had yielded just one small

sausage. She waved to the man, who tucked his pipe in the corner of his mouth, sprang up, and offered to help.

Janna dug for food and handed it to the man, who'd in the meantime introduced himself as Ivor Kalina and his wife as Greta. Janna got out plenty of bread, cheese and sausage and found a knife.

Ivor looked at it with approval. "You might need that, where you're going."

"It's meant for cheese." She didn't want to imagine why she would have to use it to defend herself.

"Hmph," Ivor said. "Still, keep it close."

"I don't even know how to use it. I'd never hurt anyone."

"You can't think that way. If it comes to someone trying to hurt you or the children, what will you do? You do what you have to."

Janna nodded, feeling she'd lost her appetite, but did her best to eat anyway. "Where are you headed?" she asked Greta.

"Not too far," she said. "If the weather stays fine, we'll walk a few more leagues tomorrow and then start back."

"Back to Kaleva? Isn't it still dangerous?"

"Shouldn't be," Ivor said. "Word is General Ensden is strict with his troops and lets them loot for just a few hours. There should be order in the city by now. In a few days, we'll be back and see what they've left us. I suppose that's what most folks are doing. They're not as well-supplied as you." He nodded toward the cart. "In fact, I'd be careful if I was you. There'll be those trying to take what you have."

"Soldiers?" Janna shuddered.

"No, just regular folk, like us. Me and Greta and the little ones, we'll be all right. But others who left the city with nothing are hungry tonight. By this time tomorrow, they'll be desperate."

"I'm happy to share," Janna said.

"It's one thing to share with another family," Ivor said, "But there might be dozens, even hundreds. That's why you need your knife handy."

Janna wished she didn't still have so far to go. They couldn't have gone more than a few leagues today. She doubted they'd reach the Sanova crossroads tomorrow.

Supper over, she made the children a bed in the back of the cart. Ivor had built a fire, which was welcome in the cool spring air. Everyone else huddled around it, wrapped in blankets that Janna got out of the cart. She wondered if she'd be able to sleep since she couldn't stop worrying about Dimir or how they would safely reach the farm. So she lay quietly, watching the fire and listening to the chirping of crickets and the murmur of other voices around other fires.

KENDRYK

After Kendryk dismissed his uncle, he sensed the crowd holding its breath, waiting for him to do something. He turned his attention to the priest, who still stood in front of the temple.

"I would speak with you alone, Father."

"Of course, Your Grace." Landrus made a small bow. "If the congregation will excuse me, we can go to my quarters in the temple."

"I'd like to speak to the people first. It doesn't seem right to just run off with you." Even though the fine mist had turned into a steady drizzle, no one standing in the square had moved.

Landrus stepped aside and Kendryk climbed onto the crate, looking into hundreds of upturned faces.

"People of Runewald," he began and paused, unsure of how to continue.

From somewhere, a man shouted, "Three cheers for our prince, and for justice!" There were a few ragged cheers and more excited chatter.

Kendryk smiled and waited for quiet. "I want to explain what just happened. The Duke of Emberg brought an improper order of arrest for Father Landrus."

"Improper because he shouldn't be arrested!" someone shouted.

"You're at least partly right. The evidence brought against Father Landrus is far from complete. I will speak with him in private since I am sure this problem can be resolved between us."

Someone cheered again, and soon the rest had joined in.

"Now go home, good people." The rain was soaking his coat. "Father Landrus will be here for your next service." He hoped he could keep his word.

Landrus led the way into the temple. It was gloomy inside; the only light came from a bank of candles burning before the icons of the Holy Family at the front. They passed through a side door and along a stone corridor until they reached a small courtyard full of fruit trees in full bloom. Beside this stood a house made of light stone where the priest lived. It was dark inside by now, but Landrus lit a lamp which bathed the room in a soft glow. It smelled of beeswax and old books.

For the first time, Landrus looked uncomfortable. "Please be seated, Your Grace," he said. "I fear I have little to offer you by way of refreshment. My cook won't go to market until tomorrow, but she can bring us tea."

"Thank you," Kendryk said. "A hot drink sounds marvelous. And please don't apologize. I realize my visit is unexpected. I was hoping to hear you preach today without being recognized. If my uncle hadn't come, you wouldn't have noticed me at all."

Landrus showed Kendryk to a carved bench with a seat of soft, worn cushions, then stepped into a corridor and spoke to someone. Returning, he pulled up a plain wooden chair for himself. "I'm glad you were here or I would be on my way to the Imperata in chains. To be honest, I'm surprised you intervened. Your reputation indicates that you are devout, conservative and intolerant of criticism of the Temple."

"I try to be devout, and I'm not fond of change for its own sake. But I came today because I believe the Faith needs renewal. It's riddled with corruption and the people are apathetic."

"The state of the Faith is indeed worrisome." Landrus frowned. "I don't wish to be a reformer, but the need for change is urgent and someone must do it. I had hoped to accomplish enough within the rules of the Temple, but it seems the authorities don't approve."

He paused as a short, wide woman brought in a tea tray. She stared at Kendryk with round blue eyes, attempted a curtsy and nearly dropped the tray.

"Just give it to me, Girda." Landrus rescued the tray and placed it on a small table nearby.

Girda wrung her hands, made a small choking noise, bobbed again, then fled.

Kendryk grinned as Landrus poured the tea. "I'm sorry for frightening your cook."

Landrus smiled back and handed him a cup of fine Temple porcelain. "Oh, don't worry. This is the greatest day of her life. I'm sure she'll never tire of telling anyone who'll listen how she served the Prince of Terragand in the flesh."

"You're taking a great risk, you know." Kendryk took a careful sip of steaming tea. "I'm sure you're aware that those who publicly disagree with Temple dogma are often executed. With that in mind, I'd prefer to find a solution without involving outsiders. I suppose I must include Julia Maxima though I have an idea she would not approve of what you are doing."

"That's a kind way of putting it. I am convinced that Julia would be the first to send me to the Imperata if she knew what I was preaching. She has told me in no uncertain terms I must not reveal these things to the congregation."

"You've spoken with her about this?" This was worrisome. "If she has forbidden these teachings, I'm afraid she or I will have to arrest you soon. It seems my uncle acted within his rights though I deplore his methods. Why did you defy her?"

"At first the changes in Moralta gave me hope. When Lucian Maximus introduced the new teachings there, many of the clergy hoped they would be spread throughout the empire."

"Moralta is paying a dreadful price for its defiance. I'd rather not follow its lead." Talk of rebellion of any kind made Kendryk uneasy.

"To be fair, the Moraltan problem is more than just a religious one. Their nobility was quick to challenge Teodora's legitimacy. I take it you have no such plans."

"I do not." Though Kendryk had misgivings aplenty about Teodora Inferrara, he was unlikely to share them with anyone besides his wife.

"In that case, challenging the Temple is a separate matter and might be accomplished peacefully."

"But I don't agree that it's separate. With Teodora so interested in religious matters, I fear she will take any challenge to the Temple as a personal insult."

"She might." Landrus shrugged. "But she will have no legal basis for action."

"She doesn't need one. Teodora Inferrara does not strike me as the most rational creature. And it's safe to say that her closest adviser, Livilla Maxima, is a fanatic. I'm certain she orchestrated the brutal response to the Moraltan rebellion. I don't wish to be next."

Landrus sighed. "Your are making very reasonable arguments. The problem is this: what the Scrolls teach defies all reasonable thought and action. We stand on the edge of a precipice and if we don't act soon, we will follow our gods off it."

Kendryk sipped more tea while he gathered his thoughts. "I'm afraid I don't quite follow you." In truth, he feared he understood all too well, though he hoped he was mistaken. "I realize that you have had access to the Holy Scrolls and know things that the rest of us don't. But not everyone who's read them agrees with you. Take Acon Benet. I studied with him for a time, and he understood the Scrolls better than anyone. Yet, he mentioned none of these things."

"You studied with Benet? He was impressive. I was always sorry that I never got the chance to meet him while he lived. I have read everything he wrote, and he had a firm grasp of the truth, in his way."

"Benet was also an adept politician." Kendryk suddenly felt the loss of his teacher with a pang. "I don't believe he was content with the state of the Faith, but he was good at making small changes, and making them often, while upsetting no one."

"Unfortunately, I lack his gift of diplomacy. No, it's true," he added, as Kendryk opened his mouth to protest. "But the time for diplomacy has passed. We must change the Faith right now. There is no more time. The final battle fast approaches and if it comes upon us in our present state, I don't dare to think of the outcome."

BRAEDEN

"Think we'll have trouble here, sir?" Reno Torresia asked. He'd been with the hussars almost as long as Braeden and was his most reliable captain.

It was their fourth stop of the day, and the sun sat just above the western hills, touching the tops of the budding trees. This was a larger town than any others they'd seen so far even though it was still a distance from the main road. It even had a high wooden stockade and a gate that swung shut as the hussars approached. This one might be a bigger challenge.

"Hard to say," Braeden said. "I'd close the gate too if I saw us coming." Until now, the villages they'd seen had no fortifications. "I'll send Dura to talk to them. She speaks the best Moraltan and maybe they won't be as frightened by a girl."

"Or they'll be more frightened." Reno grinned.

"I'll tell her to act sweet. If she can."

Prompt as always, Franca appeared as soon as Braeden called for her. "Need that gate opened sir?"

"I just want to speak to whoever's in charge here. A town this size ought to have a chief. I'll guarantee his safety. I just want a word."

Franca nodded, jumped off her horse, strode to a cart carrying the lances and found one with a white banner.

"What's that for?" Reno asked.

"So they know we come in peace sir, at least for now." Franca leapt back on her horse and started for the gate, lance straight up.

"Not used to coming in peace, are you?" Braeden laughed.

"Can't say I ever have." Reno looked offended. "What's the point of all this anyway? There can't be many rebels left after Kaleva, and even if any are on the run, they'd never come this far west."

"I agree. Still, we don't give the orders."

They both looked at the gate as Franca cantered back.

"That was quick," Braeden said.

"The person you want to speak with is already there. She's not a chief exactly; more like the last chief's widow and mother of a future one."

Braeden hoped he'd be dealing with a person of sense. So far, he'd found the Moraltan commoners to be even more proud and stubborn than their princes, which made for plenty of trouble.

Braeden picked a few others to join him. He kept the entourage small since it looked like the town would cooperate. "You too, Dura," he said to Franca. "Your Moraltan is better than mine."

As they neared the gate, it opened a crack, and several people came out. One was a woman in a bright blue dress and yellow turban. Two churlish-looking young men accompanied her. Intelligent gray eyes gleamed out of her sun-lined face, and Braeden hoped she'd be less stubborn than she was smart.

Braeden jumped from his horse, and threw the reins across the saddle, knowing Kazmir would stay put. He made a small bow as he stood in front of her. In these matters, it didn't hurt to be courteous. "Braeden Terris of the Novitny Hussars, in service of her Imperial Majesty. I have a few questions and we'll leave your town in peace."

The woman's mouth quirked upward on one corner as if she didn't believe him. "You can call me Zluba. I'm in charge of affairs here in Martiz. What do you want?"

"We are looking for rebels who've defied the empress. You might have heard that several Moraltan princes sought to overthrow her. We've defeated and arrested them, but some of their supporters are still at large."

"Are you accusing us of rebellion?"

Braeden met her glare. "No, I am not. I am asking if any strangers have come here in the past few days. People you might not otherwise see, who might attract attention. I have a list of those who are still wanted."

"I'll look over your list. But I can answer your question right now. You are the first strangers we've seen in these parts in at least a week. As you know, we are not on an important road, and the only people who come here are peddlers and farmers selling in our marketplace."

It seemed she was telling the truth, but Braeden had to press a bit more. "Yes, but that also makes it an ideal hiding place for rebels."

"That may be, but that doesn't mean you'll find any here. You're welcome to search anywhere you like, and I'll tell everyone to cooperate."

"That's very kind." He sensed he wouldn't find anyone here. Outside Kaleva there were few commoners among the rebels, and it was easy to track down nobles trying to hide anywhere other than their own estates.

"Thank you for your help." He reached back for Kazmir's reins. "We'll be on our way then." He wanted to get through the last few towns in the marches and put Moralta behind him.

She seemed surprised. "You believe me then?"

"Should I not?"

"You should, but it's unusual for armed men to leave without picking a fight."

Braeden shrugged. "It's no fun fighting civilians."

She finally allowed a real smile. "Then you are an unusual man Terris, and I wish there were more like you. Before you go, would you and your men stay for a meal?"

It was nearing supper-time, so Braeden said, "That's most kind. I won't ask you to feed everyone though. They're like a swarm of locusts."

"Why don't you and your group here come to my house? We'll send sausage, cheese and ale out to the rest."

"Thank you." Braeden looked at Franca. "Send word that everyone but the pickets should set up for supper. Then come back here."

Zluba looked at Franca's retreating form. "It's unusual to see women among the hussars."

"It's somewhat uncommon. But any girl who's good with a horse and lance is welcome in my banner."

Zluba took his arm as the gate swung open before them. "I like you. Maybe I'll keep you. We could use a tame hussar or two in these parts."

KENDRYK

If anyone else had been preaching of final battles and the end of the gods, Kendryk might easily have dismissed them as a fool and crackpot. But something about Father Landrus compelled Kendryk to at least entertain those thoughts, unsettling though they might be.

"I wish I could accept what you say." Kendryk shook his head. "But I can't recall Benet or anyone else speaking of this battle. To put yourself and others at risk because you've interpreted the Holy Scrolls in such an unusual way seems reckless."

"But that's just it." Landrus put his cup down untouched. "I'm not alone in interpreting the Scrolls this way. If you read them yourself, you would see they are quite plain on this matter. The problem is that those allowed to read the Scrolls may not speak of them in any way that opposes current Temple dogma."

"Hasn't it always been so? The Imperata and her scholars are the final word on interpretation. It would be a fine state of affairs if every priest and priestess could read them without guidance."

"Would it?" Landrus looked at Kendryk intently. "Why should interpretation be confined to the elite? With the fate of our world at stake, shouldn't everyone be allowed to seek the truth?"

Kendryk tried to order his whirling thoughts. He finished his cup of tea and put it on the table next to Landrus. Then he said, "It's never occurred to me that anyone besides Temple scholars should interpret theology or that the truth might be kept from us. A public discussion is needed. I can't be the only one who wants to learn more. Although I'm concerned that it might be seen as an act of rebellion."

"That worries me as well, but it's no excuse for inaction. Once we know the truth, we are obligated by the gods to follow it. Offending those in power is no reason to hold back. In fact, it's because those in power are trying to suppress this truth that we must expose it. If the outcome of the great battle hinges upon what's being kept from us, doesn't it make you wonder why the High Temple is doing so?"

"If what you say is true, then yes." Kendryk leaned forward, fixing his gaze on the priest. "Please, Father Landrus, understand that I am not altogether opposed to what you are doing. But my considerations go beyond the spiritual. I'd be a poor ruler if I let you run amok without regard for the problems you might cause. I can't match you for knowledge of theology, but from the little I have learned, I realize that certain truths in the Scrolls remain hidden. But Benet was one of those few allowed to read them, and he never mentioned a great battle."

"The Temple has been effective at convincing those with access to the Scrolls to remain silent. You've no doubt heard of priests and priestesses being burned as heretics from time to time. Anyone brave enough to look further into those cases would find they only wished to teach what they'd learned."

"Then how is it you hold your life so cheap?"

"I don't. But what good is my life if our world is plunged into darkness? None of us will survive if the Holy Family is overcome."

"I wish I there were some proof that what you are saying is true." A knot grew in Kendryk's stomach.

"If you read the relevant passages, you would understand everything."

"I don't think you realize how much I would like that." Since Kendryk was a small boy he'd dreamed of studying the Scrolls himself someday. "Please understand Father, I sympathize with your position. But if you continue teaching these things, I will have to arrest you. Not by my choice, but because it is my duty. If my uncle had been wise enough to come when you were alone, you would be in his dungeon, and I could not help you.

"Though I could arrest you right now if you refuse to stop spreading these teachings, I won't. I need to consider what you have said, then speak with my advisers. If I must arrest you I will try to prevent you from being tried by the Imperata in Forli. The only alternative is to try you here without fanfare and send you into exile. You cannot be found innocent under the current law. I am sorry."

Landrus's burning eyes softened. "No Your Grace, please don't apologize. It's clear you wish to do the right thing. You are bound by a great many duties that the rest of us never need consider. I am sure you will think about this at length. But be sure to spend as much time in prayer. I know that the gods never abandon those who call upon them with humility. I have every faith you will find the right path."

Kendryk wished he were as certain.

.

JANNA

When Janna awoke, her first thought was panic she'd lost the cart and the children in it. She scrambled to get out of the blanket, tangling her feet in her skirt. But they were there, right behind her. Anton was struggling to get Anyezka out of the cart, but she was too heavy for him. He pulled on her harder, and they both rolled into the wet grass.

"Good morning you two." Janna smiled at them.

"Got to wee," Anyezka said.

Janna pulled her up and took her into the trees. She caught glimpses of others stirring through the branches. When she got back, the Kalinas were up and getting ready to go. "I wish I could take you along." She wished even more she could return to Kaleva with them, but she needed to be sure it was safe first.

"You've been kind enough," Ivor said. "You still have far to go, so don't wait for us. We'll do well enough."

"I hope so." Janna reached into her pocket and pulled out two silver coins. She wasn't sure how much they would buy, but prices in the city were sure to be high.

Ivor shook his head. "I can't take your money, you'll be needing it."

"Not in the country." She pressed it into his hand. "I have everything I need. Who knows what you'll find back in Kaleva. Please, I want to help."

Ivor hesitated, but Greta shot him a look, so he said, "May Ercos keep you then," and put the coins in his pocket. "If you come back to Kaleva and need a place to stay, ask for Ivor Kalina in the baker's street. We'll do what we can for you."

Janna passed around hunks of bread for everyone by way of breakfast, loaded up her children, watered the donkey one last time, and they were on their way.

It was still early, and they were among the first on the move. If they were ahead of the crowds they might make better time. At a point where they were out of sight of other wagons, Janna took out her purse and had Anton put a few of the coins in his pockets.

"Tell no one you have these. We'll try to save them for Papa."

"Franz says that Papa is dead." Anton looked ready to cry. "I told him that was a lie. Papa got away, didn't he?"

"I'm not sure," Janna admitted. "I don't know what happened. We'll just have to wait for him and find out."

"Franz says the soldiers killed every last rebel. Was Papa a rebel?"

"What's a rebel?" asked Anyezka.

"People who fight against the empress. And yes, I suppose Papa was one of them. But we can't be sure of what happened. Franz knows less than we do. Everyone is just guessing because they weren't there."

The cart bounced down the road. The children slept in the back and Janna dreamed. She didn't want to think about the farm and Dimir's relations, so she thought of returning to Kaleva instead. Perhaps they could stay at the Sanova crossroads for a few days until they knew what was happening in the city.

The road was much emptier now since it seemed most people had already turned back, it was warm under the spring sunshine, and Janna dozed off. She awoke with a start when someone shouted in her ear. It was a messenger on horseback who'd come right up behind her.

Janna recognized the young woman's livery as belonging to the Kaleva weaver's guild. "You said it's safe to go back?" Hope surged in her chest.

"It is." The woman slowed her horse to walk alongside the cart. "I'm headed to the eastern towns to let them know it's safe to trade again. The looting has stopped, and they didn't burn anything. The rebel leaders are being hanged tomorrow and that will be the end of it."

"Hanged?" Janna gasped. "Are you sure?" She glanced back at the children. To her relief, they were still asleep. She didn't want them to hear this.

"The news was everywhere by early morning. The general wasted no time giving the leaders a trial the moment he entered the city."

36

"Have they caught all the rebels?" Janna felt it was foolish to hope, but maybe there was still a chance that Dimir had escaped somehow.

The woman shrugged. "They've caught those inside the city, though they're still rounding up their families if they can find 'em, and looking for those who've fled to the countryside."

Janna's eyes widened in alarm. She couldn't go back then. Not for anything. "Who are they looking for in the countryside?" she asked, trying to keep her voice from shaking.

"Mostly lords. Everyone with a country estate they can hole up in." She regarded Janna shrewdly. "If you knew any of the rebels, and I'm not saying you did, it's best to get as far away from Kaleva as you can and lie low for a while. Just general advice, is all I'm saying."

"Thank you for the news," Janna said. "I'll keep going."

"Find a safe place soon as you can." The messenger urged her horse on. "Nice lady like you and two little ones all by yourselves; there'll be some who'll see you as easy pickings."

Janna wished people would stop saying that. Perhaps she should buy a pistol at the next opportunity.

GWYNNETH

After such an interesting meeting with the duke, Gwynneth couldn't wait for Kendryk to return. She gave orders for fires and lamps to be lit, then paced the bank of windows along the front of the palace. It was still raining and completely dark when Kendryk finally appeared. He was soaking wet and wearing the most peculiar clothes.

"What's wrong?" he asked, peeling off his wet cloak and hat. "Was my uncle here?"

"He was," Gwynneth said, stepping in to wind her arms around his neck and kiss him once there was no danger of her gown getting wet.

"Was he in a foul temper?"

"Worse than usual, although I fear I upset him even more."

"I'm sure it was no worse than what I did." He put an arm around her waist. "I'll tell you about it at supper as long as we're alone."

"We are. It's just Count Faris and us, thankfully." They often had guests, but couldn't have discussed family business in front of them. Gwynneth might have died of curiosity waiting for everyone to go to bed.

"Perfect. I was hoping he might have some good advice."

"We have a little time before supper. Do you want to say good night to the children? And what on earth are you wearing? I nearly mistook you for a counting-house clerk."

"I was hoping for that effect." He slid his arm up around her shoulder, pulling her closer and she wound her arm around his waist. "But that's all part of the story. Let's see the children."

They walked to the end of the long hall and up the wide, white marble staircase. The nursery was at the end of another long corridor in the family wing. By the time they reached it, the night nurse had dressed the little ones for bed, tucked them in and was arranging the baby in his cradle.

Maryna popped out of her little bed like a jack-in-the-box when she saw her parents. Gwynneth smiled and watched her scamper into Kendryk's arms.

Devyn was in his bed, covers pulled up to his chin. Gwynneth leaned over and kissed his forehead. "Were you a good boy today?"

Devyn nodded, his bright eyes so like Kendryk's. "I draw castle pitcher," he said.

"That's lovely sweetheart. Is that it, over there?" Gwynneth squinted at the chalk drawing on a slate that stood at the other end of the room. It looked nothing like a castle, but she supposed it was a good effort for a two-year-old.

Kendryk was tickling Maryna as he bundled her back into bed.

"Come darling, you'll get her too excited to sleep." Gwynneth smiled at Kendryk. "We must go change."

She glanced at baby Andres, whose eyes had fallen shut.

Kendryk pulled Maryna in for a hug, then tucked the covers around her.

While he went to kiss the boys, Gwynneth ruffled Maryna's hair. "Good night, love."

"Will you play with me tomorrow, Mama?"

"Maybe if there's time before supper."

Kendryk sighed after the nursery door closed behind them. "It seems we never have enough time for them."

"Do you think so? They're well looked after. They don't need us with them all the time." Gwynneth had spent little time with her parents until she was twelve. Children weren't very interesting until that age anyway.

"You're right, of course." Kendryk paused outside her dressing room door, his eyes more pensive than usual. She could tell the day's events had made an uncommon impression on him. "But I don't want to raise them the way we were. I want them to know us long before they're adults."

"Well, it doesn't do them any good now." Gwynneth laughed and kissed Kendryk on the nose. "You have the most peculiar ideas, darling. But don't worry, we won't send anyone away to study in a strange land while they're still small." She knew that had been dreadful for him and had promised him long ago she would never insist upon such an education for their children.

Kendryk smiled, then kissed her before letting her go into her dressing room. While her maid fussed over her hair, Gwynneth couldn't help but feel a small twinge of frustration. As it was, they almost never had an hour a day to be alone together. She knew he had a vision of them sitting in front of the fire, surrounded by the little ones, like something out of a Zeelund painting. But unless they were sitting for a portrait, their time had to be spent on more important things.

JANNA

After the messenger left them, Janna heard Anton sniffling quietly in the back of the cart. Perhaps he'd been awake after all. When he and Anyezka climbed back onto the seat next to Janna, she pretended not to notice the traces of tears on his cheeks.

He was soon distracted when they caught up to a larger wagon lumbering along the road in front of them. Janna might have passed them, but now there was plenty of traffic coming the other way. Besides, the occupants looked interesting. Janna had never seen people wearing such bright and ragged clothes. At the least, looking at them would entertain the children.

"Are those soldiers?" Anton asked.

"I think so." Though the men wore the bright and colorful liveries of pikemen, they didn't appear to have any weapons, and one was wounded. He had a bandage around his head and his left arm in a sling.

"Were you in the war?" Anton couldn't contain his curiosity. Janna wished she were as brave.

"Yes." The man nodded. "But it didn't go so well for our lot, so we're off to find work."

"But you're hurt," Janna protested.

"Just a few scratches." The man shrugged. "By the time we find a recruiter I'll be mended."

"What's a recruiter?" Anton asked.

"An officer who goes around finding soldiers to fight under him. Sometimes he pays them too. This last lot didn't do us much good in that direction. But Bessi here," he pinched the rump of a slatternly looking woman sitting in the straw next to him, "she did well for us on the battlefield."

"You fought?" Janna had never seen a less military-looking person.

41

Bessi shrieked with laughter. "Not that I wouldn't be good at it dear," she said. "But I do other work. Once the fighting's done, we go out onto the battlefield to see what we can find." She scratched herself in a place no decent woman ever would.

"What do you find?" Anton asked, wide-eyed.

"This and that," she waved her hands in the air. "Bits and bobs. Once a man's dead, he don't need his things no more, so that means the rest of us can make use of them."

"You steal from the dead?" Janna interrupted, horrified.

"S'not stealing when they're dead, sweetie," Bessi cackled. "Or when they will be dead. It's a mercy sometimes, to help them on their way."

"You kill wounded soldiers?" Janna wished she could get away, or at least cover the children's fascinated ears. But now the traffic coming the other way was steady. There was no escape.

Bessi shrugged. "I wouldn't call it that. It's not like they'll live anyway. And once you see the wounds ... well, when a fellow's head is half gone, or his guts are strung out around him. .."

Janna noisily cleared her throat, then said. "I'm sorry, but I'd rather the children didn't hear such things."

"Why ever not?" Bessi's protruding green eyes reminded Janna of gooseberries. "They'll see those things soon enough if they haven't by now. War is upon us, and if you don't live with it, you'll die of it. Best to toughen them up so they can fend for themselves." She looked Janna over pityingly. "I don't mean to find fault dear, but you don't look as if you'd be much use in a scrap."

"I'm sure I wouldn't." Janna felt that as a respectable woman, it wasn't a point against her. She tried to change the subject. "So is this your husband?" she asked, nodding at the soldier.

"In a way. We've been together what, close on three years now. He says he'll marry me all official once his other wife dies. Now that war's come here, maybe she'll have a stroke of bad luck." She cackled again, and oh Holy Mother, there she went scratching again. "So where's your man?" Bessi asked.

"I don't know. He was fighting with the rebels. He went back to the walls after telling me to get out of the city."

"Dead most like." Bessi shrugged. "But it's hard to say. I had a fellow once—before this one—though he wasn't as good." This earned her another slap on the bottom. "Was sure he was dead, but his body was nowhere to be found. His comrades swore up and down they watched him fall. Good five days later he wanders into camp drunk as could be. Seems he deserted before

42

the battle, found a tavern and wanted to collect his pay after. Captain gave him a whipping for that, and then I gave him another and sent him packing. You've got to watch out for the unreliable ones. Especially if you've got children." She looked pointedly at Janna.

To Janna's relief, the cart ahead of them gradually pulled away. She and the children waved; Janna politely and the children enthusiastically.

"I want to be a soldier," Anton said, his eyes glowing.

"And get a horrid wound on your head like that poor fellow?" Janna asked, and to herself, 'and a woman like Bessi?' though no doubt Anton thought her a glamorous creature.

"I wouldn't get wounded." Anton puffed out his chest. "I will be a great fighter. No one will hurt me."

"Not until you get bigger." Janna prayed that by then, all of this would be a distant memory and Anton would be happy to follow his father into trade. Though what trade it would be, she didn't know. She was sure after this there would be no business to inherit. But perhaps Anton would get his father's good sense and ability to turn one coin into five. He could do that wherever they landed.

For she didn't intend to stay in the country any longer than she had to. There was nothing wrong with it, but Janna was a proud citizen of a free city, not a peasant digging in the dirt all day and giving most of what he grew to some lazy lord. She might not go back to Kaleva, but she would find a place somewhere. She wasn't sure how yet, but her first task was to see the children safe until the trouble passed. Then she could make plans.

BRAEDEN

Braeden and his small group of hussars passed through the town's gate, now wide open. They followed Zluba along a narrow cobbled street to a large half-timbered building on the other side of the market square. She led them through a spacious front room containing rows of benches, past a smoky kitchen and entered a long room at the back of the house packed with people, most of them young. There were a few small children and one wizened old woman seated in a large chair at one of end of the table.

Zluba waved her hand. "My children, grandchildren and mother-in-law."

Several stopped and stared at the hussars but most were occupied in running back and forth from the kitchen with bowls and wooden trenchers. It was stuffy, but the smell of pork, garlic and fresh-baked bread wafted everywhere. Braeden was glad it was noisy enough that no one heard his stomach rumble.

Everyone found places on benches at a long table, and Zluba took her place at the head with Braeden at her right and the two glowering sons on her left. Braeden kept Franca at his own right in case he needed help with the language. It had been a few years since he'd spoken Moraltan with any regularity.

While they waited for food, several young people walked among the tables setting out clay pitchers of beer. Zluba poured a large mug and slid it to Braeden. "So Terris, can we hope that the trouble with the rebellion is over once you've gone?"

"I don't know." Braeden sipped the beer, which was uncommonly good. "I hope the Moraltan princes have learned their lesson."

"Pfft." Zluba took an astonishingly long drink from her mug and wiped the foam from her lip. "Those fools never learn. Every time a new bottom sits the imperial throne, they think they can do as they please, and it always ends the same way."

"Seems to," Braeden agreed. "But I suppose if you want to change things you've got to keep trying."

"Do you?" Zluba turned toward him. "What if you never gain anything but lose everything you have while trying? Tell me, Terris, what happened to the leaders of this last rebellion?"

"They were stripped of land and titles and are being taken to Atlona where they'll be executed, most like."

"It seems severe enough, but not enough to stop them. Idiots. And what of the people on their lands, and in the cities?"

"Depends on how long their leaders resisted. If the local count surrendered, we might take some food off the population but leave them alone otherwise. If he tried to fight, we'd start by burning everything around his castle. If that didn't work, we'd destroy any nearby towns and villages. And several thousand died on the battlefield outside Kaleva."

Braeden's eyes widened as someone placed a trencher piled high with steaming pork and cabbage in front of him.

"It's plain food, but no one here eats anything else, I'm afraid."

"I'm used to much worse most of the time, and almost never any better." Braeden dug in after reaching for a piece of brown crusty bread from a basket that had also materialized in front of him.

"I wonder," Zluba said. "I can't make out your exact place. You're of high military rank, but you don't seem like an aristocratic sort, begging your pardon if you are."

"Oh, I'm very much not." Braeden washed down a mouthful with some beer. "I'm common as dirt, but have a friend in a high place."

"Those can be helpful."

"More than helpful. He's why I'm alive to begin with and the only reason I made something of myself."

"A real friend, then."

Braeden nodded and kept eating.

Zluba poured him more beer. "You're not much for talking, are you? Though you speak our tongue well enough."

"I spent a bit of time with a Moraltan girl long ago." He wondered what had become of her.

"And a romantic past, which I'll bet you won't talk about either."

"Not much to talk about." Calling it romantic at all struck him as funny.

The main meal done, a young girl put a large dish of strawberries in front of them. When Braeden smiled at her, she started, blushed, and ran off. "Didn't mean to frighten your daughter."

"Granddaughter. Don't worry. She's just discovered boys and now when she sees a man, she doesn't know what to do with herself. Although I could see how you might frighten people. Have you always had that wild hair?"

Braeden bit into a strawberry. He had seen none along the roads yet. They must grow them here in a protected garden. "I tried keeping it short for a while, but it just grows out in all directions. Easier to let it be."

"Well, in your line of work, I'm sure it helps to look frightening."

"It does."

"It was clever to send the girl with the flag." Zluba smiled at Franca, whose mouth was full of strawberries.

"The flag was her idea," Braeden said. "She's a smart one."

Franca blushed, turning redder than her hair and the berries in front of her.

GWYNNETH

By the time Gwynneth had changed and reached the drawing room, Kendryk and Count Faris were deep in conversation.

"I hope you didn't start without me," she said.

"You have missed nothing, Your Grace," Count Faris said. "Prince Kendryk was telling me both of you had separate altercations with the duke. Quite an eventful day."

"Why don't we go in to supper." Gwynneth took the count's arm. "Then Kendryk can tell us about his afternoon."

Over their meal, Kendryk recounted the events in Runewald and his conversation with Father Landrus. Gwynneth felt a thrill, like a child who has just received a long-desired toy, but she said nothing.

She waited until the servants cleared the final course away and they had moved back into the drawing room for a glass of wine. Once seated, she told them of her visit from the duke. "Landrus has done nothing more than bring to light what many have wondered about for years. And don't we agree the Temple is in need of reform?"

"That may be true," Faris said, taking a sip of his wine. "But Landrus is a mere priest, and a commoner, so he won't get far."

"I agree," Gwynneth said. "Which is why Kendryk should be the one to challenge the Temple." She smiled at Kendryk's look of mild alarm.

"It's risky," Faris said, though his gray eyes gleamed. "You might anger Livilla Maxima, who has Empress Teodora's ear, and events in Moralta have shown us Teodora is violent and unpredictable. They should have kept the Inferraras from inheriting the throne long ago. They are far too unstable."

"I agree that change is needed, and I'm shocked at what I've heard from Landrus, but we must carefully consider what to do next." Kendryk's deliberate tone was all too familiar to Gwynneth. "First, I want to verify what

Landrus has said about the Holy Scrolls. Benet used to imply there were secrets, but he never even hinted at the things Landrus claims."

Gwynneth set her half-empty wineglass on an ornate table. "But if all scholars are sworn to secrecy, how will we find anyone else to take the risk of speaking?"

"Landrus implied there might be others. What we need right now is an open discussion of these matters. I must find a way to do that."

"First we must consider if it's wise to let Landrus continue preaching," Count Faris said. "I'm sure you're aware that you might arrest him and imprison him for life on your own authority. I know you don't want to do that, but it's a choice you must consider."

"Yes." Kendryk stared into his glass. "I told him it was possible. But even if I decide he's not wanted here, I don't want him harmed before we can discover if what he's saying is true. I just worry that there's no way to do so without angering the empress. After what she's done in Moralta, I don't want to upset her without an excellent reason."

"I'm sure others in Kronland are interested in what Landrus has to say," Faris said. "But until you are sure of their support, it would be unwise to go ahead."

Kendryk was silent, his face grave.

"This is an excellent opportunity if we choose to see it as one," Gwynneth said, pushing down her impatience. Kendryk never liked to put himself forward, a decidedly odd trait for a prince, though it was also part of his charm. "The Kronland rulers have been restive for years. They tolerated the old emperor's bumbling, but Teodora is another matter. She's already shown that she's not afraid to enforce her rule with a heavy hand."

"She has far more legal authority over Moralta than she does over Kronland," Faris said.

"And she must be reminded of that," Gwynneth said. "She must also be reminded that she will need our troop levies to defend her borders if the treaty with Zastwar fails. Kronland should take advantage of its strong position right now. It's a shame no leader will step forward and challenge her." She smiled at her husband. "Although I believe Kendryk could be that leader."

Kendryk shook his head. "You know I don't want that role, Gwynn. I more than have my hands full with Terragand. I just want to know if these teachings are being suppressed, and if they are, how that can be changed."

"We should still see this as a political, instead of a religious problem." She wished at least one of them would show more enthusiasm. "If a few other

Kronland rulers can be persuaded that Landrus's claims need to be investigated you might be able to pressure Teodora to allow us greater freedom."

"That's one possibility. But it would be a bold move, and I don't believe the prince has decided such boldness is justified yet," Faris said.

There was a moment of silence, then Kendryk spoke. "You've given me even more to consider. But before I act, I'll take Father Landrus's advice and spend some time in prayer. I must act as my conscience and the gods command."

Gwynneth pasted a neutral smile on her lips. Kendryk could pray as much as he wanted. As the largest and richest of the Kronland kingdoms, she felt it was time for Terragand to assert itself, and Kendryk would understand that soon enough.

JANNA

As the sun sank lower, the road emptied and Janna found there were no other travelers in sight. The fear that she'd been able to keep at bay during daylight tapped on her spine with its icy fingers.

She'd hoped to reach the crossroads and find a room at the inn but there was no sign of it yet and she didn't want to still be on the road after dark. Making camp with no friendly faces about didn't appeal to her either, but it looked like they might not have a choice.

Janna had started looking for a likely spot when she heard voices behind her. All men, from the sounds of them, and different from the diverse chatter of the refugees. She tried to stay calm and urged the donkey off the road. Perhaps they would pass without seeing her.

She just had time to pull off the road and into the grass when they appeared around a bend. They were soldiers, but even more ragged than those they'd seen earlier in the day. Anton bounced on the seat, excited.

"Oh hey, what have we here?" One of them, wearing tattered clothes and a hat with a jaunty red feather doffed the hat into a sweeping bow. "Good evening, fair lady and lovely children." He sounded drunk.

Janna stifled a shudder. "Good evening," she said trying to keep her voice calm. "We'll just stay out of your way so you can pass."

The whole group had stopped and stared at her in a way that made her very uncomfortable.

"As it turns out, we was thinkin' of stopping for the night, weren't we boys?" said the fellow with the hat.

"I was hoping to make it to the Sanova crossroads." Janna's hands shook, but she kept her voice steady enough. "Is it very far?"

"Not too far, I don't think," another man said.

"Well then, we'll be on our way." Janna picked up the reins.

Before she could make another move, a man grabbed the donkey's harness."Not so fast, ma'am." His tone was polite, though his smile was anything but. He grinned, showing a mouth full of blackened teeth. This time, Janna couldn't hold back her shudder.

"No need to be frightened," said another man, coming up alongside the wagon.

There were at least a dozen. Suddenly, she realized she'd do anything to get away. "I'm sure you're hungry." She was talking too fast and there was no keeping the quiver out of her voice. Anyezka started crying and crawled into her lap. "I'd be happy to share my food with you, although then I must be on my way."

"That's most kind," a man said. "We like kind ladies."

"If you'll just give me a moment, I'll get something out for you." She planned to give them all the food she had since she could always buy more at the crossroads, or from a farm. She pushed Anyezka into Anton's arms and jumped down. The man holding the donkey didn't move aside, and she had to brush past him to get to the back of the cart. He leered into her face, breath sour, and she looked away as she squeezed past him. He smacked her hard on the bottom, and she fell flat onto the grass.

"Now that's better," the man laughed. "No use playing high and mighty with us when we're all of us so friendly."

Janna scrambled to stand. Another man came up next to her and held her by the arm. Her knees nearly buckled.

This one was older, and perhaps not drunk. She wondered fleetingly where they'd gotten alcohol. "There's plenty of food." She willed herself not to cry and looked up at the children, sitting in the driver's seat, Anyezka still crying, and Anton's face white and frozen. She had to hold herself together so they could get away. "You're welcome to all of it."

"Oho, she gives up her food easy enough. Wonder what else she has for us?" The one who'd shoved her loomed over her, inches from her face.

Janna slid her shaking hand into her pocket for the cheese knife. She felt nothing but coins.

GWYNNETH

Unable to sit still, Gwynneth paced in front of the bank of windows, reading Arryk's letter with mounting excitement.

"Avaron," she said to her lady-in-waiting, "Please go to Prince Kendryk's study and tell him I must speak with him urgently."

He'd be busy with everyday work, but this was important, coming on the heels of the message from Helvundala. Avaron bustled out the door, and Gwynneth went back to her desk.

"Linette, where is Prince Falk's letter?" she shuffled through a stack of papers, most of them copies of letters she'd sent out in the past week.

"It's right here, Your Grace." Linette handed Gwynneth the sheet she'd been holding.

Gwynneth took it and went to the door. "Keep working on those copies, I'll be back after speaking with the prince."

Kendryk rose from his desk as she entered. "Is it bad news?" It was unusual for her to barge in on him. Most things could be discussed during their afternoon ride.

"On the contrary." She could not hold back a smile. "I've received two very interesting letters today."

"Tell me." Kendryk followed her to a window seat and settled in next to her.

Gwynneth handed him Prince Falk's letter first. "I always thought he'd be your strongest supporter."

"Well, considering he's married to Aunt Rheda, I would expect that. In fact, I'd rather hoped he'd have a troublesome cleric of his own and be the first to make a fuss."

He said it with a laugh, but Gwynneth could tell he wasn't joking. He scanned the letter, then looked up.

"What else?"

Gwynneth handed him the other one.

"Your brother is quite enthusiastic." Kendryk's tone was not. "But it's been a long time since Norovaea had to contend with the empire in any real way. And their Temple has been independent of Forli for a long time." He put the letter down on a little table. "They are both very kind to be so supportive, but I'm afraid I don't understand what's so urgent."

"Don't you see?" Gwynneth tried to keep her impatience in check. "I think this is the sign you've been waiting for. Both of these supportive letters from powerful men, arriving the same morning." She knew Kendryk had been spending hours every day in the Birkenhof chapel, praying for an answer to the Landrus problem.

Kendryk smiled. "That isn't quite what I had in mind. For one, Prince Falk has made no concrete commitment, and as for your brother, well, he's not in a position to dictate Norovaea's policy, is he?"

"Not yet," Gwynneth admitted. "Papa is being dreadfully stubborn, refusing to let Arryk do more for him since he's so ill, but he values his opinion."

"I'm sure he does. But I doubt he will promise troops or money based on Arryk's opinion. Nor would I want him to."

"What do you mean, you don't want him to? Wasn't the whole point of marrying me to get a powerful ally like Papa?"

Kendryk laughed and squeezed her knee. "The whole point of marrying you, darling, was because I loved you, and I wanted a family. I didn't care who your father was. In fact, your rather exalted position made my suit difficult, as you recall."

Gwynneth dimpled and squeezed his hand. "I was just teasing, of course. But now you have such a powerful father-in-law, you might as well make use of him." She wasn't about to give up.

"I'm sorry love, I don't agree. I'm sure your father has no interest in getting involved in our affairs. Besides, I would hate for it to look like I'm acting on behalf of a foreign power. These problems are between Kronland and the empire, and we should try to resolve them amongst ourselves."

"I suppose you're right," Gwynneth sighed. "Still, you can't deny it's very interesting that both these letters arrived at the same time."

"There's nothing magical about it," Kendryk said. "The letters from Helvundala get put on the same boat that brings the mail from Norovaea. It would've been strange if they'd arrived at different times."

"You're no help at all." Gwynneth pretended to pout. Of course, she believed in signs from the gods far less than Kendryk did. Truth be told, she thought he was wasting his time with all of that praying, but she would never say so. She'd always found Kendryk's piety amusing, but it suited his sweet and earnest demeanor in a most attractive way. Besides, he never let it detract from his reason. Not until now, at least.

"So what shall we do now?" She kept her tone light, hoping it masked her irritation.

"We wait." Kendryk's grin meant she hadn't succeeded. He knew her too well. "It's only been a week. But as yet, Julia hasn't made a move. If she doesn't, I'm inclined to let Landrus continue while we see if his teachings crop up anywhere else in Terragand, or Kronland."

"I've asked all of my Temple contacts to write to me if anyone else says something interesting. Still, I hate for you to miss the opportunity to take the leadership role in this. Just imagine if the Kronland temples could break away from Forli because of what you did. You would be a hero."

"I don't feel like a hero." Kendryk shook his head, still smiling. "In fact, I'm probably a coward for not wanting to give the empress an excuse to march all over Terragand and return to Atlona with my head."

"I'm certain she would not respond as she has in Moralta. She doesn't have the authority, and she would have to get through southern Kronland first."

"I doubt they'd resist. Princess Zelenka worships at the Inferrara shrine and thinks that Teodora is Vica in human form."

"Now you're just being ridiculous." Although Gwynneth had to admit that he was right about Princess Zelenka, who was the most dreadful pious bore. She probably would let Teodora march straight through her lands and feast her every evening.

"No more than you are." Kendryk took both her hands in his. "Listen darling, I do appreciate all of your work, and your brother's support. I just don't know enough to do anything yet."

"Will you ever?"

"I'm sure I will. In any event, I'd like to speak to Landrus again so he can explain more to me."

"I wonder why you trust him after speaking with him just once, and yet you refuse to defend him."

"I haven't said that. Now that my uncle can't act, he might not need a defender. I don't want to cause a problem that doesn't exists. Besides, I'm not asking you to trust Landrus. I'm asking you to trust me."

Naturally, when he looked at her so intently with his large, dewy eyes, she found it hard to argue with him, let alone be angry.

"Of course I trust you." She squeezed his hands in return. "I know you'll do what is best."

KENDRYK

A wave of heat, then cold and nausea rushed over Kendryk. He wasn't sick; he recognized the signs. When he'd studied in Galladium, there'd been a few other students known for being touched by the gods. If they felt sick in this way, a vision or divine message was imminent.

His ears rang and black dots danced before his eyes, growing larger and larger until all light had gone. When the ringing subsided, and the spots disappeared, he looked down from what felt like a great height, and saw his horse, and someone wearing his armor. His hair was shorter, the planes of his face sharper and older but he still looked like himself.

His view lengthened, and he perceived a vast army stretching behind him. Banners of various colors fluttered over a sea of spear-tips and shining helmets. He recognized many of the standards, houses sworn to him, and other Kronland princes he considered friends. He spotted the black and silver of Galladium and the Roussay orange. But many more were unfamiliar.

His gaze swung around like the beam of a lighthouse. Great mountains lay to the south and east, and on the plain before them stood another host, larger than his own. He recognized imperial banners and those of Sanova, Marjatya and Moralta. There was even the dreaded golden crescent moon of Zastwar, the empire's greatest enemy. His whole life and longer, the Inferrara rulers had pleaded for help against that terrifying horde with its strange and awful gods.

He thought he was flying, but he had no body and no wings; just eyes that surveyed endless distances. He observed the enemy's endless rows of human foot-soldiers with little concern, but his stomach lurched when he spotted the cavalry. There were huge lizards with long barbed snouts, lions with gigantic horned heads, black wolves with strange, human eyes, and above them, great birds of prey. Their riders were creatures who might have been human, had they been more than gray skin stretched over skeletons, with gaping black holes in place of eyes, mouths and noses.

None noticed him, but Kendryk fled back to his army with all the speed he could muster.

"You see they have brought their gods." Father Landrus stood next to his other, older self. "Where are yours?"

Kendryk swung his far-seeing eye in every direction, but there were only mountains, forests and rivers. "Why have they not come?"

Landrus's face was grave. "Long ago, I told you why, and you did not listen. Now we are at the final battle and when we are dead, those monsters will finish what's left of our gods, and the darkness will—"

His words were cut off as a great shadow moved over the land, covering first the army of the enemy, then rolling toward Kendryk. Blacker than ink, it coated everyone and everything like hot tar. Kendryk tried to run, to fly, but the shadow caught him, black tendrils clutching at him. Where Landrus had been there was black. There was no sign of Kendryk's older self.

The tendrils grabbed him, pulled him to the ground. He reached for something to hold onto but found nothing. The shadow covered everything, and Kendryk still had one eye open to see it. When he opened his mouth to scream, it filled with black. He fought the shadow with everything in him, but he was slipping into it. If there was something he should do or should have done, he couldn't remember it. A voice shrieked at him in a language he didn't understand, but it was too late. His eye closed, and his breath stopped
...

Kendryk awoke face-down on the freezing stone floor drenched in sweat. His heart pounded in his ears. It took an eternity to get his breath back, to look around and realize that he was at home, in his own chapel at Birkenhof. When he lifted his head he saw a few candles still flickering under the icon of Ercos, the Son. He needed to do something, but he did not know what.

It had never occurred to Kendryk that he might receive a message from the gods, but this dream seemed like one. He rolled onto his back and stared at the vaulted ceiling, most of it lost in shadow. Much as he dreaded revisiting the dream, he forced himself to recall it. Somewhere in there was a sign that might guide him.

When he grew stiff from the cold, he sat up. What he was to do next remained hidden from him. Since he had done nothing in the Landrus matter, he assumed that needed remedying. He just didn't know what sort of action to take.

He stood up and stretched. First, he must find Gwynneth and tell her about the dream. She might notice something he'd missed. Then, he would speak with Landrus again. He had so deeply studied the Scrolls he could surely tell Kendryk what he needed to do.

BRAEDEN

By the time Braeden and the hussars left Martiz, it was almost dark, so they went just a few leagues before making camp. They found a pleasant spot, just off the road and next to the river. The sound of the running water was soothing and Braeden felt very sleepy by the time he'd settled under a fur rug in his tent.

He didn't know how long he'd been asleep when he heard voices. Miro Blavic, a young lieutenant, stuck his head under the door flap. "Sir, something's happened."

By the time he'd scrambled into his trousers, shoved on his boots and pulled on a shirt, Braeden was wide awake. Someone had thrown more wood on the coals of the campfire and lit a few torches. By their light, Braeden recognized one of Zluba's sons, shivering and pale.

"What is it?" Braeden asked.

"It's the town." The boy's teeth chattered. "It's burning. And Mother ... oh, gods. They've killed her."

This made no sense. "Who? Who killed her?" He couldn't imagine rebels causing this kind of trouble.

The young man was shaking so hard he couldn't speak.

"Someone get him a blanket," Braeden said. "Now, why don't you sit down and tell me what happened." He led him over to a pile of saddles. "What's your name, boy?"

"J-Jonni," he stammered.

"All right, Jonni. Tell me what happened, from the beginning." Braeden turned to Miro. "I need horses saddled. We ride in two minutes."

"After dark," Jonni said, teeth clenched. "Riders with torches. We thought it was you returning, so we opened the gates."

Braeden swore under his breath. "Go on."

"They asked for the chief, so Mother came out. There was a woman at their head, a terrible-looking thing she was. Something wrong with her eyes. Oh, gods ..." He sobbed.

Whatever it was, it was serious. A servant brought Kazmir up saddled, Braeden grabbed a helmet and a saber, then jumped onto his back.

"Pickets, return to your posts," he instructed. "The rest, move out. We make for Martiz at a gallop." They were at least twenty minutes away.

In the confusion, Braeden hadn't thought about light, but the moon had risen, and the road lay straight ahead of them. Before long, the sky glowed red and the town's stockade fence stood silhouetted against flames.

Braeden pulled up, looked around for the first time and noticed at least thirty hussars at his back, with a few more galloping up behind them. His lieutenants knew their business.

He turned to give orders. "I don't know who did this. For now, we'll assume they're hostile. Draw your blades, and if you see any armed men, try to capture them. If they resist, kill them. Bring me any prisoners." And with that, he urged Kazmir forward.

As they neared Martiz, the smoke blew toward them, making it difficult to see. The fire was too far gone for them to enter the town though a few people had escaped the flames. But in every direction, shadowy shapes on horseback were running down anyone who emerged from the gate.

Braeden went straight for those attacking the townspeople. He was looking for a leader. Everyone else he could kill. And he did. By the time he reached the gate, he'd cut down two men and one woman, mounted on short ponies, wearing long lambskin coats, leather helms and carrying curved swords.

Raiders from the east, then. What they were doing out here, he couldn't say. Probably taking advantage of the instability to sack unguarded towns. But why burn a town they wished to plunder? Braeden saw no wagons, or anyone carrying loot, nor were they bearing off civilians for the Zastwar slave markets.

He reached the gate. Behind it, the town was ablaze, but what stopped him was Zluba's body hanging from a crossbeam above the gate. Without thinking, he grabbed her legs and lifted, but a moment later realized it was too late. If the hanging hadn't killed her then the gash in her throat had. Still, Braeden stood up in the stirrups and cut the rope holding her with one swipe of his saber. Her body landed on him with a thud, and he lowered her carefully to the ground. He would have to bring it to her son. He wondered if any other family members had escaped.

When he turned back to the road leading up to the gate he saw that the fight was over.

Reno galloped up and dumped a woman's unconscious body in front of Braeden. "I don't believe it," he spat. "It's Teodora's pet wolf."

"Her what?" Braeden squinted through the smoke.

"Daciana Tomescu."

"Are you sure?" The girl laying on the ground looked peaceful, black curls framing a rather sweet face.

"I'd stake my life on it. Just wait until she opens her eyes."

"Will she? She looks dead."

"It'd take more than a wallop with my hammer to kill this bitch. Some say she's part wolf and can't be killed."

JANNA

Janna's mind grasped at possibilities, but there was no way out. The knife would have been useless anyway; there was no escape, and she wasn't clever enough to talk herself out of this.

"We could use the cart," the man holding her arm said. "Couple of us ain't walking so good." He nodded toward a man with a crutch.

"Take the cart too, then." She hoped the crossroads weren't too far away.

"Hey sprouts." Another man looked up at the children. "Time to get down from there. You and your mama is walking."

Anton was still frozen. Janna nodded at him though she couldn't manage a smile to encourage him. He finally stood up and handed Anyezka to one of the men. She looked into his face and screamed. He quickly set her down. Anton jumped down on his own, grabbed his sister's hand and ran to Janna.

He pushed Anyezka against her and turned back toward the men. "You leave Mama alone." He pulled out the cheese knife. "Or I'll fight you."

Janna stifled a shriek. The knife must have fallen onto the seat. She tried to grab Anton, but he stepped toward the man who'd shoved her.

The man jumped back a step and laughed. "Oho, a little fighter. We should take him along, turn him into a soldier."

That gave Anton pause though he detected the mockery in the man's voice soon enough. "Leave us alone." In spite of her terror, Janna had to admire how brave he sounded. "Mama is giving you food even though she doesn't have to. You can't take our cart. Ani is too little to walk."

The man laughed. "Oh, she is not. When I was that size I walked all the way from Kaltental to Kronfels, and I was carrying a basket bigger than I was."

"Stop with the lies," someone else shouted. "We know your mother carried you on your back until you was twelve."

"That's not all his mother did on her back," another man said, and they all laughed.

Janna grabbed Anton by the collar and pulled him back to her. She squeezed his shoulder, grateful that he'd stood up for her, even though she was terrified of what they might do to him.

"It's all right," she whispered. "We can walk. It's not that far."

Now the men were looking at her again.

"Well, we should be on our way," Janna said, trying to sound cheerful.

"Not so fast," someone said. "We ain't seen a girl this pretty in a good while since they all run out of the capital. Think we deserve a bit of fun after the trouble we've had these last few days."

Janna's breath came faster, and the man held her arm tighter. "Not enough to go around," he said. She wondered if he was trying to help.

"We can roll the dice for her," someone piped up.

"I don't mind going last," someone else said. "Scrawny for my taste, but better than nothing."

All Janna could think was, 'Not in front of the children, oh Holy Mother, please.'

"I have money," she choked out. "Why don't you take that so you can get enough girls for all of you, somewhere else."

"Money? Why didn't you say so?" said the man squeezing her arm. "I say boys, that's a good plan. Solid coin will do us more good than a bit of skirt this skinny." Perhaps he really was trying to help.

Janna's breath came so fast now, she had to gasp for air.

"Or we could take the money and her," someone else said.

"Except we need to be on our way. Word is they're recruiting out east and we don't want to come too late. Where there's recruiters, there's soldiers. And where there's soldiers, there's always a few girls likely to be more fun than this one. Now, out with the coin missy," he shook her gently.

Jana reached shaking hands into her pockets and pulled out every coin she had. At the sight of the silver, several faces brightened. The man with the hat stepped forward and took both handfuls.

"That's all of it," Janna said. "We didn't have much saved."

"What else is in your pockets?"

She pulled out the deed to the house. "Just this."

The man grabbed it, looked it over and stuck it in his pocket. "Might be worth something." He shrugged, then turned back to Janna. "Now the purse. Hand it over before one of these fine gentlemen looks for it under your skirts."

Janna pulled the purse out from under her apron, but her hand shook so badly she dropped it on the grass, spilling coins everywhere. The last rays of the sun glinted off the gold. The man holding Janna's arm dropped it as several others dove for the coins.

"Now!" Anton shoved Anyezka at her. "Run!"

Janna scooped Anyezka up, grabbed Anton with the other hand and ran, legs still shaking.

"Stop her!" She heard shouts around her, but the only man in her path was the one with the crutch. Once Anton pulled her past him, she didn't look back.

They crashed through some bushes and into the woods. Branches whipped at Janna's face and it was so dark she couldn't see, but Anton kept pulling. They stopped when an enormous fallen tree blocked their path. Anton climbed onto it and Janna handed Anyezka up, then scrambled up and over. The three of them dropped to the ground, breathless.

"They won't see us here, even if they look," Anton whispered. "But I don't think they will, now they have all of our money."

Janna pulled a whimpering Anyezka into one arm and Anton into the other. They sat huddled against the log, listening to the surrounding woods. They listened for a long time, but heard nothing but the rustling leaves and the occasional chirp of a bird. No one came and after a while, they breathed again.

GWYNNETH

Kendryk hadn't come to bed the night before, but Gwynneth didn't mind, since she knew where he was. Having a pious husband was sometimes a bore, but at least she never had to worry that he had spent the night at a seedy inn, tumbling the local whore. The only thing that kept him from her bed was worry, worry that made him turn to prayer for hours on end. It used to be rare that he spent the night in the chapel, but since he'd spoken to Landrus, it had happened several times in a fortnight.

Kendryk seemed surprised to find her lounging in a chair in his dressing room, wearing her prettiest lace dressing gown and reading letters while a maid drew a hot bath.

"How long have you been here?" He leaned over to kiss her.

"Not long." She smiled up at him and ran her hand across his cheek. "You need to shave."

"A hot bath sounds perfect. My legs have gone completely numb." Kendryk's valet materialized and helped him undress. The poor man had likely been up all night, waiting for him to return.

"I thought you'd be frozen. That chapel is so cold. Why don't you put icons in your study, or even in the library? It would look charming and be so much more comfortable."

"Comfort isn't the point." Kendryk winced as he slid into the steaming water.

"Do the gods give you greater credit for sore knees?" She was teasing though she suspected he held at least a small amount of suffering as a virtue.

"Wouldn't that be nice?" He slid further into the water. "It wasn't all for nothing, though. At least, I don't think so." He told her about a very frightening dream, one that included the renegade priest, the banners of Zastwar, all manner of monsters, and as if those weren't frightening enough, the Empress Teodora herself.

"It sounds horrid." Gwynneth shuddered. "I shouldn't have ordered that cream sauce for the venison. You get nightmares when your food's too rich."

"This wasn't a nightmare." His eyes were clear and serious. "It was awful, yes, but didn't feel like a dream. When I woke up I felt like I was still on that field. And I remembered all of it. I never remember dreams in such detail."

"It's true you've been praying for a sign. Though it would be nice if it had come with more specific instructions." Gwynneth had heard that some particularly gifted clergy were capable of prophetic dreams, though secretly she thought they were poor deluded souls trying to cover up some level of madness.

To her relief, Kendryk laughed at that; he had looked so upset while telling her about the dream. "I thought so too. If the gods go to the trouble of giving me a vision, the least they can do is make it helpful." He lowered himself further to wet his hair.

Gwynneth knelt next to the tub. "Here, I'll wash it for you." He loved it when she rubbed the soap into his hair.

He closed his eyes and leaned back. "Mmm, that's wonderful. You should get in, too." He opened his eyes and playfully grabbed her arm.

"Stop it." She splashed him in the face with her free hand. "I had mine last night. I waited hours for you, but you never came."

"I'm sorry." He let her arm go so she could finish pouring water over his head. "I've been neglecting you. This problem with Father Landrus has been weighing on me. If I knew what to do, I'd do it so we could get back to normal."

"Something will show itself, I'm sure." She leaned over to kiss him. "I need to get dressed. I'll see you at breakfast soon."

She took extra care with her dress, choosing one of her newest gowns; pink silk embroidered with white flowers. It felt especially springlike, and she hoped it would cheer Kendryk up a bit.

He noticed it right away when she joined him for breakfast. "I like that dress." His eyes lingered on the low neckline. "Is it new?"

"It's the latest from Galladium. They're wearing it low in front like this now, even during the day. It's not too much?"

"Not for me." He grinned, then quickly kissed her neck before she sat down, taking advantage of a private moment while the footman fetched hot coffee.

Gwynneth had just started her second cup when another footman entered. "Message from Julia Maxima." He handed Kendryk a folded paper with a Temple seal.

Kendryk opened it and Gwynneth came around to read over his shoulder. "Unbelievable," she said. "Does she have the authority to do this?"

"I suppose she does as long as I don't object."

"Then you must object." She pulled up a chair beside him. "Isn't this the sign you wanted?"

"A sign of what? Now that she's arrested him I can't demand his release without a good reason."

"Why not? She has no more authority than you do in this matter. You have every right to demand it."

Kendryk shook his head. "On what basis? He's preaching heresy according to the teachings of the Temple."

"Don't you see?" She took the message and looked it over again. "We were just wondering what you could do. Now it's obvious. You must rescue Father Landrus from Julia's clutches. Otherwise he'll be on his way to Forli by nightfall."

"I suppose he might. I still don't see how I can ask her to release him."

It seemed to Gwynneth that Kendryk sometimes forgot that he ruled over all of Terragand, Julia included. "Don't ask her; demand that she do it. Insist on a public hearing so you can buy time. I've been hearing of other priests and priestesses around Kronland who are teaching strange new things. A council might be necessary to sort it all out."

"I suppose you're right. This is a fine opportunity. But I dread facing Julia." He shivered. "She's so intimidating."

"Don't be ridiculous. You stood up to her very well when we were first married and she was being awful."

"That was easy. I knew she was wrong and trying to take advantage of my youth."

"She's wrong here too. She's overstepped her bounds."

Kendryk shook his head. "Hardly. She's allowed to discipline clerics in her temples."

Gwynneth was undeterred. "But you're allowed to intervene. Tell her that the state of affairs in Terragand is delicate and the people will resent the Imperata's interference. The removal of a popular priest could lead to a revolt."

"I doubt that very much."

"So do I. But you needn't tell her that. Just make it clear that as ruler of Terragand, you must keep order and sending Landrus to Forli will cause trouble. That will be enough."

"I ought to send you." Kendryk grinned.

Though Gwynneth secretly agreed, she knew Kendryk had to do this. "She doesn't like me. She thinks I'm a heathenish Northerner. But she likes you; just don't let her intimidate you." She kissed him, pulled him from his chair, and gave him a shove toward the door.

.

BRAEDEN

"I've heard the stories." Braeden scowled. Why had no one let him know Tomescu was also operating in these parts? And why was she attacking towns he'd already cleared?

He looked around. The hussars had taken a few captives. Braeden pointed at one close by.

Miro grabbed him by the scruff of the neck and dragged him over.

"Who the hell are you?" Braeden asked in Marjatyan. Tomescu was from its far eastern reaches.

"They call me Vlad." The fellow's tone was surly for someone who'd just been captured. A short, swarthy man with bandy legs, he looked the part. "She'd better not be dead." He pointed at Tomescu's body, still sprawled on the ground. "A favorite of the empress she is. Herself will have the head of anyone who hurts her."

"Never mind about that," Braeden said. "What were you doing here? I have orders from the empress to search for rebels in these parts. I was told no one else was here."

"Word was you weren't doing a good job of it," Vlad said. "All these villages untouched, rebels on the loose all over the countryside. We took care of things for you."

Miro kicked Vlad in the shins. "Mind who you're talking to. This here's a high officer and good friend of Prince Novitny."

"Prince who? Never heard of him. Why you kicking me? It wasn't me who didn't take care of business. You should thank us for cleaning up your mess."

"There was no mess." Braeden struggled not to lose his temper. "We'd already questioned these people and searched the town. You had no authority to attack Her Highness's subjects."

"We had every authority." The woman suddenly stood toe-to-toe with him, something no one had dared since he was fourteen. Braeden wondered how she had gotten to her feet so quickly. He looked straight into her eyes, which at first appeared black, but pulsed yellow every few seconds. Reno was right. It had to be Daciana Tomescu, and Braeden was no longer sure if the stories about her were mere superstition.

"Hand over your orders." Braeden somehow kept his voice calm and dragged his gaze away from her eyes, which he regretted when she grinned, revealing sharp incisors, long as a wolf's fangs.

"I will not." Her awful eyes turned black. "I receive my orders from Teodora Inferrara herself, and she is never foolish enough to put them in writing."

"No doubt she wants to distance herself from this sort of thing."

Tomescu threw her head back and laughed, a long shrieking cackle made worse by the sight of still more pointed teeth. "If she could, she would join me," she said, after stopping for breath. "Unfortunately, her duties keep her from these more enjoyable activities."

Braeden finally lost his temper. "You call this an activity? Slaughtering people who've done no harm?" He didn't know why this made him so angry. He was used to killing, used to the blood of dead innocents. His own rule was that he fought only other soldiers, those who had a fighting chance, but there were plenty others who had no such code.

"Who's to say they haven't?" Tomescu was inches away from his face. "That bitch certainly acted like a rebel. No respect at all." Her gaze wandered to the gate where Zluba's body had been hanging. "Tried to rescue her?" she cackled. "Believe me, she was dead when I put her up there." She smacked her lips.

Braeden's stomach turned. "I'd already questioned her. There was nothing here. I doubt you found anything in your extensive search."

"Who says I didn't? Any rebels hiding in there will be dead by now."

"And so will everyone else." Braeden thought of the girl who'd brought him strawberries. He wanted to put his hands around Tomescu's throat and squeeze it as hard as he could.

Her eyes, all yellow now, were on him, as if she were daring him to try something.

Braeden wouldn't give her the satisfaction. He took a deep breath, and unpleasant as it was, looked straight at her. "Since you can't produce any written orders, I will have to arrest you for engaging in illegal activities on Her

Majesty's lands. I'm going to Atlona, so I will take you there and the empress can vouch for you, if she likes."

"You're a brave man, Braeden Terris." Tomescu laughed, her eyes turning dark again. "Teodora won't be happy that you interfered with me and killed my people. Though I suppose that shaggy head of yours will look well enough on a spike above the market gate," she shrugged.

Braeden wondered how she knew his name, but didn't want to ask her. "Lieutenant, please secure the lady," he said to Miro, hoping his tone made it clear she was no such thing. "And Captain, please see that the other prisoners are tied together and taken back to camp."

He turned his back on Tomescu though he could still feel her eyes boring into him. He beckoned to Franca. "I want you to take a few troopers and round up any surviving townspeople. We need to find a safe place for them." He hoped the nearest big temple would take them in.

He turned to look at the town once more. The fire was going down although it would be days before it was cool enough to search. It would take a miracle for anyone to survive in there anyway. He walked over to where Zluba's body lay, and picked it up. She was rather light for someone so formidable-looking. He laid her across Kazmir's rear and walked back to camp.

JANNA

Janna had never seen anything as beautiful as the farmhouse in the distance. It looked so tidy and solid, standing in the midst of plowed fields. She would have run toward it if she'd had the energy. As it was, she didn't know if she would make it at all.

Four days had passed since the robbery and it had taken the better part of the first just to reach the crossroads inn. None of them had ever walked that far, Anyezka had to be carried much of the time and Anton was too small to help with that.

"I think you should walk so they can see what a big girl you are." Janna put Anyezka down. She didn't think she could take another step holding anything, let alone a five-year-old. Anyezka cried but Janna didn't care. She took one hand and Anton took the other and they dragged her the last half-league to the house, stumbling and crying.

She didn't want to think what they must have looked like to Dimir's relatives, but she was beyond caring. The first person to spot them was Bora, Dimir's oldest cousin, working in the field.

"Janna, is that you? Gods, what's happened?"

Janna was so relieved he remembered her, she couldn't speak.

"It's all right." Bora scooped up Anyezka, crumpled into the grass by the roadside. "We'll talk inside."

He took them to the large and inviting-looking house. It stood two stories tall, with a thatched roof. As they came closer, Janna noticed that the second floor was a hayloft. Bora took them into a tiny front room in which sat Dusek and Irina, Dimir's aunt and uncle. They were both blind, deaf and ancient, and Janna couldn't tell if they recognized her, or even noticed she was there.

Bora introduced his wife Disla, who took one look at them and disappeared into another room. Janna glimpsed smoke-blackened walls through a doorway. She'd heard of chimneyless country kitchens but never thought she'd see one.

Bora's younger brother Seko appeared next. While Bora had a friendly, open face, Seko's was pinched with small close-set eyes that looked at Janna in a way that made her very uncomfortable. "I suppose you'll be wanting to stay, then?" he asked.

"Only until we can decide what to do next."

Seko snorted and left the room.

Disla soon reappeared, a loaf of bread in one arm and a baby in the other. Bora cut off a few hunks of bread and handed them out. It seemed there was to be no butter or cheese, but Janna was too hungry to care, and wolfed down the hard dry stuff without complaint. Anton made a face, but she shot him a look and he ate his crust without saying a word. Anyezka fell asleep on Janna's lap before the bread came.

Disla stood in the doorway, the baby on her hip, its head lolling at a terrible angle. She was a bony blond woman with colorless eyes and a pinched mouth. When she spoke, Janna saw that most of her teeth were missing.

"Don't know where we'll keep them," she said over Janna's head. "We're crowded enough as it is."

Janna couldn't understand how, in a house that size.

"They'll just have to bunk down on the floor in here," Bora said.

"Oh, the floor is fine." Janna wondered if the back of the house was in disrepair.

"Didn't you have time to load up a cart with necessities?" Bora asked, sitting down and lighting a pipe.

"We did." Janna explained how they'd been robbed. "Fortunately, Anton kept a few coins in his pocket and we could buy food at the crossroads. The innkeeper there was so kind and let us sleep on the pantry floor when it rained. Then she gave us food to take along." They still ran out because the walk had taken much longer than Janna expected.

No one asked about Dimir, which Janna found odd, but she told them what she knew.

"Idiot," Disla snorted. "Getting involved in things that don't concern him. It's for the lords to decide about the empress, not the likes of us."

Janna sensed that Anton wanted to protest and squeezed his knee. She'd have to talk with him about that later. It seemed Dimir's family didn't share his political beliefs.

To Janna's relief, supper came just an hour later. But there wasn't enough room around the table for everyone, and the only food was a thin soup with more of the abominable black bread.

Janna offered to help clean up afterward and Disla sent her to get water from the well behind the house. Then she learned why there was no room. A large chicken coop and pigsty covered at least half of the ground floor. Janna hoped there would be eggs for breakfast.

Sleeping arrangements were awkward. Bora and Disla slept in a tiny nook off the front room with their baby daughter, and Seko had a little room next to the kitchen that had once been a pantry. The old people slept on a mattress that stood propped against the wall during the day and on the floor at night.

Janna and the children lay on the packed dirt floor, with just two thin blankets for the three of them. She thought longingly of the piles of heavy wool blankets that had gone with the wagon. At least the weather would warm up soon. And once the people here realized Janna and the children would be no trouble, perhaps their welcome would be warmer too.

KENDRYK

Kendryk's party made good time to Heidenhof, but by the time they arrived, there was an excited buzzing at the city gates. They trotted into the courtyard of Julia Maxima's palace and found a large troop of armed men near the main entrance.

"We expected as much," Count Faris said. "But she hasn't had time to speak with the priest, much less send him anywhere. You must insist on seeing her right away."

Kendryk dismounted and handed his horse to a waiting groom. He hoped everyone else knew what to do as he caught up with the armed men at the main entrance to the palace. His heart thudded in his mouth, but he threw back his shoulders, put on his haughtiest expression and kept walking as he reached the back of the cluster.

"Make way for the Prince of Terragand," Count Faris shouted, and several of Kendryk's men put their hands on their swords.

Everyone got out of his way.

The main palace door was open, with Father Landrus just inside with his captors. Julia was no doubt awaiting them in her audience chamber. Kendryk caught the priest's eye as he passed, and Landrus's friendly nod and composed demeanor helped calm him.

The guard captain holding Landrus made an indignant noise as Kendryk walked by.

"Where is the Maxima?" Faris asked him.

"In her office," the captain said. "She did not wish for a public commotion."

Kendryk paused and looked at the man. "I'll speak with her now. Please wait here with your prisoner."

He didn't intimidate the captain, a tall, well-built fellow with an arrogant manner. "My orders are to bring the heretic to her straightaway."

"I'm sure they are. But I am here on a matter concerning this man, and will speak to her now." Kendryk turned on his heel and strode down the hallway, hoping he remembered where Julia's private study was. Years ago, he had received a dressing-down there for getting married in a temple outside the domain of the Imperata. Another state wedding should have been held in the Heidenhof Temple, but not before Julia herself consecrated his bride since the Temple hierarchy frowned upon the Norovaean version of the Faith.

Kendryk wanted to oblige, just to keep the peace, but Gwynneth refused to budge. She was as well-versed in the Faith as any Temple-educated south-erner, and wouldn't be told that she, or her father's temple were in any way inadequate. So Kendryk had stood his ground.

When they reached the study door, Count Faris knocked and Julia's pri-vate secretary, Count Greylen opened it.

"Prince Kendryk is here to see Her Holiness," Count Faris said as Kendryk walked in.

Greylen opened and closed his mouth a few times, but no sound came out. He resembled a trout gasping for air, and Kendryk pushed down the sudden urge to laugh. Before he embarrassed himself, he swept off his hat and handed it to Greylen. Then he stepped further into the room, flinging his cloak back, forcing the secretary to take it as well.

Julia had risen from behind a gigantic, ornate desk carved in ebony, and Kendryk kept his eyes fixed on hers. "I apologize for bursting in on you, Your Holiness, but it's important that I speak with you at once."

He nodded toward Greylen, who had put Kendryk's outerwear on a chair, and now stood near the door, wringing his hands. "Alone."

"Greylen," Julia said, "Go out there and see what's keeping my guard. They should have returned with Father Landrus by now."

Greylen scurried out. When the door had closed behind him, Kendryk said, "Your guards and Father Landrus are just outside. They must have ar-rived right before me."

Julia nodded. She stood still for a moment, regarding Kendryk intently. A diminutive woman of about fifty years, her formidable presence made up for her tiny stature. Kendryk had towered over her for years now, but she still excelled at making him feel like a little boy.

"Please sit." She gestured to a large padded leather armchair in front of a blazing fire. Kendryk welcomed the warmth after his cold night and cold morning ride. Julia seated herself in a similar chair opposite him on the other side of the fire.

"Let's not waste time." Her voice was crisp as an autumn morning. "I received a message from your uncle after the incident in Runewald, so I realize you might have an interest in this situation."

Kendryk leaned forward. "I came because I was hoping to arrest Landrus under my own authority and hold him until a council could be called. As long as you agree to one, of course," he added.

"A council? "Julia looked surprised. "Whatever for? Landrus does not differ from any of the other crackpots we are cursed with from time to time."

"Given the current state of affairs, it seems unwise to ship Father Landrus off to Forli, leaving his charges unanswered by the Temple." Kendryk kept his voice steady. "The people, and the rulers in Kronland are tired of the brutal responses to any objections. They feel that the Imperata overreaches herself and infringes on temporal power."

Julia nodded. "That may be. And that's why I've handled this case differently. I will not be sending Father Landrus to the Imperata in Forli."

This was good news, but Kendryk knew better than to be relieved just yet. "That seems wise. But what will you do with him instead?"

"Send him to Atlona and the empress." Julia looked pleased with herself. "I wrote to Livilla Maxima when Landrus's activities first came to my attention. She agrees that it's best to deal with this within the borders of the empire."

This was the last thing Kendryk had expected to hear, and a moment passed before he could speak again. He took a deep breath. "I agree about handling it locally, but it would be a terrible mistake to send him to Atlona. People here bear the empress and Livilla Maxima far more ill-will than they do the Imperata."

"Interesting." Julia was unperturbed. "Doesn't the Imperata represent everything that so many here find objectionable?"

"She used to." Kendryk was still unsure of how to untangle this new knot. "At least until Teodora came to power. Delivering Landrus to her sends the wrong message to the rulers of Kronland. After what's just happened in Moralta, Kronland needs assurance that Teodora will not overstep her authority here and sending Landrus to her will do the opposite."

"You may be right." Julia looked thoughtful. "I wish to deal with Landrus without delay, but not at the cost of stability here. Just between us, I don't approve of the way the empress is handling things. While she was within her rights to put down the Moraltan rebellion, she was high-handed and brutal. I am not convinced that she realizes she cannot handle Kronland in the same way. I know that Livilla tries to temper her worse impulses, but Teodora strikes me as hot-headed to the point of being unwise."

"As far as the people here are concerned," Kendryk said, "Teodora and Livilla are two heads of one beast."

Julia nodded. "I agree with you and I can see that sending Landrus to Atlona isn't the wisest choice. But in the meantime, he stands outside this door, and we must do something with him."

Kendryk wondered what would happen if he told Julia about his dream and why he wanted to protect Landrus. But that would leave the wrong impression. Bad enough he still felt immature and inadequate in her presence; lending such credence to a dream would make him seem unbalanced. No, better to appear a political realist. He hoped the gods would forgive him a little dishonesty if it served their greater purpose.

BRAEDEN

The hussars and their prisoners reached Atlona four long days later. Braeden had wasted one of them on the Olvisyan border, negotiating with a priestess reluctant to take in so many refugees. Nineteen people had escaped both the flames and the raiders though only two of them—Jonni included—belonged to Zluba's family.

Tomescu's captured raiders were dangerous and unmanageable, wounding several of his troopers in aborted escape attempts. They were adept at cutting, gnawing and picking through restraints of all kinds. Braeden had considered either killing them, or turning them loose unarmed, but sensed he might court even more trouble that way.

Tomescu herself was the worst. She alternated terror and seduction so it was impossible to have anyone guard her for any length of time. Braeden couldn't even look at her without wanting to kill her. No one but Franca was immune to both her curses and her charm. As a result, the girl was in a foul mood after four days of guard duty with a most unpleasant prisoner.

He approached the walls of Atlona feeling relieved. It was a fine day, and the surrounding mountains were visible, their peaks still covered in snow, although the meadows on their flanks were showing bright green. It was time for cows and goats to be driven up from the valleys to feed on the fresh, tender grass.

From an impressive hill fort built a thousand years ago, Atlona had grown to a capital city that filled the whole valley watered by the River Arnach. Starting as a mountain stream, the river widened as it rushed through the Arn valley before emptying into a large lake at the foot of the Galwend mountains.

From the fortress of Arnfels, the city had spread out to the river on one side and the mountains on the other. The wall abutted the stone where the river came from the mountains, curved around the city, and turned east where it met the mountains again. As the empire grew, the city expanded past the original walls. Fifty years ago, the Empress Berenika, tired of the chilly vastness of the Arnfels, had built a larger, more comfortable palace on the other side of the river. Another wall went up well beyond it. This one was low and sloping, meant to repel cannon fire, and star-shaped with sturdy bastions at every point.

At the main gate, a bored-looking soldier came out. Since it was not a market day, traffic was slow. Braeden announced himself and handed over his imperial warrant.

"Any idea where the Sanova Hussars are quartered?" he asked.

"They're camped out on the parade ground near the Arden," the guard said. "The inns are crammed full, what with Count Ensden's army still in town. He should move out any day though, now the Moraltan executions are done."

"Ah, yes. When were those?"

"Day before yesterday. The heads are still fresh. You can see 'em on top of the inner wall."

"Something for the boys to look forward to, then."

The streets around the gate were narrow and crowded. Inns and taverns stood next to brothels and shops that catered to every taste and need. There were soldiers everywhere. They spilled out of tavern doorways and swaggered along the street in clusters of three and four. All made way for the hussars coming straight down the middle, with their frightening captives. Braeden noticed that Tomescu herself attracted a lot of attention. A fair number of those who passed seemed to know her by sight or reputation.

The street opened into a large field. This was the far end of the parade ground attached to the Palais Arden, the imperial residence. From here it was possible to see across the river, over the inner wall, to the many domes and spires of old Atlona. There were many important temples here as each ruler sought to leave their mark on the city. High above it all towered the fortress of the Arnfels, snow-covered mountains looming behind it. It was an impressive sight, and a fit seat for an empire.

It would take time to find Prince Novitny's black banners in the sea of tents covering the parade ground so Braeden brought his party to a halt.

"Find the prince and tell him we've got an interesting prisoner," he told Franca. "I'll want his help handling the empress."

Before she could go, a column of twelve women in the gold armor and red velvet of the imperial guard approached. Word of Tomescu's capture had traveled faster than he had. Braeden hoped they were here to take her off his hands.

"Braeden Terris?" a tall, red-faced woman at the head of the column asked him.

When Braeden nodded, she said, "You are under arrest by order of her Imperial Highness." So Tomescu hadn't been bluffing and Teodora really did give leave to her atrocities. If Braeden survived, he'd have to speak with Prince Novitny about finding a better employer.

Before anyone could stop her, Franca broke away and galloped toward the camp. With any luck she would find the prince before it was too late.

"All right." Braeden took a deep breath. Outrageous as all this was, it was best to stay calm. "Please let my soldiers go. I'm responsible for everything that's been done, whatever it is." He still felt certain he'd done nothing but follow orders, though that was scant comfort.

"We will take all of your officers and prisoners into custody. The rest are free to go, although they must stay within the outer walls. You will turn over your arms and come with us."

Braeden dismounted and gave Kazmir's reins to another trooper who'd see him safe to the hussar's camp. The other officers followed his lead. Their horses would be hardest to replace. The guards disarmed them, then herded them toward the Arnfels. It was to be the dungeon then.

JANNA

Janna soon wondered if they were as likely to starve to death on the farm as they were on the road. She awoke well before dawn with the rest of the family, her limbs stiff and cold. Breakfast was another hunk of bread and a bitter nettle tea. Once the men went to the fields and the old people were settled in their chairs, Janna helped Disla feed the pigs and gather the eggs. The eggs went into a basket that would be taken to market.

The children went to play outside, but Janna didn't know what to do with herself. In Kaleva, depending on the day, she'd go to market, give the children their lessons, inspect the maid's work, and spend the afternoons on sewing and embroidery.

Disla clattered in the kitchen, but Janna didn't want to bother her since she made it clear she neither wanted nor needed help. There wasn't anything that needed putting away and Janna didn't see the point in trying to clean a dirt floor.

She finally asked Disla if she could help with the baby. Disla nodded at the bundle lying on the hearth and Janna picked her up. The little girl unfortunately resembled her mother, but maybe that would change when her teeth came in. "Might I take her outside?" Janna asked. Disla shrugged, and Janna took that as a yes.

The day was sunny and warm, so Janna sat in the grass with the baby, watched the children play at the edge of the woods and the men sowing the field in the distance.

That evening, everyone sat around the table after supper, a meager bit of bread with a stew containing unidentifiable meat. Dimir had always raved about the bounty of country food, but it seemed the Kroneks had fallen on hard times, or Dimir's visits were special occasions for feasting.

Janna sat at the table, her hands in her lap. In Kaleva, there was always sewing and mending to do, but she had nothing to work on here. She helped Disla with the washing up, but that took a few minutes, since each person used one earthenware bowl and a pewter spoon. The stew-pot remained on the stove, to be refilled tomorrow.

The dying light came through the small windows, but the room was dark. In the silence, the men lit pipes. "So Mistress Janna," Bora said after puffing at his for a while. "It's time you thought of marriage."

"Marriage?" Janna gasped. "I don't know yet what's become of Dimir. And even if he's dead, it's not proper for me to remarry so soon."

"Oh, he's dead all right," Seko said

"How do you know?" Janna looked around for the children, hoping they were out of earshot. They were playing in the corridor.

"I was in town today," Seko said, "buying more seed for the northern field. A messenger came through last night, right on your heels, most like. There was a big happening in Kaleva the other day. The general put all the rebel leaders on trial and then hanged 'em."

"Dimir wasn't a leader," Janna said. "Perhaps they let him go."

Seko shook his head. He almost seemed pleased. "No, I heard it straight from the messenger. He read off a list of the ones hanged and Dimir was one of them."

"Oh, Holy Mother." Janna put her face in her hands. "What will I tell the children?" She dissolved into tears. It wasn't a surprise, but as long as there was no confirmation, there'd been hope.

"Pfft, don't carry on so," Bora put in. "Our Dimir was so old; you should be happy you'll get a nice young fellow soon and have babies of your own."

Janna looked around the darkening room, horrified. The old people dozed and nodded. She couldn't tell if they were sleeping, or agreeing with Bora. She caught Seko's eye, then wished she hadn't.

Janna fought down her panic. "That may be true." She wiped her tears with her apron. "But I would be remiss in my worship of the Mother if I didn't observe the eighty days of mourning for my husband."

"Hmph." Bora snorted. "Pious sort, are you? Well, it's nothing that needs deciding tonight. But eighty days is too long for three extra mouths to live here without doing much good to man or beast."

"The last thing I wish is to be a burden." Janna had thought of nothing else all day. "I can help get food. I've learned a bit about what grows in the woods, and it's a good time of year for berries and mushrooms." Janna at least knew what certain berries looked like and when they were in season. As to mushrooms, her mother had taught her how to spot the edible ones, just in case those offered at the market had been picked in error.

"That's all very well," Disla said. She looked less unfriendly, perhaps because Janna hadn't volunteered to help in the kitchen. "But who will look after the children?"

"Anton is almost ten," Janna said. "He's used to minding his little sister, and the two of them can help you with the baby."

"All right." Disla nodded. "Just so they're not underfoot."

No one else objected, so Janna slept a little better that night knowing she could make herself useful. Then perhaps, they wouldn't be in such a hurry to marry her off.

KENDRYK

There had to be a way to keep Landrus out of the empress's clutches. Kendryk tried again. "I still think a council is a good idea. I'm willing to host it and it needn't be large. I spoke with Father Landrus at length, and he doesn't strike me as a lunatic. He has the right to defend himself and his ideas, and for others to verify if what he says can be found in the Holy Scrolls."

Julia shook her head. "I agree that Father Landrus appears quite sane, but that's what makes him so dangerous. His reasonable manner makes him popular among the common folk, and among princes as well, it seems."

Kendryk's face reddened against his will. "I haven't been taken in by him, if that's what you're implying."

"I'm not. Father Landrus has many good qualities. In fact, I promoted him to his current position, and recommended he be given further education. While I regret that now, at the time, he gave me no reason to think he would cause trouble. In fact, knowing him as I do, I'm surprised at what he has done."

"He doesn't seem like a troublemaker," Kendryk said. "That's why I'm convinced he's stumbled onto something that must be brought to light."

"He thinks he has. But consider this. He's the latest among thousands of scholars who've read the Scrolls over the years. Don't you think someone else would have reached the same conclusion by now? In your studies with Benet, did he ever say anything of the sort?"

"He did not. But Father Landrus gave me reason to believe it was because he was not allowed to. The Temple has a vested interest in suppressing any contradictions to its dogma and will go to great lengths to do so."

Julia's eyes sparked, but her voice remained soft. "Prince Kendryk, you know very well that neither you, nor Landrus, nor I can fully understand what's written in the Scrolls. That's why we take such care in choosing those who study them, and why we've studied them for so long. Interpretation is far from simple and should only be attempted by those who show a deep and vast knowledge."

"But what if an interpretation opposes existing dogma? We know certain teachings change over time. Aren't councils used to decide when a change is in order?"

"Yes, that is what they're for, but when the Imperata decides it's merited, and not just because a priest and a well-meaning ruler decide it is."

Kendryk felt put in his place. "You are right of course." He tried not to let his irritation show. "But the problem remains that sending Father Landrus to Atlona will infuriate not just his congregation, but many Kronland rulers who will see this as another overreach of imperial power."

"Very well. I can see that. What do you propose? The fact remains he must have a trial of some sort. In the past, there've been private hearings conducted by a high Temple official, but they cannot be from the cleric's own land."

Kendryk nearly sagged with relief, but reminded himself at the last moment to maintain his stiff posture. "What about Octavius Maximus?" He didn't know what his views were, but his seat was in Helvundala, where Kendryk's aunt was married to its ruler, Prince Bronson.

Julia shook her head. "The empress will never agree to a trial so far north, especially not in the lands of your kin."

"Why should the empress be given a say in this?" Kendryk asked. "The matter has not yet passed to her authority."

"No, it has not; at least not formally. But she knows of the situation and has taken a personal interest. Even though the matter is for the two of us to decide, that she now knows about it means we must work with her."

Kendryk gave her an accusing look. With the empress involved, he didn't see how this could turn out in Landrus's favor.

Julia gazed at him, unperturbed. "I know I've caused this trouble with my letter-writing. But the truth is, Landrus would be in Forli right now, or dead already on my command, if I hadn't consulted Livilla. Of course, I didn't realize how badly the political situation would deteriorate and how harshly Teodora would handle Moralta. But what's done is done. Be angry with me if you must, but let's at least find a reasonable place for a trial; something even Teodora can't oppose."

"Somewhere further south where the ruler isn't a close relative, then."

"Yes, something like that."

"That's not so easy. I'm related to everyone, including Teodora." Kendryk considered for a moment. "What about Princess Kasbirk of Isenwald?" he asked. "She's a distant cousin and I don't know her well. I understand she's quite conservative. Not like my uncle, but no one would accuse her of fostering radicalism in Isenwald."

"I like it," Julia said. "And I can't imagine what Teodora could object to in Isenwald. Flavia is maxima there, and she's close to Livilla, I hear."

"That's not so good."

"It's not good for Landrus, true. But Flavia is fair, and she won't be influenced either way. What matters now is that the rulers of Kronland see that Landrus, and more importantly—you—were treated fairly."

"I don't care how I'm treated." Kendryk's voice rose against his will. Even though matters were now going his way, he was finding it hard to calm himself.

"Ah, but the other rulers do. If your reasonable wishes are granted, and Landrus receives a fair trial at your behest, they will believe they can also deal with Teodora."

"Very well then; let's try to get a trial in Isenwald. What happens in the meantime?"

"I will write to Livilla," Julia said. "And you should write to Teodora yourself. I recommend that you flatter her, but be firm. You are well within your rights to ask this even if it's unusual. If she has any sense at all, she'll be relieved you're offering such an elegant solution. She can wash her hands of the whole affair without losing face."

"I can manage that. What will you do with Father Landrus until then?"

"I had planned to send him to Atlona tomorrow, but I can keep him in my dungeon until we hear from Teodora."

"Could I take him instead?" Kendryk asked. "Not that I don't trust you, but his congregation might be less offended." He didn't say it, but he hated the idea of never speaking with the priest again, which would be a certainty if he was imprisoned here in Heidenhof.

Julia hesitated, then nodded. "Of course. Do you have adequate facilities?"

"Birkenfels Castle stands empty. It's quite secure."

Julia stood. "Then we are in agreement. I'll turn Landrus over to you, and we'll speak again when we receive word from Atlona."

Upon a few words from Julia, the captain of the guard turned Landrus over to Kendryk's men. After marching him back out to the courtyard, Kendryk had his hands untied, and asked to borrow a horse for the prisoner.

No one spoke until they had put the gates of Heidenhof behind them.

JANNA

Janna went out first thing the next morning after talking to Anton about his new responsibility.

"But girls are boring," he complained.

"Maybe so," Janna said. "But if we aren't to stay here forever..." She dropped her voice to a whisper. "I need to find food in the woods. And I can't do that unless you help me with this."

When he nodded, she kissed his forehead, pulled on her cloak and went out.

The morning was still cool and misty, though before long, the cloak might well be too warm. Janna walked between two fields, one sprouting small shoots of barley and the other being planted with potatoes. She saw Bora and Seko walking the furrows and waited until they had their backs turned before changing her course. She didn't want Seko seeing which way she'd gone.

The woods were dark and she could see nothing but tangles of brush ahead and large limbs overhead. There were strange sounds and nothing resembling berries, mushrooms, or a trail, for that matter. She wondered if she'd made a mistake choosing this duty.

Going back to the house would be worse though, so Janna took a few deep breaths and let her eyes adjust to the gloom. At last she spotted a narrow trail used by deer, but at least it helped lead her through the undergrowth. She wondered how she'd keep from getting lost.

The trail led her in deeper, but soon, she heard running water. If she stayed by the stream she could find her way back. That made her feel better, so she went forward. As she became accustomed to the dark and many shades of green, it became easier to distinguish shapes. The giant evergreens dominated, but there must have been a dozen other kinds of trees, most of them with newly furled leaves. Janna wondered if she'd ever know their names.

The little stream burbled downhill, so Janna followed it uphill. She walked for some time, wondering if she'd ever find anything when she spotted something red on the other side of the stream. She jumped across the stones in the middle, splashing her skirts but at least not falling in.

Sure enough, there was a cluster of waist-high bushes holding tiny red berries. They had a strawberry shape, but were much smaller than any she'd ever seen. Janna picked one and took a tiny bite, hoping it wouldn't be enough to poison her. The flavor burst onto her tongue and she laughed in spite of herself. It was without doubt a strawberry. And there had to be hundreds of them.

It took a long time to pick the bushes clean, and it looked like there were just as many not yet ripe. She could come back here in a few days. It had grown warm, and she took her cloak off as the sun climbed higher. The rays cut through the dark branches and glimmered off the water. It was too bad the farm was so unpleasant, and that there wouldn't be berries here forever. She needed a plan to get away before they married her to that horrid Seko, but found herself hungry and unable to think.

She sat on a stone by the creek, dug out a heel of bread she'd saved from her breakfast, ate a handful of strawberries and had a long drink of the creek's icy water. Feeling refreshed, she moved further upstream. She didn't know where to hunt for mushrooms, although Disla had said there should be some. It was clear there weren't any in the sunshine with the strawberries, so she looked in shady spots.

At last, she spotted one—a golden cap on a bed of needles. She plucked it and inspected it carefully. It looked just like those in the market. She decided to pick a few and see if Disla could name them. Once she'd noticed one, they seemed to spring up everywhere.

Her basket was full when she realized the sun was setting. She'd wandered far from the stream and almost panicked when she couldn't hear it. After standing quietly for a moment she discerned a faint trickle in the distance. When she found it again, she made her way down to the water, hoping she'd spot the path she'd taken from the field.

She was very close when there was a tremendous crashing through the brush. She froze in terror but burst out laughing when she saw it was Anton, pushing through the bushes, thwacking at them with a stick. Probably playing at soldier again.

"There you are Mama," he said, breathless. "They sent me to fetch you for supper. Everyone was sure you were lost."

That would suit them, too, Janna thought. "Look what I found." She showed him the basket. "Have a few strawberries, but not too many." She was about to say he'd spoil his appetite, but considering the quality of their meals, he needed the extra food.

Between mouthfuls of berries, Anton told her about his day. The baby had been good, although Anyezka cried for a long time after Janna had gone. "So I told her I would bring you back."

"I'm glad you did." Janna smiled down at him. "I missed both of you."

"I missed you too." Anton took her free hand. They were on the trail now, the setting sun shining through the trees. "But I didn't cry. Those people don't like it when you cry."

"They're rather tough. But they're good to us, so you should always be kind, even when they're grumpy."

"I know. But I'll be happy when we can go home."

"Me too." Janna couldn't figure out an alternative to returning to Kaleva and finding her own family. She had nothing to start with anywhere else and staying here was unthinkable.

Anton looked up at her and pulled her to a stop at the edge of the woods. "Uncle Seko says you'll marry him and we'll live here forever and ever."

"Oh, he's just joking." Janna attempted a dismissive laugh. "I would be a terrible farmer's wife."

"But you found mushrooms." Anton peered into her basket. "And he doesn't care that you don't know about farming. He cares that you're pretty. But you're still married to Papa, aren't you?" He looked up at her anxiously.

"Yes, I am." It seemed the children hadn't overheard last night's conversation. "So of course, Uncle Seko is just joking."

Anton looked relieved.

Back in the smoky kitchen, Disla looked almost pleased over the mushrooms—which she confirmed were edible—and the strawberries.

"We won't eat them ourselves," she said. "But if you can pick more tomorrow, we'll take them to market next week. We need the coin more right now. After the bad winter, we ate all the seed potatoes and had to spend our last bits on more."

That might explain the quality of the food. "How dreadful," Janna said. "Farming must be very hard."

Disla shrugged and pushed a damp strand of hair out of her face. "Some years are, and other years are good. It's always that way." That sounded a lot like trade, too. In the end, it was all work, though Janna had to admit that trade was less dirty. After taking the strawberries and mushrooms to the cooling shed, she stood by the well, trying to scrub the grime off her fingers.

She saw Seko come from his room, so she finished in a hurry and returned to the house the other way, so she didn't run into him. She would have to get a lot of practice at that.

BRAEDEN

Not much time went by before Braeden lost track of it altogether. Once inside the fortress, he didn't see light again, unless you counted the faintest glow of a lamp or maybe a candle that appeared once daily, when a guard shoved a wooden trencher filled with something inedible through a small slot.

There was nothing else. No sound, no light. The first time he woke up in the cell, Braeden wasn't even sure if he was alive. He had to recall the events that brought him there, and once he felt outrage rising in his chest, radiating out the tips of his fingers and the top of his head, he felt like himself again.

He wanted to kill someone, but no one came. Braeden considered hitting the wall, but reckoned the wall might come out ahead in such a contest. He hated sitting around like this, doing nothing. He didn't know if he could stand it. But it wasn't like he had a choice.

So he waited. He passed the time by pacing the cell. He knew little about it except that it took seven steps to walk from one end to the other. There was a pile of ancient, evil-smelling straw in one corner, meant to be his bed, and a small trench cut into the floor, which served as a privy. Far below, he heard the faint gurgle of water, but it was impossible to tell how near or far, and the opening wasn't large enough for a rat to slip through, let alone a man of Braeden's size. Though he might shrink fast, the way they were feeding him.

He slept a great deal. The straw was no worse than a saddle or fields he'd spent many uncomfortable nights in, and the stone cell was oddly warm and humid. Rats and fleas seemed to find it hospitable and before long, Braeden staved off boredom by alternately scratching himself and crushing the fleas as he caught them.

He'd settled into a dull apathy, so when a visitor came, he was unprepared. Even the faint light of the guard's lamp was too bright, and Braeden wondered if he was being taken to his execution. He hoped Teodora would be there; he'd die bravely just to spite her. He would have liked to think of something clever and cutting to say to her at the end, but doubted he'd come up with anything good.

Squinting and stumbling, he followed the guard down a dark corridor and into a very bright room. He realized the room was so bright because it had a window, and sunlight beamed in. Braeden had wondered if he'd ever see it again and grinned.

Braeden half fell into a chair, helped by a shove from the guard. When his eyes came into focus, he saw Prince Novitny sitting at a table across from him.

"Thank the gods you're alive." Novitny's booming voice was muted and more serious than Braeden had ever heard it before. "I worried that crazy bitch would have you killed before I could do anything about it."

"Who? Tomescu?"

Novitny chuckled. "No, Teodora. Those two make a right fine pair, don't they?"

"I still can't believe it. The empress herself."

"That's because you don't know her. But that's beside the point right now. I insisted on seeing you because I don't trust her."

"You've been talking to Teodora?" Braeden's brain was working much too slowly.

"Shouting, more like. But we're making progress though it's been an unpleasant few days."

"Please tell me the others are all right." Braeden had done his best to not think about what might have befallen his officers.

"Released this last hour, all of them."

"Thank the gods."

"Thank Dura. She got to me fast, and I barged in on the empress before she killed the lot of you, which it seems was her plan. She freed that Tomescu creature right away of course and sent her back to Moralta before the next day ended."

Braeden made an indignant noise.

"Indeed." Novitny looked grim. "But I wasn't letting her have my troopers. I did a lot of shouting and stomping around in her throne room in front of everyone. Her Highness couldn't get a word in edgewise, which I suspect was a new experience for her. She finally agreed to let all the officers go but you. She also agreed to a public trial for you. I didn't much like it, but it was enough to keep me from leaving and joining Andor Korma, that troublemaker in Marjatya."

"That was what you threatened?"

Novitny nodded. "And I would have done it, too. You had the right of it. Tomescu operates illegally by every rule of law. That she's a close friend of the empress changes nothing. There's no way you'd be found guilty."

"I hope not. Though I'm sure she can find a way."

"She'll try. But I won't allow it. Call in some favors if I have to. She knows well that my father and Queen Ottilya were childhood friends. The last thing she needs right now is Sanova causing her trouble, along with everyone else."

"But isn't Teodora's brother married to Queen Ottilya?"

"Oh yes, but that's not a point in the empress's favor. It's said he hates her with a passion and prays to Ercos for her painful death daily."

"No fond childhood memories, then."

"Seems not. Though if she was half the bully then that she is now, it's not surprising. No, her brother would welcome any excuse to start a fight, and she knows that."

"You seem to know what you're doing, and I'm grateful. .." Braeden began.

"Oh stop it." The prince snorted. "I won't have you getting all weepy like some old woman now. The bad news is you're stuck in here a bit longer though I plan to hold her feet to the fire and make this trial happen soon. Be ready."

KENDRYK

Once they'd left the city behind them, Count Faris smiled at Kendryk. "Impressive, Your Grace. Although I take it she did not agree to a council."

"She did not." Kendryk grinned back, relieved all the same. He explained the next steps, and Faris nodded.

"The letter to the empress will have to be carefully written," he said. "She is notoriously proud and prickly."

"I was hoping you and Gwynneth could help," Kendryk said. "Between the three of us, we should be able to find the best way to address her."

"I have no doubt we can. Shall I have a dungeon cell made ready at Birkenfels?" Faris asked.

Kendryk frowned. "I don't want him in the dungeon. There's no one else at the castle, and it's still easy to guard. The cells are so cold and damp that prisoners often die of a pleurisy sooner or later, and I want him alive at the trial."

Kendryk motioned the guards on either side of Landrus to bring him forward, then waved them off, so they might speak alone. Faris dropped back discreetly.

Kendryk smiled at Landrus. "I told you I might have to arrest you though it's happened sooner than I had hoped."

"You are a man of your word." Landrus returned his smile. "Although I confess to doubting your ability to remove me from Julia's clutches."

"I doubted it too," Kendryk said, then told him about the proposed trial in Isenwald, provided everyone agreed.

The priest's smile faded. "Flavia Maxima. She and I are not on the best terms."

"I tried for Octavius, but Julia felt that the empress would never agree. It seems you've already created quite a stir in Atlona."

"Good. I doubt this will end well for me, in spite of your kind efforts, but the more people who know what is happening and why, the better."

"I agree." Kendryk couldn't see a favorable outcome for Landrus either, but he didn't want to contemplate that right now. "The Kronland rulers are paying close attention to the way Teodora handles religious disagreements. Everyone expects to be offended. You've chosen an interesting time to cause trouble."

"That's because it's the right time, Your Grace," Landrus said. "I was certain of it when we first spoke, but now I'm even more convinced that everything is happening exactly the way the gods have ordained it. There is no doubt Ercos has chosen you to set all of this in motion."

"Now you sound like a lunatic." Kendryk gave a short laugh while remembering his dream with growing dread.

"It does; I realize that. I hope that this change in my situation will allow us more time to talk, so I can explain."

They were now within sight of Birkenfels. The morning mists had long ago burned off, and its pointed turrets stood in sharp relief against the bright blue sky.

"Pretty castle," Landrus said. "It looks like some cells might have a view."

"A few do, but I'm not putting you in a cell."

"I need no special treatment, although you are kind to offer."

"It's not all that special. The dungeons aren't fit for any human who's expected to survive. In fact, the castle itself isn't all that comfortable. There was a good reason my grandfather built Birkenhof as soon as he could raise the funds."

"You don't worry about me running off?" Landrus looked amused.

"I don't." Kendryk couldn't say why he trusted this man though he liked to think he was a good judge of character. "I'm sure you can outsmart these guards if you want to. But you'd be far worse off if you escaped and tried to elude all the Temple and imperial troops sent after you."

"I realize that," Landrus said, as they crossed the drawbridge and continued up a cobbled road that wound between narrow buildings clinging to the hillside at the castle's base, their horse's hoofbeats echoing off the stone. "But more than that, I would never take advantage of your kindness. You've gone to great trouble on my behalf, and I would never repay that with betrayal."

They passed below another raised gate and into the castle courtyard where everyone dismounted.

Count Faris caught Kendryk's attention. "I'll order the steward's rooms prepared for Father Landrus. They were in use more recently than any others, and most of the furnishings ought to be in good repair."

Kendryk asked Landrus, "Is there anything we can get for you from Runewald? Your clothing, and perhaps some books?"

"Yes, and one particular item, although it will need a trustworthy person to follow specific instructions."

Kendryk was nearly bursting with curiosity, wondering what Landrus needed that required such care, but knew he had to contain himself until they could speak privately.

Faris waved over a young soldier. "This is Merton. He's reliable and can read a list if you wish to send one."

"Excellent," Kendryk said. "I'll take Father Landrus to the steward's office so he can make a list, and Merton can go to Runewald later. Best wait until cover of darkness, in case anyone is observing the priest's quarters."

JANNA

Anyezka had done well watching the baby, so for the next few days, Janna took Anton with her so they could pick more. No one minded. It was more fun with him and the time flew by as he chattered about horses and becoming a soldier.

One evening, Janna said, "We should start back. I don't want to be in the woods after dark." By now, she was braver about leaving the stream, so they were much farther north of the farm. Here, the road ran parallel to the edge of the woods, so they headed straight for it.

"What's that?" Anton asked.

"What?"

"That noise?"

Janna stopped. There were hoofbeats. A lot of them. Who in the world would come to the farm in such numbers? "Be quiet," she whispered.

She couldn't see the road, but could hear the horses as they passed. Weapons and armor clanked while rough voices shouted in a strange language.

"Bandits," Anton breathed, and started for the road.

Janna caught him by the arm and yanked him back hard. "No, Anton. No. There are too many."

"But Anyezka," he began.

"They'll just steal a few things and leave." Janna tried to keep her voice from shaking. "I'm sure they wouldn't hurt a little girl, so let's sit here until they're gone."

But waiting was almost unbearable, and once the horsemen had passed they crept through the bushes until they glimpsed the road.

"Mama." Anton tugged on her skirt. "Mama, the farm is on fire."

He scrambled to stand, but she grabbed his arm and didn't let go, especially once the screaming started. It went on forever, and at last Anton stopped struggling and rolled into her arms, trembling and wetting the front of her dress with tears.

Janna felt frozen with fear, and they lay there a long time until the horsemen came back, whooping and laughing. Janna sat up and pulled Anton back from the edge of the road though they still had a view through a curtain of bushes. There was more foreign chatter, and someone came into view.

Anton gasped, and Janna clapped a hand over his mouth. This time, he didn't struggle. At the head of the group rode a woman. Her black curls fell in a tangle over a sheepskin coat. While the other men and women laughed she looked around, scanning the edges of the forest. Janna shrank back.

The woman sniffed the air, then turned and asked a question. A man shook his head. She looked in Janna's direction again, and Janna was certain her eyes were yellow, like an animal's. She sniffed again, shrugged and urged her horse on. Neither Janna nor Anton breathed until they were well down the road.

"What was that?" Anton was still shaking.

"Raiders, I suppose."

"No, that woman," Anton said. "She had awful eyes."

"Yes, she did." Janna took a few deep breaths. "Anton, stay here while I go to the farm. I'll come get you after I've made sure it's safe."

"No," he said, shaking his head wildly. "You can't leave me alone. Not like Papa did. He left and didn't come back. If you go, I'm coming with you."

"Anton ..." Janna didn't know what to say. She didn't want to go there alone, but more than that, she didn't want him to see whatever it was they might find.

He wiped his tears and looked her in the eye. "I am big enough, Mama."

"Yes, I suppose you are." Janna took his hand, and they stepped out of the woods.

The house was still on fire. Flames licked out of the windows and blazed through the thatched roof from the hayloft. The first bodies they saw were those of Bora and Seko. The raiders had cut them down where they stood.

Janna forced herself to keep going. She tried to put every thought out of her mind except for Anyezka. Finding her was the only thing that mattered now.

Closer to the house, they found Disla. That was worse. Her throat had been cut and her skirt pushed up around her waist.

"Don't look, Anton," Janna said, too late. Fighting nausea, she knelt next to Disla, pulled the skirt down and looked into her staring eyes. Blood pooled around her head.

"Poor Disla." Anton was oddly calm. "These were not soldiers. Real soldiers don't do these things."

"Some do." Janna tried to laugh, but it turned into a sob. She bit her tongue until it bled to keep the tears from coming.

"Well, when I'm one, I won't." Anton scowled, and pulled her up by her arm. "Come on. Let's find Anyezka."

They stood and stared at the house. If anyone was inside, there was no way they could still be alive. Janna thought of the old people unable to get out of their chairs without help and had to push down the sob that rose in her throat. She wasn't sure how much longer she could keep from crying.

"There has to be a way in," Anton said. "We need to get Anyezka and the baby."

"We can't." Janna grabbed his shirt in case he ran. She wondered vaguely how he could be so composed. "There's no way in, at least not until the fire burns out. But maybe Anyezka got away."

"Yes, she would run to the back door, if those bad people were in front." Anton pulled her in that direction. "She would run to the back, and to the woods."

They made a wide circle around the house because the heat was so intense. It was impossible to enter the courtyard with the well because great chunks of hay and thatch were falling from the house and from a few of the outbuildings. After skirting those, they came to the edge of the woods. Though it was too dark now to look for footprints, Janna kept hoping.

It was cool in the woods, dark and damp, and it was a relief to get away from the heat of the fire and its horrible light. They walked in deeper, calling for Anyezka, louder and louder. Perhaps she would come out if she heard their voices. They called until they were hoarse and too tired to stand. Then they curled up together on a mossy spot against a big tree and cried themselves to sleep.

In the morning, they ate part of the strawberries in their baskets and searched some more. "She wouldn't go far. Not with the baby." Janna tried to force herself to accept the worst.

"We need to search the house." Anton's face was grim. It didn't seem possible he was only nine. "The fire will have stopped by now."

"I don't want to." Tears ran down her face. Since they'd started last night, she couldn't seem to stop them.

"I don't either. But we have to find out." He took her hand, and they walked back out of the woods. The fire had died though smoke still rose from what remained of the buildings. Janna and Anton stood across from where the front door had been, then walked slowly around the edges. It was still too hot to get close, and timbers had collapsed into it.

"It's too hot to move those," Anton said.

"They'd be too heavy for us anyway." They walked around one more time although by now she was certain that there was no hope. No one had escaped.

Janna sank to the ground, then lay on her side, finally giving herself over to the tears. Anton sat down next to her and held her hands. When it began raining, he pushed and pulled at her until she stood, then pulled her some more until she stumbled along beside him, down the road toward the town.

KENDRYK

Kendryk led Landrus into the castle proper, which was dark and cold with an abiding damp clinging to the stone walls. He was glad no one had to live here anymore, at least not for any length of time.

Another soldier had rushed ahead into the steward's office and was building a fire as they entered. Kendryk lit a stubby tallow candle and carried it to an enormous desk. "The steward used this last, so there might be old account books with blank pages."

After shuffling through cobweb-draped shelves, he pulled out a leather-bound ledger with yellow pages, dust rolling off of it in waves. "Like this." Kendryk sneezed, then flipped to the back and pulled out a page. He found an inkwell, its ink hard and dry. The soldier had fanned the fire to life, so Kendryk sent him to the well for water.

"I know it's awful." Kendryk realized that the cold, the dust and the tallow stench from the candle formed a stark contrast to the cozy priest's quarters at the Temple. "I'll send books up from my library, so you aren't bored." He perched on the edge of the desk while they waited for the soldier to return.

"This is far better than any dungeon. As to boredom, if your man retrieves my things, I'll have more than enough to occupy me. And with your permission, I'd like to finish my work."

"What are you working on?"

"For the past months I wrote down everything I learned from my study of the Scrolls. Since I might not be here much longer, I'd like to leave a record of what I found. Perhaps someone else can use it." He gave Kendryk a significant look.

"What an excellent idea." This was exactly what Kendryk had hoped for. "In fact, I'd love to read everything. I still have many questions."

"I assumed you might, which is why I hope that my copy of the Scrolls can be retrieved."

This was the last think Kendryk had expected to hear. "Didn't Julia's guards take those away and secure them?"

"Yes. My official copy will go back to Julia Maxima until my replacement takes office. But I had made my own copy, expecting something like this to happen."

Kendryk stared at him, then asked the obvious. "So, you will have a copy of the Holy Scrolls here?" He still couldn't quite believe it.

"I hope so," Landrus said. "And since I should have considerable free time, I plan to translate them into the Kronland tongue, if you will allow it."

"Of course I'll allow it." Kendryk's heart pounded though now it was from excitement. Then he remembered it was illegal to possess a copy of the Scrolls without a maxima's permission. Translation was strictly forbidden. But if it meant he would find the answers he needed, he hoped the gods would forgive him. He'd worry about the Temple authorities another time.

The soldier came back with a jug of water, and Kendryk waved him out of the room, Once they were alone again he asked, "Is there a chance that, while you're here, I might look at the Scrolls myself?"

"I would like nothing better." Landrus poured a few drops of water into the dried-up ink. "I am convinced that once you read them, you will understand why I'm doing all of this."

On the one hand, Kendryk wanted to understand, but on the other, he worried what would happen if he became convinced that Landrus was speaking the whole truth. He would be forced to do something, take some action.

Landrus had found an old quill and was stirring it around the inkpot. "I don't know why you believe me now, but something has changed your mind since we last spoke."

Kendryk nodded. "I had a dream about what seemed like the last battle and it didn't go well."

"It won't go well if things continue as they are." Landrus laid down the quill. "Although you give me a great deal of hope, and once you can read the relevant passages in the Scrolls, you'll understand why. They tell of a young ruler who will stand against the forces of darkness alone, although in time others will join him as they come to learn the truth. Your dream was a message from the gods, to help you realize that you are the one prophesied."

That the gods would choose Kendryk for any work seemed incredible. He still didn't believe it. "Will the Scrolls show me what I need to do next? Or will the gods perhaps send me another dream?" Kendryk couldn't help but feel this was far more important now he had committed himself.

"The gods always give guidance to those who seek the right path; I know you will find it."

"I saw many friendly-looking banners in the dream, but they weren't enough."

"No, we will not win the battle through any strength of human arms. But when enough people practice the true faith, the Holy Family will be strong enough to prevail against the darkness. Once you study the Scrolls yourself, you will understand the importance of your role."

Kendryk slumped against the desk. His knees felt weak.

Landrus's smile was gentle. "Please, don't worry about it too much just yet. The Scrolls will make much clear."

GWYNNETH

On days like today, she often rode toward the river. The usual spring rains had ended at least for a while and the sun was warm though it had just cleared the hilltops. Gwynneth set out at a steady trot, letting the groom fall behind. She would have preferred to have Kendryk along, but he and Count Faris were huddled in his study, mapping out the eventualities should the empress respond unfavorably to his letter.

Gwynneth didn't see the point. Kendryk ruled here, and it was his right to handle Temple difficulties as much as it was Julia's.

She pulled her horse to a stop as she reached the sharp slope leading to the river. From here, she looked down on the town huddled on its banks and straight across at the castle towering over it. Birkenfels looked beautiful from the outside, though she shuddered at the idea of living in its cramped, drafty interior.

Instead of riding into the town and along the river, she started up the road that wound below the castle walls. The groom at first went the wrong way but quickly changed course and followed her. Her mare's shod hooves clanked against the cobblestones as she wound her way up the road. A guard jumped to attention at the main gate.

"Show me up to Father Landrus," Gwynneth ordered.

The man looked flustered. She knew he had orders to let in no one but Kendryk, but since he couldn't say no to her he saluted and opened the gate. She rode up and up, between the old outbuildings leaning against the walls and clustered at the bottom of the tower. When she reached the main building, she dismounted and tossed the reins toward her groom. Another guard rushed to meet her.

"I wish to see Father Landrus. Please announce me." She hoped he was up since it was still early. But the priest was already hard at work in the small castle library.

Gwynneth entered on the heels of the guard, but Landrus was already standing. He came around the table and met her in the middle of the room. He took her proffered hand and brushed it with his lips while executing a bow worthy of a courtier.

"I know I'm bursting in on you," she said, realizing he was waiting for her to speak. She placed her hat on a stack of books, and peeled off her gloves, then sat in a chair placed near the desk. She wondered if that was Kendryk's usual spot when he came to visit.

"It is an honor, Princess." His voice was both pleasant and resonant. No wonder his sermons drew large audiences. Father Landrus's looks were arresting as well. His face was stern and craggy, making it difficult to decide his age. His eyes were the most interesting; so pale as to be almost neutral, they were also very intense. Gwynneth supposed they were unnerving when directed at someone in censure.

"I confess I've been most eager to meet you." She offered her most charming smile.

He smiled back, broad and genuine, transforming his face. It was no wonder Kendryk liked him.

"Kendryk talks of nothing else these days," she continued. "Being able to study with you is quite the dream come true for him."

"He's an excellent student." Landrus returned to his seat behind the desk. "But I'm sure you didn't come here to discuss your husband's intellectual prowess."

"You're right." Gwynneth kept smiling. "I confess to having little interest in theology, though I wish to discuss other matters with you."

Landrus nodded.

"Both of us are worried about your eventual fate. Kendryk seems to believe that the empress can order him to send you to Atlona or Forli, but I disagree."

"What do you mean by that?"

"I looked up his charter myself. The emperor granted it to the rulers of Terragand over three hundred years ago, and one of the freedoms given was that of dealing with the clergy. It wasn't explicit, but it implied that even a maxima could be overridden."

"Interesting. I wasn't aware of that. I suppose Terragand has a favored position."

"It does. And I want Kendryk to take advantage of it."

"Any reason he wouldn't?"

She bit her lip and wrinkled her nose. "He doesn't like to offend anyone, and he's quite frightened of Empress Teodora."

"She's a powerful person to offend."

"In theory. In reality, she has her hands full at home and on her eastern borders. If Kendryk acts within his rights, what can she do?"

"What she did in Moralta. Those princes thought they acted within their rights as well, and they lost their heads for it. I'm sure that's what concerns Kendryk. Can you blame him?"

"But I don't think she can. I've been corresponding with the other Kronland rulers, and most agree that Kendryk is well within his rights to deal with you as he sees fit."

"That's encouraging. But are they offering concrete support, should Teodora react badly?"

"Well, no. And that's why I'm here. I wish to convince Kendryk to act boldly and perhaps even reinstate you, but I must be sure you will do whatever is required if he should do so."

"Of course," Landrus said. "The moment the prince made me his prisoner, I resolved to do whatever he would have of me."

"So if he defies the empress and Julia is upset, you'd be willing to do your work no matter what she might say?"

"Certainly."

"Good. I thought as much, but I wanted to be sure. Kendryk is very loyal, but it never occurs to him that others might not be. I do my best to make sure they are."

"Admirable of you."

"I hope you aren't offended. It's just that I don't know you and I'm asking Kendryk to take a big risk. I want to protect him as much as I can."

"Then we are very much agreed," Landrus said. "I appreciate all the work you are doing on my behalf, Princess. It matters not your reasons for doing it. If in the end the truth is made stronger, you can be sure you are doing right."

"That's the other thing." Gwynneth frowned. "You've confused Kendryk quite a bit. It seems you believe he is to take part in some sort of important prophecy?"

Landrus nodded.

"This worries him terribly," she continued. "He doesn't know what to do. He looks to you for specific instructions, but isn't receiving them."

"I know." Landrus sighed. "And it pains me a great deal that I can't be of more comfort and help to him. My confidence comes from the Scrolls, and I've shown him the passages, which appear so clear to me. But there's more than that. I've received answers to prayers and I've had dreams that confirm what's in the Scrolls. But those things are harder to use to convince him. In the end, he will need to receive his own answers."

"Yes, and I fear he is looking for more mystical and less concrete proofs," Gwynneth said. "While most rulers have been noncommittal, my own brother and Prince Falk have been quite enthusiastic, yet Kendryk does not see that as a sign he is to move forward. He's looking for something far more strange and spectacular than mere letters."

"You are right. And while it's frustrating, I can't blame him for wanting certainty."

"Yes. He has taken risks, but they are usually carefully calculated. The lack of calculation in the situation is difficult for him to accept."

"I wish I had a better response for you. All I can say is that I'll keep trying to show him the way, and promise to stand beside him whatever decision he takes."

"That's all I can ask then," Gwynneth said, standing and reaching for her hat. "I will speak to Kendryk before he comes up here later. Maybe between the two of us, we can persuade him."

JANNA

The crossroads inn was a welcome sight. Janna hated to ask for help again, but had no choice.

Maya, the owner, was watering geraniums in a pot by the door. "Why, it's you again," she said, her pleasant face creased in a smile. "You and your boy. Don't you have a little girl, too?"

Janna burst into tears.

"Oh dear," the woman said. "Something dreadful's happened, hasn't it? We've heard the most terrible stories these past few days."

"She's dead," Anton said, as Janna tried to gulp down her sobs. "That woman killed her. The one with the yellow eyes."

"Gods protect us." Maya made the sign of the Father. "Why don't you come inside and tell me what happened."

Janna didn't see the point since she couldn't speak. Even once the tears subsided, they came back the moment she opened her mouth. It was hopeless. At least Anton was tougher. While Maya bustled about, bringing fresh bread and beer, he told her what had happened at the farm.

She shook her head. "No question that was Daciana Tomescu. She and her band rode past here in the middle of the night and no one so much as breathed. No one dares even look at her, or she'll kill them."

"I was afraid she'd see us," Anton admitted. "I think she could tell we were there. It was like she could smell us. But she didn't do anything."

"And right you are to be afraid of such a creature. They say she's a friend of the empress, but I can't imagine a godly woman like Her Highness having anything to do with someone so dreadful."

Janna realized how hungry she was, and when she'd had something to eat and drink, she felt better. Maya was as kind as before even though inn was busy, with many travelers on the road.

"My kitchen maid up and left with a soldier last week." Maya shook her head. "You can have her room for a few days."

Janna slept long in the soft little bed in the bright, tidy room, but her dreams were full of fire and blood and yellow animal eyes. It was a relief to wake up in the tavern, which was about a hundred times nicer than the farm, as Anton put it.

Out of habit, she listened for Anyezka's voice, piping in over Anton's chatter. She didn't like to be left out of any conversation. It took a moment to realize that Anyezka was gone, dead, and Janna had failed her simplest task—keeping Dimir's children safe. Anton paused when she started crying into the pillow, and then she heard him clatter down the stairs.

A few minutes later, Maya sat on the edge of the bed, stroking Janna's hair just like she used to stroke Anyezka's when she cried. "Cry all you want," she said. "It's the hardest thing, losing a child, especially such a little one."

"She's not even mine." Janna wiped her tears and turned on her side. "But I married her father when she was a few months old and she feels like mine. Felt like mine."

"Of course she did. You were the only mother she knew, and you were a good one. It's not much comfort, but you know she's gone to live with the Holy Mother along with all the other little ones who die. Things are better there for her, so much better than here."

"I hope so." Janna forced herself to sit. "I can't think what to do next."

"You don't have to do anything right now. Get some rest, and we can talk about it later."

After Maya had gone, Janna cried a little longer. She wanted to stay in that lovely bed and never move again, though she had to find a way to take care of Anton. But she hadn't been able to protect Anyezka; how could she do any better for her brother? The thoughts circled in her head until she fell asleep again.

While Janna slept, Anton had made himself useful in the stable, brushing and feeding traveler's horses. By the time two days had passed, Janna knew she also had to do something in return for Maya's hospitality.

"You can bring food to the tables," Maya said. "Don't worry about taking orders since the other girl can do that. But it would help if we can get things out faster so we can feed more."

Janna didn't mention her fear of speaking to strangers. As it was, she didn't have to say much. The inn was busy that night, and the hours flew by as she ran back and forth between the dining room and the kitchen. Many of the travelers came from, or were going to Kaleva. It seemed things had settled down, almost back to normal. Janna hoped her own family and the Kalinas were well.

It might be safe to go back. She would use her maiden name and no one of her acquaintance would breathe a word about Dimir's short-lived political career. With any luck, leaving Kaleva, the dreadful farm and the even more horrible things that happened there would fade into memory. Right now she couldn't think about Anyezka without the tears welling up, but perhaps that would get better, too.

She had delivered a trencher to a table when someone grabbed her by the waist and pulled her onto his lap. "Now here's a pretty thing," the man roared. His face was too close to hers and his breath stank of ale. Janna froze. "Oh come now, sweetheart," he bounced her on his knee. "No need to be unfriendly."

Janna shrieked and leapt up with such force he fell off the bench. She ran to the kitchen, followed by good-natured shouts and roars of laughter.

"Don't pay 'em no mind," Maya said. "I box their ears and they get the picture. Oh come now, dear. They meant no harm."

"I know." Janna tried to breathe between sobs. Her breath was shallow and coming too fast and her head spun. "I just. I just can't."

Maya took her by the arm and led her to a chair. "Sit down now and catch your breath. It's all right. Why don't you stay in the kitchen for the rest of the evening? By now, there's nothing left but bread and stew. You can dish up as well as I can. I'll handle that lot out there."

Janna had trouble sleeping that night. Whenever she closed her eyes, she saw men leering in her face. But they weren't the ones from downstairs. They were the ones who'd accosted her on the road. That was her greatest fear now; that she would run into similar people on the way back to Kaleva. And this time, she would have no coin to distract them.

KENDRYK

Kendryk's days were busier than they'd ever been. As Terragand's ruling seat, Birkenhof had a steady stream of visitors and petitioners. A rotation of neighboring aristocrats constantly occupied the guest wing, and foreign dignitaries traveling through Kronland always stopped to pay their respects.

Today, Kendryk was free by early afternoon. There were several guests to be entertained and endless administrative work, but he left the former to Gwynneth and the latter in Count Faris's capable hands.

He rode out by himself, skirting newly planted fields and traveling along rows of budding trees before reaching the river. Behind the castle, vineyards climbed the steep hillsides in terraces. Wine had grown here for hundreds of years and the vintages produced were among the finest in the empire.

But right now, Kendryk cared little for wine. He sought answers, and they could only be found inside the castle, if they were to be found at all. His horse knew the way well by now, for he came here most days. Guards at the gates at the foot of the hill saluted as he went by, and those in the courtyard sprang to help with his horse.

He climbed the narrow winding staircase, pulling off his gloves as he went. The study door was ajar, so Kendryk walked in unannounced. Landrus looked up from his work. "I didn't expect to see you today, Your Grace. The guards told me you had more visitors than usual."

"No one special." Kendryk laid his hat on a stack of books and sat in his usual chair. By now, they were easy and informal with each other, like old friends. "Gwynneth can entertain them." He pulled his chair closer to the desk and opened a book, where he had a place marked.

"Eager to get to it, aren't you?" Landrus said. "I confess you are the best pupil I've ever had. Benet must have been sorry to lose you."

"Not as sorry as I was to leave him." Kendryk closed the book again.

"You weren't happy to return to your family?"

"Not under the circumstances. I'd been very young when I went to Galladium, but Prince Gauvain became like an older brother to me, and Benet like a father. Leaving them was far worse than leaving here. But I understood why my family needed me, so I did what I had to."

"You've always done that, haven't you?" Landrus's intense eyes softened. "I think most rulers are conscious of their burden, but few take it on so young."

"I suppose not. But then, I was never much like the other fellows my age, with the need to spend years wenching and drinking before taking on my responsibilities. I was always interested in Terragand, and how I might make it a better place for its people. With Gwynneth and the children my life is perfect for me. I don't think I'd trade it now for a dusty theologian's study." Kendryk looked around the room and laughed. "Although it seems I've acquired one of those as well."

"It seems so. Well, I for one am glad you weren't out carousing that day in Runewald. I feel very safe here, and quite unworried about what is coming."

"How is that possible?" Kendryk couldn't quite keep the agitation out of his voice. "I worry about nothing else. And it's not even my life at stake. It's yours." He paused and tried to calm himself. "I can't make any decisions until I hear from the empress, but I'm terrified of what her response might be. What if she orders me to send you to Atlona? I can't do it. But I also don't see how I can disobey her direct order, no matter what Gwynneth thinks my rights are."

"Have you received a reply yet?"

Kendryk shook his head. "Even a fast courier will only reach Atlona today at the earliest. I imagine it could take several days, or even weeks, for the empress to respond."

"Until you receive a reply, there is nothing you can do. Take it as a gift from the gods that you have these weeks to study and pray. As diligent as you are, they will not fail to give you guidance."

"I just wish they would give it more quickly." Kendryk hoped he didn't sound as petulant as he felt. "I had hoped that within days of reading these texts I would understand everything."

"I'd hoped so too, but what seems clear to me is still concealed from you, at least for a little while."

Kendryk sighed. "The Scrolls mention a ruler who will defend the truth, but they say only that he will be young and from the north. Couldn't he be

Prince Ossian, or my brother-in-law, or King Lennart? Why does it have to be me?"

"No one else has stepped forward in defense of the truth. That is all the proof I need." He made it sound so simple.

"Very well. So let's suppose I am that ruler. The Scrolls say nothing further except he is to be present at the final battle, along with the prophet who will bring the truth. I suppose that's you. Does that mean I have no choice except to fight the empress?"

And that was it right there: Kendryk's worst nightmare. A peaceful split from the empire was one thing, but a war could only end in disaster for Terragand.

"I don't know." Landrus was as patient as if he were talking to a child. "You wish for peaceful ways to do all of this, and it ought to be possible. But much depends on Teodora right now."

"But suppose Teodora agrees to my request to have you tried in Isenwald. Then what? In the normal course of things, you would still be found guilty of heresy and executed. I don't see how that gets us any closer to bringing the truth to the people of the empire." By now, the thought of losing Landrus felt unbearable.

"Perhaps that will be my fate," Landrus said, "although I doubt it. Much can happen before a trial, and much can happen during one. That is why I'm not worried. And even if the empress orders me to Atlona, I can bring the truth to many people before then. With your help, of course."

"What can I do?" Kendryk hoped for a concrete and specific task.

"Get these to a printer." Landrus picked up a thick sheaf of papers.

"You've finished the translation?"

"No, I've barely started. But I realize that I might not have time to finish such a large task. It will take years and may be a work that you or someone else will have to continue. In the meantime however, we can make sure that people everywhere learn the truth. I've written out the most important teachings in simple language, along with a few of my most popular sermons. If you can print several hundred copies and send them throughout the land, change may well overtake our other plans. How can these best be distributed into all the towns?"

Kendryk eagerly took the pile and leafed through it. "I'm not sure. I will start with Runewald since many of the leading citizens there support you. They will put these sheets in every public place and see that they're read aloud."

Kendryk hardly dared hope that reform might come about naturally. He might not have to do anything at all.

JANNA

The next morning, Janna and Maya cleaned the dining room before guests arrived at midday. Janna told her of her plans to leave soon.

"There's no rush," Maya said. "I'd give you steady work if I could, but most times we're not so busy as last night. Of course, you're welcome to stay longer if you need to."

"I think the sooner we go, the better. I'm not much use to you since I'm not cut out to serve in a tavern and can't cook. It's better just to get back to my parents. As it is, I can't thank you enough."

"No need. It's nice having you about. And the groom says that boy of yours is a great help. A real natural with the horses."

"Oh, he loves working there. I hate to take him back to the city. I'd send him to work at a livery stable if he wanted, but I'm sure his grandfather will make him go to school. He won't like that."

"He'll have the rest of his life to work. It's good if he goes to school. Maybe he'll go into business like his father." Maya stood up from her scrubbing and peered out the window facing the road. "Looks like an imperial courier. Wonder if he has any interesting news for us. No doubt he'll need a fresh horse."

Janna wanted to hide, but that was ridiculous. No one knew who she was. The courier had disappeared to the stable and Maya said, "He'll be wanting something to eat. You can bring it to him and hear his news."

Janna swallowed hard.

"Oh come now. This fellow will be a different sort. Not just anyone can become an imperial courier. He'll mind his manners and if I know his type, he'll cut it high and mighty with us. No need to worry about him grabbing your bottom."

Janna hoped Maya was right and followed her to the kitchen.

By the time she came back out with a loaf of fresh bread and a flagon of beer, the man was settling in at a table. He glanced at Janna without interest though his face lit up at the sight of the mug. "Ah, Maya's beer is the best between here and Sanova." He took a long drink, then wiped the foam from his mustache. "I suppose you'll be wanting the news."

Janna nodded.

"Can you read?" He rummaged in his bag.

She nodded again.

"Good. Save me time. Here." He pulled a paper from a large stack he had in his bag. "These are going up in every town square in Moralta. Tell Maya she may as well put one up here, too. That's all that's new. Now run along and tell Maya to bring me a pile of that roast chicken she always has on Tuesdays."

Janna nodded again and fled to the kitchen. While Maya set to carving the chicken, Janna read the paper. Her heart fell into her feet. By the time Maya returned from the dining room. she'd found a place to sit.

"Goodness, child. What's wrong?"

"It's this." Janna handed her the sheet.

Maya looked it over. "Now see here, just because there's a Janna on the list doesn't mean it's you."

"But it is me," Janna said in a small voice. "I'm Janna Kronek, and Anton is Dimir's son, so they want him too."

"Now that's just ridiculous." Maya laid a comforting hand on Janna's shoulder. "Anyone could take one look at you and see you're no threat to anyone, least of all the empress."

"Of course I'm no threat. But I'm sure none of the other families on that list are either. I suppose it wasn't enough to make an example of Dimir and the others. She wants to make sure no one remains to take revenge. As if Anton or I ever would. Or could." The realization came too late. "I understand if you want to turn us in. It's a lot of money."

"What sort of monster do you take me for? You're less rebellious than those chickens out in the yard." Maya frowned and folded up the paper. "I'm a loyal subject to Her Highness, but in this matter, I know better. You stay put for now, dear. No one else knows who you are, and I won't put this up until you're well away from here."

"But I can't go to Kaleva now," Janna said, a second realization dawning on her. "They'll be looking for me there, especially around my family. I have to leave, but I can't go there." She buried her face in her hands.

"No need to panic," Maya said. "You stay in the kitchen while I take care of the lunch crowd. I already have an idea but I'll work it out this afternoon. In the meantime, don't you worry. "

KENDRYK

"Your Grace." Count Faris opened the study door. "It's here."

Kendryk jumped up and hurried to take the leather pouch from Faris's hand. As he had hoped, and dreaded, it bore the imperial stamp. He pulled out an inner pouch, also of leather, then an envelope of canvas with a wax seal. He made an impatient noise, rushed back to his desk and rummaged for a letter knife. When he got through it all, there was one sheet inside, also closed with a seal. Kendryk broke it and slumped back into his chair. Count Faris sat down across from him.

The salutation, with all of Teodora's and Kendryk's various titles, was longer than the message itself. After all, there wasn't much to be said. Kendryk looked up. "Please send for the princess."

While waiting for her, Kendryk read it through again, just to be sure. He was glad that Faris was a patient sort and didn't badger him for the contents. He wasn't altogether prepared to discuss them.

Gwynneth hurried into the room alone. "So it finally arrived? What does it say?"

Kendryk handed her the letter. She sank onto a chair while she read. "Is that all?" She handed it to Count Faris.

"That's all." Kendryk had hoped for more time. Now there was none. He should have made any decision yesterday. "We must prepare to go soon, then."

"I'm coming, of course," Gwynneth said.

"Are you sure? It won't be an easy journey."

"I don't care. This might well be the most important event of your reign and I won't miss it."

"If you like, I'll stay here." Count Faris passed the letter back to Kendryk. "In this case, the princess will be of greater use to you. With any luck, many

Kronland rulers will attend, and she can lobby on your behalf so you can focus on the trial."

"The trial." Kendryk shook his head. "I can't believe it's come to that. If Flavia Maxima can't be swayed, I don't see how this will work to our benefit."

"It will, either way," Gwynneth said. "In the unlikely event she finds Landrus innocent, it will be a slap in Teodora's face. If he's found guilty, it will outrage everyone in Kronland and they will see it as a personal slight to you. Teodora loses either way."

"I must confess, I'm surprised she is coming," Faris said. "Her presence will make this far more significant than a mere priest's trial."

"She's no doubt hoping to put me in my place in front of everyone." Kendryk minded that possibility far less than he should have. "And she may well succeed." He needed a plan, but the wheels of his mind had frozen in place.

"Not necessarily." Faris stroked his small beard. "Either Teodora doesn't have all the facts, or she is choosing to ignore them. Thanks to you, Landrus's pamphlets have spread all over Kronland and even into Sanova and Moralta."

"And people are paying attention," Gwynneth added. "I've written to everyone, and every ruler in the northern part of Kronland has already heard of Landrus. In fact, Prince Bronson in Helvundala, and Princess Floreta in Brandana asked me if I can send them more of his work. They've received petitions from their clergy as well, asking for a council to discuss these matters."

"That's good." Kendryk struggled to keep despair from seeping into his voice. "But I don't see how that helps Landrus right now. If he's found guilty and executed, that's the end of it. There'll be nothing more to print, and everyone will forget about it within a few months."

"It might not help Landrus, but it can help us a great deal," Gwynneth said. "Especially if these rulers are present at the trial. They aren't friendly toward Teodora at the best times, and this might give them a real complaint." She stood. "I will send messages to every Kronland ruler today. With any luck, most of them will reach Isenwald in time for the trial. I'll also order everything packed so we can leave in a few days." She was out the door in a whirl of blue silk.

"Well," Kendryk said. "I'm glad she at least is decisive."

Count Faris smiled gently. He alone seemed to understand how Kendryk felt. "This could be much worse. The empress could have ordered you to send

Landrus straight to her, or to Forli, and you would face a much harder decision right now."

"I suppose you're right." He still felt no relief, His head whirled, trying to think of possibilities, but there were none. Perhaps Gwynneth would have some ideas. He just couldn't bear the thought of bringing Landrus all that way in chains and then having it all be over.

BRAEDEN

Braeden squinted against the bright spring sunlight. At least it was still spring. He hadn't spent more than a month in that dungeon though it seemed much longer. He had no idea why they were letting him go since no one mentioned a trial. A guard dumped him into a wagon, which bumped along cobbled streets for a while. He needed a little time to sit up, and longer to get his bearings. By the time he did, the wagon had reached the foot of the hill on which the Arnfels stood and was going through the streets of Atlona.

After the silence of his cell, the noise was deafening. People ran around the cart, giving him strange looks and dodging other wagons. Braeden looked around with interest. He'd never been in this part of Atlona. The streets were wide and the pretty buildings painted in a variety of light colors. Many had wrought-iron signs swinging over their doorways and lampposts stood all along the street. There were even pavements for people to walk on and wide gutters between those and the street. Most civilized.

The temples were even more noteworthy. Braeden's wagon must have passed at least three large ones and several smaller ones. The one built by Teodora's predecessor was the most impressive. Two great towers rose alongside an ornate facade and the towers themselves shone with gold and copper on the graceful cupolas.

Soon, the wagon was at the wall, and Braeden was greeted with the grisly sight of the rebellious Moraltan princes' heads. Or what was left of their heads. They had been up there for a few months through warm weather and plentiful birds. Braeden was grateful his head was not up there too though he reckoned he wasn't important enough for that. They might have taken the head, but they'd have just dumped it into a ditch alongside his body.

Once outside the wall, the wagon turned down a wide street with the Palais Arden at its end. Braeden hoped he wasn't being presented to the empress in this condition. But just before the palace, the wagon turned again, heading for the parade ground. So he really was returning to the hussars. Braeden breathed a sigh of relief. In front of Novitny's tent, the wagon stopped. Braeden scooted to the edge and got out. He still wobbled when standing.

Franca burst out of the tent, but the delight on her face faded fast. "Oh sir. You look dreadful. I'll go get the prince." She disappeared back into the tent, probably so she didn't have to look at him.

Novitny came straight out. "Well it's about time," he roared, clapping Braeden in a bone-crushing embrace. "Thought that bitch was going back on her promise."

"Sir," Franca tugged at his elbow. "Please don't talk about the empress like that so loud, in the middle of camp. Lots of unfriendlies about."

"They already know what I think of that wicked hag. Still, you're right. Dura's got a knack for politics." He clapped Braeden on the back while steering him into his tent. "If it hadn't been for her, I wouldn't have figured out how to release you."

Inside Novitny's tent, Braeden collapsed into a chair. He hadn't ever felt so weak. The prince sat in another chair. "Well, don't just stand around, lieutenant, go see about getting the man some food. Looks like he hasn't eaten in weeks."

"I've eaten." Braeden smiled as he heard Franca shouting at someone outside the tent. It was good to be back. "Just not very much."

"Well, Kazmir will be grateful if there's less of you to haul around."

Franca came back. "Food's on its way, sir. Oh, and I ordered a bath drawn up in your tent. Not to be rude, or anything, but you need one." She couldn't quite stop herself from wrinkling up her nose, it seemed.

"Thank you. I know I could use one." Braeden didn't worry overmuch about baths though it was nice to have one now and again when there was time and water. Besides, the Arnfels dungeon had a particularly famous aroma.

"And lieutenant, eh?" He smiled at Franca. "Congratulations; though I'd better watch my back."

"Oh sir, I'd never ..." Franca began, wide-eyed, then stopped when Braeden chuckled. "I can never tell when you're making fun, sir." Her face reddened.

"I had to reward her for her quick thinking when you were arrested." Novitny paused as a servant scurried in bearing a large tray of food. Braeden eyed it hungrily.

"Go ahead," Novitny said. "You eat; I'll talk."

Braeden dug in, washing every bite down with great swigs of the excellent ale.

"In case you're wondering, there won't be a trial. You're completely free with all charges dropped."

"That's very good news." Braeden looked at the food and settled on a piece of a large fowl. "I wasn't keen on taking my chances with one."

"I wasn't either. Can't trust that woman for even a moment. She does as she pleases and not many are brave enough to stand in her way."

"You are," Braeden said between mouthfuls.

"Eh, I have some political protection."

"Still, I appreciate the help."

"Ah well, you know ..." Novitny looked embarrassed. "Come now, don't stop eating. You should have those berry pastries before Lieutenant Dura eats them all. I'm surprised she left any."

"Oh, sir, I'd ..." Franca began before trailing off. She was getting a little quicker at spotting a joke.

"So why free me now, without a trial?" Braeden reached for a pastry.

Prince Novitny chuckled. "Her Highness finds herself in a real fix, and we're in a position to help her. And I'm not helping for free. First thing I wanted was your release with no further talk of a trial, and the second is over there in those chests." Novitny nodded at three large chests standing across the tent, wrapped in chains and secured with enormous locks.

"Gold?" Braeden reached for another pastry. To his surprise the first had disappeared.

"Every last bit of it. I had Dura count it all to be sure. You'll get your share soon."

Braeden's day was getting better and better. "So what's this problem you're helping Her Highness with?"

"A prince up in Kronland is being a troublemaker. Young Kendryk Bernotas of Terragand has taken a liking to a priest whose preaching isn't to the liking of the Temple."

"Not another one of those," Braeden groaned. "We saw how that went in Moralta."

"This is different. The Kronland states are independent, bound to the empire with individual charters. Prince Kendryk may do as he pleases in most matters, including the religious. The charter only requires him to send a certain number of troops when the empire is threatened."

125

"Which might be soon. Has there been any progress on the Zastwar treaty?"

"None yet. Ambassador Arceo is cooling her heels in Melampis, waiting for an audience with the Sultan. Which puts Her Highness in a real lather."

"Good." Braeden pushed the empty plate away.

"Yes. Good for us, and an opportunity for Prince Kendryk to press his luck."

"What do we have to do with any of this?"

"Aside from the Zastwar problem, which might turn very bad, Andor Korma has started a rebellion in Marjatya, picking up supporters everywhere. And to top it off, Prince Kendryk has asked for a public trial for his priest, in Isenwald."

"That seems odd."

"It is. All kinds of reasons behind it, according to the politicians. But in the end, Teodora feels she must go to Isenwald and make a good show of force while grinding little Prince Kendryk under her heel. The rest of the Kronland rulers might appear too, so she can intimidate them at the same time."

"I don't know much about these things," Braeden said. "But isn't she going about it all wrong? Wouldn't it make more sense for her to just let Kendryk have his way, so he and the others will send her their troops without making trouble?"

"You'd think so," Novitny agreed. "But this woman is not reasonable. She never takes the easy way if it mean showing any weakness. I think she'd sooner starve to death in the Arnfels surrounded by enemies than give any Kronland ruler the impression she might give them an inch."

"Just so long as we're not starving to death with her," Braeden grumbled. "But isn't this whole trial a concession? Couldn't she just order the priest sent to Forli?"

"She could try, but Livilla advised against it. Pretty frightening when the voice of reason in this place is a crazy old woman like the Maxima."

"I still don't see how we fit into this and how you extorted so much gold from the empress."

"Teodora needs two things right now. First is a strong military force inside Atlona, should the worst happen and Korma get across the border. Ensden's main army is stationed at the Zastwar border until the treaty is signed, or not. So he can't help right now. She also needs an impressive escort to take to Isenwald to put the fear of the gods into Prince Kendryk and the others."

"She wants you to split your force."

Novitny nodded. "I don't like to, and I don't think we're used best in fending off a siege. But she doesn't have a lot of other troops at her disposal right now. For what she's paying us, I'll do it. Now, go get your bath. Her Highness might pay us a visit later, and you should look as dapper as possible, just to spite her."

JANNA

"I can't imagine that your sister would want more mouths to feed." Janna remembered her reception at the farm.

"It won't be like that," Maya said. "Her children are grown and gone, and she's always complained about finding good help at the shop. You say you worked in a shop in Kaleva?"

"My father owned a dry goods store, and I was at the front counter sometimes."

"I'm surprised you're still so fearful around strangers."

"I hated it, but having that counter between you and everyone else made it easier. I wasn't good at chatting with the customers like my sisters were, but well enough do my job."

"You'll be able to manage?"

"I'm sure I will. But what about Anton? He must make himself useful somehow."

"Oh, he will. Zara's husband drives a wagon for hire. He's got several horses that need care, and your boy is good at that. Besides, he's good with people. Everyone likes him."

"Thank the gods for that."

"I'll send a note along," Maya said. "You needn't worry about being a burden because I know you do. Not everyone is as unkind as your husband's people. Besides, I doubt you'll be there for long. How long did you work in your father's shop before your husband spotted you?"

"Just over six months and we married a month after that."

"See here, Janna." Maya settled herself at the kitchen table. "I understand that you might not be keen to marry again, but you have to think about it. You're still young, and there's no doubt you'll catch the eye of a man or two, once you're in Trepol. If you want my advice, take the best one you can get as soon as you can get him. Anyone who's a steady sort and who'll be kind to you and the boy. Zara knows everyone around there and she'll be able to advise you. But the sooner you're settled, the better. Zara and Ivan aren't the youngest, and at some point, their children will get the business. You want to be sure you're provided for by then."

Janna saw the sense in it, though she dreaded the thought of being put on display again, like a piece of merchandise. That was how it had been in Kaleva. Once a girl of the Beran family was of marriageable age, she went to work at the front counter of the shop, so the bachelors of the area could look her over. Janna had hated the feeling, and as frightened as she'd been of Dimir at first, it had been a relief to no longer be on the market.

"I'll do whatever I have to to keep Anton safe."

"That's a good girl."

They left the next morning since there was no point in delay. The last word had been that the southern road, leading through Trepol and into Marjatya was peaceful. "There might still be packs of soldiers about." Maya loaded them up with bundles of food and a spare blanket. "Try to find a crowd of people and stick with them. Get off the road at sundown and stay in the trees."

"I can't thank you enough," Janna began.

"Oh, Psshht. I couldn't call myself a godly woman if I didn't do a little something for you and the boy. And it's little enough, though I know Zara will be good to you. She was always my favorite sister."

Janna squeezed Maya's hand and turned to the road. Anton was eager to go, once Janna told him he'd have horses to care for. He'd already peppered Maya with all kinds of questions about them that she could not answer, so he couldn't wait to get there and see for himself.

There wasn't much traffic on the road at first, and Janna and Anton made good time. She had to explain to Anton why returning to Kaleva wasn't possible.

"That empress is a bad person," he said. "You haven't done anything, and neither have I. Why does she want to punish us?"

"She's worried that when you grow up, you'll still be angry with her and start trouble."

"She's right about that." Anton arranged his face into a grimace.

"So maybe it's that she understands how boys think." Janna smiled at him. "What would you do if you were the emperor?"

"I would give Moralta independence, first thing."

"Would you? They would stop paying taxes to you, you know."

"I don't care. I'd have palaces full of gold, so I wouldn't need any stupid taxes."

"You'd be a kind emperor."

"Except I don't want to do that. I want to be a soldier." It hadn't helped that he'd seen soldiers at the tavern daily, filling his ears with lurid tales of the battlefield.

It was drizzling, but they had their cloaks and the sky cleared by midday. There were a few others going their way, but they were on horseback, so Janna and Anton weren't able to keep up.

At a small crossroads that afternoon, they fell in with a strange-looking group of people in wagons. At first Janna was afraid of the noisy, dark-skinned men who looked so foreign, but then she saw they had women and children with them. They were all rather loud and a little frightening, but as usual, Anton made friends right away.

"They're not going as far as we are. But we can stay with them until they turn off on the road to Olvisya."

"We certainly don't want to go that way." Janna shuddered. "How can you understand them?" They spoke a language she didn't recognize.

"I use my hands. And I've already learned a few words. My friend Ezmer and I are teaching each other."

Janna watched him run off to his friend. Then she smiled and nodded at a woman sitting in a wagon that had drawn up next to her. The woman patted the seat beside her and reached down. Easy enough to understand. Janna took her hand and jumped into the slow-moving wagon. The woman chattered while Janna smiled and nodded some more, without understanding a word. The woman didn't seem to mind.

When it came time to stop for a meal, Janna offered some of her food, and they took it up willingly enough. They ate a strange type of chewy, but tasty flat bread with meat so spicy it made Janna's eyes water.

They stayed with them for two days, but the crossroads to Olvisya came much too soon. Janna and Anton continued on their way after waving good-bye to the little caravan.

"I liked them," Anton said. "I want to live with them. Travel in a wagon all the time and see the world."

"You are seeing the world." Janna took his hand.

"Yes, but not in a fun way."

She couldn't argue with that.

GWYNNETH

Gwynneth was sure it wouldn't be long before Kendryk came to her, so she returned to the library to begin her preparations for the journey. They had little time, but it was important to keep up appearances. She wouldn't have Teodora thinking her decision to appear had taken them by surprise.

She dictated a letter to Halvor; he would send copies to all the Kronland rulers. While he scribbled furiously to keep up, she sent her ladies in all directions to pack.

When Kendryk appeared, he looked so pale and exhausted, Gwynneth wondered if he was ill. Was the prospect of meeting the empress upsetting him? "Sit down, darling. You look done in."

He dropped into a seat near the window. "I'm glad you're so organized. I don't feel I can do anything right now."

"Halvor, please leave us." She waited for the door to close behind him, then joined Kendryk on the bench. "You don't have to do anything right now. We have a few days to get ready and all you have to decide is which of the guards you're taking. I'll do the rest."

Kendryk tried to smile, but clearly couldn't. She looked at him more closely. "Oh. You're upset, aren't you? Wasn't this the answer you wanted?"

"It is, it was. I realize it's a tactical victory, but I'm still worried about the trial. No one is ever found innocent in these things."

Gwynneth waved away a maid who had slipped inside the door holding a stack of linens, then turned back to Kendryk. "No, I don't suppose they are. I confess I hadn't thought that far, beyond imagining how angry it would make everyone. But yes, losing Father Landrus would be dreadful." Kendryk had already lost his parents and brother; he didn't deserve to lose this friend.

He shook his head. "I can't bear the idea. I've learned so much from him. And while I still don't understand everything, I'm sure he's right and we need to make changes. If he's killed, I don't see how we will do that."

"There might be others who can carry on his work." That had to be scant comfort, but she couldn't say anything else because he was right. It was doubtful that Father Landrus would leave the trial a free man.

"Perhaps; though I'm sure the Temple will silence any others if he's executed."

"I'm sure you're right." Her mind whirled. There had to be a solution.

"It doesn't seem right that a big trial with an execution at the end is how this will end. How can this be the will of the gods?"

"It seems impossible, doesn't it?"

They sat in silence for a moment. Then it struck her. Why hadn't she thought of it before? She grabbed his hand in her excitement and waited until he looked her in the eye. "I have an idea, but you might not like it."

"I won't know until you tell me."

"What if Father Landrus escapes?"

"Now?" His tone was incredulous, but she watched hope flicker in his eyes.

"As soon as possible. We can manage it in the next few days, I'm sure."

"But then what? He'll be caught by someone like my uncle if he's out there on his own."

"He won't go by himself. He could take a ship to Norovaea. I'm sure my father would welcome him."

"Oh! You're right. I don't dislike the idea as much as you might expect. It will anger the empress, but at worst, she can accuse me of careless guarding, which I'm guilty of in any case."

"Exactly!" Gwynneth smiled in triumph. "We'll say he had Norovaean supporters who helped him. Maybe they infiltrated the guards. That's not a lie, either. I'm sure he has supporters in Norovaea."

"It's true that the timing is awkward since we've already received Teodora's message. But if she wants troops from me, she shouldn't ask too many questions." Kendryk's eyes lit up and now she was sure he would agree with her plan.

"That's right." Gwynneth couldn't stop smiling. "Now, go tell Father Landrus to be ready to travel in a day or two. We can arrange a boat to pick him up in the middle of the night, just in time to meet the next ship to sail out of Kaltental for Norovaea."

"That's perfect. I'll go see him right away." Kendryk grabbed one of her hands and kissed it before rushing out of the room.

Gwynneth was pleased to see him so happy, but it was even more gratifying to picture Teodora's reaction when she learned her prey had escaped her clutches.

JANNA

They met no one else on the road, so as the sun sank low, Janna and Anton found a quiet spot near a brook. There were no woods, but there was long grass and thick bushes by the roadside. If they laid down, no one on the road would see them. Between their cloaks and the blanket Maya had given them, they slept warm and stayed off the damp ground.

By morning, Janna felt almost optimistic. They'd be in a town tonight, behind walls, in a real house, someplace they could stay for a while.

The day was warm, and the road stretched empty ahead of them. It was noon before they met a peddler going the other way. "Where you bound?" he asked.

"Trepol," Janna said.

"Wouldn't go that way if I was you." The man shook his head.

"Why ever not?" Janna's heart sank.

"Not sure. But there's rumors of trouble."

"There's trouble everywhere," Anton said.

"Oh-ho, you've got that right, my boy. With any luck, the trouble hasn't reached Trepol from Marjatya and if you can get there, you'll be safe inside the walls."

"We'll hurry," Janna said, and they picked up their pace.

It was near dusk when they saw the walls of the city. She felt relieved, but worried because they hadn't seen anyone all afternoon. About a league from the walls, they came upon a small encampment. Anton went ahead to see if it was safe. "They're merchants. All dressed like Papa. I'm sure they'll be nice."

Before either one of them could speak, one man said, "If you're headed to Trepol, don't bother."

"Why not?" Anton asked.

"Gates are shut tight. No one gets in, or leaves."

Janna made a small noise of consternation.

"Got that right, miss," another man said. "We'd go back the way we came, but there's trouble there too. Soldiers coming up the road from Marjatya."

"Oh dear." Janna sank into the grass. Now she realized how tired she was. "What will we do?"

"Go back the way you came if you ask me. We're heading east in the morning. There's another town where we might unload these goods." He waved at a small train of wagons standing nearby.

Anton sat down next to her. "It's all right, Mama. Maya will help us. You'll just have to get used to working at the inn."

"I suppose I will," Janna said. Then a terrible thought struck her. "Will we be safe out here tonight?"

"Safe enough, I should think," the man said. "Soldiers make enough noise, we'll know when they get here, and the town will toll the warning bells in any case. Might as well stay here tonight, head back in the morning."

Janna nodded, unsure if it was safe to stay with these men, but they seemed uninterested in her, soon turning back to their talk of where to go next and what they might find there. She and Anton shared the food she had left and wrapped themselves up in their cloaks. She tried to keep one ear open for the bells, but all was silent, except for crickets chirping in the bushes. The men all fell asleep before she did.

It was barely light when she awoke, but then it was to the tolling of the bells. She usually liked the sound of temple bells, but these seemed dark and threatening. She scrambled to get up and shook Anton awake. The merchants were stirring as well and hurried to get donkeys hitched to the wagons. "Best of luck to you, miss," one of them said, as Janna got ready to go. "The soldiers will spend some time trying to get into town, so that should give you a head start."

Fear sped them on their way, and after a while, they no longer heard the bells, or anyone else.

"Is that a goat?" Anton asked after they'd been walking for about an hour.

"What? Where?"

"Right there," Anton pointed. There was a large brown goat eating grass nearby, a torn piece of rope hanging around its neck.

"It must have gotten away from someone," Janna said. "I'm sure they'll want it back. Shall we try to catch it?" It would give them some occupation while she thought of what to do.

The goat had no intention of being caught, and they soon chased it into a field. There was no one else on the road, so Janna thought it must belong to a nearby farm. She saw a small house in the distance. Perhaps they could get a drink of water since the day would be warm.

Anton had chased the goat further into the field when his head disappeared beneath the pale green stalks of barley.

"Anton?" Janna looked around, trying not to panic.

He popped back up a moment later, with a shout of triumph and a bit dirtier. He'd caught the end of the rope.

"Good boy." Janna tried to hide her relief. It wouldn't do to let Anton know how terrified she was to let him out of her sight. "Let's take it to that house."

Before they'd reached the house, they knew it was the right one. An old woman paced in front, calling for Tipi. Janna presumed that was the goat.

"We have him," Anton called, waving.

"Why thank you." The old woman turned toward him, a smile wreathing her wrinkled face. "That awful Tipi is always escaping."

"The rope is broken," Anton explained.

"He chews through them all eventually," the woman said. "My granddaughter used to herd the goats for me, but she went off to the city with the rest of the family."

"To Trepol?" Janna asked.

"No, to Pemris, off east."

"Trepol is under attack," Janna said. "We were headed there, but now I'm not sure where we'll go."

The woman looked at the two of them for a long moment, then asked, "Why don't you stay here for a while? I could use some help. The farm is too much for me. I've got a little food and I'll share it if you can help me through the harvest. Then we'll see."

Janna looked at Anton. He scratched the goat's head while it chewed on his shirt, a blissful expression on its face. "Oh Mama, please, can we stay?" He looked at the old woman. "I'll watch all your animals for you."

"I don't know anything about farming," Janna said.

"Never mind that. It's just a lot of hoeing right now and you can learn that quickly enough. Come harvest we might get help from any neighbors who are still about."

Janna looked at Anton, back at the old woman and the tidy little cottage behind her. A pot of red and white petunias stood next to the stoop. The inn was safe, but Janna had dreaded the idea of working there again. The work here might be harder, but there was no one besides the old woman.

"All right then," she said. "We'll stay through the harvest."

BRAEDEN

Braeden shifted unhappily. The time he'd spent in the dungeon was the longest he'd ever been out of the saddle since he was nine years old. He hadn't realized you could become unaccustomed to it. Still, the saddle sores weren't as painful as his overall situation.

The empress had taken one look at him after his release and decided she wanted him for a bodyguard. "He looks very frightening," she said gleefully. "He'll stand behind me at all times, in full armor. I can see why Daciana wanted me to get rid of him, but that would be a waste. She's so competitive."

"Competitive?" Braeden couldn't help himself. "I'd say she's—" He got a sharp elbow in the ribs from Franca and stopped.

Teodora jumped off her horse and stood across from him. He knew he should bow but didn't want to, though he got another elbow from Franca. The empress was tall and more attractive than he'd expected. Braeden had pictured an evil witch, with a long pointed nose and large moles, but though her nose was rather large, it was not pointed, and it fit the rest of her face well. She had large dark eyes, prominent cheekbones and a strong chin to go with it all. It was a good face for an empress, but it didn't make Braeden like her any better.

She didn't seem to mind his lack of bowing and scraping. "The dungeon didn't work on you, did it?" She laughed, showing large, even teeth. To Braeden's relief, none appeared to be fangs.

"Seems not," he said, adding, "Your Highness," before he got another jab from Franca.

"That's all right." She shrugged. "I can put you to better use. How would you like to go to Isenwald with me?"

Now here he was, in a position most courtiers could only dream of. It was a shame he didn't care for politics because he was getting a close view of the inner workings of the empire. He had to admit that Teodora took her position seriously and worked hard. Even though she was on horseback all day, she never stopped answering an endless stream of letters and issuing even more orders. If Braeden had ever harbored ambitions to rule—which he hadn't—seeing what it took would soon have soured him on the notion.

Within a few days, he was beyond boredom. Prince Novitny had stayed behind with Franca and Miro to help bolster Atlona's defenses. Reno was good company, but he spent his spare time with his wife and the two daughters he'd brought with him.

The evenings were the worst. Teodora always hosted a feast at huge trestle tables set up in the middle of camp. More often than not, as her head of security, Braeden had to sit near her. He was sure she insisted on it just to torture him.

"So, Commander." She grinned at him, showing all of her large teeth. "How are you finding the journey?"

Everyone nearby looked at him with interest. Anyone singled out by the empress might be worthy of cultivating.

"Well enough. Haven't seen so many trees in a good while."

Everyone tittered.

Teodora looked around still smiling. "True, Kronland is known for its forests. But I was rather wondering what you thought of the company. I'm sure you are not used to traveling with so many beautiful ladies."

"No, I am not." Braeden tried to look interested. While some of the ladies were pretty, Braeden knew they were not for him and gave them little attention.

"I imagine it's quite a treat." Teodora smirked.

He wondered if she was fishing for a compliment and this was his cue to say something gallant. In that case, she'd picked the wrong man for a dinner companion.

"It is." He nodded. "The company is excellent. And so is the wine." He raised his glass. That seemed to be the right thing to do because everyone tittered some more by way of agreement. Then someone proposed a toast to Her Highness and to the success of her mission.

After that, Teodora spoke with others though she often smiled in Braeden's direction. He shifted in his seat, wishing he could be anywhere else. The woman was paying him far more attention than her own husband.

The imperial consort, Prince Raynard, sat straight across from Braeden, looking unhappy. Braeden didn't know why Teodora was ignoring him. The prince was a tall, handsome fellow with hair falling in golden waves to his shoulders and eyes the color of cornflowers. The gossip was that he and Teodora both took other lovers and hadn't been seen in each other's quarters since the birth of their youngest child. If Teodora had a favorite, Braeden couldn't puzzle out who it could be. He saw no likely young man in the party.

The horrible thought struck him that perhaps she was grooming him for the position. Braeden shuddered.

"Are you all right, sir?" asked a pretty lady-in-waiting sitting next to him. Brytta Prosnitz was one of Teodora's secretaries and the one she shouted at the most. Brytta seemed to spend much of her time near tears, and they sometimes overflowed when Teodora slapped and pinched her.

Braeden put on a smile for her. "I am. Too much wine."

"It's the only way to survive these meals." She grimaced as she finished her glass and held it out for a servant to pour more.

"I've noticed that. How far are we from Isenwald, anyway?"

"About two days. But then it will be at least another two to get to Kronfels."

"That seems much too long."

"It's quite far though we are making good time. The empress is eager to arrive there before Prince Kendryk. She's worried that Princess Kasbirk will offer her palace to him, instead of Her Highness." Brytta's voice dropped to a whisper. "That would be dreadfully insulting, and would start things off worse than they are already."

KENDRYK

Kendryk was at the castle within twenty minutes. Landrus looked up from his desk, surprised, and quickly rose.

"No, please sit." Kendryk flung himself into his usual chair and tried to catch his breath.

"Has news come?" Landrus asked.

"The empress has agreed to a trial in Isenwald."

"I'm surprised. But better than the alternative." Landrus appeared calm as always. Kendryk didn't know how he managed it.

"Is it? Now it's here as a real possibility, I don't much like it. We'll be well-prepared for the trial and bring many witnesses on your behalf, but I'm not sure it will be enough."

"A verdict of innocence would be unprecedented."

"Yes. I'd hoped under the current restless political climate, Flavia might be pressured into lenience. But Teodora is to appear personally and I'm sure Flavia will find that far more compelling."

"So Teodora is coming? Interesting." Landrus seemed pleased.

Kendryk leaned forward and dropped his voice. "I've discussed it with the princess, and we've decided we can't take the risk of losing you."

"You're very kind." Landrus seemed amused. "But I'm not sure you can do much more than you already have."

"But we can. We will help you escape to Norovaea."

"Now?" Landrus looked like he was ready to burst out laughing.

"In the next day or two. A ship sails from Kaltental in three days and we want you on it. We are sure King Andres will welcome you with a personal recommendation from his daughter."

"The two of you amaze me. I am very touched you would take such care for my person, but I'm afraid I must decline."

"Why?" Kendryk was baffled. "This is the perfect solution. You can continue your work in Norovaea, and I'm sure in time, the climate will improve here so you can return."

"Forgive me if I don't share in your optimism," Landrus said. "If I leave, I fear that will be the end of any meaningful change for the Faith in Terragand."

"But I'll continue to spread your work here. It won't be that much different from you being here."

"No, I'm sorry, but it won't be the same." Landrus's eyes glowed in an unsettling fashion. "The gods have been clear on this point. My work is in Terragand, and perhaps in the rest of Kronland later. I can do no good in Norovaea."

Kendryk shook his head. "How will it be different if you're tried and executed in just a few weeks' time? How will that help change the Faith in Terragand?"

"I don't know." Landrus shrugged. "It's possible my death will help kindle some greater changes. That's happened before."

Kendryk's heart pounded in his throat. "I just can't accept that. Perhaps it's selfish of me, but I don't want you to die if I can prevent it."

"I understand. I don't want to die either. But I must do what the gods require of me, or there's no point in any of this."

"So you won't let us help you escape?"

"No, I won't. I'm sorry."

Kendryk swallowed hard, surprised at the anger welling up inside him. "You realize I could just force you to escape. Have armed men carry you off."

"I suppose you could." Landrus looked amused again.

"But I won't." Kendryk sighed. "And it seems you know it." He hated being so predictable.

"It would be out of character for you, true."

It was irritating that Landrus was so untroubled by the thought of his own death. And a painful death, at that.

"Well, I suppose that's it then." Kendryk felt deflated. "We'll be ready to leave for Isenwald in a few days. Would you prefer to go on horseback, or shall I prepare a wagon for you? There doesn't seem to be much point in having you heavily guarded."

"I'll go on horseback. Maybe we'll be able to talk on the way."

"I'd like that," Kendryk said. After taking his leave and making his way back down the stairs, he realized that the journey would probably be the last chance they'd have to talk, ever. It didn't seem possible that this was what the gods intended.

BRAEDEN

Within a few days, the empress and her entourage were on the outskirts of Kronfels, the site of Isenwald's largest temple and seat of Flavia Maxima. Princess Viviane Kasbirk, Isenwald's ruler, lived in a great palace nearby which she had placed at Teodora's disposal. Braeden would have preferred a tent pitched somewhere at a safe distance, but as her head of security he couldn't ever be more than shouting distance from the empress.

After two days, word came that the Terragand delegation was arriving, with the priest who was to be tried.

"We shall meet them in the temple square," Teodora said. She spent the next two hours changing into a very elaborate dress of stiff red brocade with a collar of gold lace that towered above her head. Braeden hoped for tall doorways.

The sun had reappeared after a rainy morning so the temple square soon filled up when everyone heard that the empress was on her way. City carpenters threw up a hasty platform and brought large chairs for the empress and Maxima.

No sooner had Braeden taken his place at the edge of the platform behind Teodora's chair, than the crowd parted for Prince Kendryk and Princess Gwynneth.

Braeden's eyes, and those of every man in the square, went straight to the princess. Gwynneth Roussay was even lovelier than rumor claimed. She couldn't have been a day over twenty-two, and next to the empress's cosmetically contrived good looks, glowed with youth and freshness. She wore a simple blue riding dress, which matched her eyes, and a small hat perched on top of her golden curls.

But Teodora's attention was on the prince. Kendryk Bernotas made a good impression as well. He lacked his wife's startling beauty, but glowed with the same youthful freshness.

While Prince Kendryk dismounted, Teodora rose and came down one step. He met her, and without hesitation, knelt on the hard stone, took her hand, and kissed it. "Your Highness. This is the greatest honor of my life." His large and expressive eyes were some kind of greenish blue and he turned their full force on the empress.

Teodora allowed a small smile, and lifted him to his feet, then nodded at Princess Gwynneth, who had sunk into a deep curtsy right behind Kendryk. "Please rise, all of you," she said. "It is a great pleasure to meet you Prince, after our pleasant correspondence."

That pleasant correspondence had led to one of the empress's noisiest tantrums. It was said that she destroyed more palace porcelain on the night she received Kendryk's letter than the barbarians did during the first sacking of Forli.

Kendryk waved over a soldier. "Bring the prisoner," he said, then turned back to Teodora. "Your Highness, I have here Father Edric Landrus, who has been in my custody these past months. As we agreed, I am now turning him over to you until his trial."

Teodora seemed surprised at the sight of the prisoner, unbound, approaching her between two unarmed guards. He sank into a deep bow.

"Goodness." She raised an eyebrow. "It seems no one worried you would escape."

Father Landrus looked up at her. "I gave Prince Kendryk my word, Your Highness. Besides, I have no wish to escape."

Braeden wasn't sure what to make of Landrus, and so it seemed, neither did Teodora. For a man who likely faced the stake in a matter of days, he was amazingly cool.

Braeden wondered if Prince Kendryk had something up his frilly sleeve. If he'd wanted to avoid this trial, he might have pardoned Landrus, or contrived an escape. But he hadn't. From the look on his face, he wasn't happy turning him over to the empress, although his slight frown disappeared almost as soon as it came. Though young, the prince was in charge of his emotions.

Teodora nodded to Flavia Maxima, who nodded to someone else, and a Temple guard led Landrus away.

"Well, I believe that concludes our business for now." Teodora offered a polite smile, and Kendryk smiled back. "I will expect you and your household tonight at the feast given by Princess Viviane at her palace."

"We would be honored, Your Highness." Kendryk bowed again, and backed up a step to his horse which stood right behind him. That was well-timed, and probably no accident. No more bowing and scraping than was necessary.

For once, Braeden looked forward to a formal dinner.

GWYNNETH

Gwynneth couldn't wait for Princess Viviane's banquet. Kendryk and Teodora would be seated together so they could converse. Kendryk was nervous, but Gwynneth was sure he would do well.

In addition, all the Kronland rulers who had traveled to Isenwald would be present. Eight out of twelve had made the journey in response to Gwynneth's letters. She knew they would watch Kendryk closely.

Kendryk and Gwynneth arrived early since Gwynneth wanted time to greet everyone before Teodora arrived. Though not as fine as Birkenhof, Princess Viviane's palace was worthy of hosting an empress. She seated over three hundred guests in her great hall. Thousands of candles blazed from chandeliers of Sanovan crystal, silver candelabras on every surface and wall sconces made of amber-studded gold.

Teodora wore a gown even more elaborate than the one she'd appeared in that afternoon. A deep red silk embroidered with gold flowers and studded with rubies and pearls, it must have weighed a great deal, though she wore it effortlessly. A red lace collar rose high over her dark hair, piled high and studded with jewels.

Several dozen courtiers and ladies flanked Teodora, and she came with an impressive bodyguard of six Sanova Hussars. The two largest and best-looking—one dark and one fair—stood behind her, faces grim. They were probably too warm in their plate armor, leopard skins and furred, feathered hats. Gwynneth thought they looked splendid and smiled at them appreciatively until the fair one turned red under his beard.

Kendryk sat at Teodora's right, Gwynneth at her left. Gwynneth took care to engage Princess Viviane in conversation so Kendryk could devote all of his attention to and use his considerable charm on Teodora. This was all the more effective because it seemed so sincere and unpracticed; almost puppyish and clumsy. When Gwynneth had first been its target she fell in love instantly. Teodora might be less susceptible.

Kendryk began as soon as everyone had settled in. "I am grateful to Your Highness for agreeing to meet us here. I know it's unusual, but under the circumstances it was necessary."

"Was it?" Teodora asked. "It seems a great deal of trouble for a common heretic."

"The problem is, the people don't see Father Landrus as a common heretic. To them, he's a savior with the answer to all of their problems. Normally, he wouldn't be so important, but in these unstable times, removing him might lead to political unrest."

"Which you could control." Teodora's voice seared like acid. What an unpleasant person she was. "Do you not command many troops?"

"In theory." Kendryk smiled, seeming unfazed by her tone. "But, those troops are part of a militia comprising the same citizens who adore Father Landrus."

"They should still do as they're told," Teodora persisted.

"They should." Kendryk kept smiling. "But just because they should, doesn't mean they will. I'm sure you've found that to be the case?" He softened the barb by turning his luminous gaze on her full-bore.

"There will always be rebels." Teodora waved her hand.

"Will there? It seems possible that people won't rebel if they are content. Although I'm sure that's harder to accomplish in a diverse and far-flung empire."

"You have no idea. Whenever I please one group, another is offended. This whole affair is a good example."

Kendryk nodded. "No matter the outcome of the trial, someone will be unhappy."

"What would make you happy?" Teodora asked.

Kendryk's eyes flew to Gwynneth's.

Teodora didn't miss a thing. "Oh come. Surely your wife need not approve your opinion."

A gasp went up around the table. Even though conversation flowed between the rulers of Kronland and members of the imperial court, everyone was listening with one ear to the discussion at the head.

"Of course not," Kendryk said, without the slightest hint of offense. "Although I always value her thoughts."

"Quite a good husband then, aren't you?" Teodora sneered at her own husband, seated near the table's middle. Prince Raynard ignored her. "Unlike some."

"I try to be," Kendryk said. "But in this matter, my own feelings are immaterial. I wish for the truth to be made known, but a trial of this nature doesn't seem like the correct forum for that."

"Oh? Why not?" Teodora finished a goblet of wine and waved for more. Gwynneth had lost count of how many she'd had already. They hadn't even finished the second course.

"Its purpose is to prove whether Father Landrus's ideas are heretical," Kendryk replied. "It's possible they are. Yet at one point, most of the beliefs we take for granted were heresy."

"Long, long ago, before there was an Imperata who could offer correct interpretations."

"But since then, there have been many councils, many of which have changed our dogma. It's been two hundred years since the last one. Don't you believe it's time for another?"

Teodora laughed. "I certainly don't. I believe our current beliefs have served us well and continue to. That they are being questioned at this moment strikes me as politically convenient more than anything."

Kendryk was unperturbed. "That would be the cynical view. I'm no cynic, however."

"You are probably alone in this room on that count."

"Perhaps. But then, I've never been one to follow a crowd."

"You seek the truth instead. How noble." Teodora's tone was mocking, but Gwynneth could tell she was unnerved. Kendryk had spoken frankly, as to an equal, and it was obvious she was not accustomed to that.

Worse for Teodora, many at the table approved of Kendryk's words. The imperial councilors were wise enough not to make a peep, but the various Princes and Princesses of Kronland agreed with Kendryk openly. Those of the northern lands, Bronson Falk, Floreta Bensen, Andret Klemens and Ossian Dahlby had all made the long journey, and were most vocal in their support. Gwynneth tried to hide her pleasure. It wouldn't do to gloat so soon.

KENDRYK

To be sure the trial didn't start without his input, Kendryk asked to see the empress the next morning. She received him in private; only her chief adviser, Count Solteszy, and a pretty blond secretary were present. The setting was informal, in Princess Kasbirk's somber study. The wood paneling and carpets were so dark that even the sunlight streaming through the long windows seemed dulled.

Kendryk also felt muted. Perhaps it was the weight of his obligations, or perhaps it was his outfit. Gwynneth had taken great care in picking out a suit of a sober deep blue. Wearing it made Kendryk feel old and responsible.

Teodora was waiting for him when the door opened, standing in the middle of the room in a pool of light. Today she wore a different dress of deep red, this one far less stiff and formal than what she had previously worn. The low neckline showed off her still lovely skin.

Kendryk kept his eyes on hers as he bowed over her outstretched hand. "Your Highness, Thank you for seeing me. I realize this is unorthodox."

Teodora raised an eyebrow. "Everything about this is unorthodox, but here we are." It was hard to know what to make of her cool tone. She led him to a corner of the room, where Count Solteszy already stood, greeting Kendryk with a bow. The pretty secretary sank into a deep curtsy until Teodora slapped her arm, at which she quickly straightened up.

They sat facing each other across a little table holding a dainty tea service. The secretary poured. Kendryk set his cup on the table after taking a perfunctory sip.

"I suppose you wish to get started," Teodora said. "I have several unhappy courtiers who had hoped to be present at these negotiations."

"So do I. I thought that the trial might take a great deal of time already, and the two of us might come to an agreement more quickly."

"Maybe." Teodora sipped her tea. "I'm surprised you brought no one with you. I was sure that wife of yours would want to be involved."

If she'd buried an insult there, Kendryk ignored it. "She's far more interested in seeing old friends who've also come." He didn't bother to mention that Gwynneth was buttonholing those old friends to offer political support against Teodora. "Shall we discuss the trial?"

"If you wish. Though I can't imagine what there is to talk about." She leaned back in her chair, her eyes challenging.

"I have a few specific requests."

"Oh, you do, do you?"

He pretended not to notice her tone and pulled a small book out of his pocket. In it he had written everything he, Gwynneth and Count Faris could think of that might work to Landrus's advantage. "First, I'd like to call witnesses on Father Landrus's behalf, in equal number to those called for the prosecution."

"I don't like it. It's not the way tribunals are done."

"But this isn't a tribunal, with only Flavia here to judge." He could see from her face he had her there. "And in any other imperial court, it's customary for the defense to call witnesses."

"Oh, all right. Though I don't see what difference it could make. Please don't tell me you want a lawyer for the accused. That would go too far."

"A lawyer won't be necessary. But I would like to speak." Kendryk's own lawyer had already briefed him on everything he might say to make a good case for the priest.

"Hmph. I don't much like that, either. But if I don't allow it, every ruler here will take offense. Very well. You may speak."

It was going well, but Kendryk didn't expect her to give way on every point. "And one more thing. Father Landrus ought to speak on his own behalf."

"No. He's said more than enough to condemn himself already."

"This is a trial. Doesn't he have the right to explain himself?"

"He has whatever rights I say he has." Spots of color appeared on her cheeks.

Kendryk concentrated on breathing evenly and leaned back. Whatever she did, he had to stay cool. Most people didn't fare well when Teodora lost her temper and there was too much at stake here for him to crumble in the face of it.

"This has gone far enough." She set her cup on the table with a clatter. "I don't know what you're trying to do. But if you believe you can take advantage of the newness of my rule, or of some perceived weakness in my position, you are wrong."

"I believe no such thing."

"Then what are you playing at?" She appeared a little calmer though still breathing hard. It seemed she was accustomed to flying off the handle whenever she felt like it, but knew she shouldn't do so in front of Kendryk.

"I am sympathetic to your situation." He kept his voice even, hoping she might notice its contrast to her agitation. "I understand what it's like to be in the early phases of consolidating one's rule since I did it just a few years ago. I remember what it was like to have others try to exploit your position. You are my sovereign, and I wish to be a good subject." He saw she had calmed down a little and was regarding him warily.

"I did not request this trial to cause you problems," he continued. "In fact, your interest surprised me, and I was even more surprised that you came. My goal is not to cause you embarrassment or inconvenience of any kind. I simply wish to avert a rebellion."

"Is that a threat?" She didn't seem angry anymore even though her question was.

"It's not a threat. I understand your other kingdoms have kept you busy, but things are going much the same way all over Kronland. Terragand is less volatile than some of the others, but there's trouble enough. Father Landrus stands for every grievance, real or imagined, that many citizens have against the empire. If he's not given a fair hearing, there will be trouble before this trial is a day old."

"Then we're back to the question of why you don't put a stop to any trouble?" Teodora asked.

"Perhaps. But perhaps you also noticed I came with a large contingent of armed men. They aren't here to threaten you; they are here to show everyone I intend to enforce the law, which also is your law."

"I can't make you out." She shook her head. "You've already caused me a great deal of trouble, and I fear a lengthy trial will cause more. If Landrus may speak, the people may well go wild."

"They may," he agreed. "But they are almost certain to if they find he may not speak. The common folk know nothing of protocol and procedure. They care about what they perceive to be just. It's in both our interests if you appear to be so. Don't you agree?"

Teodora looked at him long. The secretary refilled their cups. "I can see why you don't need a lawyer; you might as well be one yourself. I will need time to consider this."

JANNA

Janna reached the end of the row and straightened up. Her back still ached, but at least her hands holding the hoe had a heavy layer of calluses and no longer felt like they were on fire. She wiped sweat from her forehead and put the straw hat back on straight. Without it, she would burn bright red.

She looked back down the row, satisfied with herself. The cabbage plants finally looked like something someone might eat someday. Even the plants she thought she'd destroyed several weeks ago when she was first learning to hoe seemed to have recovered. Next, she'd do the beans.

She wondered if Betha had planted enough to even feed one person through the winter. It didn't seem likely. Janna hadn't realized how much work it took to grow so little food. She had been fortunate, buying just about anything she wanted from the market. She wondered if she'd ever be able to do that again. Even if she found a market, she would probably never have money again, the way she had with Dimir.

She shook her head and got back to work. She was halfway down the next row when she heard Anton calling for her. He ran toward her, two goats at his heels.

"Anton, keep those animals out of the field." She hated the goats, but Anton loved them and the feeling was mutual.

"People are coming, Mama."

She dropped the hoe. "What kind of people? Raiders?" Her first and greatest fear was that Tomescu would find Betha's farm and attack it.

"I don't think so. They have a wagon."

"All right, I'll come." She couldn't imagine who it might be. The neighbors kept to themselves and the farm wasn't visible from the road. It might be a peddler. "Put the goats in their pen and wash your hands." The goats wouldn't stay in the pen long, but with any luck the visitor would get into the house before being attacked.

Whoever was coming had already arrived. Janna first went behind the house and washed her hands and face at the bucket that stood next to the well. From the kitchen she heard voices from the front of the house. She took a deep breath and walked out. She had seen no one new these past several weeks and had liked it a great deal. It couldn't last, of course.

Betha stood in front of the house with a man, a woman and a girl of perhaps fourteen. Their wagon was small; not much larger than the cart Janna had taken out of Kaleva, but was mostly empty and the horse pulling it was skinny and sad-looking.

"And who are you?" the man asked. He was a short, bandy-legged fellow with small close-set eyes and a mouth set in a thin line.

"This is Janna," Betha said. "She and her son have been helping me on the farm." Anton had come up from behind and stood next to her.

"Don't look like they'd be much use." The woman sniffed. She was a full head taller than the man and her face was so red Janna reckoned she must have gotten a sunburn, or was angry, or both.

"They've been a great help," Betha said. "Janna, this is my son Havil, his wife Gerda and their daughter."

Janna managed a polite nod. "You've come to visit." She said. "How nice."

"Not to visit." Havil snorted. "We've come to stay. They were fighting in Marjatya, but now it's here too. Our town is full of soldiers. They was going to quarter them on us, but I wouldn't allow it, not with a sweet thing like our Petra around."

"Such a fool," Gerda said. "He goes whimpering like a little girl and they turfed us out. Don't know what he thought would happen."

"Oh dear," Janna said. "I can see why you might be worried." Although she really didn't, as poor Petra bore an unfortunate resemblance to Havil, but with a weaker chin. Janna was already thinking she and Anton would have to sleep in the barn. The house was barely big enough for the three of them.

"Come in then," Betha said. "You must be tired. We'll feed you and get you settled."

Janna went straight to the kitchen to look for food. Betha was right behind her.

"Listen Betha," she began, "Anton and I will sleep in the barn, or the shed. I know the house isn't big enough."

"Oh dear. I can't let you do that. It's too dreadful. I wish Havil hadn't objected to the soldiers. I'm sure Petra is in no danger, scrawny little thing that she is."

"Some soldiers don't care about that." Janna shuddered, remembering. "I don't blame him."

"It's just," Betha whispered. "I can't abide that Gerda. Always ordering everyone around. She'll just take over."

"Don't let her. It's your house." Although Janna couldn't imagine standing up to that woman, either.

Anton had disappeared when Janna and Betha laid the table. It would be a scanty meal to begin with and stretching it to three more people would hardly do. From the way they fell on the cabbage soup and the bread, it had been a while since they'd eaten. Janna didn't eat. Maybe she could find something later.

KENDRYK

Kendryk and Gwynneth spent two days hunting in the beautiful forests of Princess Kasbirk's estate and being feted by one prince after another. Kendryk felt rather popular. It was clear however, that most of Kronland's other rulers were only interested in the political implications of this trial. Most didn't seem to care in the least what happened to Landrus.

Kendryk was sure Teodora hoped to unnerve him by making him wait so long, but he received a summons on the third day.

"I've considered your proposal," Teodora said, as they settled down in the same chairs, to similar cups of tea. "And I will agree to all but one condition."

Kendryk could guess what that was, but he said nothing.

"I don't see a problem with calling witnesses, as long as Flavia approves of the individuals, and I assume she will. I'll let you speak even though I don't like the idea. But I like even less these Kronlanders complaining about it, so there you are. I can't however, allow Father Landrus to speak. I agree with you that the situation is inflamed, but disagree that allowing him to speak will make it less so. His presence at the trial alone will be a problem. So, what do you think?" She leaned back in her chair, looking obliging.

Kendryk let her wait for a long moment. "All right," he said, when she looked like she was about to spring out of her chair with impatience. "I'll agree, but with one more condition. I don't want to close the possibility of Landrus speaking."

"Whatever do you mean by that? Either you agree, or you don't." She was getting angry.

"I agree with most of it and even agree that for now, it's all right if Landrus doesn't speak. But I might change my mind. After all the witnesses have spoken for both sides, let's talk again."

"And if I don't agree to that right now?"

"Then we aren't done negotiating, it seems."

"You really are an insidious little troublemaker." She got up and paced along the windows.

Kendryk stood up too, just to be polite, and fixed his eyes on her. He didn't want her to think the conversation was over.

"Oh, don't look at me like that. You are too used to getting your way, aren't you?"

"I'm used to having civil conversations with other rulers." He walked to the windows and stood next to her.

"And now you lecture me." She moved just a little too close, her hands on her hips. She was a little taller than he was, which unnerved him.

"I'm not lecturing you." He was unhappily conscious of the flush rising up from his neck. "I just don't appreciate your implication that I'm trying to manipulate you. It's insulting."

He wasn't the only one getting flushed. Teodora's cheeks were bright pink. "You dare to speak to me like that." She stamped her foot. "Have you forgotten who I am?"

"Not for an instant. But it seems you've forgotten who I am." He wondered if he'd pushed her too far. As far as the empire was concerned, he wasn't remotely her equal. But here in Kronland, he was the senior ruler, and she was a privileged guest, no more.

"I was wondering when you'd bring that up." Her tone was accusing.

"I didn't want to. But I won't be treated like a Moraltan count or Olvisyan vassal. We have a bond, but not a close one, and it benefits from careful cultivation."

They stood staring at each other angrily for a moment. From the corner, Count Solteszy cleared his throat. Kendryk had forgotten that anyone else was in the room.

"Shall we start again?" He managed a tight smile and gestured back toward the chairs.

She stared at him a moment longer, then nodded and walked back. They both sat down again. Kendryk smoothed his palms over his breeches, surprised that they'd become sweaty. He took a deep breath. "Your counter-offer was a reasonable one, and I accept it, for the most part. Is that all right?"

She nodded though her dark eyes were still stormy.

"All I ask is that we discuss Landrus speaking one more time after all the witnesses have testified. I have a reason for this," he added quickly, seeing she was about to protest again. "If you are right and Landrus speaking will further inflame the situation, then I will agree that he should not. If the populace be-comes more unruly and starts muttering about justice and so on, it might be wise to reconsider. Does that seem reasonable?"

She stared at him for a time, one corner of her bottom lip caught in her teeth. "It seems reasonable." She'd probably been wondering what sort of trap he was setting. "But I'm not committing to anything." She shook her head and a hint of a smile crossed her face. "It seems you would have made quite a law-yer, Prince Kendryk. I rather wish you'd become one so I could deal with someone else right now."

"I was meant to become a priest, or maybe even a maximus someday, but I never considered law." Kendryk smiled, relieved that the interview was near-ly over.

"Oh, well, religion is very similar, you know."

GWYNNETH

Gwynneth and Kendryk took an open carriage to the temple for the first day of the trial. Their route took them past the city hall with the jail that held Father Landrus, and the wagon bearing him pulled out right in front of them. That seemed fitting, somehow.

Gwynneth tensed up at the first angry shouts from the crowd. But she soon realized that the people weren't angry with the priest; they were angry with his imprisonment. The shouts turned to cheers, and those became even louder when Kendryk and Gwynneth passed. She nudged Kendryk to smile and wave. Even though the townspeople would not decide the outcome of the trial, there was always a possibility that Flavia Maxima might be swayed by her congregation.

The crowds grew denser and friendlier as they approached the temple. Gwynneth couldn't help but wonder what sort of reception Teodora was receiving, coming to the temple by another route.

The Kronfels Temple was one of the largest in the empire, but there still wasn't enough rooms inside for all the interested parties to attend. All rulers and their courtiers found seats, but commoners had to make do with standing in aisles, and even spilled out into the square. Gwynneth was sure whispered dispatches would be relayed outside from those lucky enough to see everything firsthand.

Princess Kasbirk, as the hostess, sat in front of the high altar. Kendryk, Gwynneth and the rest of the Terragand party sat on her left, with Teodora and her court on the right. It allowed Gwynneth an excellent view of Teodora since the benches all faced the center at a slight angle.

Based on the empress's expression, her reception en route had been less than wonderful. A large contingent of Sanovan cavalry accompanied her, and her two favorite troopers now stood glowering over her shoulder. Two red spots had appeared on Teodora's cheeks, and Gwynneth wondered if they were about to be treated to one of her famous tantrums. According to Kendryk, she'd barely kept a check on her temper during their negotiations. It would be very helpful to them if Teodora lost it here, in front of everyone.

Gwynneth had to admit the color looked well on her. Teodora used cosmetics to keep her skin an unblemished white sheet, but it didn't show off the planes of her face and her superb coloring to advantage. Not that Gwynneth would ever tell her.

The excited buzzing inside the temple heightened as four guards led Father Landrus into a docket, chains on his wrists and ankles. Gwynneth could feel Kendryk stiffen in outrage, and she squeezed his hand. To his credit, Landrus looked unconcerned by his altered state.

The buzzing died down as soon as Flavia Maxima took her place at a seat in front of the high altar, followed by a string of underlings. Flavia was a large, grim-faced woman who did not appear to look forward to her task. She shot angry looks at the empress and Kendryk though Kendryk didn't seem to notice.

The Maxima called the trial to order and then led a religious service that lasted two hours. That should have calmed even the most frazzled nerves.

Next, Flavia asked Father Landrus if he understood the charges against him.

"I do, Your Holiness, but please make note that I disagree with them and question your authority to try my case in the sight of the gods." His sonorous voice rang through the temple, so everyone heard. There was a collective gasp at his audacity. Flavia raised her eyebrows and Teodora's red spots returned. Perhaps she would explode after all.

"Are you quite finished?" Flavia asked.

"For now," Landrus said. A murmur ran through the temple again. Gwynneth was pleased. Father Landrus hadn't lost his nerve.

"In that case, I call the first witness for the Temple."

This was Julia Maxima, and Gwynneth worried Kendryk would take this hard, even though they had known she would appear. He still seemed to see her unwillingness to support Landrus as a personal betrayal.

Julia gave Kendryk a long look while Gwynneth squeezed his hand again. Kendryk's excellent composure didn't fail him though the hand that returned the pressure was cold and clammy. Julia spoke for a long time. She told of how she'd recognized the young priest's scholarly gifts, first promoting him, then after some years, trusting him with the study of the Scrolls.

"Not only did he break the trust I placed in him, he broke a sacred vow that all who study the Scrolls must take. This vow exists for a good reason. We have long understood that the Scrolls hold many mysteries. The Faith is ill-served if any one person—no matter how learned—takes it upon himself to trust in his own understanding. We realize that the gods grant each of us a small part of all that is known. The Imperata alone is granted greater insight."

She carried on like this at length. Landrus had violated the sacred traditions and laws of the Temple and had broken his sacred oath. Gwynneth wondered how he had justified that to Kendryk, who took these matters seriously.

After Julia's testimony, there was a break and Kendryk and Gwynneth dined at a nearby nobleman's home. Teodora went elsewhere. It seemed the local aristocracy was doing its best to keep the two parties separated.

Upon their return, Flavia Maxima called witnesses against Landrus. These included several noted theologians and each of them read from written versions of Landrus's sermons and dissected them. Line by line, they read each sermon aloud, and refuted every objectionable item, sometimes at great length. It was all terribly boring, but Gwynneth could sense Kendryk's fascination.

At supper that evening, he tried to explain the theologians' errors, but she just laughed. "Oh darling please, I've heard nothing else all day. You realize it all doesn't make a bit of difference. You've called your own witnesses, haven't you?"

"Yes, but I worry that Flavia has already decided."

"I think Flavia will hew to the official line. We expected as much. Our only chance is letting her see the public sentiment against a conviction. Try not to worry so much. You've done everything you can."

"I hope so," Kendryk said, looking pale and picking at his food.

The prosecution went on for days. Even Landrus's chambermaid testified that she had seen him copying from the Scrolls when she was quite sure "he dursen't."

Gwynneth knew that Landrus had his own copy of the Scrolls at Birkenfels, but she hadn't realized how illegal that was. Kendryk must have known this and gone along with it anyway. If he was willing to break the letter of the law in this way, perhaps he wouldn't shrink from other methods, especially if it would save his friend.

JANNA

The room was silent while everyone ate. "So," Havil pushed his plate away. "Where do you belong, young lady?"

"Kaleva," Janna said.

"Why aren't you there?"

"It's a long story."

"We have time." Havil smirked. She did not care for the way he looked at her, and neither did Gerda, judging from the way she glared at him and at Janna in turn. Petra kept her head down. Janna didn't think she'd seen her eyes yet.

Janna opened her mouth, but Betha interrupted. "Her husband was killed in the fighting in Kaleva and it's not yet safe for her to go back."

"A rebel then." Gerda let her spoon clatter to the table. "I won't have my daughter around those who don't respect the lawful empress."

"Oh, I'm not a rebel," Janna protested. "I have nothing against the empress. My husband had strange political ideas, I suppose."

"Then you should have convinced him he was wrong," Gerda said. "It's our job to keep our husbands on the straight and narrow."

"Well, I couldn't." Heat rose up Janna's cheeks. "I wish I had, or he'd still be alive. It's too late though, isn't it?"

"Oh see, now you've upset her," Betha said. "Don't be unkind, Gerda."

Gerda snorted.

As she and Betha were cleaning up, and the others were bringing their things in, Janna said, "I insist on sleeping in the barn. It's not a problem. We'll take a few blankets. The nights are so warm right now." She didn't say she wasn't interested in sleeping under the same roof with Havil, whose leer had become more pronounced as the evening wore on.

163

When she and Anton settled into the hayloft, he said, "I don't like those people, Mama."

"I know." She sighed. "I don't either. We'll try to leave as soon as we can. Perhaps by the time we get back to Kaleva, it will be safe."

"But Betha needs our help."

"Not anymore. She'll have a grown man and woman, and the girl."

"But who will look after the animals?"

"I suppose Petra can."

"She can't. She'll be afraid of the goats and they won't behave."

"Maybe. Or you can teach her how to handle them, hmm?"

Anton huffed and rolled over.

When Janna came into the kitchen in the morning, Gerda was at the stove.

"Oh, you're letting Betha rest. How nice."

Gerda snorted. "I told her to make herself scarce. It's time you and the boy left."

Janna stopped short. "Right now?"

"The sooner the better." Gerda turned toward her, holding a wooden spoon like a weapon. Janna shrank back.

"We were planning on leaving soon anyway, but I thought ..."

"I don't care what you think. But I care about the way my husband looks at you and I'm not having it."

"I'm not interested in your husband."

"You'd say that. A bit of baggage like you, it's plain as day, isn't it?"

"What is?" Janna backed into a corner.

"That you're looking for another man. Useless little thing like you can't get by without one."

"I can," Janna whispered. "I did."

"Well, you're not having mine."

"I ... I don't want yours. I swear I don't."

"Well, I don't care, and I'm not taking the chance. Havil's always had a roving eye and if I don't watch out, he'll wander off one of these days. You're just the thing to tempt him."

"I would not." Janna mustered up indignation through her fear. "I'd never do anything to tempt your husband."

"Well, lucky for you, all you have to do is be under the same roof. No, you've got to go."

"All right," Janna said, bewildered. "I'll go say goodbye to Betha."

"That won't be necessary. She'll just carry on and try to get you to stay."

"I'd like to see her."

But Gerda advanced on her with the spoon, looming over her, and Janna decided not to push her luck. "I'll get my son and we'll be on our way."

Anton cried at leaving the goats and it wasn't until they were back on the main road that Janna realized they hadn't even had breakfast. Another meal didn't seem likely anytime soon.

BRAEDEN

After several witnesses unfriendly to the priest had appeared, Braeden's job became more difficult. The crowds lining Teodora's path rumbled angrily and one morning on the way to the temple, someone shouted, "There goes Vica's whore."

"Do something," Teodora said under her breath between gritted teeth. Braeden directed the other hussars to move in closer and scanned the crowd. He saw unfriendly faces, but no obvious culprit. He ordered a few other hussars to keep a close eye on the crowd and arrest anyone who misbehaved.

It was an exercise in futility. The crowd was large and even if the hussars saw someone act, they'd never reach them before they disappeared. They were too few to overcome the people and doing so would have been disastrous anyway.

Teodora dined in the city that evening, so they could return to the palace after dark. As soon as they arrived, Braeden followed her inside. "Might I have a word, Your Highness?"

She whirled around. "Why don't you do your job? You should have arrested those people and anyone stopping you should have suffered the consequences."

He felt his temper rise. "Your Highness, Kronfels isn't Atlona. I can't break heads because someone shouted an insult."

"Why not?" She seemed astonished.

"With all respect Your Highness, you do not rule here. Princess Kasbirk does. Should I ask for more guards from her? They will be better able to handle the crowds."

She flounced into a room and Braeden followed her. Just inside, Brytta squeaked in protest, but Braeden ignored her.

"Shut the door," Teodora said, and Braeden closed it behind him. She flung herself into a chair. "This is intolerable."

Braeden was silent.

"This is my empire and I ought to be able to do as I please. When did this happen? Which one of my incompetent predecessors let Kronland get away?"

Braeden assumed she didn't expect an answer. He didn't know it in any case.

"I don't want Kasbirk involved in this. Oh, she'll offer her guards while crowing over my unpopularity behind my back. I shouldn't need her. It's maddening. Do you ever say anything?"

"I did, Your Highness. A few minutes ago." Braeden shifted to his other foot.

"That's not what I meant. You look fearsome enough as a bodyguard, but I do wish you had better conversation."

"I am very sorry I don't, Your Highness."

"It's not your fault, I suppose." She sighed. "I pay you to fight, not to talk, and you seem to manage the fighting bit well enough."

She stood up again and paced the room. "Let's not involve Princess Kasbirk for now. I'll deal with these Kronlanders later. Oh, I realize they have their precious charters, but charters can be rewritten. Once the Zastwar situation has settled down, I'll make them sorry they ever so much as looked at me sideways here. Especially that little Prince Kendryk. I don't believe a man has annoyed me so much since my husband last ..." She stamped her foot, then turned to Braeden again. "So, what do you propose we do?"

Surprised, since he'd fallen half asleep while she rambled, Braeden pulled himself together. "I suggest a closed carriage, Your Highness. And those of us guarding in plain liveries, not our hussar regalia. You could pass for just another noble that way."

"Not draw attention to myself, hmm. That seems ridiculous. What's the point of being empress when you can't let people see you are?"

"I don't know, Your Highness."

"I wasn't expecting an answer. You really are dense, aren't you?"

"Sometimes, Your Highness."

"Don't take that tone with me, Terris. Your Prince Novitny isn't here to help you should I decide you need to disappear."

"No, he's not, Your Highness." Braeden found the thought depressing. He missed the prince and his other comrades. It wasn't right they'd been split up like this.

167

"Oh gods, don't look so sad. I don't plan to kill you, at least not right now. I'm just very frustrated."

Braeden nodded, hoping that wouldn't make things worse.

She sighed heavily. "Very well. I'll take a closed carriage. But I still want the lot of you in full armor and looking fierce. I refuse to be anonymous. We'll put it about that I have a headache and the sunlight makes it worse. I would hate it if anyone thought I was intimidated."

Braeden shifted to the other foot again. This wasn't a good time, but he had to know. "Your Highness, I've heard rumors about Andor Korma."

"Do not speak that name in front of me," she screamed.

Braeden jumped.

Teodora pulled herself together with visible effort. "Yes, yes it's all true. He's crossed the border and is a mere fifty leagues from Atlona. General Ensden is too far away to stop him."

"Perhaps we should head back. If we hurry, we might make Atlona before Korm—I mean, the rebel does."

"No." She shook her head so vehemently, hair spilled out of its pins. "If I leave now, no matter how good the reasons, the Kronland rulers will never respect me again. I must see this trial through, and we'll go as soon as there's a guilty verdict. Your lot will hold the city, won't they?"

"Oh sure." Braeden was on firmer ground here. "No one will get past them. Problem is getting out once a big army is there."

"Yes, I know." Teodora dropped into a chair. "Gods, I'm tired. If I'd known that being empress would be one annoyance after another, I never would have bothered. My cousin could have had the job. All right, Terris." She closed her eyes. "I'll use a closed carriage. You can stay in that armor. You seem to frighten people. Let's get this priest convicted and we'll make for Atlona with all speed. With any luck, the Zastwar treaty will soon be signed and Ensden can meet us so we can take on that Marjatyan monster. I refuse to say his name. He is a nobody."

"I'll say good night then, Your Highness." Braeden backed out of the room before she screeched at him again.

The trial dragged on. Kendryk assembled an impressive array of witnesses, including two priests and a priestess who were old friends from Landrus's school days. They must have been taking considerable risk to do this, not just to their careers, but to their lives, should they ever leave Terragand.

These clerics also dissected Landrus's sermons and appeared to come to opposite conclusions from those found earlier. It seemed to Braeden that the confusion was now so complete it would be impossible to find if heresy had in fact been done.

Civilian witnesses spoke after the clergy. These were prominent citizens who belonged to Landrus's congregation in Runewald.

Even Flavia Maxima's hatchet face softened visibly when Prince Kendryk finally testified. He spoke of Father Landrus's good character and his loyalty to both faith and Temple. Young, earnest, attractive, and already popular, Kendryk made a good impression on the audience, and judging by the many big words he used, seemed to have a firm grasp of theology.

Not that it mattered. Little as Braeden understood, he understood well enough that Flavia would never proclaim the priest's innocence in front of Teodora. Kendryk was wasting his time.

KENDRYK

Kendryk rode at Teodora's side, his horse treading silently on a needle-strewn path, a vast canopy of branches overhead. It was dark here, but sultry, and even though it was early in the day, Kendryk was already much too warm.

Teodora glanced at him sideways. "That's a fine cuirass you're wearing. Are you worried I'll get you alone in the woods and kill you?"

"The thought never crossed my mind. But it crossed my wife's, and that's why I'm a bit overdressed." He tried to keep his tone light and friendly since there was a good chance matters wouldn't stay that way for long.

Teodora seemed amused. "I knew your wife hated me. I can always tell."

"She doesn't hate you. She just doesn't trust you."

Another sideways glance, almost flirtatious. "She's probably right, in general. Though I give my word that no harm will come to you here in the deep, dark woods. You're well-guarded in any case."

Kendryk glanced back at his twenty-man escort. "That was mostly for the sake of protocol. And I'm not as well-guarded as you are."

Teodora had come with an escort of thirty Sanova Hussars. He saw she had the same enormous blond fellow with her who stood behind her at the trial. If it came to a fight, Kendryk doubted his men would prevail.

It had rained the night before and the rising sun warmed the earth, making the ground steam. Kendryk supposed it wouldn't be long before he steamed inside his armor as well. Perhaps if he started sweating, Teodora would think she was wearing him down.

"I'm sure you remember what we discussed a few weeks ago," he began, since Teodora did not try to start the conversation. In fact, he doubted she would have raised the subject again if he hadn't sent her a message by way of reminder.

"We discussed several things," she said.

"We did." Kendryk reminded himself to be patient. "And we agreed to discuss one of them again when the trial was nearing its end. We are just a few days away from the last witnesses for the defense, so it's time."

"There's no point in talking about it. I haven't changed my mind."

"Might I ask why not?" She had to be aware of the deteriorating situation.

"I don't see how allowing a heretic to speak will make these unpleasant people any less unpleasant." So she was aware.

"I am sure that if he doesn't speak, they will only get worse."

"Oh, you are? How can you be certain?"

"I can't. But I'd rather not find out, and I assume you feel the same way."

She looked at him out of the corner of her eye again. "Oh, I don't know. In some ways, I would welcome open rebellion because it would allow me to put a stop to it without all of this endless prevaricating."

Kendryk felt his temper rise. "You'd prefer violence just so you could enjoy putting it down?"

She laughed. "You make it sound so terrible."

"It is terrible. Especially when it's preventable." He hoped it wasn't his anger taking over, but he decided it was time to bring up the one thing he hadn't yet dared. "And besides, you won't receive the troop levies you need from Kronland if you've just slaughtered its inhabitants."

There was a long silence.

Kendryk finally ventured a look at her.

Teodora stared straight ahead, a bright red spot on her cheek. "You are the most ..." She said through gritted teeth. "Disrespectful, insolent puppy I have ever, ever ..." Her voice rose.

Kendryk's mouth fell open, and he quickly clapped it shut again. Not even his uncle dared speak to him in that tone. He took a deep breath and let it out before speaking. "Please believe me, Your Highness. I intend no disrespect. I merely wished to point out that. .."

"Point out what?" Teodora pulled her horse to an abrupt stop. Kendryk followed suit. "Point out that you and the other Kronland rulers will refuse to abide by the terms of your charter if I don't give you what you want?"

"It's not that simple." Kendryk's heart hammered against his ribs. "Our charters don't just dictate our responsibilities; they give us rights as well."

"I don't want to hear about your rights!" Teodora shrieked, accidentally spurring her horse, which bolted down the path. The large hussar went after her and grabbed the reins before it went far.

Kendryk followed at a more sedate pace. Merton came up to his elbow. "Should I stay closer, Your Grace?" he murmured. "She seems unpredictable."

"That's one way of putting it. Yes, please stay a little closer. I'd like a friendly witness if she becomes too uncivil." Perhaps Gwynneth had been right about the armor after all and Teodora would become uncivil enough to try to kill him.

JANNA

They walked in silence for a while, then Anton said, "Those are nasty people. Poor Betha. What are we supposed to do now?"

"We'll go to Kaleva. It's been a few months since we left and perhaps they've stopped looking for us. But to be safe, we'll use my old name, all right? I'll be Janna Beran, like I was before I married your Papa, and you'll be Anton Beran. You can remember that, can't you?"

Anton nodded. "Will we stop at the crossroads?"

"We must. I think it's the first place we can get food. It's a long walk, but I'm sure we can make it." She tried to sound more hopeful than she felt. Neither one of them had had much supper the night before, and they hadn't received breakfast either.

"I think we can do it. But isn't Trepol closer?"

"Yes, it would take us less than a day. But I don't know what's there. It sounds like things are worse in Marjatya now, so I don't want to go in that direction."

It soon became clear they would need water before food. The day was hot and the road dusty. There was little traffic. They saw one peddler and one farmer hauling a wagon of hay. Both told Janna to get back to where she came from. "There's marauders about, and soldiers," the farmer frowned.

"We have nothing for them to take."

"Oh yes you do," the farmer said. "At least stay off the road if you can."

"We have no food. We need to get to the Sanova crossroads."

"You're in a right scrape, aren't you? I'd give you something to eat, except I don't have none myself. I'm taking this hay to Count Manek's estate, in hopes they'll trade me some."

"Do you think they'd help us there? We'll work for a bit to eat."

"They won't help you, at least not at a price you'd be willing to pay. In fact, if I were you, I'd go nowhere near that place. Every father who knows what's what keeps his daughters well away from the count, and his son's even worse."

Janna felt even more hopeless by the time the farmer left them. At least he gave them directions to an abandoned farm nearby that still had a good well. They drank their fill and tried to rest through the worst heat of the day. Janna hoped they'd be able to keep walking after dark. The moon was near full, and with the road so empty, perhaps no one would bother them.

It got cooler after dark, but the hunger and thirst were much worse now. With no landmarks and no one to ask, Janna did not know how far they still had to go. The moon was bright, and it was possible to see far ahead on the road. So they had plenty of warning when they noticed the soldiers.

The soldiers saw them, too. Janna pulled Anton off the road and into a stand of trees as fast as she could, but the men were on horseback, and were upon them before they could hide.

"Don't fight," she whispered to Anton the moment she knew they couldn't escape. "They'll just hurt you and it won't do any good."

"I have to do something," he whispered back fiercely.

"We'll both do what we must to stay alive. Let's do it for Papa, hm?"

A man jumped off a large horse, strode to where Janna stood in the brush and grabbed her by the arm. "Someone get the boy," he said, as he yanked her toward the road.

Another man picked Anton up and carried him toward the horses. Anton struggled, but he was too small. The man just laughed and threw him on the ground, then held him there, a boot planted on his back.

"Please let him go. He's just a little boy." To her surprise, her voice didn't shake. Perhaps she'd gotten stronger. Still, not strong enough for this.

"We noticed," one man laughed. "I'm sure we can find a use for him."

"Just don't hurt him, please. I'll do whatever you want."

Several men laughed at that, and one said. "Oh, you'll do whatever we want anyway. You're not in a good place to make a deal, girl."

"I have nothing," Janna said. "Not even food."

"Got thrown out, did you?" Someone laughed. "The wife likely found out the little maid isn't as innocent as she looks."

Janna gritted her teeth and said nothing. A few ribald jokes were the least of her worries.

"Looks like you're in need of a new position. Till then, though, I'd say you're available for sampling," another fellow put in. By now, they were crowding her. Several were still mounted, and the horses were uncomfortably close, stomping and snorting hot breath into her face.

"I'm a respectable woman." Her voice shook now. "My son and I must get to Kaleva. If you were gentlemen, you wouldn't cause us trouble on the way."

There was laughter. "Never claimed to be gentlemen," one man said. "Though I've been called worse. Anyway, I've had enough of this refined chit-chat. I don't know about you boys, but I ain't seen a wench this pretty in weeks, and I for one intend to enjoy myself."

Janna jumped back, but hands grabbed her on either side. Anton was still on the ground and she couldn't see his face. She hoped he'd have the sense to look away. "Not in front of my son, at least." Tears slid down her face. They had taken surprisingly long to come.

"For someone in such a bad place, you sure have a lot of demands," one of the men holding her said. She cringed away from his sour breath, and he laughed into her face. "No matter, you won't be near so picky once we're through with you."

Panic-stricken, she tried to count them. Not even a dozen. Maybe eight. The blood roared in her ears. What did it matter how many? She doubted she could survive it. They probably wouldn't let her.

She prayed. First to the Mother, to save her life and to give these men pause, and perhaps some compassion. Then to Ercos, for strength to endure it. That didn't seem forthcoming as her legs turned to water when a man dragged her to the side of the road.

He threw her down hard, and stars flashed before her eyes as her head bounced off the ground. She rolled to her side, and tried to crawl away, but a boot landed in her stomach, and the breath whooshed out of her chest. She opened her eyes, saw nothing but black, so she squeezed them shut again, and prayed Anton had done the same.

KENDRYK

Teodora threw off the guard and turned her skittish horse to face Kendryk. Her breath came hard and her face was aflame.

Kendryk stopped his horse and looked straight at her. When she seemed to have mastered herself, he asked. "May I speak, Your Highness?"

"That's more like it," she muttered under her breath.

Kendryk reminded himself that most people deferred to her, and his typical haughty manner might have added to her rage.

He waited until she said, "You may speak. Just don't forget who I am, and who you are."

He attempted to look contrite. "Of course. And I apologize if gave offense." He didn't mind giving ground if it ended with him getting what he wanted.

"Oh for gods' sake. Stop looking at me like that and say what you must."

"Thank you, Your Highness. I know you don't trust me, but I am not trying to make things difficult for you. I wish to bring this trial to a speedy and peaceful conclusion so you can be on your way. You have much to worry about, and I do not wish to take advantage of that."

"Then you'd be the first," Teodora grumbled. "And you're right; I don't trust you."

"Can you at least believe that I don't wish for violence on the streets of Kronfels?"

"Oh, I believe that. You Kronlanders are far too enamored of your precious citizens. You seem to forget they are also subjects, and they are mine as well as yours."

This wasn't quite true, but Kendryk decided not to press the issue. "Then you agree that bloodshed before the trial does not help you. Most of Kronland still believes you are acting in good faith and wish for Father Landrus to receive a fair hearing."

Teodora snorted, but Kendryk continued. "You may not feel that way, but it's what most assume, and you can't deny it works to your benefit."

He waited for her agreement and got another snort.

"Even if Father Landrus speaks, I'm sure you'll get the verdict you want." He hoped the heaviness in his heart didn't show in his voice and he averted his eyes, knowing he couldn't conceal it there. "That alone will make many unhappy. But if he can speak, no one will accuse you of being the least bit unfair. In fact, you'll be able to say with complete justification that you went far above and beyond what everyone expected."

"I'm not required to do any of this," Teodora spat. Her eyes were sparking again and her guards looked alarmed.

Kendryk backed away a little and noticed Merton moving closer.

Teodora pulled herself together with visible effort. "Still, I'd rather have this conversation over with soon." She took a deep breath. "You want Landrus to speak. I will allow it. But I have a condition."

Kendryk waited, too worried about what she wanted to feel any real hope.

"I want twenty thousand Terragand troops delivered after the trial. I will renew the Zastwar treaty somehow, but then I must deal with Andor Korma."

Kendryk stared at her. "Our troops aren't to be used against threats within the empire." And twenty thousand was double Terragand's usual obligation.

"I don't care. I need them to fight Korma, and if you want your priest to have his say, you'll swear right here and now that I shall have them."

Sweat prickled on Kendryk's scalp while a frozen knot grew in his middle. This violated his charter, and Teodora knew it. "I can't make that decision here and now." From her triumphant expression, it was clear she knew she had him. "This is a serious matter, and I must consult my advisers ..."

"You know what they'd say," Teodora snapped. "That's why you must promise me right now."

"Then my answer is no." Kendryk told himself that Landrus speaking made no difference to the outcome of the trial. "If I must decide right now, I choose not to violate my charter and the law of the empire." He emphasized the last words. "Father Landrus won't speak. And since you expect to renew the treaty with Zastwar, I'll assume you won't need my troops for some time."

The look on her face made it clear she hadn't expected this. Did she think him so in the thrall of Landrus that he would violate the law to help him? "Very well," she said, turning her horse in his direction.

Kendryk backed up and turned around to fall in next to her. He was glad to have a moment to compose himself. He wondered if he'd been too rash in upholding the letter of the law, sealing his friend's fate.

Teodora pulled up as she drew level with him. "Listen carefully, little prince. You are toying with treason right now."

He opened his mouth to protest, but she continued. "Oh and stop going on about your precious charter. It's outdated and no longer fits the empire's needs. Be assured I will revisit all the charters, and yours first of all."

She looked straight at him and he forced himself to meet her gaze, aware of the color creeping up his face. By now his shirt was soaked with sweat under the armor.

"I will be clear, and I want you to remember what I say." Her voice was low but oozed menace.

Kendryk was conscious of Merton drawing closer and felt a bit comforted.

"When this trial is over, and your darling priest a mere bit of crispy meat on that stake, I shall return to Atlona and defeat Andor Korma. I will have the Zastwar treaty renewed and my armies recalled from their border. Then I will take back what my weak ancestors gave away too freely. I will start with you."

"Kronland and all of its states belong to the empire. Terragand is not an independent kingdom, and no more special than Moralta or Marjatya. You are not and never will be my equal. It may take time to bring you lot to heel, but I will and Terragand will be first on my list. If you give me any trouble at all, I will crush you like I did Moralta, and I will do it gladly. In fact, given what you've already cost me, I'm inclined to crush you anyway."

In the back of Kendryk's mind, he knew that much of this was bombast. Teodora's power in Kronland derived from the pleasure of the aristocracy and it would take more than threats to alter that. That didn't change the fact that she was in front of him, her eyes blazing hatred.

His mouth was dry, but he forced the words out. "Your Highness, I am not your enemy. Until you make the reforms you wish for, we are both bound by the law as it stands. You can't fault me for not wishing to be in rebellion against the laws you yourself swore to uphold at your coronation."

Her lips trembled, and a vein throbbed in her temple. "Never. Ever. Lecture me again," she forced out, then spurred her horse violently and disappeared down the forest path.

BRAEDEN

On the day of the verdict, Flavia decreed that the temple would not be open to spectators. Clergy, any rulers present and members of the imperial council could attend. This didn't stop an enormous crowd from gathering in the temple square and spilling into the streets.

Braeden and the hussars got Teodora's carriage into the city, through the crowded streets, and into the temple in time. Conditions on the way back were sure to be worse, especially if there was a guilty verdict.

The large temple seemed sinister and empty. Without the press of bodies, words echoed off the stone archways and sometimes it was hard to make them out.

Landrus, calm as always, sat in his docket. Kendryk looked pale and tired, and for the first time, Princess Gwynneth's cheeks were colorless.

Flavia Maxima stepped up to the podium, then asked Landrus to stand. "I have heard all of the evidence, as has everyone else present. As a person, I cannot find great fault with the character of Edric Landrus. No one who knows him can dislike him. And yet, the Faith has nothing to do with popularity. It is concerned solely with the truth and the worship of the Holy Family. The Imperata is the final word in this.

"The Temple gave Edric Landrus an unusual opportunity, then placed its trust in his discretion and his willingness to be guided by his superiors. He broke that trust. He didn't work within our traditions to make his views known. Though some of you might disagree, the Faith is not static. Our Imperata and her scholars work always to understand the Scrolls, interpret dreams and spend hours in prayers seeking further enlightenment.

"Edric Landrus sought to work outside our order, an order which nurtured him and gave him great authority. As he has misused that authority, I hereby strip him of his position as priest and scholar of the Temple." She paused while a murmur swept through the temple. If this was the full punishment, it was a light one.

Braeden watched Prince Kendryk. His eyes had lit up in his pale face, and he squeezed his wife's hand.

Flavia cleared her throat and silence fell once more. "Edric Landrus's behavior as a Temple official is the smaller issue here. Far more serious are the charges of heresy. While his words might seem reasonable to many of you, they are not part of the Faith. Even worse, many of them contradict the Faith outright. And in that matter, I have no choice but to find Edric Landrus guilty of heresy."

There was an uproar among the Kronlanders and their retinues. Prince Kendryk's face remained white and set.

Flavia raised her hand. "However, this trial has been irregular from the beginning. In most cases, a verdict of heresy carries an automatic death sentence. Due to unusual circumstances, I wish to offer the guilty party a choice." She turned to face Landrus, who still betrayed no emotion. Braeden wondered if he'd consider a military career, now he could no longer preach. He'd never seen a cooler head.

"I wish to offer you the chance to confess your heresy and admit your guilt. In exchange, I will commute your death sentence to exile. You would be required to live outside the empire, though I'm sure you could find patrons elsewhere. And you must swear never to set foot in it again, nor publish your teachings so they could be in any way disseminated within your lifetime. I will give you a day to consider this offer if you wish."

The effect of her words was extraordinary. No one had expected this development. Teodora started out of her chair, then sat back down again. No doubt she wanted to protest, but she must have realized that would have been a mistake. Flavia had just given her the gift of potential reconciliation with Terragand and Kronland.

Kendryk's eyes were full of hopeful light and fixed on Landrus.

After a few moments of excited buzzing, Landrus raised his voice. "I thank you, Flavia Maxima," he said, his tone humble, but his demeanor unruffled as always. "I am aware of the special treatment you have just given me and am honored." The crowd was silent.

"However," he said, "I cannot accept your kind offer. It is impossible for me to confess to something I know is false. I am not a heretic, and this trial has shown me I am not alone in my beliefs. The gods sent me here for a reason, and I cannot carry out my mission outside this empire. For the empire in particular needs my help."

"Enough!" Flavia snapped. "So you will not confess and agree to exile?"

"I will not," Landrus said, then bowed his head.

"In that case." She raised her voice over the growing pandemonium, "I sentence you to death by burning, to be carried out in this temple square three days hence."

Teodora rose.

"Your Holiness," she said, her voice low but carrying. "I would like to propose an alternative. It will have greater impact empire-wide if the execution takes place in Atlona. I will bear sole responsibility for the prisoner's security until that time."

Flavia looked at her, then looked at the temple doors, which now opened onto the square. News of the verdict had gone out already and the mood of the crowd was ugly. If the woman had any sense, she'd take Teodora's offer. The last thing she needed was the public execution of a popular rabble-rouser on her front door, especially while so many rulers were still present. She'd clearly sought to avoid that in the first place by giving Landrus a way out.

She looked back at Teodora. "That is an excellent idea, Your Highness, so long as Princess Kasbirk is agreeable?"

The princess was agreeable and plainly relieved to have the troublesome fellow offer her hands.

Prince Kendryk had gone from looking stricken, to hopeful again. Landrus was receiving another stay of sorts. It was a long journey to Atlona, and much could happen on the way.

GWYNNETH

Kendryk sat across from Gwynneth at a small table, staring down at his plate. He hadn't wanted to eat, but she insisted on having something sent up to their bedchamber in the borrowed house.

It seemed he could not accept several things. To him, the verdict was incomprehensible after all the discussion that had made it so clear that Father Landrus had discovered something important.

"Then," he said, pushing his food around the plate with a knife, "The compromise Flavia offered seemed like an answer to my prayers, only for him to refuse it."

"I guessed he would." Gwynneth reached across the table to take his other hand. "Once he turned down our offer to help him escape, it would have surprised me if he had agreed to it now."

"If only I had one more chance to speak to him," Kendryk said. "I know it's hard for him to confess to something he isn't guilty of, but isn't it much more important that he stay alive and continue his work?"

"It seems not. Would you confess to heresy you hadn't committed?"

"I don't know. My first answer is 'of course not,' but if faced with the stake in three days time, I might decide to live so I could redeem myself later."

"So would I." Gwynneth couldn't bear seeing him so unhappy. "In a heartbeat. But your Father Landrus truly differs from the rest of us. And that's why he's doing something the rest of us can't."

"But when he dies, then what? If no one else can replace him?"

"If he dies." Gwynneth buttered a second slice of bread. She wasn't suffering from loss of appetite. "A lot can happen between here and Atlona, especially in these uncertain times."

"I don't know what you mean."

Gwynneth raised an eyebrow. Was he deliberately misunderstanding her?

"I mean there is still hope," she said putting down her knife. "You still have a role to play."

"I think my role is finished. Why didn't he choose exile? It would have been the easier way."

"For you." She smiled. "But not for him. He told you. His work is in Terragand, nowhere else."

"Now it looks like nowhere at all." Kendryk crumbled a piece of bread onto his plate.

"On the contrary. The empress has granted him a stay of sorts, which buys us time."

"I wonder why she did that."

"Oh, she's not stupid. She sees which way the wind is blowing here. And she still needs your troop levies. The worst thing that can happen to her right now is Landrus being executed in front of all of her enemies. She's far better off presenting him as yet another rebel in a city where more people are fearful. Besides, the word is that Andor Korma has crossed the border and is making for Atlona. Even if she leaves today, she might not get there before he does."

"I don't see how that helps us, though I don't mind seeing her inconvenienced," Kendryk said, still glum.

"It helps us because she'll be distracted and in a hurry to get back. So you should be able to act and get away with it."

He shook his head. "You amaze me. Exactly what can we do at this point?"

Gwynneth pushed her plate away and took a long drink of wine. "You rescue Father Landrus and take him back to Terragand."

"What?" It was clear Kendryk had never considered the possibility. "How in the world am I supposed to do that?"

"We've brought plenty of armed men. It will be easy enough to see how well Landrus is guarded on the way to Atlona and find a good time to break him out. The empress will have all of her best troops in front, riding for Atlona as fast as they can. Landrus will just be baggage and guarded as such."

"Baggage? He's far too valuable for her to be casual about security. Besides, she might guess we would try something."

"Oh, I doubt it. I think you've done well to give her the impression that you are firm but not belligerent. You've been all charm and courtliness, so it's unlikely she'll suspect you of any violence."

"She thinks I'm too soft."

Gwynneth shrugged. "Too soft to make a bold move, perhaps. But that's a good thing. She won't be expecting any action from you besides an appeal to the imperial court or to the Imperata. She won't expect you to break Landrus free."

"Even I don't expect that." Kendryk pushed his plate away, his food still untouched. "And what if I swoop down on the imperial baggage train and rescue Landrus? It's possible we'll injure or kill people to do so. The empress could interpret that as an act of aggression."

"Maybe. Though I doubt she'll declare war. Just look at the reception she's received here. She's already fighting on two fronts and Zastwar could open a third. Even if she wants to fight you, she can't. Oh, she might throw a tantrum, but that's as far as it will go. You'll have the support of at least eight Kronland rulers; I'm sure of it."

"What does that mean? Will they stand with me against the empress if the worst happens, and she invades Terragand?"

"At least some will, I'm sure. And she can't invade because she doesn't have enough troops. What's more likely is, that by the time she has things straightened out on her eastern border, she'll complain, take you to court and you can put her off indefinitely."

"That's not how I like to do things."

"But just think of the possibilities. With the time you buy, Landrus can preach and write and his works can be published and spread all over Kronland. By the time the empress can react, you might have set up your own branch of the Faith. And with that, it's also possible that Kronland will find it doesn't need the empire either. Now is the perfect time to start this."

"I don't even want all of that," Kendryk said. "All I want right now is for Father Landrus to stay alive, to keep working and for me to learn more. I don't care about the rest."

"You may not care." Gwynneth was feeling more excited than she had in weeks. "But many others do and Father Landrus himself has said that change is essential if we are to survive."

"But you don't even believe all of those things about the final battle, do you?"

"I don't know, but I'd like to learn more and I can't do that if Landrus is dead. Listen darling." She leaned across the table and took both his hands in hers. "I know you've been waiting for a miracle, and you just got it. Now you have to do something with it. The gods will help, but they need you to act, too."

Kendryk smiled wearily and squeezed her hands, then stood. "I need to find a place to pray," he said. "I might be there all night."

Gwynneth got up and kissed his cheek. "There's a chapel down the street. I got the key for you."

Now all she could do was hope the gods gave him a push in the right direction.

BRAEDEN

Braeden wasn't sure how long he'd been asleep, but it hadn't been long. Teodora's maid looked like she hadn't had a wink. "Come quick, sir," she said. "Her Highness is in a real rage." Not that Teodora being in a rage was anything new. Braeden jumped up and made for the door, pulling on his clothes as he went. He shoved his boots on, then grabbed his pistols, fastening the belt as he followed the maid into the corridor.

The maid led him into Teodora's dressing room. Another maid was helping her fasten on a traveling cloak. If the empress was angry, it wasn't the usual; Braeden could see that right away.

"Get your troops ready, Terris." Her voice was hard as a brick, her face set and pale. "We ride for Atlona within the hour."

He nodded and prepared to leave the room.

"If it makes you hurry more, I'll tell you right now, that bastard Korma has Atlona besieged it with your precious hussars inside."

He'd expected as much. "Yes, Your Highness. We'll be ready to go soon."

He rushed back to his room and sent his servant Gergo to rouse his troops. He struggled into the rest of his clothes and what armor he could put on without help. If they were to ride fast, less was better anyway. As he strode into the corridor, he met Gergo coming back.

"Pack up my things," he ordered. "I'll meet you at the stables."

By the time he reached them, a saddled Kazmir was dancing around a nervous groom. Gergo was efficient when he needed to be; he gave him that. A good half of his hussars were also ready. He started a head count, hoping no one had celebrated the end of the trial with a drinking bout and was sleeping it off in a tavern somewhere. Anyone missing would have to catch up.

He heard shouting and another imperial servant elbowed his way through the crush.

"Message from Her Highness," he shouted at Braeden. "You're to secure the prisoner before we go."

"Is he coming with us?"

The man shook his head. "He'll be in the baggage train, but she wants him well-guarded." He handed Braeden a scrap of paper.

It looked like Teodora had scrawled it in haste, and Braeden had to take it to a nearby stable lantern to make it out. It said he was to pick twenty guards from her household troops and set them to guard the priest, and another twenty to guard the wagon bearing her children.

"Torresia," he barked, spotting Reno in the crowd. "Make sure everyone is ready within the quarter hour and go with Her Highness. I need to see to the baggage." Braeden jumped onto Kazmir. He wasn't sure where the baggage was but he found it on the other side of the stables. These were enormous since Princess Kasbirk was an exemplary breeder and always had at least five hundred head of horse. It looked like more than a few would be pressed into imperial service tonight.

The courtyard was bright with torchlight and crowded with wagons and servants rushing around. It was less chaotic than he would have expected, but when he spotted Count Solteszy, he knew why. With him in charge, the train would be no more than a few hours behind the rest of them. He cantered straight up to Solteszy.

"I'm to secure the prisoner," he said.

Solteszy nodded, his face grim. "Over there," he pointed to a heavy wagon with a barred window.

Braeden trotted over and jumped down when he got there. "Prisoner inside?" he asked an officer who might have been in charge.

The man nodded. "Aye, sir. We're waiting on further orders."

"I have them. Her Highness wants twenty guards detailed to the prisoner and twenty to the children."

"Is that all?"

"Yes. I reckon she wants the rest at the walls of Atlona as soon as possible."

"Does she realize it won't be enough?"

Braeden shrugged. "Not my problem. Or yours. I don't know the household guard as well as you, so pick the best fellows for the job and send the rest round the other side. The empress is ready to go."

"Now?"

"Within minutes. My troops are already saddled up."

"Quick work."

"Slower than I would have liked, but we'll get going soon enough. If yours aren't ready, tell them to catch up as quick as they can. We'll be on the main road south."

The man nodded and had already motioned over another officer. He shouted several names at him, the fellow ran off and he turned back to Braeden. "Tell Her Highness that Kerzer will come with near four hundred. They'll be as fast as they can."

KENDRYK

Perhaps Gwynneth was right and even a temporary stay of execution could be considered a miracle. Kendryk just didn't know what to do with that miracle.

The tiny chapel was warm, and candles burned before the icons. Kendryk paced in front of them for a time. He knew he needed to pray, but he was unsure of what to ask for. Until now, requesting guidance had resulted in nothing but a series of confusing events.

He wanted any solution except the one Gwynneth suggested. The rulers of Kronland always spoke of more independence from the empire, but until now, that was nothing more than talk. No one had done anything vaguely rebellious in a long time. That Kendryk should be the one to do so felt wrong. He just wasn't the sort. Someone like Prince Bronson seemed so much more likely. He was older, and had military experience. Why shouldn't he take the lead?

Kendryk breathed in the scent of candle wax and paused in front of the Father. The icon stared back at him with large, blank dark eyes. Even though the Holy Parents rarely intervened in human life, the Scrolls made it clear they must be worshiped and their blessing sought.

They stood for all that was sacred and alive about the land. The Father created all—the mountains, the deserts, the oceans and the rivers, the whole of earth itself. The Mother gave life to all—the creatures of the fields and the plants in them. She gave life to the first humans, but it wasn't until she gave birth to Ercos and Vica that people received understanding and strength to rise above the other animals.

Kendryk didn't know who would help him now, or if he should expect no more. Perhaps the discussions with Landrus, and his own readings of the Scrolls should have been enough to tell him what he needed to do.

He moved from one icon to the other, sending up his prayers and waiting for a response. He hoped to fall asleep again, and dream as he had before. Maybe that would spur him to action. Or perhaps there would be another sign. He wondered how many signs he needed before he'd be comfortable enough to act. He wished he could speak to Landrus one more time.

Kendryk lay on his back on the hard floor, staring straight up, into the flickering shadows vanishing into the blackness of the vaulted ceiling. His limbs were heavy with despair and exhaustion, but his head pounded and sleep would not come. He tried letting his mind wander from the immediate problem.

He recalled the hours spent in the castle's little study, reading over the Scrolls while Landrus translated other parts. It reminded him of his years in Galladium, sitting in Benet's cluttered library, poring over the ancient tongue. He loved Benet like a father, more than he loved his own father. Edwyn Bernotas had been an intimidating stranger until the last year of his life. And in that year, broken by the death of Kendryk's older brother, the prince was not himself.

Benet died less than two years later, leaving Kendryk bereft. Count Faris filled some of the gap as both a friendly and competent adviser. But Faris and Gwynneth were both entirely practical. Neither of them were interested in discussing religious stories, myths and deep theological puzzles. Gwynneth excelled at philosophy, but she liked to apply it to reality. To her, pondering the meaning of something written thousands of years before was an exercise in futility.

When Landrus came to Birkenfels, Kendryk felt like he'd found a long-lost family member. To lose him after such a short time was intolerable. When Landrus refused the maxima's offer of clemency, Kendryk was sure his heart would shatter.

Why had the gods sent Landrus to him, only to take him away again so soon? Sure, he'd learned a great deal, but in doing so also understood that he was scratching the surface. There was so much more.

Landrus had made progress on the translation, but would need at least another year to complete it. And now it looked like it would never be done. Kendryk lacked the ability and the time, and the chances of finding someone else to do it seemed minuscule. All the same, he couldn't let it end now. There must be a solution.

Kendryk saved his last prayer for Vica. He needed wisdom more than anything right now. Before he started, he silently apologized for any hard feelings he might have harbored toward the goddess. It wasn't her fault that empress and Imperata were putting her forward. The gods were not like people, who gloried in being held above others. He was sure Vica wished for a return to the proper worship as much as Ercos did.

Kendryk said his prayer, then waited. He waited until his legs cramped under him and the candles guttered. A pounding on the chapel door and someone shouting his name broke the silence. Kendryk leapt to his feet, wondering if the gods had sent him an especially noisy messenger.

BRAEDEN

Braeden hurried back around the stables though the press had increased a great deal. He spotted the empress at the head of the column and joined her. "Your Highness, a Captain Kerzer will join you with four hundred troops as soon as he can gather them. I told him to catch up to us."

"Very well," Teodora said. "We go now."

Braeden took his place right behind her and at the head of the Sanova Hussars. It was the middle of the night, so most of Kronfels was asleep by the time they reached the town. The column made a fair amount of noise, shod horses hooves clattering on cobbles, weapons and armor clanking. Torches flickered, and the commotion brought some sleepy residents to the windows overlooking the street. No doubt they'd be happy to see the back of them.

Silence reigned as the southern gates swung open, setting them onto the Tirilis road. Braeden felt relieved as they left the city behind them. It had been a tense place.

"So it's true?" Reno asked in a low voice. "About Atlona and Korma."

"It is," Braeden said. "We can only hope Novitny and the others stay inside the walls."

"Korma is said to have at least five thousand. Novitny won't take them on."

"I'm sure he won't. His orders were to defend the city, and that's best done from inside. You've seen those walls. Korma may have a lot of soldiers, but I doubt he has many guns, and he'd need hundreds or more to take them down."

"I hope you're right. I suppose Adela will be safe enough, though I hate being so far away and feeling useless." Reno's eldest daughter had recently married an Atlona merchant and was expecting a baby.

"We all do." It was times like these that made Braeden glad he didn't have to worry about a family.

"But the empress can't hope to take Korma on with just us and those few hundred household guards."

"I doubt it. She's probably hoping Ensden will make it, or even Tomescu."

"Not her." Reno shuddered.

"Better than no one," Braeden said, though he hoped never to lay eyes on that woman again. "Will Senta and the girls be on their way soon?"

"I hope so. Senta got up with me and dragged the girls out of bed so they should be packed by daybreak."

Teodora was in deep conversation with Solteszy, so Braeden moved forward to eavesdrop.

"But I can't give them up," Teodora said. "If I do, and Zastwar attacks again, they'll be leagues into Marjatya before we can hope to stop them."

"If they do," Solteszy said. "That's in the future. You need your army right now. It's troubling yes, to think of losing Girosna and Lubardol, but far more troubling to lose Atlona."

"I will not lose Atlona." Teodora spoke through clenched teeth. "Livilla will hold, no matter what, and I believe I can rely upon Novitny. The Sanova Hussars have never surrendered, and he wouldn't dare to be the first."

Braeden and Reno exchanged glances. She was right.

"I'm sure that's true, Your Highness," Solteszy said. "But the longer you wait to make concessions to Zastwar, the more they will demand, especially as the weakness of your position becomes known."

"I hate that word." Teodora's teeth were still clenched from the sound of it. "I am not weak and I will not allow anyone to treat me like I am. I've experienced a setback, but there is no doubt I will get my capital back and make Korma wish he'd never been born."

GWYNNETH

Gwynneth watched the empress and her guards ride down the deserted street. A moment later, Kendryk burst into the room.

"I received your message," he said, breathless.

"The empress just went by, riding for Atlona with the Sanova Hussars at her back. If you were waiting for an answer from the gods, it looks like you've received it."

"This isn't anything like the last sign." He looked exhausted.

She shook her head. "Darling, it should be obvious by now that the gods aren't always as specific as you'd like."

"That's one way of putting it," Kendryk grumbled.

"But consider this. If you do nothing, Teodora will take Landrus to Atlona and have him executed as soon as she can. Even if the city remains besieged, she can do what she wants with him. If she ever gets it back and her fortunes improve, it sounds like she plans to act against you anyway."

"If she wants to do as she threatened, she will first have to bring her aristocrats in check," Kendryk said. "And that's before any reaction she gets from Kronland if she mentions altering charters. I doubt she'll do it."

"Maybe not. But you can't deny she has it in for you now, and will do everything she can to cause trouble. I could even see her starting something with Zastwar so she has the satisfaction of forcing you to supply troops."

"I'd still prefer not to provoke her."

"You already have." Gwynneth was very serious. Her heart pounded with excitement, but she had to stay calm until she brought him around. "Teodora won't expect you to rescue Landrus, but if you do, she'll take it as yet another insult in a line of several you've delivered already."

"I didn't intend to be insulting."

"Of course you didn't. But she can't be certain of that, and the result is the same. But after everything, I don't understand how you can't see the clear message here."

"You truly believe it's from the gods?"

"Yes. Between Flavia's stay and Teodora's intervention, it's clear they wish Landrus to stay alive. And who else but you will do it?"

"There must be someone, surely."

"You know there isn't." She was sure she had him; he would only need a little more convincing. "Besides," she added. "Landrus is counting on you. He wouldn't have refused Flavia's offer otherwise."

"You can't be sure of that. He already turned down a similar one from me."

"But that was different. Death is a certainty this time. He's a tough fellow, but anyone facing the stake in three days would welcome having it deferred."

"You don't know him like I do," Kendryk muttered.

"That doesn't matter. The fact is, he has more faith in you than you do in yourself. Please don't disappoint him." She gave him her best pleading look.

He grinned, shaking his head. "I can't say no to you when you do that. And I trust your judgment; I don't want you to think it's because of that."

From the window, they watched the tail of Teodora's entourage make its way down the dark street, then sat down to a quick breakfast of bread and coffee.

Moments later, Gwynneth's maid Catrin interrupted them. "Word just came, Your Grace." She bobbed a curtsy while running into the room. She did everything quickly, including mercifully, Gwynneth's hair. "The prisoner leaves the temple at dawn. He will be in the middle of the baggage train. Most of the empress's household will be in that, including her children."

As usual, Gwynneth had cultivated a network of sources in every household of significance in Kronfels. Her kind manner with servants and generosity with silver meant that a steady stream of information poured into her bedchamber via the loquacious Catrin.

"How many are guarding him?" Gwynneth asked.

"Twenty. But that's not including the armed escort for the baggage. The empress left two hundred infantry behind for that."

"They'll be spread out thin," Kendryk said. "But those twenty will be ahorse, and well-armed. They will be able to pursue for a great distance."

Gwynneth dismissed the maid. Her nerves clattered as if she'd had too much coffee. Perhaps she had. Still, it was clear this was the perfect moment to act. Helping Landrus escape to Norovaea paled in comparison. A prisoner snatched out from under Teodora's nose would establish Kendryk as a force in his own right, a leader who was not to be crossed.

Unable to contain her excitement any longer, she turned back to Kendryk. "We can manage it."

"I suppose so." Kendryk still looked miserable. "I wish Count Faris were here. He would know how to do this sort of thing."

"He's taught you well, and we have three hundred soldiers. That should be more than enough."

"We need to think this through," he said. "Whatever happens, I don't want to risk you falling into imperial hands. Before I do anything, I want you on the road to Terragand, with at least a hundred guards."

"I can help." She didn't want to miss out on the excitement of a rescue.

"Yes, you can help by making it appear we are returning to Terragand right away. Did Selwin Mikus come with us? He grew up in the woods around here."

"Yes, he's here. I remember him asking you if he could come along since he has family here."

"Good. He'll help me disappear into the woods. We can do our best to stop those guards from pursuing us, and we need to be well away before she can send the Sanovans after us."

It was a relief to see him decisive now. "You'll never have a chance like this again."

"I know." Kendryk still looked pale and worn, but now it was just from fatigue. His eyes were alive and sparkling again. "Let's send for Mikus and make a plan."

KENDRYK

Kendryk hoped the empress had gone without leaving any spies behind to report on his movements. That the entire Terragand delegation left Kronfels so quickly must have looked suspicious, but it was the only way to act without putting his people in danger.

Gwynneth rode out in front, surrounded by a hundred troops. Once out of sight of the city, she would ride ahead as quickly as possible. Stopping only to rest the horses a few times, she would make the Terragand frontier in a day and a half. Once there, she would be safe.

Retainers, baggage and more troops came next. This group would be slower, but if the weather held, they could be in Terragand in three days. Kendryk assigned another fifty troops to guard them. If he must lose anything, he would risk this group.

Kendryk brought up the rear with a hundred and fifty men handpicked for loyalty and skill. He wore plain and serviceable borrowed armor, hoping he'd look like a regular soldier.

Two leagues from Kronfels, he watched Gwynneth's group pull away. His heart beat faster, but now he knew he was doing the right thing. Any impatience he felt was because he couldn't wait to see Landrus again. He couldn't say why, but he knew the gods had answered his prayers and laid a clear path before him. Once he returned to Terragand, he hoped they would guide him further.

They rode another half-league when Mikus said, "It's up here, Your Grace." They'd come to a small trail going into the woods.

"You're sure this will put us on the Tirilis road?" The path wound into the woods and soon disappeared.

"I'm certain of it," Mikus said. "If we keep a good pace, we should come out less than a league behind the empress's train."

Kendryk gave the order to turn. The trail was so narrow, they could ride no more than two abreast, and he worried about exposing such a long column. But Mikus assured him that there was no one dangerous in these woods. Princess Kasbirk had rooted out the last outlaws many years ago, and now all they saw was the occasional woodsman's cabin.

They rode for hours. Even at its highest, the sun's rays barely penetrated the dark branches overhead. Mikus stopped him at a small crossroads and pointed to a trail going east. "That will be our way when we come back."

"So we'll come back on this path and then turn here?"

"Yes. We'll also ford a stream that might help put them off our trail if we're pursued. There'll be several paths leading from the stream. Stay close to me so you take the right one."

"Oh, I will."

This forest was confounding. The land was flatter than in Terragand, and the massive fir trees went on forever, with a soft undergrowth of light green shimmering underneath them. It all looked the same to Kendryk. He thanked the gods for Mikus.

They carried their own supplies, so there would be no need to stop for food. The horses would find plentiful forage here, and there was water in the little streams that criss-crossed the forest floor. They wouldn't stop to make camp, sleeping in the saddle and eating biscuits and dried meat until they reached Terragand.

The sun was low in the western sky when they reached the Tirilis road. A great company had passed recently, but no one was yet in sight. Kendryk gathered everyone around and explained his plan.

Without exception the men were excited about retrieving Landrus, especially since some among them had guarded him at Birkenfels, becoming his friends during that time.

Kendryk sent two of his fastest riders ahead to scout and they returned with word that the caravan lay less than a league ahead, but would make camp in the first likely spot. The empress and Sanova Hussars were much farther ahead; out of sight. Landrus was in a wagon in the middle of the baggage train.

"One more thing," Kendryk said. "The empress's children will be in the train. Under no circumstances do I want them harmed. And try not to hurt any unarmed person. Take down anyone who tries to stop you from getting Landrus, but no one else."

"Wouldn't an imperial child make a useful hostage?" someone piped up.

"Absolutely not. We aren't here to pick a fight." It sounded ridiculous as soon as he said it, but he didn't care right now. Some of his elation had subsided during the long ride, but now they were close, it had returned. "We want to get Landrus, and we can negotiate later. The empress will be angry, and she's unreasonable enough as it is." Not to mention, trying to escape with a little archduke or archduchess would make their task more difficult.

As they reached the edge of the woods, Mikus grinned and tied a piece of red cloth to a nearby tree branch. "So we don't miss the trail. I'll pull it down once we're in. With the ground so trampled around here, they might never see where we leave the road."

Kendryk didn't want to imagine what might happen if a force like the Sanova Hussars pursued them into the woods. He ignored the knot in his stomach and urged his horse onto the road and into the open.

JANNA

She woke up to rain falling on her face. When she tried to lift her head, she saw stars. Janna wondered if she was dead. A moment later, she wished she were, as memories returned. She'd lost consciousness for most of it, but not enough.

The rain fell harder, and she wiggled her toes and her fingers. She breathed, although it was excruciating. Janna was cold and noticed her skirt bunched up around her waist. She lay in the grass at the side of the road and knew she must move before someone came. She struggled to sit up and cried out in pain, but gritted her teeth and forced herself to stand. She needed to get off the road, and she needed to find Anton.

Swaying on her feet, she stumbled into the trees before she fell. The rain changed to drizzle and moonlight peeked through the clouds. She hoped Anton had escaped somehow and was hiding nearby. Perhaps he got a chance when the men were busy with her. Just thinking about it made her vomit, but her stomach was empty, so she heaved and whimpered from the pain. By now she was sure that those kicks had broken her ribs.

Well, they'd heal. Everything would heal, given time.

"Find Anton," she whispered to herself, and whispered his name more loudly. There was nothing but the soft rustle of leaves, so she tried calling out loud. No sound came out. She tried again but had no voice. Her throat felt swollen under her hands though she didn't remember screaming.

Janna stood again, then lurched from tree to tree, keeping the road in view while whispering Anton's name. She did that until the sun rose. When the first voices came from the road, she disappeared into the woods, walking for leagues until she collapsed from exhaustion. Out of habit, she found water and crawled along the creek for a while. For a day or two she did nothing but sleep and drink water from forest streams.

When her voice returned, she called for Anton again although she no longer expected to find him. Before she could stop herself, she prayed to the Mother to help her find him and to the Father to protect him if he still lived. Then she cursed herself for a stupid, ignorant girl. Everything she'd learned about the gods was wrong. They were supposed to protect the good and punish the wicked. But that was a lie.

Janna was good. She'd always done what everyone expected, did her duty to her parents, her sisters, her husband, his children. Even though she wasn't perfect she had done nothing to deserve this punishment.

It felt strange to lose that comfort, that knowledge that someone powerful was looking after her, but she didn't care. She was too tired and hungry to be angry. And it was better not to think at all because sooner or later those thoughts would always come back to every dreadful thing that had happened.

After several days of wandering, she lost count altogether. She became like a wild animal. Her shoes fell apart, but she kept going. There were three kinds of berries she could safely eat, and two kinds of mushrooms. They never satisfied her hunger but were enough to keep her alive and moving. Streams provided water and once she followed a river until she heard voices in a clearing. A few times, the sound of an ax sent her the other way.

She was glad now that she didn't have the children with her. They couldn't have survived this. She wouldn't for much longer either. At some point, she would just fall onto the ground, and be covered by leaves and needles. Scavengers would come, and before winter ended, no one would know she'd been here, or been alive at all.

Her family, if they still lived, would wonder what had become of her, but in time they would forget her too. That should have made her sad, but she was too weak to care. She didn't even cry anymore. The weather remained warm, so she stayed dry, but she didn't want to imagine how she must look. Her hair was a wild tangle, her face filthy. She didn't bother to wash it anymore. Her feet were a horror of dirt, cuts and blisters, although she was growing an impressive layer of calluses.

It would have been impossible to picture herself this way as a merchant's wife in Kaleva. Always so clean and tidy and proper. Janna laughed, first softly, then louder. There was no one to hear, no one to think she'd lost her mind, which she probably had.

KENDRYK

It was almost dark as they came upon the camp. The few soldiers about were busy putting up tents and starting fires. The scout pointed out the wagon with Landrus in it. Most of its guards were making camp, but Kendryk noticed four wandering around the wagon. Though armed, they weren't paying much attention. Best to move before they noticed anything amiss and alerted the others.

Kendryk gave the signal. They charged into the camp, running over a fire or two and upsetting a tent. People fled into the woods screaming, and a few soldiers ran for weapons. Kendryk let those behind him worry about them; he focused on the guards. By now a few more had run back toward the wagon. Kendryk drew a pistol and fired at the guard who stepped out to block his path.

The shot missed, and the guard jumped out of the way. Another stood right in front of Kendryk, holding a musket. He raised it, but it misfired. Now Kendryk was too close for more shooting and pulled out his sword. There was gunfire around him, but Kendryk focused on the wagon ahead of him. He swung his sword down and the guard moved aside. Out of the corner of his eye, he saw the man fumbling for his own weapon, but then he'd left him behind.

At the wagon, Kendryk saw he was not alone. Several guards lay on the ground; whether they were dead or wounded, he couldn't say. His own men were rounding up a few more. They had to hurry, for the alarm was no doubt raised by now and troops accompanying the rest of the train would be here soon.

Kendryk looked at the wagon with a small barred window and heavy lock on the door. Perhaps they'd have to break it. But then, his captain shoved a man forward. "He's got the key, Your Grace." Kendryk winced, since he had instructed them not to address him in any way that might reveal his identity. It didn't matter. Teodora would suspect him before anyone else.

"Open the door." By now it was dark, and someone brought a torch forward to cast light on the lock. The door swung open and Landrus blinked at the torchlight. "Unfasten his chains." The same man held the key for those as well. He was nervous and fumbling and took an eternity.

Kendryk looked back to see a riderless horse brought up. "Can you ride?" he asked Landrus, who was rubbing his wrists rubbed raw by the chains.

"I can, Your—" he caught himself before giving Kendryk away yet again.

His chains removed from his ankles, Landrus stood up unsteadily. His legs had likely fallen asleep, bolted as they were to the bench in the wagon. Kendryk grabbed him by the hand and pulled him out. Before letting go, so he could mount his horse, Landrus looked Kendryk straight in the eye and said, "Thank you."

"I'm sorry I took so long to do the right thing."

Landrus swung stiffly into the saddle. "There is nothing to be sorry for. All of this is happening how the gods ordained it."

"I hope so."

Kendryk's efficient captain bundled the guards who were still standing into the wagon and locked the door. He flung the key into the woods, but they'd break the door soon enough. It was time to go.

They rode out of the camp in all haste. By now, word had spread, and there were shouts and hoofbeats in the distance. With such a large party, they couldn't make a silent escape and would have to rely on speed and their ability to lose themselves in the woods.

It was dark, but they extinguished all torches. Kendryk hoped they'd be able to find the path back into the woods. They came upon the spot soon since they were now at a gallop. Mikus leaned from his saddle and pulled the piece of cloth from the branch. "Just where we left it," he said, grinning.

"Thank the gods." Kendryk turned on the path, Landrus at his side. They would go first, with the bulk of the men guarding their rear. "And thank the gods for you too, my good man."

Mikus grinned some more. "We're not there yet, Your Grace. Finding our way will be tricky."

"I imagine we can light torches in a while."

"Perhaps. But we want to be leagues away from any pursuit."

Moonlight glinted through the trees, lighting their path. Kendryk was grateful for it. Without it, he wouldn't have dared to follow this little trail at night. They moved at a good pace at first so that all the men would be off the road and in the trees as quickly as possible. At some point, they heard shouting far away, and even spotted the gleam of a few torches on the main road. Everyone stopped and held their breaths, but it seemed their pursuers never noticed the forest path. This would buy them at least a little time.

They rode in silence for a time, the moon rising higher. Finally Landrus asked, "What comes next?"

"I don't know," Kendryk said. "First, we see you safe to Terragand."

"Back to the castle?"

"You're no longer a prisoner, so I'd prefer to have you as my guest at Birkenhof."

"That is kind. But I have much work to do and don't know how much time I'll get to do it."

"We'll find a quiet room in the palace for you to work as much as you like, though I'm sure Gwynneth will insist on having you join us for dinner."

"Did I ever tell you I like your wife very much?"

Kendryk grinned. "Who doesn't?" Then his mood shifted. "I don't know what will happen after we get there. Teodora has her hands full right now, but if she dislodges Korma and renews the Zastwar treaty, I imagine she will stop at nothing to get you back."

"I expect she will," Landrus said. "But just as all of this has happened as it should, the gods will continue to guide and help you. You will not be alone in this fight."

"So you think it will come to a fight?" Even though Kendryk had trained for battle since he could stand and could acquit himself well in a tournament, he'd never thought he would have to use those skills. Today was the first time in his life he'd used a weapon with intent to harm.

Landrus nodded. "I believe it will. Any other ruler might have been willing to negotiate. But you've injured Teodora's pride, and she will not forgive you for that. I am sorry for anything I have brought down upon you."

Kendryk shook his head. "No, I believe it had to come to this. You saw what the mood was in Kronfels. I hear it's that ugly everywhere in Kronland. Teodora is at her weakest and someone had to act. I was hoping it wouldn't be me, but here we are."

"Here we are, indeed." Landrus smiled in the dark.

GWYNNETH

The rescue party traveled quickly, but so had Gwynneth, and they all arrived at Birkenhof on the same day. After moving into the palace, Landrus was very eager to get back to work and he and Kendryk headed to the study they'd set up for him right after breakfast the next morning. Gwynneth also had much work to do, so she settled in the library where Halvor was scribbling away.

She wrote letters until noon, explaining what had happened at the trial and how this translated into a severe overreach of imperial authority. Technically, Teodora should not have intervened at all, let alone have any say in the conduct of it.

"The lines between Temple and empire have become blurred," she wrote. "This contradicts our holiest teachings and traditions. The Kronland rulers received authority over Temple matters in their own lands because it became clear long ago that the empire shouldn't be involved in these matters. That the empress now feels entitled to intervene is at best, worrisome, and at worst, illegal."

She set Halvor and her ladies to making at least five dozen copies, which she sent to every political and Temple leader she knew. With each copy, she sent a note of her own. She didn't think it wise to come straight out and ask for direct aid, but she hinted that anyone supporting Kendryk now would benefit when he prevailed against Teodora.

They worked right through luncheon, eating cold meat and bread in the library. Gwynneth felt exhausted, but couldn't stop until she'd dispatched every letter.

A footman interrupted her mid-afternoon. "It's Julia Maxima, Your Grace. She wants to see the prince."

"I'm sure she does." Gwynneth stood. "Show her into the drawing room and I'll see her."

"Shouldn't Prince Kendryk speak with her?" Linette asked.

Gwynneth shook her head. "No. He's much too intimidated by Julia. She'll try to get him to agree to something, and then he'll feel bound. It's better if I handle her."

"Your Holiness," Gwynneth said, entering the drawing room. "I didn't expect you to be back already."

Julia had come straight from the road though she looked unruffled as always. "I hurried as soon as I heard of your husband's escapade. I don't suppose he's here?"

"Not at the moment, though I expect him to return soon. Won't you be seated and take refreshment?"

Julia sat, then said, "I wish only to clear this up."

Gwynneth sat across from her. "Nothing needs to be cleared up. It should be obvious."

"The only thing that's obvious is that Prince Kendryk has declared himself a heretic right alongside former Father Landrus."

"We don't believe that Father Landrus is a heretic."

Julia pursed her lips. "I can see you don't take this the least bit seriously, but perhaps you should. If your husband doesn't hand Father Landrus over to the Temple authorities, he will follow Landrus into excommunication, and you and the children will join him."

"I'm not interested in remaining part of a faith that has such antiquated views. In Norovaea, we already believe the things Father Landrus teaches and I can assure you, they are not heresy."

"We are not in Norovaea." Julia restrained her temper with obvious effort. "By the Mother, I knew I should not have given in to the prince when he insisted you understood our ways. It is clear you do not, and now you have pulled him into error with you."

"Or saved him from it." Gwynneth looked her straight in the eye. "I have no quarrel with you, Your Holiness, but my husband's actions speak for themselves. I'm sure you know him well enough to realize he did not take them lightly. He spent untold hours in prayer and study and took them with great reluctance when he saw there was no other way."

"Praying and studying under the influence of that man." Julia spat the last words. "And that man knows exactly what he is doing." She stood. "He has your husband bewitched and is leading him down a path that will lead to war and the ruin of everything."

Gwynneth stood up and faced her without flinching. "I don't believe it needs to come to that."

"Then you don't understand power, and you understand Teodora Inferrara even less. She will not rest until you and your family are destroyed. If you want your children to survive this, you should send them to your father without delay."

"Is that a threat?"

Julia chuckled though her eyes were cold. "Oh, you needn't worry about me. I can deplore the prince's actions as much as I want, but I cannot force him to my will. The empress is another matter."

"The empress has her hands full."

"Right now she does. But if you think she will forget about this once her other problems are solved, you are mistaken." She swept to the door and turned to Gwynneth before opening it. "You can tell your husband I'll see him any time he wishes to speak with me. He knows where to find me." She continued into the hallway and out the front door without another word.

Gwynneth clasped her hands behind her and walked to the window. It was hot and humid and the entire bank of front windows stood open. In the distance, she could hear the shouts of the children playing in the garden. She wondered if she should send them to Norovaea, although the wrong people might misinterpret that as cowardice.

The best thing now was to stay resolute and show no fear. There was nothing to be fearful of anyway. Teodora had her hands tied with her capital besieged and Gwynneth's sources told her that Zastwar would demand serious concessions before agreeing to a renewal of the treaty. Knowing Teodora, she would never give in, and Zastwar would soon march on her eastern frontier.

In the current climate, she wouldn't receive speedy help from Kronland, and least of all from Terragand, which supplied the largest number of troops. With any luck at all, she'd be deposed or killed, or both. Gwynneth smiled to herself. At that point, it would be easy enough for Kendryk to step into the breach, secure a peace, send Zastwar home, and then who knew? He might be seen as the savior of the empire.

BRAEDEN

Teodora pushed them hard, so they didn't stop to make camp and the messenger didn't catch up to them until after midnight. Both she and her horse looked exhausted. "Your Highness," she gasped. "It's the priest. He's gone."

Teodora wheeled her horse around, forcing Braeden to a sudden stop. "What do you mean he's gone?"

"They took him."

"What are you on about woman? Who took him?"

"A large group of armed men. No one is completely sure who led them though a few of the guards say they might have recognized Prince Kendryk."

"Tell me precisely what happened." Teodora held her temper in check with visible effort.

The messenger hadn't been present, but recounted what she'd heard. Someone had swooped down on the baggage train, overpowered the guards and taken the priest away.

"Surely you gave pursuit?" Teodora asked.

"Oh yes, the guards went after them, but they'd disappeared into the woods."

"They'll make for Terragand of course," Teodora said. "Terris, get your troops ready. You're going to catch Prince Kendryk and retrieve the prisoner. If you happen to kill the prince in the process, I'll be very grateful."

Braeden turned to give orders, but Count Solteszy said, "Just a moment, Your Highness. I'm not sure this is the best course of action."

"What do you mean?" Teodora's tone was dangerous. Braeden expected her to blow at any second and he didn't want to be there when it happened.

"It might take the hussars several days to catch Prince Kendryk and bring him back." Solteszy seemed to be the only man immune to Teodora's tantrums and never failed to give his opinion. For such a gray little fellow, he had nerve.

"I don't care." Teodora spat. "I want him right now, preferably dead."

"You won't get him right now. It will take days at best, and those are days Andor Korma will use to dig in. We can't hope to stop him without the hussars."

"I can't let Kendryk get away with this."

"Of course not. You will deal with him soon enough. But getting your capital back is far more important than dealing with an insubordinate prince."

"This is intolerable." Teodora fumed. "I can't believe that ridiculous little boy had the nerve to do this. I had him completely intimidated. Don't you agree, Terris?"

"Yes Your Highness, I believe you did." Braeden had seen the alarm in Prince Kendryk's eyes when faced with Teodora's temper, but he'd also noted his devotion to the priest.

"That doesn't matter right now," Solteszy said. "What matters is defeating Korma and dealing with Zastwar. Once that is done, you will be able to throw all of your force at whoever has done this. We need to verify it was Prince Kendryk and not another Kronland ruler. There's a small possibility it was Bronson or Ossian, so we must be sure before acting."

"Get away from me, all of you!" Teodora shouted. "I can't stand the sight of you." She suddenly spurred her horse into the forest.

"Best keep an eye on her," Solteszy told Braeden. "But keep your distance. She'll settle down before long. We don't want to lose her in the woods in the meantime."

Braeden followed Teodora until he watched her dismount and demolish several small trees and bushes with her sword. She only stopped when it got stuck in the bark of a large oak tree. Then she yanked on the hilt until she slumped against the tree in exhaustion. When it seemed safe, Braeden rode up and pulled it out, then helped her back on her horse. She was silent all the way back to the road.

By the time they reached Atlona, it was too late. Andor Korma had a good six thousand troops well dug in behind impressive fortifications. No one had expected him to be so efficient. Braeden and the hussars might have done some damage, but the odds were long even for them, since Korma had his own hussar unit, the only cavalry in the empire who could give the Sanovans a serious fight.

Stymied, Teodora found a stout castle twenty leagues to the east. It belonged to a Countess Rabatin who had no choice but to offer her hospitality for an indefinite period.

Once settled in, Teodora called for her advisers and military officers, including Braeden.

"Write to Beatryz Inferrara," Teodora said to Count Solteszy. "Ask her if she has any troops going to Floradias, or coming back. I know they've just signed a truce there, so she should have soldiers at loose ends."

"It will take too long for them to reach us," Solteszy said.

"I know," Teodora snapped. "But there might be an army in transit over the mountains right now. They could be here within a few weeks."

"Are you sure you wish to ask for help from the queen?" Solteszy asked.

"I don't like to. Beatryz is an idiot and the wrong person to rule Maladena right now. But there's nothing I can do about that. She's very good at squandering all of that gold, so she might as well spend some of it helping me. You know how to ask so she'll agree." She waved at Solteszy who was already writing.

Braeden prepared for weeks of boredom while awaiting a reply.

KENDRYK

Kendryk rode between the ragged ranks. Their disorganization wasn't the real problem; it was a mere symptom of their complete lack of training. It had been over thirty years since Terragand had mustered a significant number of troops, and none of these recruits had ever seen military service.

"The equipment should arrive soon," Count Faris said, riding next to him. "They will look much better in proper uniforms and armor."

"I'm sure they will," Kendryk said. "Though I'm more concerned about how they wield the weapons we still don't have." One of the first orders of business upon returning to Terragand had been to place a large order for firearms, swords, halberds and pike from Zeelund's largest armorer. Aside from being shockingly expensive, the time required to put together and ship such a large order was worrisome. If Teodora or anyone else attacked before they arrived, he would have no way to fight her.

"They can practice with farm implements," Faris suggested. "I'd be happy to drill them."

"Please do. I don't know what to do about the muskets. Those take the most practice." Kendryk was an excellent shot, but practiced several times a week and went hunting often, and had been doing so since he was five. Most of these recruits had never even seen a firearm.

"I've asked the Zeelunders to send the muskets first. But we can drill with what we have and borrow from your household troops. They can help with the instruction, too."

It still didn't seem like it was enough. Kendryk continued up and down the rows, smiling at the soldiers and greeting those he knew by name. But with about twenty thousand here, most were strangers. They all recognized him though, and were happy to be there. For many, it was likely to be the greatest adventure of their lives.

211

As he came to a new unit, a cheer went up. This lot were to be grenadiers, but they had no weapons. Kendryk sighed. In the meantime, they'd have to be fed and housed. Faris had set up a large encampment on a field near Birkenhof with strict sanitation. So many people packed into close quarters often led to epidemics.

With any luck, they could receive training and be sent home with their weapons, keeping up a local drill until the danger from Teodora had passed, if it did.

Kendryk hoped all of this could happen before the harvest. He was glad that Faris was in charge. He had considerable military experience and was ruthlessly efficient. If anyone could turn this lot into a fighting force, he could.

He turned to Faris and said. "Do all of that. Send extra money to Zeelund if they'll speed up their shipments. I don't care about the uniforms, but we need the firearms as soon as possible."

Faris waved to a young officer and dictated a message.

"In the meantime," Kendryk said, "I'd like to help with the training."

"Good idea. That will be excellent for morale."

Kendryk agreed, but didn't mention it would also be good for his. Any action was better than waiting for the sign from the gods that never seemed to come.

Several days of training left Kendryk even more discouraged. He understood it took a long time to become proficient with a firearm, but the results were terrible. No one had hit a single target.

"Let's practice reloading." Kendryk tried to keep his tone upbeat. The recruits were eager to learn and excited that he was teaching them. They were doing their best.

"Men don't learn anything fast, begging your pardon, Your Grace," a young woman said. She'd been practicing with the pike nearby and wandered over to watch the musketry.

"It's difficult." Kendryk smiled at her. About a third of his recruits were women. So far, Kendryk had found them rather easy to train, but he didn't know if it was for the reason she described. "I've been shooting my whole life and am still far from an expert."

"Your Grace is too modest." The woman looked him up and down while he tried to keep from blushing. He hoped she'd be as bold in battle.

"I don't believe I caught your name." Kendryk tried to cover his embarrassment.

"Sabina Martyn. I come from the lands outside Runewald."

"I appreciate you coming, Miss Martyn. It must be difficult to leave your home and family."

"Oh, I was glad to leave," Sabina said. "I was dying of boredom out on that farm. And I was the biggest, so I always had to work the plow. Flinging a pike around is ever so much easier."

She was a tall, sturdy girl, the kind Kendryk always thought of when someone mentioned good Terragand peasant stock. With a broad, rosy-cheeked face and snapping brown eyes, she was pretty in a rough way. Kendryk wondered why she was unmarried, though it could be hard to meet someone in a small village. She might do much better in the militia. He already saw several fellows eying her with open appreciation.

"Thank you anyway," Kendryk said. "I hope to have you home in time for harvest."

Sabina made a face at that, but dropped a quick curtsy before strolling back to the ragged-looking pike square.

Kendryk located Count Faris, showing some recruits how to reload a pistol. It seemed his progress wasn't any better. When he saw Kendryk, he left them and came over.

"I'm not encouraged," Kendryk said. "If Teodora makes a move soon, we're finished."

"It seems so," Faris said. "Weapons or not, these troops will be no match for Ensden's veterans. We should have a mercenary force at the ready."

"I hate to do that." Kendryk sighed.

"So do I. But with the truce in Zeelund right now, a lot of soldiers are looking for work. It's a good time to hire."

"You're right, I'm sure. I just feel like once we do, we have to use them."

"Not necessarily. We can offer a short contract, subject to extension. Ninety days at most. In that time, you'll know more about Teodora's reaction."

"How many do you think we need?"

"At least twenty thousand—thirty if we can find them."

"That will be expensive." Kendryk had never worried about money, but he'd never spent it at this rate before, either. Fielding armies of any quality was a costly venture.

"It will be." Faris seemed unperturbed. "But well worth it. Why don't I go to Zeelund and see what I can find? I still have good contacts there."

"All right. The sooner you go, the better. See what you can do."

GWYNNETH

Gwynneth was encrypting a dispatch to her source in Zastwar when Count Faris interrupted her, bearing a letter. "It's addressed to the prince." He sat down across from Gwynneth and handed it over to her. "But you might as well see it right away."

It was from Princess Zelenka of Arcius, the southernmost Kronland kingdom. The princess was not the most literate woman, and she had been distraught while writing. Gwynneth read it over twice before saying, "She sounds quite mad. But let me see if I understand this correctly. She says that a certain Arian Orland, an ally of Kendryk's, has attacked her lands. Is that Duke Aidan's son?"

"It is." Faris nodded. "Arian is a younger son and last I heard, was a soldier of fortune in Floradias. I don't suppose you've heard from him or his father?"

"I haven't. Oh, wait. I received something from the duke before we went to Isenwald, but I don't recall seeing anything of importance." Like most of the responses to her first round of letters, Duke Aidan's had been equivocal, if polite. There was no point in wasting time on those types of messages.

She turned to Halvor. "Can you find the last letter from Duke Orland?"

Halvor nodded and went to a large bureau with many drawers in it. He had an efficient filing method which no one else understood.

Gwynneth turned back to Faris. "It was difficult for me to tell why Orland was targeting Zelenka's lands. She didn't seem to understand herself."

"We received word that the empress stayed with Princess Zelenka on her way back to Olvisya and persuaded her to supply several thousand troops at some future date."

"Oh, maybe that's what she means when she writes 'only doing my duty to my sovereign.'" Gwynneth took Duke Orland's letter from Halvor and scanned it for references to Arian.

The Duchess sent her greetings, but she was a silly woman and Gwynneth usually ignored her. The duke went on at length about their daughter, the heiress to the duchy, being betrothed at last, and "here it is," Gwynneth said, then read aloud. "Our son Arian is returned to us after the truce in Floradias. He has married the widow of my cousin, the Baron of Engelstein, and we hope he will settle down and manage her estate, held in trust for her young son."

Gwynneth put the letter on her desk. "That doesn't sound as if he plans to become a marauder. It's rather domestic in fact. If I recall, the baroness was young and lovely and I felt sorry for her having to marry that horrid old baron. Perhaps it's worked out well for her, and for young Orland."

"Perhaps." Faris frowned. "I'll make further inquiries, but the fact remains that in the meantime, someone is committing atrocities on Prince Kendryk's behalf. That is not acceptable."

"No, it's not," Gwynneth said. "We must find out who is doing this and stop him."

That evening, they discussed it with Kendryk after supper.

"I remember Arian Orland." Kendryk frowned. "He was a few years older than me, and a friend of my brother's. By the time I came back from Galladium, he'd already gone soldiering. There was some kind of trouble with a girl so his father sent him away. Back then, he would have been fifteen or sixteen."

"So he might be a troublemaker." Gwynneth was still trying to put the pieces together.

"He was then," Kendryk said. "He was always getting my brother into scrapes and was a terrible bully. I stayed away from him. But that was long ago; perhaps he's changed."

"Fighting for a living rarely changes a personality for the better," Faris said, his face grim. "If we didn't know that he had just come into a bride and an estate, it's not beyond comprehension he might try to start trouble as a way to gain employment. The Floradian truce has been hard for mercenaries who have nothing saved. Which is most of them. But it's possible that Orland has the resources to build up a force of his own. It's common to terrorize a region and then extort protection money from its ruler. But I don't understand the benefit of doing it in your name."

"I don't see that Princess Zelenka mentions being forced to pay him." Kendryk looked at the letter again.

"Would she?" Gwynneth wondered. "I'd be likely to keep such humiliating circumstances to myself."

"It's hard to say," Faris said. "The whole thing is odd, and problematic. Delicate as the situation is, we need no one stirring up extra trouble. Right now, it might still be possible to treat with Teodora since you've committed no act of aggression. Should Orland attack Olvisya in your name, we might have a serious problem."

"I'll write to him," Kendryk said. "We'll send one copy to Engelstein castle and ask his wife to forward it to him if he isn't there. I'll also send a messenger into Arcius and see if he can be located. If Orland is leading a force large enough to cause the princess real distress, he shouldn't be that hard to find."

"What will you say?" Gwynneth asked.

"As I'm his liege lord, I'll tell him to stop it right now. I authorized none of this and I don't appreciate help of this sort. I'll order him to leave Kronland and take his trade elsewhere."

"Why not here?" Faris asked. "A large force might be a useful addition to your militia."

Gwynneth sat up straighter. "It would indeed. A few of our friends have made encouraging noises, but no one in Kronland or elsewhere has offered any concrete help. If Arian Orland is operating on Kendryk's behalf, he should be placed under his direct command, where he can be of real help."

Kendryk pulled a face. "I'd prefer to not have him around at all."

"Why not offer him a choice?" Faris asked. "He can either leave Kronland altogether, or he can work for you."

"I don't know if I want to pay him," Kendryk said.

"Why should you pay him?" Gwynneth asked. "You're his lord and as regent for the Baron of Engelstein, he's responsible for delivering a certain number of troops to you, is he not?"

"Militia troops," Kendryk said.

"Experienced mercenaries are better," Gwynneth said. "I like the count's idea. Give him a choice. If he intends to act in your best interest, he'll join you. If not, you can publicly disavow him and order him away."

"I suppose it can't hurt to try," Kendryk said. "Let's write that letter tonight."

BRAEDEN

Whenever the waiting seemed unbearable, Braeden reminded himself how much worse it must be inside the walls of Atlona. Teodora seemed to think the city had enough provisions to hold out for months, but right now there was no end to the siege in sight. Besides, Braeden knew that most hussars didn't like long periods of inactivity. Those inside would be crawling out of their skins worse than he was.

Braeden suspected that Reno Torresia didn't mind the quieter schedule. With his wife and two daughters around him, he had a nearly normal family life. They worried about Adela, the eldest, pregnant and living in Atlona with her husband's family, but they had lived with war for years now. In fact, Reno had met his wife Senta while sacking a town in Cesiano—Braeden forgot which one.

Braeden had hoped that the middle girl might become a hussar herself. Cara was a wild little thing and sat a horse like a natural. But she'd turned fifteen and all of a sudden it was frilly skirts and making eyes at the best-looking of the young troopers. The baby, Trisa, was coming up nicely though. At twelve, she had the lanky, athletic build that made a good cavalry trooper, and idolized Franca. But with Franca inside Atlona, Trisa pestered Braeden to teach her how to use a lance, even though she was still too short. He also suspected she rode Kazmir when she could get away with it.

Teodora called for Braeden and he went, with some misgiving. He couldn't remember a personal conference turning out well for him. She was reclining on an ornate sofa, wearing a lacy gown unlike her usual clothing. He wondered if it was underwear and averted his gaze. At least she was in a good mood; rather uncommon these days.

"I've had the most brilliant idea, Terris," she said, smirking. "I'm sending you to Marjatya."

That caught him by surprise. "Marjatya, Your Highness?"

"That's what I said. There's no sense in you lot sitting around here wasting your time when you could be causing trouble for Korma's followers."

"I see. I'd hate to miss out on lifting the siege, Your Highness."

"Oh, you won't. You won't be far away, and when I receive word that help is on the way I'll send for you. You'll have plenty of time to get back."

No reasonable objections then. "Yes, Your Highness. What are your orders?"

"Nothing too difficult. I have here a list of Marjatyan nobility that support Korma. Most are in the field with him. I want you to attack and destroy as much of their property as possible. When you can, get at least one hostage from each family and send them back here."

Braeden wondered how well he could keep his feelings from showing on his face.

Not well, it appeared.

"Don't be ridiculous, Terris. These are not innocent civilians."

Braeden raised his eyebrows.

"They are not. They've rebelled against me and by maintaining their estates they continue to derive income that helps support the rebellion. I'm not asking you to kill peasants and townspeople, although if they get in your way, no one will fault you."

"Most will die if their homes and crops are destroyed," Braeden ventured.

"Not my concern." She shrugged. "The aristocracy is responsible for its actions and the people on their lands should hold them accountable." She sat up and looked straight at him. "You don't believe me, but I'm well acquainted with your type, Terris. Once, I was like you, and had definite ideas about how good soldiers behave. I don't have the luxury of those ideas anymore."

He was obliged to look back at her. She had never seemed so earnest; there was a softness about her. Once he noticed her bare feet he was certain she was in a state of undress. He felt a flush creep up his neck and hoped his beard covered it.

She rose and walked toward him. It took everything he had not to step back. She stood right in front of him. Tall as she was, she still had to look up, which made her seem young and uncharacteristically vulnerable. "You must help me with this," she said, her voice soft and throaty.

Braeden wasn't sure if she was seducing him. If she was, he wasn't sure how to handle it. He needed to get out of there. "I will, Your Highness," he said.

"Good." She smiled. "I'd prefer you didn't see me as a monster, but in the end, people will think what they will."

"You're not a monster," Braeden said, thinking of Daciana.

"It's charming of you to say so, but I doubt it's the truth. That's all right. There's no one living who understands what I'm going through right now. There is no ruler anywhere with an empire so large and so fraught with trouble. I also realize that no one else thinks so, but I know that I'm the best person to hold it together and restore it to greatness."

"I have no doubt about that." Braeden meant it.

She seemed startled. "Thank you. It's a difficult task, but I'm capable and prepared to do whatever it takes. There are few willing to support me right now and I will not forget those who do."

"I want nothing special for doing my job," Braeden said. "Carrying out orders I don't like is nothing new."

"I think we understand each other." She placed a rolled-up paper in his hand. "These are the names of the estates you will target." Her voice had hardened again. "Start at the border and work your way east. If you run into Daciana, send her here. She'll stay out of your way if you stay out of hers."

"That is my intention, Your Highness."

"Good," she smiled her usual cold smile. "Then I shall see you when we are ready to march on Korma."

GWYNNETH

"That's all for tonight, Halvor." Gwynneth put her quill down and rubbed her eyes.

"Just let me finish this one, Your Grace," Halvor said, still scribbling. "That way I can send it with the morning messenger."

"All right. But you must stop after that. We have all day tomorrow."

After being closeted with Faris most of the day, Kendryk had gone to Landrus's study, as he did most afternoons. "Don't wait up for me," he had said, giving Gwynneth a quick kiss while she sat at her desk.

In her room, Gwynneth shrugged on a velvet dressing gown and sent Catrin for her supper. She collapsed into an armchair, then picked up a pile of letters that had come in with the afternoon's messenger. One was from her agent in Zastwar. As one of the imperial ambassador's many secretaries, he had a great deal of interesting news.

He wrote that Ambassador Arceo had been in daily talks with the Zastwar foreign minister. After four twelve-hour days of discussion, a temporary treaty appeared imminent.

Gwynneth sighed. She was too tired to panic. She read more. The agreement would be good for two years and require the empress to give up two of her disputed frontier forts. It was far from certain she would agree to such humiliating terms, but the ambassador was very much in favor, under the circumstances.

Gwynneth put down the letter. Her maid brought in a tray and put it on the table next to her. "You can go to bed, Catrin," she said. "I'll see you in the morning."

Sipping wine and picking at her food, she went through the rest of the letters. There were few responses to the dozens she'd sent to every ruler in Kronland and everyone else she could think of, including family.

So far, her father's response had been the most disappointing. "It makes no sense for Kendryk to risk his kingdom over some preacher," his last letter had said, even though she had explained to him how this was more than a religious disagreement. If her father helped, they wouldn't need anyone else.

She spotted a letter from Natalya Maxima in Galladium, one of her oldest friends. As the maxima in Allaux, Natalya had the ear of King Gauvain, a good friend from Kendryk's childhood. Gwynneth read it eagerly, but friendly as it was, it offered nothing concrete.

So he couldn't escape without talking to her, Gwynneth took her pile of letters and found a place in Kendryk's dressing room. She sent his servant to bed since she could help with any clothes that needed unfastening.

After working through all the letters, she was dozing in a chair when Kendryk entered. The candle had burned itself out, and it was well after midnight.

Kendryk started when she moved in the chair. "Oh, it's you," he said. "No, stay right there." He knelt on the floor in front of her, leaned into her lap and kissed her. "This is a nice surprise. You didn't have to wait up."

"I know." Gwynneth kissed him again. She'd noticed a distinct decline in kissing since they'd returned from Isenwald. Maybe because they had so little time alone. "I'm afraid I've got bad news and thought you should hear about it as soon as possible."

Kendryk looked alarmed. "You could have sent for me. I would have come straight away."

"It's not urgent—" there's not much to be done right now." She told him about the news from Zastwar.

Kendryk sighed and laid his head in her lap. She ran her fingers through his hair.

Finally he asked, "What will we do?"

"I don't know. I've written to everyone at least twice. My father is being horrid although I'm sure if it comes to real trouble he'll help." Then she told him about the letter from Natalya. "You should write to Gauvain. He trusts Natalya, and she's at least sympathetic. Perhaps a personal appeal ..."

He stood. "No, Gwynn, I won't do it. This is not something friends and family can help us with. If we are in real trouble, we need proper alliances and definite commitments."

"We aren't getting those right now."

He paced the room. "But it doesn't matter, does it? If Teodora attacks us, we'll get help, or we won't. We've done our best."

Then she stood. "We? I've done my best. Do you know how many letters I've written? Two hundred twenty-four! I can't do this alone, Kendryk." To her chagrin she noticed her voice quivering. She was so tired.

"Darling," he said, coming over and taking both her hands in his. "You don't have to do any of this. I started this, and I must find a way to see it through."

"But if I don't do it, who will?" Now the tears spilled over. "I know you need to spend time with Father Landrus, to figure out what to do, but it doesn't seem like you're making any progress. At least none I can see."

"It doesn't work that way," he said, pulling her to the edge of the bed, until they were both sitting. He kept holding her hands. "This will not be a normal war. We can't fight it the usual way."

"Then how are you going to fight it? Are you going to wait for imperial troops on our land before deciding it needs to be defended? This may be a religious fight, but we still need soldiers and weapons."

Kendryk sighed. "So far, none of this has gone the way I expected." He pulled her close. "I'm sorry darling, I appreciate everything you're doing. And when it bears fruit, you'll get all the credit. I would help you, except that Father Landrus is sure we will find more answers in the Scrolls."

"I wish I had your faith." Gwynneth snuggled into his chest. She'd missed this so much.

"So do I," Kendryk said, stroking her hair. "But I understand why you don't. If I were anyone else, I'd think I was mad, too."

"I don't think you're mad," Gwynneth said into his shirt, suddenly very sleepy.

"Yes you do."

"All right, I do. But I love you anyway."

He laughed a little. "Good. That's all that matters. We must trust the gods. They have taken care of us so far, and they won't abandon us now. I am sure we are doing their will right now."

"I hope you're right," Gwynneth murmured, then pulled him down onto the bed next to her.

KENDRYK

Kendryk rode out early, with as many men as he could spare. Count Faris had already taken ship for Zeelund to hire an army. Kendryk didn't like leaving Birkenhof undefended, but the danger was on his borders, not here at home. Maryna cried when he said she couldn't come. First they'd gone to Kronfels without the children, and now he was leaving without her again.

"I have to leave Mama here, too," he explained.

"But you are always gone, Papa." Tears ran over her chubby cheeks.

"Not always." He felt guilty because he spent so little time with her, even when he was here. "Can you be a big girl and help your mother?" Not that Gwynneth ever needed help.

Maryna nodded and hugged him one more time.

Gwynneth saw him off in the courtyard. She looked pale and tired, like she always did these days. "If good news comes from Zastwar, you can stop writing letters for a day or two," he smiled at her. "And if Arian Orland gets here before I return, don't let him leave."

"Can I at least give him a piece of my mind?"

"All right. But don't frighten him too much."

"I'll try not to." She lifted her face for a kiss. "Please be careful and hurry back."

They headed south at a brisk walk. It would take all day to reach the nearest frontier outpost. He hated this state of affairs. All the time spent poring over the Scrolls hadn't yielded a single clue. He knew that Father Landrus understood more, but by now Kendryk wondered if he'd read the signs incorrectly.

The prophesied ruler seemed much more sure of himself and quite a glamorous figure. Gwynneth assured him he was, reminding him of swooning girls on the streets of Kronfels, but he was sure that was because they were excited about the trial. Under normal circumstances, anyone could see he didn't cut quite the dashing figure he ought. He was too short and his nose wasn't altogether manly. His brother would have been better at this and Kendryk wondered again why the gods had let someone so well-suited to his role die so young.

They reached the first outpost within a day. Karrebad was a town of some size on the border with Podoska. An ancient baron held the tiny castle.

"No one's bothered us here since my brother fought Prince Martinek for the girl," the baron said, before dissolving into a fit of wheezing. Kendryk wondered if he'd die on the spot. The famous feud over the girl had happened at least sixty years ago.

"We have other problems now." Kendryk recounted the events in Kronfels. He knew that Gwynneth had written the baron at least one letter, but he appeared to be almost blind, and clearly didn't remember it.

The old fellow clucked and shook his head. "What in the name of the Father were you thinking, Your Grace? No good can come of this. Back in my father's day, when old Princess Benda feuded with the emperor, he put an end to it so fast, her family still hasn't found her head. Though they got the body back after a time ..."

"Yes, yes," Kendryk said, uncomfortable with the talk of heads being separated from bodies. "This is different, I assure you. I have the support of everyone in Kronland this time." The lie was out before he could stop himself. "We're just taking precautions. The empress will have to fight Zastwar when the treaty expires, and no one will bother us here. I want to fortify the border, out to Sanova."

The old man frowned. "Princess Martinek won't take kindly to imperial troops marching through her lands if the empress comes."

"I'm sure she won't. But I also doubt she has enough soldiers to stop a force of any size. We don't either, but I need your help to slow them down, should the worst happen and we're attacked."

"I can do that." The baron brightened. "Wouldn't mind putting on the old armor one more time though I doubt I can sit a horse."

"Why don't you lead the castle defenses," Kendryk said diplomatically. "I'll leave a few of my troops to man the town walls and train up the city watch. Please also call up your militia for training. They needn't be mobilized just yet, but they must be ready."

"Very well, Your Grace. I can't say I approve of all this trouble-making, though things are awful dull around here these days."

"I hope there won't be any trouble."

"Begging your pardon, but for someone who feels that way, you've sure done your bit to stir it up. And here I thought when your brother died, we were in for a long, boring, peaceful time. Well, you never know how these young fellows will turn out. When I was your age, I never even dreamed of starting a fight, except in a tavern. Once, when I was nineteen, my cousin Elfred and I. ... ."

"Yes, yes. Everyone keeps reminding me what an awful thing I've done. I appreciate your help all the same."

Rather than pray for guidance as he was supposed to, Kendryk prayed that Teodora wouldn't attack. He prayed for something to happen, something that would keep her out of Terragand. Though he didn't wish for war with Zastwar, a small amount of trouble on their border would suffice. Even though he would admit it to no one, Kendryk wondered if the gods were listening to him at all. Maybe they never had, and he had interpreted chance events as the signs he wished for so fervently. If this path led to disaster, he had no one to blame but himself.

JANNA

Janna heard a stream running nearby, so she stumbled to it. The day was hot and her feet hurt. She sat on a rock and put them in the fast icy water, letting the hem of her skirt swirl around her ankles. It tickled a little, so she laughed. Then she laughed harder until she couldn't stop. She laughed until tears ran down her face, and she didn't stop until she saw the girl leading a horse to the water. She had long black braids and wore breeches.

Janna stopped laughing long enough to say, "You look funny."

"I do not," the girl said.

"You're wearing breeches." Janna giggled. "What kind of girl wears breeches?"

"A smart one." The girl turned to peer at her more closely. "Are you all right, ma'am?"

"I'm well, thank you." Janna's giggles turned into hiccups. "And you?"

"Sir," the girl shouted, "You'd better come see this."

"Who's sir?" Janna asked and hiccuped loudly. "Excuse me." It occurred to her that these might be soldiers, but she no longer cared. She reckoned there wasn't a single thing they could do to her that could hurt her anymore. It was a lovely feeling.

She was still laughing when "sir" appeared. He was an enormous brute, with long yellow hair that curled out in all directions. He wore armor and a belt of pistols, but Janna didn't find him very frightening. From the way he stared while she giggled and hiccuped, he might have been frightened of her.

"So you found her right here?" He asked the girl.

"Just sitting right there, laughing. Do you suppose she's mad?" she added in a loud whisper.

"I can hear you, you know," Janna said. "And I'm not mad. At least, not most of the time. At least, I didn't used to be."

The man nodded and took a step closer. "Where do you live?" he asked. "We'll take you home."

"Live?" Janna stopped giggling. "I don't live anywhere. Everyone is dead. Everything is gone."

"Hmm ..." the man said.

"What should we do?" the girl asked.

"We can't leave her here." They were speaking Moraltan, but his had a strong accent she couldn't place.

"Yes, you can." Janna smiled. "In fact, I wish you would. You seem to be a soldier and I don't like soldiers. It's not personal," she added, not wanting to seem rude.

"All right," the man said. His eyes were bright blue, and they twinkled, she noticed. She hadn't at first because the beard that seemed to cover his whole face was so distracting. She'd never seen anyone with a beard like that.

"Are you foreign?" she asked. She knew it was rude, but he didn't seem to mind. The girl was smiling, but trying to hide it behind her hand.

He nodded. "I'm not Marjatyan if that's what you mean." He delivered a rather courtly bow. "Braeden Terris, of Prince Novitny's Hussars."

"Goodness. What sort of name is that?"

"Oh, Novitny's Sanovan. Surely you know of the Sanova Hussars?"

Janna shook her head, and the girl snorted. It seemed it was rude not to know this. "Are you Sanovan?" she asked, to cover her embarrassment, then remembered that she could no longer be embarrassed.

"No, I'm not." His tone was conversational, as if he were sitting in her parlor in Kaleva.

"Because Braeden Terris is a strange name."

"It is," he said cheerfully. "And what's your name, ma'am?"

"Janna Kronek." She'd forgotten she shouldn't use that name. Not that she cared anymore. If this fellow wanted to kill her for being a rebel, she'd welcome a quick end.

"So Mistress Kronek, what are we to do with you?" He took a few steps closer, and she flinched.

"It's all right," he said softly. "I won't hurt you. I'm not one of those kinds of soldiers and I don't allow my men to be."

"It's true," the girl added. "They're a good lot."

He turned to the girl. "Trisa, would you run to your mother and ask if she'd be willing to help this young lady for a day or two?"

The girl pulled the horse she'd been leading away from the water, and went back into the woods, looking over her shoulder as she went.

"I don't need help," Janna said.

"Yes, you do," the man said quietly. "How long since you've eaten?"

"I had two handfuls of strawberries last night. I'm fine."

"A real meal. And what about a bath?"

"That's been a bit longer."

"Slept in a bed, under a roof, with a full belly?"

Janna started crying.

"That's what I thought. Listen ma'am, I won't force you to come with me. But I don't like to leave you out here by yourself. The next people to find you might not be friendly."

"They usually aren't," Janna muttered.

"Right. But Trisa's mother, she's a good sort. She's married to one of my officers and has raised three girls. She'll take good care of you."

"And then what?"

"Let's not worry about that right now. We'll get you cleaned up and fed and rested and then we'll figure something out." He'd come closer now and held out a hand.

Janna hesitated, then looked straight into his eyes. They were clear and still sparkled. She saw none of that look that so frightened her. She put her hand into his. Like the rest of him, it was huge and swallowed her own. He pulled her up off the rock and she stood in the water, her feet numb by now.

"Shoes?" he asked, looking around.

She shook her head.

"That's no problem." He smiled, then whistled. A gigantic black horse appeared at his shoulder. "Lucky I didn't unsaddle him yet."

Janna shrank back.

With one swift movement, he picked her up and set her in the saddle. She squeaked and held on for dear life. The horse looked at her sideways, but held still. It looked like it was a mile down to the ground.

The blue eyes twinkled up at her again. "No need to be afraid of Kazmir. He only pretends to be fierce. He's gentle as a lamb and loves ladies."

Janna doubted she qualified as a lady at this point, but was too frightened to protest. Still, it was a nice change to be frightened of a horse instead of its rider.

KENDRYK

They were traveling a boring stretch of the Podoska road, when one of Kendryk's scouts spotted a large party of horse ahead.

Kendryk's heart lurched. "Sanova Hussars?" He'd feared the empress would send them ahead.

"Doesn't seem so, Your Grace." The scout was young and nervous.

"Were they bearing a banner?"

"Yes." The boy brightened. "A black falcon on a purple field."

"The Orland standard," Kendryk said. "Bring Arian Orland to me straight away."

"Yes sir." The scout galloped off again.

He was back within a quarter hour, accompanied by a lone horseman in fine black and silver armor, mounted on an enormous black warhorse.

Kendryk rode forward and took off his helmet, handing it to a page. "Count Orland?"

The man dismounted. He swept his own helmet off and went down in the mud on one knee. "Your Grace, a most unexpected honor."

Taken aback, Kendryk dismounted. "Please rise. There's no need to stand on ceremony. You haven't done so until now."

Orland stood, then threw back his head and laughed, showing a mouth full of white teeth. Black hair fell to his shoulders, framing a singularly handsome face. He stood a good half head taller than Kendryk, who had the fleeting notion that maybe this was the ruler Landrus was always going on about. He looked the part.

Kendryk frowned. He would have to be stern. "It should come as no surprise I'm displeased with you. Have you received my messages?"

"I have," Orland said. "I was on my way to Birkenhof and didn't expect to meet you on the road. Is all well?"

"Hm." Kendryk didn't want to offer any information before receiving an apology, and Orland appeared in no hurry to offer one. "Before I give you any news, I wish to discuss your activities."

"Oh yes, those." Orland grinned, looking at Kendryk from under long dark lashes. "Apologies. I'm afraid I got too excited when I heard what had happened in Isenwald. I had just assembled my force, and it seemed the perfect way to put it to use."

He didn't sound very sorry. "Hm," Kendryk said again. "Well, it wasn't the thing at all. What made you attack Princess Zelenka? If we ever had any hopes of gaining her support, they're gone now."

"Oh, she was hopeless." Orland tossed his head. "She's always been in the empire's pocket. But my little ploy worked. As far as I know, she hasn't sent the empress any troops."

"Your little ploy?" Kendryk felt his face redden. "Your little ploy killed several dozen innocent Kronlanders, and now people blame me for it. Exactly what are you playing at?"

Orland had the good sense to look abashed. "I was sure it wouldn't hurt to show those southerners you're serious, and that you can well defend yourself, perhaps even attack when needed. To be honest, I remember what you were like as a little boy and thought you might not be intimidating enough on your own."

"I see you're as insolent as always." Kendryk used his haughtiest tone. "For your information, I'm barely able to defend myself and as yet have no army I can use to attack anyone anywhere." He hadn't meant to say all that, but he was angry.

"I wondered if that was the case." Orland didn't seem offended in the least. "That's why I thought I should put on a good show."

He turned to face the troop coming down the road toward them. Kendryk stifled a gasp. He stood on a slight rise and could see the road as it sloped away below him. There was no end to the horsemen. Magnificently armored and equipped, and riding Maladene horses, from the looks of them. This was serious heavy cavalry.

Kendryk swallowed hard. "How many?"

"Ten thousand, give or take a few dozen. The baggage train goes on twice as long."

"Those are a lot of mouths to feed."

"They are." Orland nodded. "But they're rich in plunder from the Olvisyan frontier and can pay for all they need in good coin."

Kendryk tried to picture this enormous host camped in the Birkenhof gardens. "I suppose you'll want payment at some point, too."

Orland waved dismissively. "All in good time. No need to discuss details right now. Besides, you are my liege lord and I should fight for you anyway, shouldn't I?"

"Yes, my thoughts exactly." Kendryk turned to one of his officers. "Let's stop here. I'd like to speak with Count Orland before we continue." In truth, he desperately needed military advice, and Orland seemed to know what he was doing.

An ensign set up a table at the roadside while Orland shouted a few orders, and the horsemen dispersed into the meadow on both sides of the road. Once they sat down over a bottle of wine, Kendryk told Orland how things currently stood.

"There's no need to be upset about any of this," Orland said. "The empress is tied up well and good outside Atlona, and there's no word about the Zastwar treaty."

"Our sources tell us they're talking."

"Pfft. It's all talk right now. Teodora might get a treaty, but she must give up a great deal. And from what I've heard, she's so proud and stubborn, she'd rather die than give an inch."

"That's true. She's difficult to deal with, even when her temper doesn't get the best of her."

Orland grinned. "Ah, a spirited woman is such a joy, isn't she? I hope I can witness Teodora Inferrara's temper at least once. Is she as beautiful as they say?"

Kendryk was bewildered by the change in subject. "Not really to my taste, and well, a bit old, but most would find her attractive."

"Oh, but older women are wonderful. None of that trembling, shrinking virginal business. You must try one."

Stunned, Kendryk stammered, "Er, I'd rather not. I'm quite happy with my wife."

"Of course you are. Rumor is that the Princess Gwynneth puts every other lady in the empire in the shade. You are a lucky devil, you know." Orland smiled and flashed a dimple.

"I know," Kendryk said sternly, not liking the conversation. "Where were we? Oh, the Zastwar treaty. I don't want to take anything for granted and be prepared for the worst."

"That's the correct approach," Orland said. "Although, I'd recommend moving against Teodora now, while she's weak. If we marched into Olvisya right away, you could kill or capture her within a few weeks."

"I don't want to do that. I want her to leave me alone."

"That's unlikely. But now I'm here, I'd like to help."

"I don't know how to fortify the border. We've tried to keep the buildings and walls in good repair, but we don't have enough trained soldiers."

Orland shrugged. "I doubt there's much you can do there, although I can advise you on training and how to best man the fortifications. You'll have to take the fight to Teodora."

Kendryk didn't like Orland's assumption that attacking the empress was the best course, but it was a relief to have someone at his side who understood his business. Orland had the bulk of his force make camp near a larger town, and then he rode with Kendryk toward the Sanovan border.

Things weren't any better there, but Orland's cool competence made even the peasant soldiers stand up straighter. Kendryk felt more confident just listening to him. Orland had taken part in many sieges in Zeelund and Floradias and had defended against besiegers as well.

But best of all, whenever Kendryk worried, he would think of that magnificent cavalry, waiting for them back at the crossroads. With that and with whatever infantry Count Faris could find, he might have a chance of winning.

GWYNNETH

"Goodness!" Gwynneth jumped as Devyn grabbed her skirts and burrowed into them. He was hiding from Maryna who collided into her other side.

Kendryk laughed and snatched Maryna while Gwynneth untangled Devyn and passed him back to the nurse. Maryna shrieked as Kendryk swung her onto his shoulders, crushing his collar. Gwynneth made a face, which Kendryk saw.

"Oh come now, darling. They're happy to be out in the garden. So am I."

It had rained for a solid week before Kendryk returned two days ago with Arian Orland and an enormous force of sodden cavalry troopers. They were probably all occupied in polishing their armor. This was the first fine day, and it promised to be hot.

"It's difficult to talk when they're running about screaming," Gwynneth said, aware of how sulky she sounded. With Orland here, Kendryk couldn't think about anything except troop dispositions. When he wasn't poring over scrolls with the priest, he was poring over maps with the soldiers. He'd had Orland and his top officers move into the palace, so even their meals centered on military talk.

Gwynneth also wished Kendryk had consulted her before bringing them all into the palace. Count Orland was civilized enough and two of the Maladene officers were courtly in the extreme. But Ossian Schurtz, a rough mercenary colonel, was another matter and not proper company for anyone else here. She had no idea who he was or where he was from, but his manners were horrid. Worse, he regarded Gwynneth with a frightening leer and had once cornered Linette in a dark corridor. Only a passing footman had saved her from gods-knew-what.

Kendryk put Maryna down. "Go play with your brother now." He kissed the top of her head and gave her a gentle shove, then turned to Gwynneth. "I'm sorry darling. But we see the children even less than we see each other."

"I doubt that." She tucked her hand under his elbow. "But you were telling me how Count Orland proposes to man the border."

"Yes. He believes we can spend much less time training the militia if we have them guard fortifications, rather than drilling them for the battlefield. With Orland's cavalry, and whatever Faris finds in Zeelund, we should have enough force to meet whatever Teodora throws against us."

"That's encouraging." Gwynneth squeezed his arm. "Much as I dislike Orland's type, we can't deny he arrived at an opportune time."

"Yes, the truce in Floradias has been fortunate for us. But I fear it might also be fortunate for Teodora since it will make Maladena's troops available to her."

"Do you think so? She's not on good terms with Queen Beatryz."

"She's not on good terms with anyone, but that doesn't keep her from getting what she wants from them."

"True." Gwynneth frowned. "In that case, we should act before she gets help from Maladena."

"That's what Arian says, too."

"Oh, so it's Arian now? You two are rather friendly."

"He's been very helpful," Kendryk said. She regretted the bit of defensiveness in his voice that seemed to be there almost every time they spoke. "And unlike everyone else who claims to wish me well but offers nothing useful, he's doing more than his share."

"It's his obligation. Besides, the truce freed him up, and he needed employment."

"Unlike everyone else, he's not asking for immediate payment, and I appreciate that."

"I wonder what he wants," Gwynneth mused.

"Probably a good fight."

"How does the treasury look? I'm afraid to ask these days."

Kendryk frowned. "There's not much left after accounting for what the Zeelund army will cost. More is coming in, but not as fast as it's going out."

"How long will you be able to pay the Zeelunders?" Gwynneth tried not to show how appalled she was. She'd always thought they had an unimaginable amount of money.

"Three months; give or take a few weeks."

"So something has to happen within three months, or they go home."

"Yes."

"In that case, you should move as soon as they arrive."

"Move where?"

"Attack Teodora. We know where she is, and she's undefended right now. My sources in her camp tell me she's sent the Sanova Hussars into Marjatya, so she can't have over five hundred troops, total. You have more than enough to defeat her."

"Yes, but ..."

"But nothing. She needs to be removed and you are in the perfect place to do it."

Gwynneth took a deep breath and walked ahead. The children were playing with a ball on a large circle of grass nearby. She stopped at the edge of it.

Kendryk caught up and put his arm around her, pulling her close. "So I remove her. Who would replace her?"

"Who cares?" Though Gwynneth very much cared, she realized Kendryk didn't agree with her ambitions. "It's time they looked outside that family with it's half-crazed blood."

"Only half?" Kendryk joked. "But you know I don't want the job."

"I know. What about an independent Kronland? Let the rest of the empire sort out who rules them, and we go our own way, including a complete break from the Temple."

"Maybe. I just can't be certain it's the right way and I'm so tired of trying to figure out what is." He sat down on a stone bench, and she sat next to him, sliding an arm around his waist and resting her head on his shoulder.

"You think I'm always so certain about what to do next, but I'm not. I'm trying to look at the situation clearly, and Father Landrus isn't helping, for all he started it."

"It's not his fault." There was that tone again.

"Of course it's not. But we have a real opportunity and we ought to take it while we can. What if the Zeelunders disperse when the money runs out and Teodora attacks us then?"

"The money won't run out," Kendryk said. "I can borrow at least six times as much as I've spent."

"But for what purpose? So you can fight Teodora after she has a treaty with Zastwar and is back at full strength?"

"What if Korma attacks her right now? He could do all the work for us."

"Korma is like a dog with a bone and won't let Atlona go for anything. He should go after Teodora herself, but he's not an intelligent man. He's decided on Atlona and he will have it. It's probably never occurred to him how unprotected she is right now. And those around him are no better. There is nothing so thick-headed as a Marjatyan who's decided on something. Except for you, when you haven't," she teased.

"I'm close to an answer," Kendryk said. "Or at any rate, Father Landrus is. He's working his way through a difficult part of the text and he's sure something important is hidden there. It's just a matter of uncovering it."

"He's been saying that for months now." Gwynneth sighed.

"I know." Kendryk's face was a picture of misery. Her heart went out to him in spite of her frustration. "I've committed to this thing because of what he's learned and what he's taught me. It would be folly to try something else. Please, just give me a little more time."

"I needn't give you permission." She forced a smile. "You should take whatever time you need. The rest of us are here to support you in whatever you decide."

"Thank you darling," He kissed her hand. "Something will turn up. I promise."

BRAEDEN

Braeden had finished his supper and was contemplating bed. Teodora would be pleased at the villages burned and the crops destroyed that day. Somehow, that work was more tiring than battle. He had risen from the campfire where he'd been talking with the other troopers when Senta Torresia bustled up to him.

"Signor," she said, although he'd told her to call him Braeden a thousand times in the past twenty years. "Might I speak with you alone?"

"Of course." He gestured toward his tent.

Gergo had lit a lamp and made everything ready, so there were a few camp chairs sitting at a table.

"Sit down, if you have time." He grinned at her since she was always in a hurry.

"What is it?" He asked though he had an idea.

"It's that girl you and Trisa found in the woods the other day." Senta dropped her voice.

"Is she all right?"

"Oh, she will live. And she is not crazy though Trisa is not sure. Reno says she acts like normal girls, but I know he is teasing."

"So she'll live and she hasn't lost her mind. It sounds like she's doing well."

"She will get better, but it's difficult. She is so very frightened."

"I noticed that. I imagine some soldiers mistreated her."

"Yes, they did." Senta wrung her hands and dropped her voice to a whisper. "She would not say, so I asked her, with great care of course, if those bad men had their way with her."

Braeden didn't want to hear this. "Hmm. And?"

"She wouldn't answer, but every time I ask, she cries."

"That seems natural."

Senta shook her head. "She is afraid of Reno even though he is so kind. She tries to hide whenever she sees him, or any man."

"That's a shame," Braeden said. "I'm sure she'll get better. What do you want me to do?" Senta always had a task to be accomplished.

"Perhaps you can talk to her."

"That will just frighten her more."

"But you're different. She already knows you won't hurt her."

"What would I say?"

"Oh, not much. Stop by sometime and ask how she's doing. Just a friendly check up on her."

"Hmm. You're sure it will help?" In Braeden's experience with Senta, objections were useless.

"Yes, I do. I understand girls and I can help this one, but I need you to do something too."

"All right. I'll visit her tomorrow."

"You should come right now." Senta smiled.

"Now?"

"The sooner the better. It's a quiet time and you can talk for a few minutes. Come along now."

Braeden followed her, knowing it was easier than arguing. Better to get it over with anyway.

The Torresia tent wasn't far away. It was large and comfortable, having at one point housed the entire family of five. Since Cara had stayed with the court, there was plenty of room.

The girl sat on the edge of a cot, doing some mending. She started when Senta bustled through the flap, and her eyes widened when she noticed Braeden behind her. She jumped up, dropping her work on the floor.

"See who I found wandering around the camp," Senta chirped. "It's your rescuer."

Braeden forced a smile and said, "Please sit down, miss. I wanted to say hello and see how you're doing."

She sank back on the cot and Braeden sat on a stool so he didn't tower over her.

She looked at her hands and was silent. Senta had melted, not altogether quietly, into the background.

"Are you feeling better, Mistress er, Kronek is it?" he asked.

She looked up and back down. "Yes, much better, thank you." Her voice was so soft he could barely hear her.

"Good. I told you Signora Torresia would take care of you."

"She has been most kind, and so have you." She looked at him, but he could tell it cost her some effort.

"Oh, it's nothing. No trouble at all."

"But that's the problem." The girl glanced in Senta's direction. "I worry I'm being a great burden to all of you. I can't do anything except a little sewing." She looked at the work back in her lap. "Everyone here is so busy and capable."

"You don't have to do anything except get better."

"I know I need to." She swallowed and he could tell she was working herself up to say something. "When I'm better, I must search for my son. He disappeared after ... well, I'm sure the soldiers took him."

"Any idea whose soldiers?"

"No." Her eyes welled up. "It was dark, and I was so frightened. I didn't pay attention to anything important."

"Now, now," Braeden said uncomfortably, seeing she was about to cry. "We can ask around for your boy. Could be someone's seen him, or even picked him up." Though it was doubtful, it was better she had hope right now. "How old is he and what's he look like?"

"Almost ten." She dashed tears from her eyes. "Tall for his age but skinny, with dark hair getting too long and dark eyes. His name is Anton."

"Aren't you young to have a ten-year-old?" She didn't look a day over twenty.

"He's my stepson. But he's been mine since he was four."

"Where did you last see him?"

"South of the Moraltan border, at the top of that hill."

"How long ago now?"

"I'm not sure." Her eyes filled with tears. "I went into the woods and lost track. A few weeks, perhaps."

It sounded hopeless, with dead children everywhere these days, but Braeden tried to sound cheerful. "I'll spread the word and we'll all keep an eye out. Maybe he'll turn up. Boys that age, they can be tough little buggers."

"Oh yes." Her eyes lit up. They were large and hazel and quite beautiful, he noticed for the first time. Too big for her pale little face, though. "He's tough, ever so much tougher than I am. I'm certain he could survive."

"Then he probably has," Braeden said. "Now Miss, please don't worry about a thing. Let Signora here take care of you, do little jobs for her if you can, and we'll do what we can about your boy. All right?"

She nodded and looked down again.

Braeden stood, not sure if he'd done any good. "I'll go now, but I'll visit you again soon, if you don't mind."

"Not at all." She looked up at him and stood. "Thank you for being so kind."

From over her shoulder, he saw Senta smiling at him.

KENDRYK

Though Kendryk had warm memories of the times in the castle's cramped library, having Landrus here at Birkenhof was far more convenient. Instead of riding to the river, he only had to walk to the guest wing of his own home. He found the priest hard at work as usual, in the little study they had improvised for him.

"You should try to get outside for a bit." Kendryk sat down across from the desk. "It's beautiful out there."

Landrus glanced at the window with little interest. "There's no time," he said. "I feel such a strong pressure to work even faster right now."

"I won't keep you long."

"That's not what I meant." Landrus put down his quill. "I find talking to you as helpful as poring over these scrolls and sometimes more so. By seeking to answer your questions, I often find interesting answers, even when they aren't the ones you want."

"I'm glad I'm not too much of a bother then." Kendryk smiled. "To be honest, I am under great pressure too, though of a different sort."

"I imagine you are. It seems everyone else in this household is eager to march into Teodora's camp without delay."

"Eager doesn't begin to describe the enthusiasm for that plan." Kendryk let the frustration creep into his voice. "And I understand why. We've learned that Teodora has sent most of her guard into Marjatya, which means she would be easy to kill or capture. No one understands why I'm not keen to do so."

"It is hard to understand in the normal way of thinking." Landrus pushed back from the desk and stretched.

Kendryk winced at the sound of several sharp cracks from his back. Sitting at this desk day and night was taking its toll. He had it from the servants that the priest seldom slept over three hours at night. Kendryk wondered how long he could continue.

Landrus slumped back into his chair. "Striking at Teodora while she's so helpless is sure to turn many against you. The opposite must happen. You make the case against her so that allies are drawn to you."

"That's what we've been trying to do. Gwynneth has written dozens of letters, with your pamphlets in every one of them. Many rulers have expressed interest in your ideas, but no one yet has offered any real help. No one except for Arian Orland that is."

Kendryk caught Landrus's brief grimace. "You don't like him, I realize that." He sighed. "But you must admit, he's here with a large force and a great deal of experience. No one else can stand against Teodora right now. My militia is close to useless and won't improve."

"I understand. And I don't wish to speak against Orland since I know so little about him. I get a bad impression from him though it's nothing specific. But my prayers for guidance have so far gone unanswered."

"Perhaps there's nothing." Kendryk had to believe that. He couldn't face yet another problem. "Though it's true his manner can be abrasive."

"It's not that," Landrus said. "I'm a fair judge of character and something is wrong with his. But I haven't spent enough time around him to discover what it is."

"Do you suspect him of disloyalty?" Kendryk frowned. "That he might be an agent for Teodora?"

"No, nothing so obvious." Landrus shook his head. "Your Grace, I don't wish to cause you unease, but I wish you didn't need to rely upon him."

"I won't much longer. Count Faris's latest message says he's assembling a large infantry and artillery force and will march this way as soon as he can. He also has contacts in the Zeelund government and might enlist more help from them."

"That's good. Zeelund is the ally you need. They practice a far better version of the Faith and are wealthy enough to offer meaningful help. "

"But what should I do in the meantime? I have enough troops to attack Teodora before she gets help, so no one understands why I don't."

"You're in charge." Landrus smiled. "You needn't do what everyone else wants. You must please yourself and the gods, and no one else."

"I wish the gods made themselves clearer." Kendryk knew he should trust his own judgment and the guidance he'd been given, but it wasn't enough to stop the dread rising inside him.

"Have they not so far?" Landrus asked. "They haven't spoken to you again as they did in the dream, but that is not always their way. And yet, you've always received guidance when you most needed it. They will not fail you now you've come this far."

"You're right. But I pray and pray and study as much as I can and yet I understand less than I did when I first brought you back here." No one else seemed as frustrated as Kendryk, but then, no one else had his responsibilities.

"It's not wrong to doubt," Landrus said, his voice softer now. "It's natural, especially in this very difficult situation. You are handling it brilliantly. Just don't let anyone force you into action that doesn't seem right to you."

Even though he hadn't resolved anything, Kendryk felt better. He made to get up, but Landrus said, "If Your Grace has time, there's another matter I'd like to discuss with you, soon if not today."

JANNA

Janna ran outside the tent again as her breakfast came back up. This was the third time since last night. When she came back in, Senta looked concerned. "You might be sick. You should ride in a wagon today."

Janna shook her head. "I'd rather not. I'm all right otherwise. Do you suppose it might be ... oh gods, I can't even bear the thought." She put her head in her hands.

Senta led her to a cot and made her sit. "Listen, little dove," she said with her lovely accent. "You might be, or you maybe ate something too rich last night. You were starving not so long ago, and it takes time to get back to normal. But a baby is not the end of the world."

"Isn't it?" Janna couldn't hold back the tears. "I can't ... I won't know who the father is. The only certain thing is that it was one of those horrible men. What if I hate the baby? What if every time I see it, I remember...."

"Ah, it won't always be like that." Senta patted her back. "You will be so busy with a baby, which will be so sweet, you'll forget all about those men after a while."

"How do you know? Unless it's happened to you, how could you know?"

"It hasn't happened to me, true," Senta said. "But in my time with the hussars, I watched many women go through the same thing. It's one of the most common things to happen in wartime and often babies come afterward. Those women always manage. And you might not believe it, but a husband adds difficulties. Even if the baby looks like him, he will always wonder."

"Oh, that would be too dreadful." Janna couldn't imagine Dimir reacting to her plight very well. She was sure he never would have put her aside, but she wondered if he might have always held it against her. But then she thought of something else. "How will I survive with a baby? Must I leave it at a temple?"

Senta shook her head. "Of course not. No matter what happens, we will not abandon you."

"But I can't impose on you forever," Janna wailed.

"You won't. A pretty girl like you—and you are pretty as soon as you gain a little weight." Senta had an obsession with girls having ample figures. That her own daughters all had athletic builds was a source of distress for her. "You will get a husband in no time. You should choose a high-ranking officer though. More money and nicer things, better quarters in the towns." She made it sound as though Janna would have her pick of suitors, a ridiculous idea.

Though she found the idea of a husband repulsive at the moment, Janna saw the sense in it. She was no good at taking care of herself. But while the hussars were all kind enough, she still found them foreign and frightening. The men were large, rough and loud, and she'd seen them kill without hesitation. Being married to one of them seemed a terrifying prospect. But when the time came, she'd have to do it. Baby or not, she mustn't live on the Torresia's kindness forever.

"How will I find a husband if I already have a baby?" she asked in a small voice.

Senta shrugged. "Easily enough. There are plenty of widows with children around and they nearly always find someone. You're so sweet and you'll look good once you're plumper. It's possible you'll be snapped up before the baby is born. If there's a baby at all."

Janna wiped her tears and got to work, helping pack up the tent. She hoped Senta was wrong about the baby. It would be too cruel of the gods to take the children she loved and give her one she would probably hate instead.

BRAEDEN

"We're done here, sir." Reno's eyes watered from the smoke.

"Move out," Braeden shouted, and the hussars gathered from the various points they'd scattered when the fighting started.

Braeden saw no survivors. With any luck, the folks that stayed out of the fight were hiding in the woods somewhere.

"What's left?" Braeden asked.

"Just the village below the castle," Reno said. "I think it might be empty. A scout reported people running for the castle right after we got here."

"Let's burn it anyway. Sends a message. Get everyone to gather round, and then we'll deploy around the castle." Braeden's orders were to take Count Andarosz's castle by any means necessary. The count was one of Andor Korma's most fervent supporters.

Braeden squinted at the castle. Built on flat land, it was small and old. It hadn't served as a fortification since the Zastwar armies last came through here a hundred years ago. With any luck, the defenders were ill-prepared. Most of the fighting people in these parts had marched to Atlona with Korma, leaving behind the elderly, and women with young children.

The air cleared as they moved down the road toward the village. "Round up any livestock," Braeden said. The villagers hadn't had time to take everything to the castle on such short notice. It was nice having fresh meat on hand, now they were deep into rebel territory with not a supply line in sight.

A few troopers rode off and some time later, drove a herd of cows and goats down the road toward their camp. When he'd received word that the village was stripped of valuables, Braeden gave the order to burn it. They'd be sure to see that at the castle.

It was near evening by the time he approached the walls. Many times, they'd gone around the castles, burning everything else, but Braeden needed to get a hostage here. Any Andarosz would do, according to Teodora's list. The count's wife and children ought to be here.

Braeden rode up to the gate. He'd put on his wings, just for effect. A crossbow bolt whizzed past his ear, snapping at the feathers. A few more bolts flew by. He wondered if they didn't have firearms. More likely, they had a few, but were saving their ammunition. He waited a few more minutes until the shooting stopped. Their aim was terrible, which meant there were no older soldiers here. Few youngsters these days learned how to shoot a crossbow.

A head poked up over the battlements. "What do you want?" a man shouted.

"I'd like to speak to the Countess Andarosz, if she is at home," Braeden shouted back.

"She is, but she doesn't want to speak to you."

"I'll wait." Braeden turned Kazmir around and rode away. When he reached the hussar line, he sent them off in twos, until they surrounded the castle in a thin circle. It wasn't an impressive show, but then the castle wasn't very big either. When he gave the order, everyone fired their arquebusses at once. They were to aim over the battlements, and with any luck, a few balls would reach over them. He didn't expect they'd hit anyone, unless it was an accident, but it would give the defenders an idea of what they were facing.

A gratifying racket echoed off the stone walls. Braeden waited for the smoke to clear. Nothing from the castle. He ordered a few more rounds, and this time they moved closer. A few crossbow bolts flew, but hit nothing.

At last a shout came from the castle. "The countess will see you."

Braeden rode to the gate. A face poked through a slit in the wall next to it. "You're to come in, alone."

Braeden dismounted and handed Kazmir's reins to Trisa, who'd just ridden up behind him. He handed her his weapons and unstrapped his wings. These were no hardened killers, and if any harm came to him, they wouldn't live much longer.

A small door in the gate opened and closed right behind Braeden. The countess already stood in front of him.

"We won't surrender." Her voice was firm, although panic showed in her dark eyes.

"It's better if you do," Braeden said, hoping she'd give up quickly.

GWYNNETH

Gwynneth watched the children play for a few minutes longer, then made her way back to the palace. Kendryk would be with Landrus, as usual. She asked for a tray to be sent to the library for luncheon and got back to work. Halvor had copied letters all morning while Avaron opened the messages as they arrived.

"Your Grace, you should see this one right away," she said, as soon as Gwynneth sat down at her desk. It was a note from Princess Martinek of Podoska, a small kingdom southeast of Terragand. Raiders from Moralta were crossing her borders and burning crops and villages before disappearing again. She didn't know who they were or who sent them, but blamed Teodora and Kendryk for starting the trouble.

Gwynneth tossed the letter onto her desk and put her head in her hands. It didn't matter who was behind it if she could somehow convince Kendryk that Teodora was attacking Kronland. After a moment she said, "Avaron, send for Count Orland and ask him to come here as soon as he can." She'd seen him return to the palace earlier, so perhaps he was still nearby.

He entered the library with an easy saunter that wasn't quite the thing off the battlefield, but it suited him well enough. He bowed with a flourish as Gwynneth rose from her desk. "Princess, I am honored." He straightened up and took her hand, brushing it with his lips while regarding her with his too-bold dark eyes. "I was beginning to wonder if you'd ever speak a word to me."

"Don't be ridiculous," Gwynneth snapped, more sharply than she meant to. She had spoken to him, in dinner conversation at least. It was true there'd been nothing beyond that since she was in here the rest of the time, leaving Kendryk to entertain the men afterward. "Please, sit down," she said, taking a seat across from him.

He slouched back, his legs outstretched and unapologetic about the mud on his boots. "What have I done, Princess? Since I'm sure you wouldn't bother to speak to me unless you wished to call me to the carpet for something."

"You must have a guilty conscience." She smiled, then cursed herself for falling into flirtation. "But no, you are not in trouble, and I don't wish to hear any lurid confessions," she said firmly, changing her tone.

"That's a relief. I was wondering if I'd offended you."

"Not at all. I've been busy. I apologize for being such a poor hostess. The times are ..."

"Difficult." He leaned forward, his tone serious now. "I understand that well Princess, and I should be the one apologizing for imposing upon you so. Now, how may I be of service?"

That was better. "I'd like your opinion on what Kendryk should do next, from a military perspective."

"We should march on Olvisya right now. Teodora is so weak at the moment, we could overcome her easily with my troops alone. She's surrounded by so few Sanova Hussars that we might have a chance."

"My sources tell me the Sanova Hussars are in Marjatya."

"That's welcome news. In that case, we should act now. Anyone Faris brings can serve as reinforcement should Ensden be able to come to her rescue."

"That's what I was thinking. The hussars won't be far and could probably relieve Teodora within a day or two, so you'd have to sneak up on her."

"I could do it."

Gwynneth sat back in her chair, pushing down her excitement. "Kendryk thinks Andor Korma might attack Teodora, but if he hasn't yet, I doubt he will."

"He won't. I've met the man. He's brave, but stubborn and rather an idiot. Even if the other Marjatyans see the possibilities, which I doubt, they'll never be able to talk sense into him."

"That's what I thought. So you believe now is the best time to attack Teodora?" It was a relief to finally have someone agree with her.

"Absolutely. I've been trying to convince your husband, but he seems averse to making the first move."

Gwynneth sighed. "He doesn't want to be seen as the aggressor."

"No one would fault him for being aggressive against Teodora, though I take it he has other considerations. He spends a lot of time with that Landrus fellow, a queer enough sort from the looks of him."

"Oh, he's all right. He's just got Kendryk tied up in knots over an obscure theological problem. At first I thought he would support quick action because he has the most to lose should Teodora prevail. But it's not so simple. It ties in with something about the gods and a big battle and so on."

"How annoying," Orland said.

"It is. I have nothing against the man, but he's holding us back now."

"That won't matter if we can find a reason for the prince to act anyway. If there's a worry of imminent danger, for instance."

"Linette, get that letter from Princess Martinek on my desk." Linette brought the letter and handed it to Gwynneth, all while staring at Orland and blushing. Gwynneth rolled her eyes. Orland caught that and smiled. Gwynneth handed him the letter. "Do you have any idea who might have done this?"

He glanced over the letter, shook his head and handed it back. "No idea. It might be Daciana Tomescu, although last I heard she was in Marjatya. Could be bandits, or partisans trying to start trouble. It doesn't matter. How much proof does the prince need before he's willing to act?"

"I don't know. I wish Count Faris were here. I'm sure he'd agree with us, and Kendryk always listens to him."

"I thought he always listened to you."

"He does. Or rather, he did, until Father Landrus came here. Now it seems the religious reasons will forever trump the practical."

"How did you ever get him to rescue Landrus?"

"I convinced him that Korma besieging Atlona was a sign from the gods. Now he's waiting for the next one."

"So, it will need to be impressive. I doubt these little raids on Podoska will do it."

"Oh, it's frustrating!" She flung the letter onto a little table.

"Is there any chance of convincing Landrus to help us?"

"I doubt it. Though perhaps you should talk to him."

"Oh no." Orland laughed. "Not me. He doesn't care for me in the least. I hate it when he's at dinner because he has that disapproving glare. .."

"Oh, I know what you mean. He makes me feel like a little girl who's misbehaved."

"I think we must let the good priest be and try to convince Kendryk from the practical standpoint. If we can't do it right away, I'm sure Count Faris's arrival will help."

"I wish he'd hurry," Gwynneth fretted. "I'm so disappointed in the response from the rest of Kronland. You've been the only one to offer real help. I hope you realize we appreciate it."

"Why thank you." He flashed a blinding smile at her. "I'm just doing my duty, but it's nice to be appreciated, by you in particular."

"I don't want to keep you from your work, and I must get back to mine," she said, standing. He rose as well.

She walked him to the library door. "I suppose for now, we'll keep mentioning the threat from the south and let him draw his own conclusions. Beyond that, we need to wait for Faris to arrive."

BRAEDEN

Countess Andarosz may have been frightened, but she was also angry. Braeden doubted she was as old as he was, but judging by the lines on her face, life hadn't been easy. It often wasn't for minor aristocrats. Only one step above peasant, survival was almost as much of a struggle. "Of course it's better for you," she said, her dark eyes flashing. "What good does it do me to surrender?"

"I'm sure you know what happens when a castle is sacked." It wasn't a threat; just the way it went.

"There are children here," she said. "And many villagers. They have no part in this fight."

"Ah yes, children." Braeden hated doing this. "That's one reason I'm here. My orders are to escort one member of the Andarosz family to Atlona to be a guest of the empress."

She paled. "A hostage? There's just me and the children. The oldest is only eleven. He can't go."

"He must. If you let him go, we'll ride away in the morning and leave you alone."

"And if I don't?"

"We'll wait you out since we know you're not provisioned for a siege. You're almost out of water, too."

"We have a well."

"Going dry." He'd picked up this useful bit of information from a villager they'd questioned earlier in the day.

The look on her face showed the man hadn't lied.

"We'll fight."

"With crossbows? Come now countess, we both know that while your walls may be strong, there aren't enough fighters here. We'll break your gate down within a few hours. If you don't surrender, our orders are to kill everyone."

"Everyone? You'd slaughter innocent women and children? What kind of knight are you?"

"Not really a knight." Braeden shrugged. He didn't tell her he'd let most of the civilians get away.

She stood silent for a moment. "What if we surrender without the hostage?"

"That won't happen. If you surrender, we take a hostage. Those are my orders."

"You can take me," she said. "I can't bear the thought of Karil ... no, it's too awful."

"Lady." Braeden shifted onto his other foot. "Think about it. How many children do you have?"

"Five." Her voice quavered.

"How old is the youngest?"

"Two." Tears spilled from her eyes.

"You can't leave them. You can't leave your people here. When I go, you will have whatever is within these walls, but everything outside them is gone. The months ahead will be hard for everyone. What will they do without you? Your husband, if he comes back, won't do so for some time. Stay, for your children and your people. We'll treat your boy well. We won't put him in a dungeon and someone will look after him. Eleven is old enough."

"For some," she said, the tears still falling. "But not for him. He's just not ready."

"I am sorry," Braeden said, and he was. But he hoped she saw the sense in what he was saying.

"Not sorry enough." She sighed. "But I suppose we always knew the risks."

Indeed. And losing one child was a small price for rebellion, compared to what others had, and would, pay.

"All right." She wiped the tears from her face with her sleeve. "I will get him. He'll need time to gather his things."

"There is no hurry," Braeden said. "Have him ready to go at first light. And please, don't substitute someone else's child. When I find out, I'll come back, and then you won't have any choices." Braeden made a small bow, turned on his heel and walked through the door that opened in front of him, and shut behind him again just as quickly.

In the morning, he rode to the gate with a small contingent. The door opened once more, and a boy came out, carrying a small bundle. Braeden dismounted and took the bundle. "Your name?" he asked.

"Karil Andarosz." He was small for eleven, with his mother's enormous dark eyes in a narrow, pale face. Braeden could see why she hadn't wanted to let him go.

"Can you ride?"

The boy nodded.

Braeden had a horse brought forward. It was a spare, and the smallest he could find. It was still too big, and he could see that the boy was frightened. He'd probably ridden nothing larger than a pony until now.

There was no way he could mount on his own, so Braeden picked him up around the waist and lifted him onto the saddle. "This is Zoltan. He's a battle charger, and well-trained. He's big, but will respond to the smallest command from you. You'd be riding something of the sort in a few years anyway, wouldn't you?" He gave the boy a small smile.

Karil smiled back tremulously. From the looks of him, he wasn't warrior material, but in a few years he might grow quite a bit. Braeden himself had been a scrawny little thing until he shot up at thirteen. Maybe he'd tell him about that on the way to the empress.

"All right, Karil. Wave goodbye," Braeden said. "You won't be back for a while."

Karil waved, and a red flag fluttered from the battlements. The boy gulped back tears.

"Move out," Braeden said, then turned to Karil. "Think of it as an adventure. It's boring around here, and you're about to meet the empress of the land."

This seemed to rouse the boy. "She is not the rightful one."

"You aren't the only one who thinks so," Braeden said. "But you should keep those ideas to yourself. Think what you like, but don't say it, and it'll go easier for you."

KENDRYK

"Let's talk now." Kendryk sat back down.

"We must discuss the changes the Faith has undergone in Terragand," Landrus said. "I receive a great deal of correspondence from temples around the land, and most now embrace the new form of worship."

"I've heard similar things. I can't imagine Julia has endorsed them though she's been silent since our return."

"Julia is finished," Landrus said rather dismissively considering how close he and the Maxima had once been. "Though she still holds the office, she has no power. Priests and priestesses are ordering the worship as they see fit and reading the passages I've translated from the Scrolls to their congregations. They ignore any orders to stop."

Kendryk shifted in his seat. "I don't suppose Julia can do what she did with you."

"She'd need to arrest every cleric in the land at this point. Except for a few hold-outs, their congregations have removed them and replaced them with lay clergy."

"I didn't know about that," Kendryk said, appalled.

"It's done with little fuss. The Duke of Emberg is still a threat, and no one wants to cause you any more trouble."

"I wouldn't let my uncle interfere."

"Not everyone knows that. But the Faith is undergoing great changes and it might be time for you to consider making some of your own."

"What sorts of changes?" Kendryk didn't want another thing to worry about.

"Julia could be removed and a new hierarchy put into place."

"We would choose a new Maxima?"

"No, you can do away with the office altogether."

"But who would oversee the temples? If Julia is gone, you should be maximus. I'd be happy to appoint you."

"I appreciate that. But I don't want the job. I can be more effective the way I am, at least for now. In that post, I would become bogged down in administrative tasks and another set of politics. No, it's time congregations received more power and worked with their priest or priestess to set up a temple they like."

"That sounds like anarchy." Kendryk's head ached.

"Not at all," Landrus said. "According to the Scrolls, all of this Temple hierarchy is heretical. Nowhere is there any mention of Imperata or maximus. It's the gods, the priests and the people. That's all."

"That seems radical."

"It is. And it might take time before it settles into a workable state."

"What about those who don't want change?"

"They are wrong. Most are frightened of change, or misinformed. Their fellow believers will guide them to the truth."

"This is the first I've heard of this. I don't know what to think. Given my current problems, I'd rather not confront Julia."

"What's the worst she can do?"

"She's not without her own power. My uncle is not in open rebellion, but he's made no secret of the fact he finds the course I've taken illegal and appalling. He would welcome the chance to throw his weight behind Julia once she has a grievance."

"True." Landrus didn't seem upset at the prospect.

"Can we leave her in place for the time being? Once I've dealt with Teodora, it will be a simple matter to remove her, although I still don't quite understand how we go ahead from there."

"It will be simple. Though there will be no religious head of the Temple, the priests and priestesses will still need to be bound by a few rules. Those would come from you. You would oversee the practical side of the Temple, or appoint someone who does."

"I am not fit for that role," Kendryk said, alarmed.

"You will be when the time is right. Soon, you will head the Faith in Terragand and the people will decide how to worship."

"I'm not sure I like this. I don't wish to start a new religion or be the head of it. I liked much about the old one and don't wish it destroyed altogether."

"It won't be completely. But if we're to prepare for the last battle, we must make significant changes, and soon."

For someone who wasn't a rebel, Kendryk was overseeing changes so radical they made Andor Korma look like an amateur. He didn't like the feeling.

GWYNNETH

Gwynneth seldom joined the rest in the drawing room after supper, but she'd written all the letters she could stand. Besides, she felt guilty leaving all the hosting duties to Kendryk, who had more than enough to do. She also realized she looked particularly well today; her cheeks rosy and her eyes bright, and she sensed the appreciation at supper.

Kendryk shot her a grateful look when he saw her take Landrus's arm as they left the dining room. Once they reached the drawing room, Kendryk drew Landrus into a corner to pore over a strange-looking document, while Ossian Schurtz and the two Maladene officers took up a card game.

Arian Orland waved them off when they asked him to join.

"Don't they need a fourth?" she asked as he followed her to another corner.

"Not for this game. Besides, I hate to leave you alone since you so seldom join us."

"I've been a terrible hostess." She sat on a sofa, letting her skirts billow out around her. Arian took a seat in a chair next to it.

"Not at all." He smiled. He smiled often, probably because he looked so good doing it. His teeth were white and straight, a pleasant contrast to his olive skin, and he had a dimple in his left cheek. "Everyone is busy right now and you most of all. A great deal depends on what you're doing."

It was about time someone acknowledged the importance of her work. "I'm glad you're here with your wonderful cavalry, but if we're to challenge the empress in any meaningful way, we will need several powerful allies."

"I agree." Arian leaned forward and dropped his voice. "Have you had any luck persuading your husband to move now?"

259

She shook her head. "He's preoccupied with religious matters. And I'm certain that Father Landrus has counseled patience because he's said no more about doing anything. It's so frustrating," she added in a whisper.

"It is," Arian said. "But he's the ruler, and we must do as he says."

"Yes though I can't help wondering if he's making a dreadful mistake." Once the words started they wanted to pour out. She'd prided herself on not complaining, but now she wondered if that was because she had no one to complain to.

Arian wasn't the right person either but now she could not stop herself. "And I worry that no allies will step forward until he takes action. Once he does so I'm certain others will follow, but if we wait for Teodora to move, they may be too frightened."

Arian shrugged. He never seemed to worry much about anything. "All we can do is keep showing him the best way and hope he'll take it."

"That's not enough," Gwynneth said. "Even if it's difficult, I would rather march on Teodora instead of sitting here, waiting for something to happen."

"Something will happen soon enough. It always does."

"I wish I could relax about it like you do."

"I wasn't always like this. It comes from spending so much time in the military. You become accustomed to waiting. In fact, you spend little time fighting. You're either on the march, or sitting in camp."

"It sounds awful. I always pictured military life as glamorous and exciting."

"Everyone does until they experience it. Still, I prefer it to sitting in palaces all day. An evening like this one is a pleasant diversion, but I find endless talk of politics and religion boring. I prefer to make things happen rather than waiting for events to unfold."

"So do I. And that's how my life has been so far. This is the first time I feel I have no control."

Arian leaned toward her. "To be honest, Princess, I am surprised at your husband. If you were mine, I would do whatever you asked."

Gwynneth blushed, quite against her will. "Pretty words notwithstanding," she said, "I doubt that would happen, the first time you disagreed with me about something."

"Don't be so sure. You seem so intelligent and logical, I doubt I could disagree with you about anything."

No one had flattered her like this in a long time, and it was going straight to her head. She hoped she kept it from showing. "It's kind of you to say so. I like to think I'm right most of the time."

"I'm sure you are," Arian said, his head cocked in a most attractive fashion.

Gwynneth sensed she was at a disadvantage. Maybe it had been too long since she had engaged in flirtatious banter.

Long after Kendryk went to sleep that night, Gwynneth mused that Kendryk and Arian combined would create a perfect man. Kendryk was all thought while Arian was all action. Since Arian was a younger son, he'd had to make his own way in the world and it seemed he'd done so rather well, showing both enterprise and ambition. While she admired Kendryk's intelligence and thoughtfulness, they seemed to hinder him right now. Decisive action was needed, and she was certain Arian would have handled all of this differently.

She didn't see Kendryk again until the next evening when he stopped into the library to say good night. She yawned. "I'll come too. I've had more than enough tonight."

Kendryk took her hand as they went up the stairs. "You needn't keep up this pace, darling. You've already written to everyone at least once. I imagine if they intended to reply they already would have."

She shook her head. "It's not that simple. Many are wavering and just need persuasion. I'm sure that the moment you act, they will join you. Until then, some ought to come around if they hear from me often enough."

If he caught the barb, he ignored it. "You might be right, but I worry about you. You work much too hard."

"I don't mind." She stopped at the door of her dressing room. "I want to help."

"You do," he said, kissing her cheek.

He was waiting when she crawled into bed next to him. She snuggled up under his arm and he said, "I don't quite know how to bring this up."

"Bring what up?" She looked into his eyes. Their troubled look was nothing new.

"Father Landrus has concerns about Arian."

"What?" She sat up and turned toward him. "Whatever is he worried about?"

"Nothing specific," Kendryk said, though he was frowning. "He's just apprehensive about him."

"That's ridiculous. How can he think that about the only person who has offered to support you and his cause in a concrete way?"

"I'm not sure. It's about his character, or something like that."

Gwynneth took a moment to slow her breath. "You know what I think? He's jealous. Since Arian has come, you've spent a lot more time in the field and a lot less time with Father Landrus."

Kendryk opened his mouth to protest, but she continued. "He's not even conscious of it. I'm sure Father Landrus doesn't mean to be possessive, but he must miss the time you used to spend with him. I can sympathize." She kept her tone light.

"Now I feel guilty."

"I'm sorry." She snuggled back into his arms. "You have a lot of demands on your time and that's fine. It's part of who you are and what you are trying to do."

"If only I knew what I was trying to do." Kendryk chuckled into her hair.

"Funny. At any rate, it's likely that Landrus resents you being pulled away from him, and by someone who doesn't always agree with his way of doing things."

"You might be right. I find it difficult to distrust Arian. As you said, he's the only person who's come through with meaningful help, and his behavior has been exemplary. You have spent little time with him, but he's not been inappropriate in any way?"

"Oh heavens, not at all," Gwynneth said, with more conviction than she felt. "He's the perfect gentleman. Not like that horrid Schurtz fellow." She shuddered.

"All right then." He kissed the top of her head. "As usual, you've made me feel better."

BRAEDEN

As they rode across the countryside, Braeden made a point of checking on his hostage from time to time. Karil still looked unhappy and clung to Zoltan as if he feared falling off at any moment. Braeden hoped he'd get used to it. A few hours later, he looked again, and saw Karil on the pack horse that Janna had been riding. She was on Zoltan, looking wary, but resolute. Braeden smiled to himself.

When he looked again an hour later, they were still riding side-by-side and talking. There were traces of tears on Karil's face, but now Janna was making him laugh.

They followed a wide road into the interior of the country. The hussars rode in full armor with weapons at the ready. The Marjatyan rebels were forward about attacking forces of any size. Those remaining here were disorganized and desperate, but determined.

The land had flattened out with long grass rippling all the way to the horizon. Settlements and farms were visible from a distance, which meant they were usually deserted by the time the hussars arrived. Braeden preferred this to having to evict everyone first. Their only trouble that day had been an obstinate farmer who refused to leave.

"Take what you can load in that cart," Braeden urged. "We'll burn the rest."

"I'll take no orders from the likes of you," the old man spat. "No empress will tell me what to do. I'd sooner die."

"And at this rate, you will," Braeden said.

The man stood his ground. "You'll have to kill me."

"We won't kill you." Braeden motioned to a few troopers, who bodily removed the man from the barn, led out the few livestock and set the place afire. Braeden let him keep his livestock.

He was weary. They'd burned four villages and a half dozen farms with no further resistance, but it was dirty, unpleasant work. When they made camp, Braeden could taste the ash in his mouth and see the soot on his skin. Everyone around him had blackened faces, so he was sure he looked no better.

In his tent, he called for water and set to cleaning himself. He wiped his face and hands until the water was black. He stopped once the rag he was using came back only a little gray. There were noises around the cook fires outside, but it would be awhile before any food was ready.

He didn't want to lie down because he would fall asleep, and he didn't want to talk to anyone, so he paced the floor. He missed Novitny, Franca, Miro and the others. That, combined with the work he did here left him restless and dissatisfied.

There was a slight rustle outside the tent, then a cough and a faint "hello?" He wasn't sure if it came from outside his tent or another one, so he waited. There was another "hello," louder this time. He poked his head out the flap. Janna stood just outside, looking nervous. "I wanted to knock," she said, "but ... well, tent."

"We don't bother with knocking here," Braeden said. "If it's not tied off from the inside, just come right in. Did you need to speak with me, Mistress Kronek?"

"Yes. Oh, and please call me Janna."

"Of course." That was a good sign. Maybe she wasn't as frightened as before. Several servants and two troopers cleaning their armor stared at her with frank curiosity.

"Let's go inside." Braeden didn't want the others unnerving her.

She went in ahead of him. He tied one flap back, so it didn't feel like a closed door.

She found a chair and sat down, working her hands in her lap. He wondered what in the world had got to her.

He sat across from her, but not too close. "Now, tell me what's going on."

"It's Karil Andarosz," Janna said. "The little boy we took along this morning."

"How is he doing? I saw you'd traded mounts with him. That was good of you, though I'm surprised you don't mind riding Zoltan."

"He is rather enormous, but well-behaved. I was all right as long as I didn't look down."

"We'll make a hussar of you yet," Braeden said, hoping she realized he was joking.

"I doubt that." She almost smiled. "But since I'm around horses so much, I must learn to be braver."

"That's the spirit. Horses behave when they realize you're in charge."

"That's what everyone says, so I'm trying." She twisted her hands some more. "I wanted to ask you about Karil. He's sure you're taking him to the empress to be tortured for information about Korma's army. I told him I didn't think that would happen, but I'm not certain. I hoped you might reassure him."

Braeden hoped he could, too. "The empress is not a kind woman, but she wouldn't do anything terrible to a child. She has children of her own."

"That didn't keep her from sending people to kill mine," Janna burst out. She clapped her hand over her mouth as her eyes filled with tears.

"It doesn't make sense." Braeden pretended he didn't notice her distress. "But whatever happened to your children wasn't personal. Just like the work we're doing right now. The empress doesn't bear these people any ill-will."

"I can't believe you'd defend her," Janna said in a small, tearful voice.

"I hate the way she does things, but I also understand why she has to do them that way."

"I'll never understand it." Janna dropped her hands, letting the tears run down her face. "And I can't understand why anyone would work for her. You seem like a kind person; you've helped me so much and been kind to Karil. Yet today, you've made several hundred people homeless. You might as well have killed them." That was the most he'd ever heard her speak at once.

After a few sobs, she continued. "I'm so sorry. You must think me ungrateful."

"I don't."

"It's wrong of me to be disapproving when you've saved my life and helped me so much."

"It's not wrong." This conversation was far too awkward for Braeden's liking. "You can feel grateful and be angry at what we're doing, all at the same time. I don't like what we're doing either, but my job is to follow orders."

"Even when they're wrong?"

"If I were too picky, I'd never find work. Besides, I don't work for the empress directly. I work for Prince Novitny, who saved my life many years ago, and I do whatever he says."

"I can understand that." She dried her eyes on her apron. He noticed her dress was too big; it was probably one of Cara's old ones. He'd have to get her something better when they returned to civilization. "I'm very sorry I shouted at you. Seeing all of those farms and villages on fire reminded me, well, it reminded me of something awful not too long ago. But that was different. The people there never had time to get away."

"That's not right. There are some who work like that, but I don't." He thought of Tomescu and what stopping her had cost him.

"So what can I tell Karil? What will happen to him?"

"He'll be a hostage," Braeden said. "He'll be kept as a prisoner, but a privileged one. Teodora wants his father to surrender and he won't, if he thinks she's killed his son. He might not be too comfortable, but he'll be sheltered and fed well enough."

"How long will he be there?" Janna asked.

"No idea. With any luck, the empress will negotiate something within weeks. If not, she'll try to defeat Korma on the battlefield."

"What if she does? Then she won't need him anymore."

"I don't know what happens then," Braeden admitted. "He might be kept to assure his mother's good behavior, or sent home when there's no more threat from Marjatya. He's in no danger of being killed or hurt."

"I'll tell him that then. It's not wonderful news, but it's better than his fears." She stood up and smoothed her apron. "Thank you so much. He'll sleep better tonight knowing this. Is it all right if he stays in the Torresia tent with me? I'm sure he won't run away."

"All right," Braeden said. "But his guards will be right outside. And no helping him escape." He was half serious.

Her eyes widened. "Oh, I wouldn't do that. It would be a dreadful mistake."

"Aye, it would be. You're a sensible woman, Janna." He found he liked saying her name.

"Sometimes." She nearly smiled. "I'll leave you now and thank you again."

He showed her outside, then saw that supper was ready, so he joined the others at the fireside.

GWYNNETH

One morning, after she'd been at work for several hours, the footman announced Father Landrus. Gwynneth looked up in surprise. "Show him in," she said, rising from her desk.

The priest came in and bowed to her. Since his defrocking, he no longer wore the traditional robes, but simple, everyday clothes in black. They suited him. Perhaps when he and Kendryk were in charge of the new version of the Faith, they could create a new uniform for the clergy. "Please sit down, Father," she said.

"Might I speak with you alone?"

Gwynneth hoped he wasn't bearing horrible news. She told Halvor and her ladies, "Go take a half hour in the garden."

Everyone left, and she motioned Landrus to a chair. She sat down across from him. "Can I send for anything?"

"No, no. I shouldn't be long."

"Is everything all right?"

"More or less." She had never seen him look this ruffled. "Something has come up that requires your attention."

"All right," she said, with an encouraging nod.

"It's Arian Orland."

"Goodness, he seems to be all the topic of conversation these days."

"So the prince has spoken of him to you?"

"He said you had concerns about his character."

"Yes," Landrus said. "But I fear the prince doesn't take me seriously. I was hoping you might influence him."

"Prince Kendryk always takes you seriously, Father. The problem is the lack of any specific reason you have to mistrust Orland."

"I worried that might be it." Landrus sighed. "I wish I had something, but I don't, at least nothing concrete. I'm also concerned at the attention Orland pays you."

Gwynneth felt a twinge of indignation. "Attention? He has said nothing the least bit inappropriate. As to anything else, I'm sure he's just being polite."

"Perhaps. But one thing I know for certain about Arian Orland is that he has a bad reputation where women are concerned."

"Goodness, I've never heard anything about that."

"You are shielded from such talk, but men have different conversations amongst themselves."

"Even in front of priests?" Gwynneth hoped she could keep the conversation light.

Landrus allowed a small smile. "They don't hold back like you might expect. But, it's just talk. I felt it best to tell you so you can take precautions."

"Precautions?"

"Such as making sure you are never alone with him."

Gwynneth pushed down her annoyance. "Father, if you suppose I would spend time alone with him, you don't know me very well."

"I am very sorry if I've caused offense. I have no reason to expect you would do any such thing, but I wanted to mention it. He's so important to the prince, it would be terrible if there were any kind of incident."

"There will be no incident," Gwynneth said firmly. "Thank you for your concern, but it is unfounded as regards my virtue. As to the other things, unless you have a specific reason, Arian Orland is far too important to Kendryk right now to act on a hunch. I'm sure you understand. I will be vigilant, so you needn't be concerned."

"That will have to do." Landrus took his leave, but she had the strong sense he was unhappy with the outcome of the conversation. What was she to do? There was nothing to worry about. And men like Orland always had rumors swirling around them. Most other men probably resented his success with women. Gwynneth sighed and sat back down at her desk after he had gone. These days, she scarcely had time to eat, let alone engage in idle flirtation.

One evening, Kendryk, Gwynneth and Arian sat around a table in Kendryk's study. "I don't like to leave Birkenhof unguarded," Kendryk said. "My uncle continues to make noises and he might take advantage of the situation if I'm gone." Kendryk was leaving with the bulk of the militia to oversee their deployment along the border.

"Attack us?" Gwynneth asked. "He wouldn't dare."

"It's unlikely," Kendryk agreed, "but I still worry."

"I'll stay close," Arian said. "We'll patrol the area, and I'll leave at least two thousand in the near vicinity."

"But after Faris arrives with the rest of the troops, you'll all march south to meet me."

"Once he knows you have that many troops, he won't try anything," Gwynneth said.

"But if none of those forces are here ..." Kendryk frowned.

"Even after I go, I can spare a few hundred," Arian said, "And Faris can leave some. It shouldn't take too many to make the duke hesitate before betraying you."

"He's not brave enough to do it." Gwyneth resented being treated like a helpless child. She was more than a match for Duke Evard.

"We'll leave next week." Kendryk turned to Arian. "I'm glad you'll be here. I won't be the least bit worried about Gwynneth, the children and Father Landrus with all of your troops surrounding Birkenhof."

Gwynneth was glad too, for a different reason. If Arian left, she would miss the little thrill she got every time she glimpsed him. It wasn't as though anything would happen, but it was a bit of excitement missing from the rest of her life right now.

Her only concern was Landrus. Since being rebuffed by both Kendryk and Gwynneth, he had made a point of watching Arian and expressing his disapproval at every turn. It was growing tedious. Gwynneth wondered how she could get him out of the way while Kendryk was gone.

When Arian had gone, Gwynneth asked, "Do you have time for us to talk longer?"

"Certainly, though I promised Father Landrus I'd look in on him later."

"That's perfect. I wanted to speak with you about him anyway. I think it's time to do something about Julia. Who knows what she might get up to once you're gone."

"Do you expect her to cause trouble?"

"I'm sure she will. She's been much too quiet, considering how badly Landrus has undermined her. It isn't like her."

"True." Kendryk frowned.

She hated to cause him more worry, but a solution was at hand. "It's important you do something before she gets help. She might be waiting for Teodora to take back Atlona."

"I can't have her arrested for doing nothing."

"I'm not thinking of anything that dire. But it's high time you put Landrus in her place."

To her surprise, Kendryk laughed. "That's exactly what I've been thinking."

"Then do it before you leave."

"I've already mentioned it to Father Landrus, and he isn't keen on the idea. He feels it's not the best way he can serve right now. And he thinks the office should be done away with altogether."

"He may be right." Gwynneth tried to appear unconcerned. "But that's not something that can be decided right now. And if it's not what he wants, I don't care."

"Gwynneth!"

"Really, Kendryk. You've done everything to protect him and now you are risking your entire kingdom to see his teachings prevail. The least he can do is indulge you in this. It needn't be permanent. Just someone to displace Julia and keep things running for the time being."

"You make a good point. I would feel much better knowing he's in charge in Heidenhof. I'll ask again."

"Do more than ask. Tell him, as his sovereign, you require this service of him right now. He can't refuse."

"No, I don't suppose he can." Kendryk stood, and she rose with him. "I'll talk to him now. Thank you darling for the excellent idea."

She was more excited than she ought to be and the thought of the priest's glowering presence no longer haunting her filled her with relief.

JANNA

They'd been riding along a main road in a long column. The flat land seemed to stretch out forever, so monotonous that Janna had stopped looking at it. For a time, she and Karil had tried playing a game, but it involved spotting different shapes and colors and there weren't any here. Sure, there were the green and golds of the endless grass, but nothing else. No trees, no bushes, and not even a river in three days. Few people lived here, and the few that had, had disappeared. They hadn't even found a farm to burn in two days.

Janna didn't mind. As kind as everyone had been, the sight of farmhouses and barns on fire still made her short of breath. A few times she hung onto her pommel and hoped the black spots in front of her eyes didn't result in complete darkness.

It upset Karil as well. "This is wrong," he said. "These people are not the enemy of the empress. Papa and all of them are far away fighting her."

"I know," Janna replied. "But it's easier to attack those who can't fight back. They hope that if they destroy enough farms, the empress's enemies won't have the food and money they need to keep their armies going."

"They're wrong. Someday I will show them. Someday, I will find their people and show them how it feels to have everything destroyed around you."

"I understand. But it doesn't help, does it? Everyone keeps trying to destroy each other, and it never ends."

"It shouldn't end," Karil said. "Until the empress is dead. Then it will be over."

"Perhaps," Janna said. "But what if that makes her children angry, and when they grow up, they'll try to kill those who killed their mother?" Though it seemed hard to imagine the children of the empress having any love for such a horrid woman.

"She has children?" Karil looked amazed at the idea.

"Of course. I think she doesn't want to make the mistake the old emperor did and leave the succession in doubt."

The wound their way along the road. Janna got sleepy and wondered how any of the troopers stayed alert through these endless hours of nothing. She wound her hands through the reins and looped them to the pommel. If she fell asleep, the jerk would awaken her before she fell.

She was already very comfortable on Zoltan. He was terribly tall, but never did anything sudden. After a few days on his back, she worried much less about falling off. It helped that she wore split skirts, as most of the women here did. Sitting astride seemed much safer.

Suddenly there was a shout, and Zoltan came to a halt. The air filled with the piercing shrieks that Janna recognized as the Marjatyan battle cry. Familiar panic surged inside her, but she mustn't black out right now. She counted to five, trying to slow her breathing, which was long enough for the whole convoy to stop. The hussars faced outward. It was hard to tell where the attack was coming from. Both sides, perhaps. Pistols fired all around through shouting and screaming.

Soon she couldn't see through the smoke from the guns and the dust kicked up by horses. She heard the whistle of bullets and leaned over Zoltan's neck. "Keep your head down," she shouted at Karil. It wouldn't help if anyone had good aim, but a smaller target was better. Karil hunched over his horse's neck.

She peered through the smoke and noticed a few bodies on the ground. She wondered whose they were. Then there was a gap in the line and the outlines of someone who wasn't a hussar. She couldn't be captured by someone else now. To them, she would be the enemy. It occurred to her that Karil considered these his people.

It seemed it had occurred to him at the same time. He glanced at Janna, and dug his heels into his horse's sides, making for the gap. Without thinking, she grabbed his horse's halter and held tight. Zoltan was much stronger than Karil's mount and dug in his heels.

Karil looked back at her incredulously. "Let me go!" he shouted.

KENDRYK

With Arian Orland and Ossian Schurtz close on his heels, Kendryk didn't slow down for the guards at the doors. He'd brought enough men that there wouldn't be trouble. At the door to Julia's study, Kendryk paused. "Wait here. I won't be long."

"You're sure you want to do this alone?" Arian asked.

Kendryk nodded. "I'll send the secretary out. See he stays out."

He opened the door without knocking. Count Greylen jumped to his feet, but Julia remained at her desk.

"You can't come in here," Greylen said.

"Out," Kendryk said, holding the door open. Arian took one step inside, his hand on the hilt of his sword and Greylen scurried past him. Kendryk let the door fall shut behind him and turned back to Julia. She was standing, but stayed behind her desk.

"I'm sorry to be unpleasant," Kendryk said.

"I fail to see how it could be otherwise." Julia was as calm as usual. "Don't worry, I imagine you can do this quickly."

"That would be best. And yet, I don't wish to make you think I am disrespectful of you or your office. You have been a fine Maxima."

"What you wish has no bearing on how I feel." Julia's voice was flat, but her eyes burned.

"I understand." Kendryk took a deep breath. "This is overdue anyway. It has been some months since you've had control of the Terragand temples."

"I suppose Landrus put you up to this."

"Not at all. He doesn't want this position, but I need him in it."

"While you pursue your ill-advised war against the empress and the Faith."

"There is no war and I have no quarrel with the Faith. I can't say the same for all of its leaders."

Julia sniffed. "The outcome will be the same."

Kendryk sighed. "Let's not get off track. As Prince of Terragand, I am relieving you of your post of Maxima."

"On what grounds?" Julia's voice was tight.

"On grounds of failure to fulfill your duties effectively. No priest or priestess in Terragand now follows your directives. I have already sent a letter to Forli to that effect."

"I thought you were no longer following the Imperata."

"I am not, though I still prefer to do things correctly."

Julia snorted. "Only those things you choose, it seems."

Kendryk ignored this. "You are removed from your position at once. A carriage is ready to take you to Olvisya. Please be ready to leave in three hours and take no Temple property. All of your travel expenses are covered." Kendryk put a purse on her desk.

She stared at him. "You can't imagine that I would accept anything from you at this point. I will leave, but I will take my carriage and my own guards. And I won't return until I accompany Teodora Inferrara's army."

"Good enough," Kendryk said. "Please be away before noon."

"Might I say a few words?"

Kendryk wished she wouldn't, but felt he should allow it. "Go ahead."

"I know you are still young, but until now, I did not consider you foolish. In fact, I still don't find you foolish, just misguided."

Kendryk scratched his itching nose. "That's no secret."

"I don't dislike you; in fact if I had a son, I should be pleased if he were like you. But you have made some dreadful mistakes and will pay dearly for them."

"Maybe I have," Kendryk said. "But not acting as I did would be far worse. "

Julia came out from behind her desk and stood in front of him, looking up into his eyes. "I cannot wish you success in your venture, but I can hope you will see your errors in time to correct them before it's too late. And now, if you'll excuse me, I must get ready to go."

She swept past Kendryk and out the door.

JANNA

Janna gritted her teeth and tightened her grip on Karil's bridle. Someone ran up to her from the other side, waving a long curved blade. Zoltan reared up and knocked them to the ground. A moment later, hussars filled the gap, and the intruder disappeared.

Karil slumped over his saddle, crying. Janna held on, just in case.

It was over a few minutes later. The attackers were better-organized this time, but still no match for the disciplined, well-armed hussars.

"You should have let me go." Karil sobbed. "Those are my people. They would have helped me."

"They don't know who you are. Do you think every Marjatyan peasant knows what you look like?"

"No." Karil wiped his face. "But I would tell them, and they'd take me home. Don't you hate the empress too? I thought you would help me."

"It was too dangerous. You saw how quickly the hussars defeated them. They might have killed you if they caught you getting away."

She could tell he hadn't thought of any of those things. "I'm so sorry," she said. "I don't want you to be the empress's prisoner any more than you do, but trying to escape in the middle of a fight is too dangerous. Even if you end up with the empress, you'll survive it. And that's the main thing. You just have to stay alive long enough to get through all of this."

"If I'm dead, she can't use me as a hostage." Karil wiped his nose. "I couldn't bear it if my father stopped fighting because of me."

"I doubt he will. I've heard you Marjatyans are most stubborn." She smiled at him, showing she was teasing.

"We are." Karil sat up straighter. "It's our best quality. No one can defeat us because of it."

"Good. Then the empress won't defeat you, will she? You'll outlast her."

"I will," Karil said.

They moved ahead slowly. After a time, she spotted Braeden and Captain Torresia coming back down the line. They were on their way to the baggage train. The raiders often went after the wagons holding food and other supplies. To Janna's surprise, she was happy to see the two of them. She already knew Captain Torresia was kind in spite of being dreadfully loud. And Braeden seemed a decent fellow who looked more frightening than he was. While he was fierce in battle he was always gentle with her, his voice soft. She'd watched him treat skittish horses in similar fashion.

She wondered if he was looking for her and Karil, so she waved. He looked relieved when he saw Karil. No doubt he'd been worrying about the same thing she had. He lifted a gauntleted hand in response. Blood ran down the steel, but she was sure it wasn't his. Perhaps she should have been glad to see any of the empress's creatures hurt, but she couldn't bring herself to wish him harm. He had been good to her and to Karil when he didn't have to be. He might have left her in the woods, or worse.

The column was moving at a normal pace again when Janna felt a sharp pain in her stomach. She gasped and doubled over, holding onto the pommel.

"What's wrong?" Karil asked.

"Can you pass the word for Signora Torresia?" she gasped.

There was another sharp pang and Janna gritted her teeth to keep from crying out. Suddenly Senta was by her side, pulling on Zoltan's reins.

"You must get down," she said, her voice urgent.

Senta pulled Zoltan behind her own horse as they left the column. When they reached the grass by the side of the road, Senta slapped Zoltan on the rump and he laid down. Janna half fell out of the saddle with the next painful jolt. Senta laid her down in the grass, making soothing noises in a language Janna didn't understand.

The horses blocked the view from the rest of the column, and Senta pushed Janna's skirts up a little. "As I thought." She turned and shouted something at the column, then turned back to Janna. "It's all right. It will hurt a bit, but should be over soon."

"What's happening?" Janna gasped as another pain hit and she felt something warm run down her leg. "Is that blood?"

Senta nodded. "There will be quite a lot, but it's all right. It's happened to me a time or two. Did Zoltan jump during the attack?"

Janna nodded.

"That will do it. That's why it's best not to let pregnant women ride war-horses."

"Oh. So that's the end of it?"

"Yes," Senta said, smoothing the hair back from her face. A horse thundered up in a swirl of dust and Trisa jumped down holding something.

"Here are the bandages, Mama." She shoved something into Senta's hand, then knelt next to Janna. "Will she be all right?"

"She will. It happens sometimes."

"I'm glad," Janna said, in a small voice.

"Yes, it is for the best. Now Trisa, help me stop the bleeding."

There was some lifting and arranging, and Janna stopped feeling the blood. The sharp pains had abated, but her abdomen was still sore. At least the column kept moving; the last thing she wanted was everyone looking at her.

Senta and Trisa were both helping her sit when Braeden galloped up with Karil in tow. "I heard Miss Kronek was hurt," he said, jumping down and lifting Karil to the ground.

Karil ran to Janna and took her hand. "Are you all right?" he asked.

"I felt a little sick." She didn't miss the glance Senta exchanged with Braeden.

Braeden frowned. "She shouldn't have been riding Zoltan. Put her in a wagon for the rest of the day."

"But I love Zoltan," Janna burst out. "He was protecting me. Besides, I'm glad this happened."

She hoped she wouldn't need to elaborate, especially in front of Karil and Trisa.

Braeden's frown didn't leave his face. It was the first time she'd seen him look so grim.

With Karil and Trisa each holding an arm, she struggled to her feet. "I'm all right," she said, then almost fell over from light-headedness. "I'll ride in the cart for a while. But please, I want to keep riding Zoltan later."

"We'll see," Braeden said. "Let's get you into that cart." He scooped her up and carried her over to a baggage cart that had pulled off to the side. Someone had piled blankets onto sacks to make a bed for her. It was nice to be cared for like this. Tears sprang to her eyes, but Janna held them back. Maybe she really was getting tougher.

KENDRYK

Kendryk waited until the next morning to make sure that Julia was far away, in case the mood turned ugly. After breakfast, he and Gwynneth set out with a large party for Heidenhof. Gwynneth had felt it would be best to turn it into a celebration. It would be a happy occasion for Kendryk to show himself to his people. He rode next to Landrus all the way.

"How things have changed, since last we took this road," Landrus said.

"In the other direction." Kendryk grinned. "I remember it well. It was the day everything changed."

"You are right in requiring this of me. I cannot expect you to do everything. Someday this post will no longer be needed, but until then, it's fair I take on some of the burden."

"I've tried to lighten it. Mother Leiza is coming to help with day-to-day Temple administrative tasks. She's done wonders with the Engelstein temple and you won't have to worry about a thing."

"She's in Heidenhof?"

"Not yet. I sent for her yesterday after Gwynneth heard the Duchess of Kaltental singing her praises. I don't want you distracted with clerical tasks since you must continue your work on the Scrolls. Though if you like, you can lead some of the temple services."

"I don't mind doing that. I've missed having a large congregation." He had been leading services at the Birkenhof chapel, but that was for a small group of family and servants.

"They've missed you, too," Kendryk said.

And it was true, the crowds in Heidenhof were considerable. News of Julia's removal had spread and everyone was excited about Landrus returning. The procession made its way to the main square where a hastily erected podium stood ready.

Kendryk spoke first. "This is an important day for Terragand," he said, once the cheering had died down. "Yesterday saw the end of the old, improper version of the Faith. Julia Maxima did her job well, but her time is over. With the help of Father Landrus, of you and countless others in Terragand and around Kronland, we will overthrow the old, corrupt ways and begin something new.

"Upon my request, Father Edric Landrus will take the office of Maximus of Terragand." The crowd roared. Kendryk waited. "Though most temples have already taken on the changes he has requested, he will make sure that all of Terragand now worships the Holy Family the way the Scrolls require. Priests and priestesses who refuse will be replaced by clergy that teaches the truth. Anyone refusing to worship in the new way will be asked to leave the kingdom."

This was a sore point for Kendryk. He did not like to force belief on anyone; in fact he didn't think it possible. But under the circumstances, he had little choice. If he allowed some to worship the old way, temples would spring up in opposition to what Landrus was teaching. In the current climate that could quickly lead to instability. Once Teodora's threat diminished, they could work this out.

He introduced Landrus, who as yet refused to wear the maximus robes. He insisted that he should not be set above any other worshipper. The crowds cheered louder and longer for him. "You are a fortunate people," he said, as Kendryk rejoined Gwynneth and Maryna, who had come along for the big day. "You are blessed with a ruler who understands the importance of true worship." He stopped while the crowd cheered again and Kendryk blushed.

"Without Prince Kendryk's help, the Imperata would have had me executed long ago. Fortunately, none of us need worry about this, ever again. Today marks the beginning of a new faith. We have cast aside the rule of the Imperata and imperial interference. We have taken the worship of the Holy Family into our own hands. Before long, every believer will be able to read the Holy Scrolls in our tongue, so you can see the truth of what the gods ask of us.

"You will see that much of the pomp insisted upon is unnecessary and sometimes even wrong. The new way of worship might seem simpler, but that's only true on the surface. In reality, the gods require a harder service. They ask you to look within yourself, to examine your heart and to put aside all selfish thoughts. They ask you to spend less time in the temple itself and more in prayer and quiet contemplation. You were taught to venerate Vica, but now you must learn about the rest of the Holy Family, and that will take time and diligence.

"I believe this new faith is better, but it will need more work from all of you. This change might also bring down the wrath of Imperata and empress upon us."

"Her Highness can rot!" someone shouted.

Landrus smiled. "There is no need for disrespect. The empress continues to rule the empire."

"For now," Gwynneth whispered to Kendryk, squeezing his hand.

"But she no longer has any say in our worship," Landrus continued. "In time, Prince Kendryk will have a greater role in overseeing the temples. But for now, he has asked me to do so, and I do so gladly." He paused. "Welcome to a new era."

The crowds erupted in a loud cheer.

After the service, everyone joined the new maximus at his palace for a feast. Tables had been set up in the square for the common folk, and wagons of food brought in, but the wealthy and upper class, along with any clergy near enough to come, joined Landrus and the rest.

It was a merry time, and Kendryk looked around with regret. He sensed there would not be a gathering this happy for a good long time. He was leaving in the morning, and when he came back, it might well be to rally his forces to face Teodora.

BRAEDEN

The lieutenant came galloping back. "Armed men ahead," he gasped. "But this time, they're on the road, acting like they own it."

"Not partisans then," Braeden said. "Still, I want everyone on alert, arms at the ready."

He rode out ahead of the column, taking an escort of ten. As far east as they'd come, he guessed who it might be. There couldn't have been more than a hundred, but they looked fierce as ever, with their long coats and shaggy ponies. Daciana Tomescu rode at their head.

"Braeden Terris," she said, almost friendly. "I never expected to see your head again, at least not attached to your body."

"Sorry to disappoint. You're not the only one with powerful friends."

"Why are you so far east? Aren't the hussars trapped inside Atlona?"

"Not all of us. Teodora took us as an escort to Isenwald. Until she gathers enough troops to attack Korma, she sent us here to attack his base."

"Back doing the work you love so well." She smirked, looking past him at the smoking remains of a village. "Though knowing you, you let all the people go, so they can die slowly."

Braeden ignored this. "I have a message for you from the empress. She thought I might see you, and if I did, I was to tell you to meet her at Rabatin Castle."

Tomescu made a face. "How boring. I've heard little of what happened in Isenwald, but I wonder if she has plans for Kronland."

"I'm sure she does." Braeden was unwilling to give her any further news. "But I don't know what they are. All I know is that you're to meet her. You should leave as soon as possible."

"Eager to get rid of me, are you?" She grinned at him, her black eyes gleaming.

"Yes, I am."

"I can't blame you," she said, shrugging. "Though most men become friendlier in time. I can be charming." She cocked her head and fluttered her eyelashes in a ludicrous imitation of coquetry.

Braeden almost laughed, but stopped himself. "I don't see the point in being friendly. You haven't given me much reason."

"True. Though that could change."

"Don't bother on my account." Braeden wished she would go. "Is there anything else you need before you go on your way?" he asked, hoping she'd get the hint.

"I wouldn't mind a decent meal. These idiots slaughter the livestock right along with the peasants, so we haven't seen fresh meat in quite some time."

"We'll stop here for the midday meal. Set something up for these fine folks," Braeden said to the officer next to him.

Once the food was ready, the raiders ate greedily and there wasn't much conversation. Tomescu spoke little. The only disturbances came as messages from the baggage train. A few of the raiders were looking things over and some of the children were frightened.

"Would you control your people?" Braeden snapped, annoyed.

"We'll be on our way." Tomescu licked remnants of stew from the bottom of her bowl. "Thank you so much for your excellent hospitality."

Braeden accompanied them along the line to make sure there wouldn't be more trouble.

"Word is you have an interesting hostage," Tomescu said.

"Just the Andarosz boy. I'll give him to Teodora when I return."

"I'll be happy to take him off your hands."

Braeden tried not to shudder. "I'm sure you would, but I have my instructions. Besides, Teodora wants him alive and unharmed. I doubt you could manage that."

"I wouldn't hurt him. Much." She laughed her horrid laugh.

They were nearing the middle of the baggage train. Janna still rode in a cart. He wondered how she was doing and glanced over at her. She was sitting up and staring at Tomescu with wide, horrified eyes. Braeden couldn't blame her.

"Poor frightened little thing," Tomescu cooed. "You'd think I'd killed her children."

"Maybe you did. You've killed enough of them."

"You're no fun at all," Tomescu said, as they reached the open road.

The message came two days later. "Thank the gods you're here," the messenger said. "I ran into that Tomescu bitch, begging your pardon miss." He nodded at Trisa, who was shadowing Braeden. "She can't say anything straight, and when her eyes turn all wrong, you forget what you're about. I thought she said you were out here, but couldn't be sure."

After his meeting with Tomescu, they had turned south to cover an as yet untouched area. "What's the news?"

"You're to return to the empress. Troops from Maladena should reach her in five days. Once all of you have gathered, she plans to assault Korma."

"Thank Ercos," Braeden said. "It's about time. Any word on who is coming from Maladena, or how many?"

"It's to be Demario Barela. He was bringing an army over the mountain passes when Maladena and Zeelund signed the truce. At least four thousand infantry. Good luck for Her Highness."

"Good luck indeed. Barela is one of the best. He lifted that siege at Mensen a few years ago. Made short work of Emilya Hohenwart before her sappers could mine the walls. Now go get some refreshment. We'll be moving out in a few hours."

Braeden went back along the baggage train. They'd have to step up the pace, and he wanted to see how Janna was doing. If she still wasn't well, he'd have to arrange a slower wagon for her, which he didn't care to in this dangerous area.

He found her sitting in her cart, playing a children's card game with Karil. "We're getting ready to go west," he said. "Run along boy, and make sure your horse is ready." Karil scowled at him, but climbed out of the cart and went in search of his horse.

Braeden leaned over the side of the cart. "How are you feeling?"

"Quite well." It was true her color was much better. It was even possible she was putting on weight. He knew Senta would do her best on that score. "I can't wait to get back on Zoltan. Riding in the cart is so boring."

"That's good," Braeden said. "We've received orders to rejoin the empress at Rabatin Castle. I want to move at a good pace, and if you can ride, so much the better."

She frowned. "We're going to the empress?"

"She's received reinforcements so she can attack Korma. She promised me I would get to be there too."

"You make it sound like it's a party she's invited you to, rather than a battle," she said, with a half-smile.

"A battle is always better than a party." Braeden grinned.

"I won't have to meet the empress, will I?"

"Only if you want to. I'm sure I can arrange an introduction."

"Oh gods, no. I'd rather not. Seeing that horrid woman the other day was more than enough."

"Tomescu? Real piece of work, isn't she?"

"I've seen her before," Janna whispered. "In Moralta. Do you know if she was there?"

"She was in Moralta all right." Braeden didn't care to revisit the circumstances just then. "With any luck we won't see her again. The empress will likely send Tomescu into Kronland since she's not much use in lifting a siege."

"Those poor people." Janna shuddered.

"Don't worry. As long as you're with me, neither she nor the empress will bother you. Now, get into your riding clothes and we'll get Zoltan saddled up."

As he rode away, he found himself pleased that she was better. He also, less expectedly, found himself pleased that she wasn't pregnant. Since she was more or less his responsibility, it made things less complicated. Senta would find her a husband soon, and it would be easier without a baby.

JANNA

The closer they got to Olvisya, the more Janna worried. It seemed ridiculous to go straight into the mouth of the monster after everything she'd endured. She was worried because she had told Braeden her real name. What if he let it slip around the wrong people and someone pieced it together and had her arrested? It was too awful to contemplate.

Worse, she worried that if she told Braeden, he might turn her in. There was a large reward after all. He didn't look like he needed it, but since he was willing to fight for someone like Teodora for money, he might be capable of anything.

It got so bad she couldn't sleep at night and started planning a way to escape with Karil. But that was impossible. To leave the Sanova Hussars now meant death, or worse. She'd be better off cutting her own throat and getting it done quickly.

At last, she could bear it no longer. She gathered up what little remained of her courage and went to see Braeden. That evening, he was sitting around the fire with the other troopers, listening to one of their stories. Janna moved tentatively into the light, but Braeden didn't see her.

Another man spotted her. "Oh hey sir, it's that little bit you picked up in the woods."

Janna swallowed hard, glad that the darkness covered her blush, and took a few steps forward.

Braeden looked at her, his eyes twinkling. "Hello Janna," he said, his tone so easy and friendly she felt better right away.

"I was wondering if I might speak to you for a moment, er, sir." She wasn't sure if that was the correct way to address him, but that's what everyone else called him.

He stood. "Of course. Shall we take a little walk?"

She nodded, glad she didn't have to go into his tent in front of all these eyes.

Once they were out of earshot she said, "I'm sorry to be such a bother, sir."

He roared with laughter. "You don't have to call me sir. If I can call you Janna, then you must call me Braeden."

"All right, sir. . I mean, Braeden." He took long strides, and she had to trot to keep up with him. As they cleared the edge of the tents, he looked down at her again. "I'll slow down now, but I wanted to get away from those gossipy old hens. Here, we'll walk around the edge."

The picket lines were several yards away, hidden in the trees. It was comforting, knowing they were there. It didn't hurt to be in the company of such a huge, fearsome-looking man, either.

"Now, what can I help you with, Janna?"

"It's hard to explain, but I'm worried that I will be so near the empress."

"You keep going on about that. It's as though you think she has a personal interest in doing you harm. I'm sure she does not."

"But she does." Janna explained about Dimir and the proclamation. As terrified as she was about how he might react, it was a relief to tell him.

Braeden stopped short. There was a half moon, but it was bright, and she saw his face clearly. At first he wore a puzzled expression, then burst out laughing.

She took a few steps back, not sure what to make of this.

He stopped laughing when he saw her face. "I believe you, but you are the unlikeliest rebel I've ever seen."

"But I'm not a rebel. It's by association. Someone told me that a good wife would have talked her husband out of such foolishness, but I couldn't ..."

"I am not one of those people," Braeden said. "I met your husband, and he seemed a resolute man. Once he turned his mind to something, I doubt there was anything you could do."

"You met Dimir? How did you find him?" She wasn't sure she wanted to know the answer.

"Slightly wounded and brave. He knew his fate and never flinched. Many of his betters did far worse."

"Did you see him die?" She hadn't expected the conversation to take this turn, but she wanted to know.

"It was quick. He didn't suffer. I'm sure the worst of it was knowing it was coming, but he faced that brave as anyone I've ever seen."

The tears came all of a sudden. Until now, Dimir and her old life in Kaleva had seemed years away.

"Oh come now." Braeden looked uncomfortable. "He really did well. You should be proud you were married to such a man."

"I am proud." Janna sobbed. "Very." She forced herself to stop crying and wiped her tears. "He was a good husband, and his children were wonderful, too."

She couldn't think about that now. It was obvious her tears made Braeden uncomfortable, and she still had business to discuss. "Maybe another time you can tell me more about what happened. I'm afraid it's still too fresh."

"Naturally." Braeden chewed on an end of his mustache, looking at her with concern. "Though we still have the problem that you are a wanted rebel."

"I understand if you want to turn me in," Janna said in a small voice.

"Don't be ridiculous. I may have to follow the empress's orders in battle, but I don't have to hand you over to her. I probably should, but I won't."

"Thank the gods." Janna couldn't hide her relief.

"You didn't think I would?" He seemed a bit insulted but also amused.

"I wasn't sure, to be honest. But I hoped you wouldn't, otherwise I wouldn't have taken the risk."

"Still, you shouldn't be going about with the last name of Kronek. Is there another you can use?"

"Beran was my maiden name."

"Good enough. From now on you're Janna Beran. Where should you be from? Not Kaleva, in case someone gets nosy."

Janna considered for a moment. Her family had always been from Kaleva. "What about Nitrany? It's a small town on the Sanova road. That horrid Tomescu woman burned it."

"Good enough reason for you to be out on the road for us to find you. Chances are, no one will suspect you, and if your name doesn't draw attention, you should be in the clear."

"I can't thank you enough." Janna forced herself to look into his eyes. "And again, I'm sorry that I'm nothing but trouble."

"What are you talking about? You're no trouble at all. Senta misses her girls and likes having someone to fuss over. She already loves you like one of her own. She said so."

"She did?" Janna was touched. "I love her too; she's wonderful. But I know I can't live with them forever."

"Don't worry about it right now. They like having you and something will work out, I'm sure of it."

GWYNNETH

Since Kendryk was away, Gwynneth needed to be a proper hostess. Except for Ossian Schurtz, who might as well have been born in a gutter, Arian Orland's officers were all noblemen of Maladena with courtly foreign manners. Next to them, Arian seemed rough and unpolished, though she couldn't say she disliked it, it was so different from what she was accustomed to.

Suppers were intimate, informal affairs. With no other visitors there was no need for ceremony. Besides, after working all day, it was nice to have civilized company.

Most evenings, she left them to card games in the study, but now and then, she would spend an hour before retiring. Captain Lanza was an accomplished guitarist and sometimes played songs from Maladena. Gwynneth found them lovely and filled with longing.

One evening, she sat listening to a particularly poignant song when she couldn't stop herself. She had been aware for some time now that Arian Orland's eyes were always on her, and she made a point of not looking at him. But the song made her feel soft and weak. When she dared to glance Arian's way, the intensity of his eyes shocked her. She looked away again but sneaked another glance soon. A shiver went over her.

As soon as Lanza finished the song, she excused herself. She considered going to bed, but it was still early and she needed to calm herself. She turned to Avaron and Linette. "Why don't you retire? Tell Catrin I'll be up in a few hours. I'll find something to read."

With all the letter-writing she'd done in the past months, she'd neglected her books. She had a stack building up in the library of ones she'd ordered and those sent as gifts by friends. It would relax her to read for a while.

It was a warm night, so the windows stood open to the garden. She sank onto a sofa with a sigh. Perhaps she was too tired to read after all. Or maybe it was something else. Her cheeks burned and her mind raced. She wondered what had gotten into her.

She started as the door opened behind her. "I don't need anything," she said, supposing it was Avaron checking in on her one last time.

"Are you sure?" a deeper voice asked.

It was Arian. "Goodness. I wasn't expecting you." She didn't bother to cover her consternation. He was the last person she wanted to see right now.

"Really?" He sat down next to her, but not too close. "I was being rather obvious."

She forced a laugh. "I hoped you had better sense than that."

He sighed. "I'm afraid sense has nothing to do with it. I've never fallen in love like this before, Princess. It's rather upsetting."

"It should take more than that to upset you. I've heard you are accomplished at this sort of thing."

"Rumors are cruel. People don't understand."

"What is there to understand? You have a habit of seducing ladies and leaving them."

"That was in the past. I'm a happily married man now. Or rather, I was, until I met you."

"Don't be ridiculous." Her tone was much too sharp. The best way to handle this was with light banter, and she wasn't managing it.

"It is ridiculous," he said softly. "But I can do nothing about it. You know how it is when love strikes. No reason or logic can stop it."

"Distance works rather well," she said.

"The thought of being away from you is unbearable. I'm amazed at your husband, that he would leave you without a thought."

"He left because he must. I can assure you he thought about it a great deal."

"Perhaps. Still, in his place, I would have taken you along."

"You are not in his place. Best to remember that."

"I know." He hung his head, which was so uncharacteristic of him she almost laughed. "I am sorry for being inappropriate, but I had to tell you how I feel."

Gwynneth stood up quickly. "I am very sorry, but I can't reciprocate. It's impossible."

He stood. The moonlight streaming through the windows reflected off his dark hair and illuminated his eyes just enough so she could see their flash. She stepped back into shadow.

"It's not impossible," he said, in a more serious tone than she'd ever heard him use. "Not at all. I want you to be all mine, but I realize that can never be. I would take a few stolen moments whenever I can get them. Anything at all ..."

"That will be enough," she snapped, and made for the door. To her relief, he didn't stop her. She opened it and stepped into the corridor. "Good night," she said. "We will speak no more of this." And she fled down the hallway and up the stairs, not slowing down until she had burst into her dressing room and closed the door firmly behind her.

JANNA

Senta had been waiting for Janna. "There you are!" she exclaimed when Janna returned to their tent. "I couldn't imagine where you'd gotten off to. And after dark. You should be more careful."

"You told me I was safe here in camp."

"You are. But I would hate for some fellow to be rude and frighten you."

"I'm becoming less easy to frighten." Janna sat down next to Senta. "I needed to talk to Braeden."

"So you're on a first-name basis now?" Senta looked pleased.

"He insisted. I wanted to speak with him because I was anxious about something." Senta listened to Janna's tale, her mouth opening wider as Janna finished her story.

"I am amazed. You look so innocent."

"I am innocent," Janna said firmly, then mentioned that Braeden had met Dimir.

"The world is a strange place." Senta shook her head. "I am sure that things happen for a reason, but often I have not the slightest idea what that reason is. But I still try to take comfort in it. Did I ever tell you how I met Reno?"

Janna shook her head.

"It started as the worst day of my life. I was fourteen and our city had been under siege for two months. We had eaten the horses and were looking at cats and dogs with great appetite. I lived in a small city in Cesiano, but our defenses were strong. Someone betrayed us and let in the old empress's army, including the Sanova Hussars. I hid under the kitchen table and watched some dreadful men kill all of our servants. They probably killed my family too, though I didn't see them do it, thank the Mother. I just know I never saw them again.

"They were trying to drag me out from under the table. I was never so scared in my life. Then there was a commotion and a moment later, someone dragged me out, but it wasn't those men. It was Reno, and he wasn't a day over eighteen. Your Braeden was with him, and not much older."

Janna wondered if she should correct Senta about "her" Braeden, but decided not to bother.

"They'd chased off the other soldiers, but I was sure they meant me harm. I was crying and shaking like a leaf. I'm sure I looked awful. My nose turns so red when I cry, and I was much too skinny because of the siege. I don't know what Reno saw in me. But he made sure I got safely out of the city. I was still so frightened, but he put me in his tent and wouldn't let anyone bother me. I learned he was also from Cesiano and spoke my language. We talked all that night and the next, and I was pregnant with Adela within a month."

"Goodness," Janna said faintly.

"So yes, the worst day led to some of the best things of my life. I missed my family, but have never been sorry that I met Reno and had the girls. It has been a good life."

"Isn't it hard, always being on campaign?"

"You get used to it. Now I like it. I have seen so much more of the world than I would, had I stayed in my little town. Perhaps your adventure has just started."

"I wish I could see it that way. So many bad things have happened, and so few good. You and Reno and Trisa, and Braeden," she said after a second's hesitation.

"Yes, Braeden," Senta said. "He is a good man. He will always do the right thing."

"That's why I told him. I knew he would help."

"Yes, he would. But we must take this a step further if we are to pull the wool over the empress's eyes."

"Why?"

"The empress is a practical woman and very unromantic. She is sure that everyone has their price, and she may be right. However, she would not for a moment believe that Braeden would help you just to be kind. He would help you in exchange for something."

"I suppose I knew it was a possibility. I just wanted more time ..." And some choice in the matter.

"You misunderstand me. Braeden expects nothing from you. He helps because he wants to. But the empress would not believe that, and neither would many around her. Normally, we wouldn't worry, except that the empress has a special interest in Braeden and pays attention to everything he does. It needn't be true, but it should appear that you are his woman. A pretty young girl discovered in the countryside, now living in his tent would seem natural."

"I wasn't raised to be like that." Janna didn't wish to offend, but she couldn't see how this set her apart from the worst slattern in everyone else's eyes.

"Of course you weren't. But there is no harm in you living in his tent. No one here will think worse of you for it."

"Won't it be awkward?" Janna squirmed, feeling she was losing the argument.

"At first," Senta admitted cheerfully. "Braeden is such a dolt around women and he will be shy. You are shy too, but it will be all right. Don't worry. I will arrange everything." And she bustled off before Janna could protest any more.

GWYNNETH

Gwynneth tossed and turned that whole night, falling asleep at last when the sunlight found its way between the curtains. After sleeping for a few hours, she awoke with a start, bathed in sweat, and feeling an odd sense of urgency. Looking critically in her mirror while Catrin dressed her hair, the sleepless night showed. It would be marvelous if she could avoid seeing anyone today.

She sat up straighter. If she didn't look her best, what did it matter? She wasn't here for the viewing pleasure of mercenary officers. She sniffed and tossed her head, making Catrin lose the pin she had been putting in. "Just leave it," she said. A few strands still hung down, but looked rather becoming with her face so pale.

Once in the library, she found it impossible to concentrate on her writing. "It's pointless anyway." She threw down her quill. "I write and write and all they do is respond with pretty words and prevarication if they respond at all. I'm wasting my time." She jumped up and paced the room.

"I'm sure that's not true, Your Grace," Avaron said in a soothing tone, which annoyed Gwynneth even more. "You write the finest letters. You've had a bad night and the terrible heat doesn't help."

"Oh, would you be quiet!" Gwynneth snapped, then regretted it after seeing Avaron's crestfallen face. "I mean, perhaps you're right. Let's spend some time in the garden before it gets hotter."

She walked out through the open doors, down the path between the fountains until she reached the shady path under the trees. In the distance, she could hear the children playing on the lawn, but she didn't want to see them right now.

It was much cooler under the trees, so she slowed down and took a few deep breaths. Linette and Avaron hung back, probably worried about another outburst.

Gwynneth turned down another path, remembering. She and Kendryk used to come here when in the early days of their marriage they wanted more privacy than the palace afforded. Yes, it was still here; a little pavilion over-looking a brook. Even though she hadn't been here in at least a year, it was still well-maintained with soft cushions on the bench and a little table ready for a picnic. Gwynneth sighed and sat down. It was cooler here and very peaceful. It might have been leagues out in the country rather than in her own garden.

She sat quietly until her mind calmed and her heartbeat slowed. It was hard to say how much time had gone by before she stood up, smoothing her skirts. Linette elbowed Avaron, who had fallen asleep, curled up in a corner.

As they walked back under the trees, they spotted others coming their way. They weren't the only ones trying to escape the heat. Gwynneth flinched when she saw it was Arian and two of the Maladene officers.

"Ooh, it's Captain Lanza," she heard Linette titter into Avaron's ear. "He's so handsome, don't you think?"

"Hmph," Avaron said, while Gwynneth hid a smile. The captain wasn't handsome exactly, but he had long-lashed dark eyes, and anyone hearing him play the guitar was likely to fall in love with him, or someone nearby.

"Good day, Princess." Arian's eyes were no less intense than before.

"Good day. I suppose you're trying to escape the heat as we are."

"We are," Lanza said. "We sent the troopers off to bathe in the river. Their tents are most uncomfortable."

"We just came from the loveliest spot." Linette told them about the pavil-ion by the brook. Gwynneth wondered if she was hinting at an assignation. She'd have to keep a close eye on the girl. It was true her husband was an un-pleasant fellow, but that was no excuse.

After returning to the palace, Gwynneth managed a few more hours in the library. The heat broke right before dinner when a short and violent thunder-storm passed through. The servants rushed to close all the windows before rain blew in, and opened them all again after the storm had ended, letting in the fresh evening air.

In the cool hour before supper, Gwynneth resolved not to speak with Ari-an alone again, ever. She was in dangerous territory. Whenever she closed her eyes, she saw Arian before her, looking as tempting as the strawberry tarts she loved but of which she never ate more than one.

She realized she often denied herself small indulgences, priding herself on her strength and self-discipline. Perhaps she deserved a little treat, a diversion. Kendryk need never find out.

Gwynneth pushed the thought away. She was not one of those weak, immoral women who threw themselves at the first attractive man to pay them attention. She was just a bit lonely and missed her husband, and the feeling would pass soon enough.

"You were right about the pavilion," Captain Lanza said at supper. "What a beautiful place. Cool and secluded."

"Prince Kendryk built it for me, for my birthday, just after I arrived here." Gwynneth smiled, remembering.

"A lovely gift."

She was surprised at the tears that sprang to her eyes. Perhaps she just missed Kendryk.

There was no card game that night since the heat had worn everyone out. Arian monopolized her attention, but since they were sitting in a group, it wasn't as conspicuous. Gwynneth was still sure that Father Landrus wouldn't approve and was relieved he was in Heidenhof.

"I liked that pavilion too," Arian said. "You should visit there more often, especially when it's hot."

Gwynneth kept her gaze averted.

The next day was as hot as the one before, but more humid after the previous evening's downpour. There would probably be another that night, but in the meantime, the palace was much too warm. Avaron had a toothache, so Gwynneth sent her to her room with instructions for a poultice. It was hard to get any work done. By afternoon, she'd had enough. "Let's go to the pavilion again, Linette. It was so much cooler."

Linette was happy to agree. When they reached the path leading to the pavilion, Gwynneth paused at a stone bench in a small grove of aspen. The leaves shivered at the slightest breeze. "Can you stay here? I'd like to be undisturbed for a while."

Linette arranged herself on the bench. She would be happy if someone came by, just so they could appreciate how much she enhanced the scene.

Gwynneth sank into the cushions and closed her eyes. The rushing of the brook was the best music, and the air smelled cool and fresh. She thought she might doze off when she heard footsteps and someone sat down next to her. Her eyes flew open.

"I told you no one—" She stopped when she realized it was Arian again. "Linette wasn't supposed to let anyone in here," she said weakly.

"I told her you meant anyone except me. Why else would you want to remain undisturbed?"

"Because I'd like time alone? Is that so hard to understand?"

"Why would you want to be alone when you are lonely? It makes no sense."

"It makes more sense than the alternative." Gwynneth tried to move away, but the fabric of the cushions clung to her dress.

"I can make you forget all that."

"I doubt it. You don't know how guilty I'd feel."

"Is that what's stopping you? Guilt?"

"What's stopping me is that I love my husband and don't want to betray him."

"He can't feel betrayed if he never knows." Arian moved closer, and she froze. "There's no reason he should ever know."

"Linette is not my most discreet lady-in-waiting."

"She won't say a word since she's busy having an adventure of her own right now. I'm sure she'll see the sense in keeping quiet."

"Oh," Gwynneth said in a small voice. "You've thought of everything, haven't you?"

"I like to be prepared." He grinned. "Also, I like your husband and don't wish to see him hurt. It's unfortunate I would fall in love with his wife, but I have no control over that."

"How convenient for you." Gwynneth's breath came fast now.

He moved closer. "There's nothing wrong with it," he murmured in her ear. "Your husband is gone, and it's hard for you to be alone. I won't leave you alone."

Gwynneth backed away. "Only until its time for you to join Kendryk."

He shook his head. "I'll stay."

"And miss out on a battle? That's hard to believe."

"I enjoy fighting, true, but I'd rather be with you."

Suddenly he was right there, his breath in her hair and his lips brushing her cheek. Against her will, she leaned into him, trembling. Her head turned just far enough so her lips met his. She thought he would be rougher and more insistent, but he let her take the lead.

She hadn't expected to like kissing him so much. But then, she'd never kissed anyone besides Kendryk. The danger and the wrongness of it was thrilling. Fear of being caught niggled at the back of her mind, but stayed there. She stopped for breath, and he turned the tables. He pushed her back onto the cushions while expertly unfastening her dress. She wanted to tell him to stop, but the words caught in her throat.

It was as though he sensed that tiny hesitation. He stopped, looking down at her, eyes liquid pools of black. "I'll stop if you want me to."

"I don't want you to," she said, reaching for him.

BRAEDEN

Janna moving into his tent was at least as awkward for him as it was for her. Senta arranged everything. Since Braeden had a large tent, there was room to curtain off a corner and put Janna's cot there.

"I hate to be such a bother." Janna seemed distressed at his servant Gergo's grumbling.

"You're not," Braeden said. "He's bothered by everything and you aren't taking up any space at all." It was true. She had nothing to call her own except for two dresses handed down from Cara Torresia.

The awkwardness soon went, too. Janna was so quiet he could hardly tell she was there. She joined the rest of them at meals, but was always in her corner by the time he went to bed. The tent was becoming tidier too, with his things put away instead of strewn across the floor, as they usually were.

He noticed something else. One morning, he got dressed and went out to the cook-fire. Janna was helping dish out porridge and pour coffee. When she brought him a bowl, he pulled her onto a bench next to him. "You don't have to mend my shirts, you know. Gergo's good enough with a needle."

She flushed. "He might be, but he leaves them too long and the holes just get bigger. It's the least I can do. You don't mind, do you?"

"Of course I don't mind. And your work is much neater than that dolt's." He grinned at her. "Just don't feel you have to."

"I like doing it." She smiled shyly. "I'm not good at a lot of things, but at least I can sew."

He smiled back. "Now, go get Zoltan saddled. There's a long day of riding ahead if we're to make the empress's camp by nightfall."

Braeden attended a council of war the next morning. Set up in Countess Rabatin's library, Teodora gathered what generals she could. It still wasn't many, but with Demario Barela present, her odds looked much better.

The Maladene general was happy to see Braeden. "Your hussars are famous," he said, his ugly, engaging face creased with smiles. "It will be a great pleasure to fight with them."

Barela wanted to know the exact numbers Korma had and spent a good two hours poring over a map of Atlona and its fortifications. Then he marked out positions.

With somewhere between five and six thousand men, Korma had an impressive force, but its quality was mixed. His own army was small, and he relied upon what the Marjatyan nobility could muster. There was also a hussar regiment, seasoned veterans of the war with Zastwar, but they were the only troops of professional quality. "Korma has had time to drill his infantry," Barela said, "But most are inexperienced in combat."

After making their plans, Teodora's forces moved on Atlona. Besides Barela's four thousand infantry, she'd scraped together another thousand from nearby estates. With the Sanova Hussars, they numbered just over five thousand. It wasn't enough to outnumber Korma, but their better-trained troops might be able to surprise him.

It was now mid-summer and warm, so traveling in full armor was not enjoyable. General Barela asked Braeden if he'd ride with him for a time, at the head of the Maladene troops. Though no older than Braeden, Barela had been fighting even longer, seeing his first combat at thirteen.

"I was never good at anything else," he smiled, though Braeden suspected that wasn't altogether true, since women seemed to love him. "However," he went on, "I have spent too much time marching back and forth between Maladena and Zeelund. There are many mountains to cross and sometimes fighting along the way. Each time can take many months, and I have done it fifteen times. I am tired of that area and happy to be somewhere new."

Braeden shrugged. "Fighting is the same, no matter where you are."

"Maybe true. But the landscape here is new and interesting. Zeelund and Floradias are so flat. Every siege is the same. Here there are many hills, rivers, and then the mountains around Atlona. It is very interesting. Having the empress involved is interesting too. My queen does not care for anything military and leaves it all to her commandant. What is the point of all this fighting if one's sovereign does not care what happens on the field? I don't understand it." Barela shook his head as though he couldn't fathom why Queen Beatryz didn't find siege machinery and infantry tactics fascinating.

"They don't care about what happens on the field as long as you win."

"I suppose. Still, it pleases me that our beautiful empress is so interested in what we do." He cast an admiring glance at Teodora, lightly armored and riding nearby on a white palfrey.

"That's because you don't know her," Braeden said

Barela laughed. "Ah, you don't like her. I understand. She is a challenging woman. Not always pleasant to be around. But, I like challenging women, and very few are as lovely as she."

He looked her way again, long enough to make Teodora look back. She gave him that intense stare she had, but he didn't flinch and instead smiled that broad, charming smile of his that engulfed his whole face. Braeden wondered if the man knew what he was doing.

When they were within a few leagues of Atlona, they made camp on the other side of a mountain ridge. It was possible that Korma had spotted them although Barela had been careful to watch for scouts and have them killed before they could report back. There was still a chance that a few had gotten through, so they couldn't rely on the element of surprise.

Barela sent scouts to get detailed reports of Korma's positions, and asked Braeden, "Is there any way we can get a message to your troopers inside the city?"

Braeden shook his head. "Place is shut up tight as a tick. But the hussars will come out when they hear Korma being attacked. I'm sure they'll be eager for a good fight."

Barela seemed to consider that enough. "I hope they have not yet eaten their horses. We will push hard at Korma from the east but we cannot prevent him escaping down the other end of the valley."

The only way to get there was to cross a steep, snowy range of mountains. It was possible to do so, but would have taken the better part of a week. "We'll have to watch our rear, in case Korma gets away and tries to attack after, but if this works, he will be in no condition."

Everyone turned in early that night because they would attack at daybreak. Janna was still up, helping Gergo polish Braeden's armor and making sure all of his weapons were ready. She looked pale.

"Are you all right?" Braeden asked.

"You'll be in danger, won't you?"

"No more than usual. I expect we'll win. Barela knows what he's doing."

"Yes, but you might be hurt, or killed."

"I've been fighting longer than you've been alive and never had more than a few scratches from time to time. Nothing to worry about." He hid a smile as she tried to appear unconcerned. Truth be told, he didn't mind having a girl worry about him. It hadn't happened in a while.

GWYNNETH

Gwynneth's meetings with Arian went on for a week, then two; nearly became a routine. They never talked about when they'd next meet, but the weather continued hot and clear during the day, and Linette seemed as eager for their walks to the pavilion as she was. Avaron's toothache continued, but Gwynneth counseled waiting for the surgeon until it got worse. Having a tooth pulled seemed very horrid.

Every day she went to the pavilion intending to tell Arian this was their last meeting. She had hoped just the one time would be enough, but she felt half-crazed with desire. Was it because she and Kendryk had spent so little time together in the past months? But the reasons didn't matter; it had to end.

Arian couldn't stay here after Faris's arrival without arousing considerable suspicion. Besides, his cavalry was worth twice as much with him at the head of it and Kendryk needed every advantage. She had to end it now. But each time, the words wouldn't come. They didn't speak much anyway, and afterward her next thought was 'just one more time.'

She was in the library one morning when the footman announced Edric Maximus. Her heart pounded. Somehow, she was sure he knew. Or maybe she had a guilty conscience.

"Why don't you go walk in the garden," she told Halvor and Linette, who left much too slowly. She closed the open doors with a bang, rattling the glass.

"Please, be seated," she said, giving Landrus a chilly smile.

"I am sorry to trouble you again, Princess." He lowered himself into a chair, clearly reluctant to speak.

"Something tells me I'm about to be more sorry." Her heart pounded in her throat.

"So, I don't have to tell you why I'm here," he said as a statement rather than a question.

"There's no point in talking in circles."

"I suppose you're wondering how I found out."

Gwynneth shrugged. Now that it was out, she could breathe again. "The servants here are friendly toward you. I suspected there might be at least one informant."

"It's less that they are friendly toward me, but that they love your husband."

She flinched, feeling like she'd been punched in the stomach. It was hard to breathe again. "I've tried to end it," she finally managed. "I never meant to start so much as a flirtation. I have no excuse." She lifted her head and looked at Landrus with some effort. He seemed sympathetic, which surprised her. She had expected a sermon on the damnation she was bringing on herself.

"I realize this has been difficult for you, Princess. But an affair with someone like Orland is not the answer."

Tears started into her eyes. "I can't bring myself to end it."

"You shall." The steel had crept back into his voice. "I will give you three days. After that, you will leave here and take the children with you to Norovaea. You will be removed from temptation, safer as well. Who knows, you might prevail upon your father better in person."

"Leave? I can't leave now. Kendryk needs me."

"He does. But if this is your idea of help. .."

That hurt even more and she had to bite her tongue until it bled to stop herself from whimpering. Until now, she'd been able to push the vileness of her actions to the back of her mind. Confronting the enormity of what she had done made her wish she could melt into the floor and disappear forever.

Landrus went on. "If you don't do this; if you aren't on the Helvundala boat four mornings from now, I will write to Kendryk and tell him what is happening."

She gasped. "You wouldn't."

"I don't want to. Far better it be over and you far away from temptation."

"Wouldn't me leaving arouse suspicion?"

"It doesn't need to. Everyone knows you're trying to get help from your father. Better to take the children since Kendryk isn't here. It would be strange if you went without them."

The tears spilled over. Landrus was silent and let her cry. She couldn't bear to look at him. It would have been easier if he'd looked stern and disapproving, but he appeared to pity her and that was much worse. When the sobs subsided, she wiped her eyes with the lacy end of her sleeve and said, "All right, I'll end it. I know I must. But I won't go. I can't. Kendryk would see that as a betrayal."

"Isn't that better than the alternative?"

"He doesn't have to know about that at all."

"I am not sure you can resist temptation as long as you stay here."

"I'll shut myself in my room and say I'm ill."

"You're never ill. No one would believe that." Landrus shook his head. "No, you must go." He leaned forward. "It seems harsh, but I know what I'm speaking of. Do you think you're the first woman or man I've seen led astray? It's all too common."

"I always thought I was better than that." Gwynneth felt another sob rise in her throat.

"That is the problem with pride." Landrus was now in full priestly mode. "When we rely on ourselves, we always fail. You must pray to Ercos for strength, and to Vica for the wisdom to see your way. They will always give you what you need. Just because you are a princess, doesn't mean you are less in need of their help."

She had to admit that was exactly what she'd always thought. It seemed she was wrong. "Very well, I will end it. But I won't go. If my father isn't moved by my letters, seeing me in person will be no better. And I must be here for Kendryk. It's the only way I can make it up to him, even if he never knows."

Landrus regarded her silently, his eyes colder now. "Do that first. Once it's done we can talk again." He rose. "I'll leave you with that, Princess. May the gods keep you."

BRAEDEN

Braeden was up before anyone else, except Barela. Dressed in mail and plain black leather, the general sat at a campfire and sipped something hot from a cup. Braeden got a bowl of porridge from the cook wagon and sat down across from him.

"It's good to be fighting again." Barela smiled. "Sometimes I hate it, but when I have gone a few weeks with no action, I can't think of anything I like better."

Braeden nodded by way of agreement. They sat in companionable silence as the camp awakened around them. Everyone was quiet, because they wanted to avoid any loud noises that might alert scouts in the area, but also because of the contemplative mood that struck many before a battle. A few soldiers prayed, and a small cluster of Maladene pikemen gathered at an impromptu altar holding a crude icon of Vica.

Barela followed his gaze. "I don't know about you, but I don't believe all that."

"I don't either. Gods that allow the things I've seen, I want nothing to do with."

"And yet we might soon fight about gods again."

"It seems so." Braeden had spared little thought for Terragand, but he was sure that once Teodora had Atlona back, she would look north while she still had Barela at her disposal.

"Foolishness, all of it," Barela said. "And yet, you and I would have no work without this foolishness. Perhaps the gods really are looking after us."

Braeden smiled at the thought, then got up. Gergo and Janna helped him with his armor. He could tell Janna was doing her best to act as nonchalant as everyone else.

There was a great deal of armor, and each piece had innumerable hooks and buckles. He started with a padded linen tunic and a shirt of mail. Over that went a heavy plate cuirass, thick enough to stop bullets. Several dents proved it had done just that. Then came smaller pieces like pauldrons, gorget and vambraces. Finally, he put on his helmet, leaving the visor up. Gergo fastened the wings on their tall frames to his belt, then Braeden sheathed his saber and holstered his pistols.

Once mounted, Gergo handed him his hammer, and a short arquebus that went into a holster on his saddle. All the firearms were loaded. He didn't want to know how much all of it weighed, but Kazmir danced about like a colt, sensing the coming action. He didn't carry a lance since they were unlikely to run into tight formations. If they did, a wagon full of them traveled right behind his banner.

The army moved, the hussars in its van. Barela hoped that if the hussars inside Atlona spotted them, they would come out right away. Besides, it was best to swoop down on Korma with cavalry.

The sun rose behind them as they crested the ridge overlooking Atlona. The city lay dark and quiet, Korma's camp spread out along its wall. They couldn't outflank Korma, although the hussars would break to the left and try to squeeze him against the wall as the infantry pushed down from the east.

Braeden urged Kazmir to a trot as the ground leveled out. There was still no sound from the camp. By now, they should have run into outposts. Braeden realized that Korma must have known they were coming. That would make it more interesting. He kept Kazmir at a steady trot, holding him back from galloping. The outer line of tents was now in clear view.

There was a blast of fire and smoke in front of him. Muskets. Braeden urged Kazmir to a gallop, pulled out a pistol, fired into the smoke, let go the reins, and pulled out the other. Both pistols spent, he drew his saber, and waded into a squad of musketeers trying to reload.

Lined up among the tents, they weren't in proper formation. Still, he could see the rising sun glinting off the tips of pikes up ahead. Once he'd dealt with these fellows, he'd circle back for a lance and get more loaded pistols as well. The musketeers scattered, though one or two had a chance to draw their swords. They weren't quick enough. Braeden slashed wildly, in a hurry to get back. Out of the corner of his eye, he could see Reno and a few other hussars working over the muskets on his right.

He paused for a moment. "Fall back and get lances," he shouted, pointing his saber at the gleaming helmets marching toward them. Reno nodded, cut down one more man, then wheeled around to join Braeden.

As Braeden rode back, met the next rank of hussars coming forward. "Pike coming," he shouted. "Lances." Everyone turned back with him, but in good order. As they reached the wagons holding the lances, Braeden spotted Barela, also ahorse and speaking with Teodora.

"Nothing better than a bloody saber to start your day, eh Terris?" He laughed, his teeth white under his black helmet.

Braeden grinned. "Seems they were ready for us."

"Thought they might be. But no matter. You did just as I'd hoped. Their first rank of muskets is in confusion and we can meet their pike properly. And they are constrained by still being in camp. This will be over soon."

Braeden grabbed a lance from the cart. "Wonder how long before Novitny and the rest are on their way?" he asked Reno.

"I expect they're armoring up right now. Should be here soon."

Barela waved the infantry forward. The hussars would ride into the first rank of the enemy, and Barela's muskets would follow. His pike had already engaged on the right.

Braeden found his banner, already in good order. "Time to go. Maybe we'll meet Novitny on the other side."

There was a great din from the other side of the camp, and Braeden could see occasional black wings fluttering beyond the square of pike. The Sanova Hussars inside the city had come out and were attacking. That made his job much easier. The pike were still in formation, but nervous, knowing the hussars were attacking their rear.

Braeden charged before they could get their nerve back, and they scattered on the first try. He galloped straight through, his lance broken but still useful. He would let the rank behind him mop up while he connected with his comrades.

He came up on the backs of both musket and pike fighting hard hand-to-hand with the hussars. The hussars had no lances, but were doing well enough.

"Good morning, sir," Franca said, while she used her hammer to stave in the helm of a man in front of her. His mouth sprayed blood, and he fell at her horse's feet. Without pausing, she swung the hammer again, and caught a musketeer in the chin. He'd been trying to come up behind her and use the butt of his musket to unhorse her. Her instincts were perfect.

"Took you long enough." Novitny took down two pikemen with one slash of his saber.

"I missed you too," Braeden said, and it was true. He helped by shooting another pikeman as he circled around, holding a saber. Pike were not so used to hand-to-hand fighting, and these were unseasoned troops.

"What's the plan, sir?" Franca asked.

"We regroup and do our best to outflank. Barela is coming down from the northeast."

"We can't outflank," Novitny said. "They're strung out too far down the valley, all the way to the mountains."

"We know that. Some will get away, but very few. Any idea where Korma is?"

"Probably in the thick of things. At least, he likes to talk about how he always is."

"All right, let's go."

By now, Braeden's troops had followed him, and the rest from Atlona had joined them. They'd lost a few, but surprise had been on their side. Even though Korma might have been aware there were hussars inside, he wouldn't have known how many.

There was no point in getting more lances now. Braeden hoped to find and engage the Marjatya Hussars. Before heading south, Braeden looked back. Barela's squares were mowing over Korma's. Discipline and experience always told.

"Oh, *that* Barela." Miro rode up to join them, blood dripping from his saber.

"He knows what he's about," Braeden said, "and best of all, the empress listens to him, so it all goes off easy; no arguments. Who else was inside the city?"

"Not many," Novitny said. "Livilla ordered the city watch to stay inside. Otherwise, it's less than a thousand regular infantry. They should be out here somewhere. They were as eager to get into it as we were. Where's Ensden?"

"Long story," Braeden said, as they cantered along the edges of the camp. Most of the fighting was behind them, where Barela was attacking, but there were still troops ahead of them. Their orders were to cut down anyone they saw and prevent the retreat of as many as possible. As they curved around to the west, Braeden saw a familiar banner. It was Count Andarosz, taking his troops to the fight. Braeden let him go. With any luck, Karil would still have a father tonight.

They were still on the edges of the camp when the tide turned. Braeden could have sworn he'd been out there no more than and hour, but the sun was high in the sky, and now he felt its heat. It had to be near noon. The smell of battle wafted over him too, and he hadn't noticed the flies until now. The Marjatya Hussars thundered past, making for the river. They would probably escape, but Braeden wanted to make it difficult. "Stop them," he ordered.

They caught a fair few of them, and once the rest disappeared, there was fleeing infantry to chase. All the while, Braeden kept an eye out for Korma. If he could catch or kill him, the revolt in Marjatya would end today.

GWYNNETH

Gwynneth sat in the pavilion and tried to compose herself.

Arian walked right to her, sweeping her into his arms. "What is it darling?" he murmured into her ear. Perhaps he noticed her stiffening at his touch. She tried to disentangle herself. If she let it go further, she wouldn't have the strength to tell him. He didn't release her, but let her pull him down on the bench next to her.

"We've been discovered," she said.

"That didn't take long." She wondered why he wasn't more bothered. He was probably used to escaping out of bedroom windows when irate husbands came home. This was tame by comparison. "Who did it? If you punish them you'll discourage others from telling tales."

"It doesn't matter. We haven't been discreet."

"So Kendryk knows?"

"Not yet. We can keep him from finding out, but we must end it now."

"That's ridiculous. Who's threatening you with this?"

"Edric Maximus. He came to see me yesterday. If it's not over in three days, he'll tell Kendryk." She didn't tell him about the demand she leave as well.

"The nerve of that man. He has no right." Arian stood up and paced the floor. This was the angriest she'd ever seen him. "I can kill him if you like. That would solve several problems."

"Are you mad? Kendryk would stop everything. Not to mention, you can't kill people because they inconvenience you."

"You'd be surprised. It wouldn't be the first time."

He couldn't mean that. "Please don't say those kinds of things."

"Why not? I only want to take care of you. Of us." He sat down again and took her hands.

"There is no us." She pulled her hands away. "Edric Maximus is right. It needs to end now." It helped that Arian had reacted so strangely. If he'd been sad, it would have been much harder.

He took on a wounded expression. Perhaps she'd been premature. "What do you mean there is no us? You're the most important thing that's ever happened to me. I've never been in love like this. Please don't say this was just a dalliance for you."

"Not a dalliance," she said more softly. "But a mistake. It's wrong and I should never have given in to you. I do not wish to hurt you, but this can't go on."

"I don't think you understand." Arian's eyes lost all their warmth.

Gwynneth shivered and edged away.

"You can't just end this," he went on. "Both of us are involved and both of us get to decide."

"It seems we disagree. Now what?"

"Nothing. We carry on and if the maximus makes trouble, I'll deal with him."

She hoped she could hide her rising unease. "Maximus or not, I must end this for my sake. I'm not the kind of woman who can do this."

"Are you sure? You do it rather well."

Her hand struck his face before she could stop herself. He caught and held it so tightly it hurt.

"Let me go," she said through clenched teeth, "and never insult me like that again." It was a relief to let anger wash away her fear, at least for a moment.

He squeezed her hand tighter. "Don't play the virtuous little princess with me."

She struggled to free her hand, and he released it with a laugh, though his eyes still held a dangerous gleam.

She scrambled to back as far away from him as she could. "Why are you being horrid? You say you care about me, but you're doing every thing you can to make me miserable right now."

"I'm not through with you yet. Perhaps I never will be. You don't believe me, but I have fallen in love with you, and I can't bear the thought of being without you."

"I am very sorry." Gwynneth tried to keep her voice even although her whole body shook. "It's not like I don't care about you at all. I do. But I can't do this and be married to Kendryk."

"Then don't be married to him."

"That's impossible and you know it."

"Only because you can't imagine not being a princess."

"That has nothing to do with it. I've made a mistake with you, but I love him."

"I suppose I can accept that, though I don't like it. What I won't accept is ending this now. It will end when it's time for me to join your husband. But it continues until then."

"He'll find out." Tears started to Gwynneth's eyes. She would do anything to keep Kendryk from learning about this.

Arian shrugged. "What's he going to do? He'll be upset, although I'm sure he'll forgive you, if the alternative is sending you away. If he were smart, he'd know it's best not to expect much from a woman, even one like you. It's a hard lesson, but one he must learn. Don't worry about him too much. He'll be away on campaign with plenty of distractions of all kinds. Who knows, maybe you doing this will make him feel free to indulge himself. No reason he shouldn't have fun as well."

"I can't believe how awful you are. I suppose I didn't know you at all."

"You don't. It's not like we've spent all of this time in deep conversation. In any event, this continues until I say it stops."

"And if I don't go along with this?" Her heart pounded wildly. If he could so coldly contemplate killing Landrus, what might he do to her?

"I leave." His eyes were hard again. "I'll take my troops and never come back. What's more, I'll ride straight for Olvisya and offer my services to the empress. I'm sure she would be very grateful. Who knows, I might even meet Kendryk in battle someday. That would be poetic, wouldn't it?"

"You can't be serious." This possibility had never occurred to Gwynneth. "You'd be a traitor."

"No, I'd be changing employers. From one who hasn't paid me at all to one who will pay me well."

Gwynneth wiped her eyes. "Tell me what Kendryk owes you and I will settle up right now."

He laughed and leaned back on the bench. "That's not the payment I want. Now come here sweetheart, and stop crying. All will be well."

She was too frightened to resist. All she could hope for now was Ruso Faris's arrival before Edric Maximus found out what was happening.

KENDRYK

Kendryk worked his way along the border, garrisoning each fortress, but things looked no better than they had earlier. The situation was especially abysmal along the border with Sanova. There had been no threat from that direction in two hundred years and many fortifications had fallen into disrepair. In addition, the land was flat here, with no natural barriers.

Kendryk was sitting down for an evening meal in another drafty castle when the tired messenger arrived. "Didn't expect to see you this far east, Your Grace," he said. "You've made good time."

"Not good enough." Kendryk took the bag. He saw a few messages from Ruso Faris, who was marching from Zeelund with twenty thousand men. To Kendryk's relief, they were getting closer, though he didn't know what to do with them when they arrived.

Then he spotted Gwynneth's hand on a message and smiled. She wrote short notes daily sent in bundles. This one had "Very Important!" written on it in Linette's messy scrawl. Kendryk opened it with a sense of dread. Good news was unlikely.

"My agent in Melampis tells me that negotiations are nearing their conclusion," Gwynneth wrote. "Ambassador Arceo has received instructions to make any concessions necessary to reach an agreement, even a temporary one. Teodora is desperate. She will give up the fortresses of Girosna and Lubardol in return for a two-year peace. It's not long, but it's enough to give her time to deal with Andor Korma and with you.

"If all goes as planned, Ensden will need no more than a few hundred garrison troops at the frontier and can march on Atlona with force. If they succeed there, she can march into Kronland well before winter. I believe it's important to meet her as far south as possible so you can get help from your aunt and keep the fight from Terragand. I love you so much and miss you desperately."

Kendryk looked up. This was bad news, but he'd half expected it. As proud and impetuous as Teodora might be, she understood that Zastwar was by far the biggest threat she faced. In her unfavorable position, major concessions made a great deal of sense.

Kendryk's grandfather had fought hard for those fortresses and sacrificed many Terragand soldiers in their taking. Still, it made no sense to keep them for sentimental reasons. It would be an unpopular decision, but Teodora never worried about that.

He put the letter down and picked up the last one. It was from Landrus. He smiled. Perhaps he'd get more information gleaned from the Scrolls or something Landrus had missed before. But the letter was unnervingly short. "Please return to Birkenhof in all haste," it said. "There is an important matter that concerns you which you must deal with before you go anywhere else." That was all. Kendryk shook his head. He couldn't imagine what it might be.

Kendryk called for his adjutant. "Send the word we are leaving for Birkenhof in the morning."

Kendryk had plenty of time to think on the long journey back to Birkenhof. The Zastwar treaty concerned him more than anything else. It was unlikely that Ensden would take back Atlona and then invade Kronland before Faris arrived, but recruitment had taken far longer than expected. Kendryk wondered if he should take Orland's force south without delay while waiting for Faris to catch up.

For the thousandth time, he wished Faris were here already. He knew that Arian and Gwynneth would counsel moving right away, no matter how unprepared he felt. He'd prefer to be backed by a cooler head.

He also knew that Ensden's large and professional force would make short work of Korma's rabble. They would sustain little damage and be ready to march on Terragand in less than a month. He needed to write to his aunt in Oltena again and warn her of the coming crisis. She was still his most stalwart supporter in the south and would throw every possible obstacle in the empress's path. It wouldn't be enough. Her militia was even smaller and worse-equipped than his and she had no mercenaries.

He would hate to see her country laid waste, almost as much as Terragand. Maybe Gwynneth and Arian were right, and it made sense to take the fight straight to Olvisya. He sighed and shifted in his saddle, wondering about Landrus's letter. It was unusual for him to be so brief and so vague. He wondered if Julia had come back and was causing trouble. But then he would have said the trouble was at Heidenhof. Kendryk couldn't and didn't want to imagine yet another problem.

BRAEDEN

Braeden never found Andor Korma and hoped it was because his mangled body lay somewhere on the battlefield. There were plenty of those, almost all Marjatyan. It was well after noon before Braeden found Barela again. The general was pleased. Not only were the Sanova Hussars reunited, but word spread that those breaking out of the city might well have turned the tide. Barela seemed to think so.

"I am so impressed, Prince," Barela told Novitny. "The initiative! The discipline! I doubt I've ever had troops who behaved so well. Are you sure you would not like to go with me back to Floradias when it is time? I could use cavalry like yours. And just imagine all of that lovely flat ground!"

Novitny smiled. "Flat ground covered with ditches. You are kind to offer, General, but for now, I'm committed to the empress."

Barela shrugged, still smiling. "Contracts end," he said.

Braeden wished he could work for Barela. Anything to get away from the empress. But it looked like Barela himself had no interest in doing so.

Teodora was flushed and smiling after the battle, blood splattering her armor. Rumor was she had broken free of her bodyguard and done some fighting herself. There was also no denying the heated glances flashing between her and Barela. It seemed if she had her way, Barela would stay in Atlona for a while.

It took the rest of the day to get the victorious army into the city. Conditions hadn't been as dire as many had feared. Livilla Maxima had managed well, imposing reasonable rations, and keeping up morale. Even Novitny praised her.

Teodora planned lavish entertainments as if the city had suffered no deprivation. Barela was a celebrity, his name on the lips of every lady at court.

After giving everyone a few days to settle in, it was time to make plans. Teodora called a large meeting in her great hall. This included the imperial council and all of her generals.

"There is much news," she said without preamble. She was smiling and her eyes shone. Braeden looked sideways at Barela, but his face gave nothing away.

"First the bad. Korma has managed to get back into Marjatya." Normally, something like this would have put her in a week-long rage. "However," she went on, "He's much weakened. Our scouts estimate he has a few hundred men at most. We need not worry about him for a while.

"There is good news too. Ambassador Arceo just signed a new treaty with Zastwar." There was a happy roar from those who gathered. She stood smiling until the noise died down.

"But we can't rest yet. Most of you already know that we have another problem on our hands. Right before this siege, Kendryk Bernotas of Terragand engaged in an act of open rebellion by abducting the convicted heretic, Edric Landrus and taking him to safety. Temporary safety." The familiar, fierce Teodora was back. "As if that weren't bad enough, Prince Kendryk has taken advantage of our other problems to invade our borders."

There was another gasp.

"I have heard from several of the rulers in southern Kronland. Not only has he ravaged our own lands, but Bernotas has sent his dog, Arian Orland to intimidate Arcius and Tirilis. Orland has burned villages and sacked towns. Anyone who professes loyalty to me is a target. I cannot let this continue, so I will deal with Bernotas next."

She turned toward Novitny and Braeden. "The Sanova Hussars have served me well, and will continue to do so. Your next mission is to invade Terragand. Until Count Ensden returns, I cannot launch a full-scale invasion. But we can show Kendryk that we are coming for him."

Braeden looked forward to some real fighting. With the hussars at full strength, they might be able to run right over Prince Kendryk before anyone else got there. Once Teodora's problems were solved, Novitny could go to work for someone else. Braeden was ready for a new employer.

KENDRYK

Kendryk galloped into the stable courtyard at Birkenhof just after noon, startling a groom dozing in the sunlight. He tossed him the reins and dismounted. By now it had been several days since he received Landrus's letter and his anxiety had reached an unbearable level. He wanted to find Gwynneth right away and make sure she and the children were all right.

The palace dozed in the sun. The main hall was cool, but aside from a lone footman, deserted. Kendryk went straight to the library, but found no one. Strange for the middle of the day since Gwynneth spent most of her time there. Perhaps she was ill. He hurried along the corridor, poking his head into every room. No one was about.

He ran up the stairs, taking them two at a time and finally spotted Avaron, sitting on a bench in the corridor.

She jumped up when she saw Kendryk. "Your Grace, we did not expect you today."

"I know." Kendryk was breathing hard. "Where is the princess? Is she well?"

"Well enough." Avaron's tone was strange. "I believe she is, um, in her dressing room."

"Why? Is something wrong?"

"She might have had a headache from the heat," Avaron said, her eyes blinking rapidly.

Now Kendryk expected the worst. Was Gwynneth horribly ill, and no one dared tell him? Was she dead? Where was the doctor? He paused at her dressing room door. He heard raised voices, one of them Gwynneth's. Breathless but relieved, he opened the door.

He couldn't quite believe the scene before him.

Gwynneth and Arian sat side-by-side on the chaise lounge, absorbed in an intense conversation. Gwynneth was angry, but Arian held her hands in a way he shouldn't have been and Gwynneth wasn't trying to pull away. Time seemed to slow. Kendryk stood in the doorway breathing hard, unable to say a word.

Gwynneth noticed him first, gasped and yanked her hands from Arian's grasp. There was no doubting the guilt on her face. Arian turned and jumped up when he saw Kendryk. They all stared at each other.

Arian spoke first. "See here, it's all right." He took a few steps in Kendryk's direction.

"It's not what it seems?" Kendryk finally managed.

"Not quite," Arian said.

"Let me explain," Gwynneth began.

Kendryk stared at her. "How can you possibly explain this? There is only one reason he would be here."

"Nothing was happening, or going to happen," Arian said. "She was ending it."

Which meant there was something to end. Arian took one more step and Kendryk's fist shot out and hit him square in the jaw. Pain flashed up Kendryk's hand, momentarily clearing his head.

Arian stumbled back, but rather than reach for him, Gwynneth stepped out of the way. At least that, Kendryk thought. If she had rushed to Arian's aid, he couldn't have borne it.

Kendryk took a deep breath. "I have to know. Did he force you?"

Gwynneth gave him a long look, her eyes filling with tears. "No." She shook her head as they spilled onto her cheeks. "No, he didn't."

That was all he needed. Turning on his heel, Gwynneth's shocked, tearful face burning into his brain, he sprinted back down the stairs. He hurried along the corridor, passing the footman holding his hat. Storming into the courtyard, he shouted for a horse, any horse. While he paced waiting for one to be saddled, he heard Gwynneth calling his name. He ignored her until she stood right behind him and put her hand on his shoulder.

"Kendryk, please," she said through tears.

He flung her hand off. Fortunately, the groom brought up a horse so he could get away.

"Don't talk to me," he said through gritted teeth. He'd never before used that tone with her.

She stood there stunned, while he jumped into the saddle and galloped out the courtyard toward the forest.

JANNA

Flames grabbed at her like fingers, and though Janna ran as fast as she could, the fire was faster. But instead of burning her, it snatched and threw her to the ground. Her breath flew from her chest and her mouth filled with dirt. When she rolled to her back, something fell on her, knocking the rest of her wind out of her. It was a body, one of the men who'd attacked her. He was dead, but no matter how hard she pushed, Janna couldn't get him off her.

She gasped and panted and pushed until suddenly the weight lifted. Janna sat up, gasping for air, just in time to see Daciana Tomescu fling the body to one side as if it weighed nothing. Then she pushed someone toward Janna. It was Anton, looking pale, but taller than before.

Janna opened her mouth to thank her, but Tomescu's eyes turned yellow as she loomed over Anton. She laughed, loud and shrieking, showing long, sharp fangs that kept growing until they were the size of a wild boar's tusks. She lifted a long, curved sword.

Janna tried to stand, but her legs wobbled like jelly and refused to lift her. The blade flashed toward Anton and Janna shrieked, "Kill me! Please, kill me instead. Please."

But the blade swooped down and Anton collapsed in a small bloody heap. Janna screamed and screamed while Daciana licked the blood from her blade, grinning at Janna sideways.

She screamed and shook and shook harder until another voice pushed in from somewhere behind her. It was Braeden, shouting her name and shaking her.

"Janna, wake up," he said over and over again, until she did, much too slowly. The wolf eyes and the blood were replaced by the weight of a large hand on her shoulder and the sight of a boy holding a candle, standing in front of her cot, staring at her. It took a long time to remember that the boy was

Gergo and why she was in a Sanova Hussar's tent. Braeden said nothing once she was fully awake, just knelt next to her cot, rubbing her shoulder.

"It was awful," she said when she'd caught her breath and could move her limbs again. "Fire, and Tomescu, and she killed Anton and there was so much blood."

"Just a dream," Braeden said. "A nightmare. It's normal to have those after something bad's happened."

"But why didn't I have them right after? Why now when I'm safe?"

"I don't know." Braeden didn't seem inclined to explain and for some reason she was grateful for that. "Here Gergo, give me that and go back to bed." He took the candle and set it on the ground next to Janna's cot. The flame cast enormous shadows against the wall of the tent.

Janna shivered. "I'll just sit here for a while. You should go back to sleep."

"I don't mind sitting with you for a bit." Braeden moved away from the cot and sat against the wall of the tent, the flickering light shadowing his face from below. "Did your mother ever tell you the story about the peasant who tricked his lord with a big white goose?"

"Of course. Everyone knows that story."

He leaned forward, his voice low. "I don't think you've heard this version. It's not generally told around ladies, but it might make you laugh."

Janna leaned forward too, in spite of herself. He was right, it did make her laugh, and it made her blush too, though she hoped it was too dark for him to notice that. Best of all, when she went back to sleep, her only dreams were of a fat lord, his breeches around his ankles, chasing a white goose down a busy street.

KENDRYK

Kendryk gave the horse its head, using his spurs to keep it moving. The heat was less intense in the woods. He turned off the road onto a smaller path, and the branches reached down to slap his face. He tasted blood on his lip. The pain comforted him, distracting him from the tight knot in his chest.

After a while, he let the horse drink from a brook which ran alongside the path. He was thirsty too, but dismounting took too much effort. Kendryk tried to calm himself, but as soon as he did, the unbearable memory of what he'd seen washed over him.

He stayed in the woods for hours. The horse wandered where it wanted, down different paths, stopping to eat grass and getting water a few more times. The shadows were long before he made himself see where he was though he didn't fear being lost. He had known these woods his whole life.

He couldn't return to the palace pretending nothing had happened. That was impossible. Everything had changed and he couldn't see his way forward. He wished he had someone to talk to. Normally, that would have been Gwynneth, but he wanted nothing to do with her right now.

After two hours of riding, Kendryk entered Heidenhof just as the sun went down. He realized he must look terrible, dirty from the road to begin with. No hat, no cloak, no company. That didn't matter. Landrus would always see him.

They recognized him at the palace and he told the stable-boy who took his horse to rub him down well and give him extra water.

Someone had already sent word to Landrus, so he stood near the main door as Kendryk came in. "Come in and sit down," he said in that calm tone he had, leading Kendryk into a small, comfortable room near the entrance. Kendryk fell into a chair. He wasn't sure he'd be able to speak, and Landrus didn't push him. He called for refreshments, then took his time closing the door and coming back in. "Speak when you're ready. If it's any help, I have a good idea why you're here."

Kendryk took a few moments to master himself. He had a childish desire to throw himself into Landrus's arms and cry on his shoulder. But he hadn't had that luxury even as a child.

A servant came with a tray, and Landrus handed Kendryk a small glass. "Drink this. It might help calm you."

Kendryk took a sip. It was some kind of brandy, sweet, but with a sharp bite. He gulped it all down, though it made his eyes water.

"Another?" Landrus asked.

Kendryk held out his glass.

After emptying that one, he felt calmer. The sharp pain in his chest had dulled and a wave of exhaustion swept over him. He'd been on horseback since sunrise and the day had been hot.

"I think I know now what your letter was about." Kendryk set the glass on a table.

"I didn't know what to say. Perhaps I should have remained silent, but that seemed wrong. Someone needed to tell you."

"Yes, you're right. I still can't quite grasp it, and I don't have the slightest idea what to do about it."

"I won't ask how you found out, but I'll assume there was no doubt what was going on."

"No doubt at all. She looked far too guilty though Arian said she was trying to end it."

"She probably was. I spoke with her last week, telling her she needed to do so right away. I learned that she had tried, but Orland refused. He made many dire threats."

"I'll kill him," Kendryk said. "I have never wanted to kill anyone, but I want to kill him right now. Perhaps I can challenge him."

"That would be unwise. He's deadly in a duel. You must rise above it since he is not your equal."

"I won't ask how you got your information. Though no doubt it wasn't too difficult. It doesn't matter. But I can't go back and act as if nothing has happened."

"You cannot," Landrus said. "I won't tell you what to do, but this is what I told the princess when I found out. Arian Orland must be banished and leave your service altogether. And the princess should leave too, at least for a time."

"Where would she go? I don't want it to appear as if I am casting her off."

"It seems plausible she would go to Norovaea to plead your case with her father in person."

"I suppose it does. I was about to say I would miss her, except I don't think I can bear to look at her right now. Maybe I never will again."

"It's hard to say if your marriage can be saved. Perhaps it can. I've seen worse situations remedied with the help of the gods. She still loves you and would do anything to make things right."

"How can she?" Kendryk asked miserably.

"Perhaps she cannot. But the shock of this is still very new. In time, you will feel better, though it's hard to believe right now. However, you must act in the meantime."

"Getting rid of Arian would be satisfying though I realize it diminishes my chances against Teodora."

"You will miss his cavalry, though he won't go over to Teodora, as he threatened the princess."

"He told her he would do that?" Anger surged up inside him again.

"Yes when she tried to end it. I doubt he was serious, though she might not have realized it. The Orlands are by far the most rabid anti-Imperialists in Terragand. He would sooner fight for Maladena. And besides, Count Faris can't be far away now. With the force he has assembled you should have no trouble challenging Teodora."

"That settles it then. Arian must go. But what about Gwynneth? It seems harsh to send her away."

"It does. But some distance between you might be helpful. She might find success pleading with her father in person. Also consider that you will soon be away from home again. I don't believe she will betray you a second time, but if Orland refuses to stay away, there could be trouble."

"Yes, trouble as in, I'll kill him without the courtesy of a challenge." Kendryk couldn't believe how belligerent he'd become. "It's hard to believe he'd be so brazen."

"It is. Though you are far from the first man he's hurt because they underestimated him."

"I should have listened to you." Underneath the anger, the pain threatened to overwhelm him.

"It's understandable that you didn't. You have a good heart and expect others to behave as you do. This has been a hard but necessary lesson."

Kendryk sighed. "I'll send them both on their way in the morning. I suppose I'll sleep in my dressing room tonight."

"Don't go back tonight," Landrus said. "You're done in. There's plenty of room here and you will more likely sleep better. Your horse will thank you. I'll send a message so the princess doesn't worry."

"Why?" Kendryk felt angry about that consideration. "Let her worry."

"It would be cruel. Tomorrow will be a hard day for her. Let her sleep tonight knowing you are safe."

"All right." Kendryk stood. "Thank you for listening and for your counsel. I'm glad you were here."

"It was because of me you had need. It's the least I can do."

BRAEDEN

"Now this is interesting." Prince Novitny handed Braeden a sheet with some fancy writing on it. "We're all invited to the palace for a feast before we go. Those with wives should bring 'em. But you'll notice at the bottom, that bit of chicken scratch? That's Teodora herself, requesting you bring your girl."

"I don't have a girl," Braeden said, then remembered Janna's corner of his tent.

The prince's eyes twinkled. "No one else knows that. Peculiar set-up if you ask me. The least the girl could do is repay your kindness with...."

"We don't have that kind of arrangement." Braeden had to admit he was a little sorry they didn't.

"You surprise me." Novitny turned and walked between tents to the hussar's camp. "Sure, she's not your usual type, but that's a good thing, considering your history."

"True, I like women with more to 'em. More personality, I mean," Braeden added.

Novitny laughed. "She's on the scrawny side true, but coming along nicely, the way Senta's feeding her. And it won't hurt you to have someone sweet who makes you happy rather than causing nothing but trouble."

"I don't mind trouble." Braeden remembered the fiery blonde he'd found in Briansk and lost in Cesiano.

"Trouble can be fun. But at your age, you should consider settling down, and this one looks right for that."

Franca had come up next to Braeden and rolled her eyes. "Do you two ever talk of anything besides women?"

"All the time," Novitny said. "In fact, we talk about horses more than anything."

"Doesn't sound like it to me," Franca said.

"That's because you like talking about horses, but not about women. Time always goes by slow if the talk is boring to you," Braeden said.

"I can't say I approve of this Janna person."

"Why not?" Braeden wondered.

"There's no saying what she's up to. Isn't it strange you found her the way you did?"

"Not really. There are refugees everywhere right now."

"She was awful far from home. I can't help wondering if she's a rebel come to infiltrate us."

Braeden struggled for a blank expression while Novitny roared with laughter. "Her? She couldn't look less like a rebel if she tried."

"See? Perfect spy material. Don't tell me you're taking her to the empress's banquet."

"Seems I have to," Braeden said. "Though if you wanted, you might come instead. Her Highness would never know."

"I'd have to wear a dress, wouldn't I?" Franca asked fearfully.

"Something with lace, most like. And it would be best if it were pink." Braeden somehow kept a straight face.

Franca's turned pale. "Oh sir, not pink. I'd go if you ordered me to, but it would be a dreadful hardship for me."

"I know." Braeden didn't dare meet Novitny's eye. "But if you're so worried about Janna assassinating the empress, you should do your part to prevent it."

"She couldn't assassinate anyone." Franca tossed her head. "She's afraid of everything, even me. When I asked her if she wanted to race Zoltan against my new charger, she nearly died of fright. I've never seen such a ninny."

"Not a good spy then." Novitny managed a straight face too, as Franca sniffed and walked on. "It's true, she seems easily frightened. You think meeting Her Highness would do her in?"

"I hope not. Though she has reason to be frightened. She's had some dreadful things happen to her."

"I'm not surprised. Soft little thing like that out on the road by herself."

"She wasn't always by herself. She had two children. Seems both of them are dead now."

"Terrible shame. All the more reason to make her happy and give her more babies."

"I'm not sure it works like that," Braeden said, alarmed at the prospect of a squalling infant in his tent.

"It does," Novitny said cheerfully. "Women like her, all they want is to have babies. If they don't, they'll mother you instead. Just wait. If it hasn't happened already, it will."

Braeden was silent, thinking of his clean and mended shirts. He wondered if he'd gone soft in the head, though the softness was more in the chest area. It only happened when he looked at her. Or thought about her. It was no use. A girl like Janna was too fine for him. He should speak to Senta about finding her a nice Atlona merchant to marry. But the notion filled him with such misery, he put it out of his mind and resolved never to think of it again.

GWYNNETH

Gwynneth took the message with a mixture of excitement and worry. What if Kendryk had met with an accident? She'd never seen him so upset. It was a short note from Edric Maximus saying that Kendryk was spending the night at his palace and would return to Birkenhof in the morning. Dropping the note on the floor, she dismissed the messenger. Though she was glad Kendryk was all right, she wished he were here instead. She needed to talk, to explain, to apologize; anything to take away that awful, wounded expression in his eyes.

After sending her ladies to bed, Gwynneth spent the night pacing on the terrace in front of the library doors. It was a warm perfumed night, one she and Kendryk would have loved walking in. She wondered if they'd ever enjoy that kind of companionship again. At some point, she fell into a chair and an exhausted sleep. Once sunlight came through the open windows she made her way to her dressing room to repair her ravaged looks. She put on her plainest dress and arranged her hair simply. This was not the time to appear as a fashionable flirt.

She picked at a breakfast tray and listened for any sign of Kendryk. He would have to speak to her sometime. There was a knot in her stomach and her hands trembled. It might have been hunger or lack of sleep, but she knew better. Terror at what Kendryk might do gnawed at her. Until yesterday, she had only feared hurting him, but his anger was unexpected. Now she worried that he might tell her to leave and never come back. And there would be no protesting because she deserved it. She chewed on a nail while walking back and forth to the window.

After what seemed like an eternity, the door between her dressing room and their bedroom opened. She jumped up. It was Kendryk, and he didn't appear to have slept any better than she had. She wanted to run to him and fling her arms around his neck, but stopped short at his expression. His jaw was set and he wouldn't meet her gaze. She noticed pain in his eyes, the expression she hated more than anything, but she didn't know how to make him understand that she was hurting too.

"Might we speak for a moment?" Kendryk asked, far too formally. "I won't be long."

She sat down, her heart in her mouth. He sat across from her at a slight angle, still avoiding her gaze.

"I just spoke with Ossian Schurtz. It seemed better that I not speak with Arian at all. I gave him a formal decree of banishment, to pass on. It applies to Arian alone though I expect his men will follow him. He has until nightfall tomorrow to quit Terragand, or be considered an outlaw."

Gwynneth wanted to protest, but feared Kendryk would take it the wrong way. She realized now she didn't care for Arian Orland, and never had, but she worried at Kendryk's chances without his cavalry.

As always, Kendryk read her thoughts. "We don't need him. He would help, but Faris will bring enough troops to face Teodora."

Perhaps he would consider banishing her lover punishment enough. He probably assumed she cared for him a great deal.

Kendryk swallowed and bit his lip. "Now, as to you," he said, his voice shaking a bit.

Gwynneth looked at her hands, twisting a handkerchief in her lap. When she looked up, Kendryk was staring somewhere over her head. He sighed heavily. "It's best if you leave."

"Oh, no," Gwynneth whispered. "Not forever, please," she said, her voice breaking.

"I can't say, Gwynneth." He sounded so hard and cold, like a stranger. "At this moment, I never want to see you again. Edric Maximus tells me I might not always feel that way, and I don't want to deprive the children of their mother. I can't be certain how long it will be."

The blood roared in her ears and for a moment, she thought she might faint. That Kendryk, her husband, the only man she'd ever loved, could sit across from her and say these words was too much to bear. Gwynneth thought she would cry, but the grief welling up inside her was dammed up by something that wouldn't break.

"You can go to your father," Kendryk said. "We'll tell everyone you want to lobby for his support in person. We needn't tell anyone the real reason, though I'm sure everyone will suspect. I think it's best the children stay here. If it appears that they will be in any real danger, I'll send them after you."

She concentrated on his fingers, drumming on his knee. He was right; the children should stay close to their father. Kendryk was the better parent anyway. That she'd never been an interested mother hadn't bothered her before, but now it served to compound her failings as a wife.

"I don't want to go." Her throat was so tight she could hardly force any sound out.

"That has no bearing on the matter. I'm ordering you to go."

The coldness of his voice frightened her. She wondered what it was costing him to be so hard and calm. If it was costing him anything.

When she raised her eyes he was still not looking at her. "Will you ever be able to forgive me?"

"I'm not sure," he said. "I hope so. Right now I'm confused and angry and shocked. It's very hard to think straight."

"Perhaps we should wait a few days before I go. Perhaps you'll change your ..."

"No." His voice was harsh. "You're going today. I can't even begin to feel better if you're here." He stood. "Get your things packed. I'm picking an escort that will go with you to the boat when it comes. You should be able to reach Kaltental in time to catch the next ship to Norovaea. You will see you father and brothers within the week. That should make you happy." He turned on his heel and left.

Gwynneth found it hard to contain her shock. This Kendryk was a stranger to her. She wondered what Landrus had said to him to make him so angry. Probably that she'd thrown herself at Arian like a common whore and would pine after him forever. She wondered if there was any way she might persuade him otherwise, but there seemed to be no way to engage him in conversation. If only he would grant her a few more days! He must soften at some point.

She called Avaron and Linette. "Please tell my maids to pack my things. Write to your families and tell them we are going to Norovaea for a time. Prince Kendryk and I have decided that it's best I go speak with my father in person." The lie was ridiculous because these two had all but conspired with her, but it was important to keep up appearances.

Linette burst into tears, no doubt because she'd be leaving her Maladene lover behind.

"Stop it," Gwynneth said a bit too harshly. "Orland and his cuirassiers are leaving today. Best to send a note down to the camp with your goodbyes."

She waited to visit the children until it was closer to time. That way she'd be gone before they realized what was happening. She packed little because she had no intention of spending much time away from Birkenhof. She wasn't sure how, but she would return. In the worst case, she'd reach Norovaea and ask her brothers to help her get back. They would, she was certain of it.

She put on her newest riding dress, so Kendryk would remember her looking pretty instead of her worn and tear-stained face.

When she said goodbye to the children, Maryna cried because she wanted to come and Devyn cried because his sister did. Baby Andres grabbed at her hair.

She went to the foot of the stairs waiting for Kendryk, but only Merton appeared. "We are ready to go, Your Grace. Everyone's gathered in the courtyard."

Gwynneth preceded him out, but she didn't see Kendryk. "Where is the prince?" she asked as casually as she could manage while she mounted her horse.

Merton's eyes were full of sympathy. "He sends his apologies, but wasn't able to get away. He will write to you soon."

She nodded because she couldn't speak. It was beyond possibility that Kendryk wouldn't say goodbye. What if she never saw him again? Thankfully, Merton gave her horse a push, so she didn't have to do anything.

At the end of the drive, she looked back at the palace. No one stood in front of it and the windows stared at her like empty eyes.

KENDRYK

Kendryk waited until he received the message that Gwynneth and her escort had boarded the boat. A small riverboat, it would meet a larger seafaring vessel at the port of Kaltental. He hoped she would be safe. Kaltental was the domain of Arian Orland's father, and he didn't know what the duke had heard of the situation. Gwynneth was traveling without fanfare, so with any luck, she would come and go unnoticed.

He needed to talk to the children before they went to sleep, but his limbs were so heavy, he could hardly make himself move. At his desk, he pushed papers around and stared at the tray of food someone had brought without touching it. The house was silent, as though someone had died. Not someone, Kendryk thought. Something, My marriage.

He tried to pull himself together. No matter what had passed between him and Gwynneth, someone had to take care of the children. Since he was leaving soon, he would have to make those arrangements. When the shadows covered the wood paneling of his study wall, he forced himself to stand and go up the stairs. He felt like he was a hundred years old.

The children had just come out of their baths and the nurse was tucking Andres into bed. Kendryk kissed his forehead and turned to the other two.

"Why did Mama go away?" Maryna asked.

"Didn't she tell you?"

"Yes, but I didn't understand."

"She has to go talk to your Grandpapa about some important things."

"She should take me," Maryna said. "I am good at talking."

"Yes, you are." Kendryk sat on the floor and pulled her into his lap. "But they have to talk about grownup things and you would be bored."

"Why?"

"Because you're not a grownup."

"I'm big enough. I can help."

"I need you to help me here. Come here Devyn," he said, pulling the little boy, just released by the nurse, onto his other knee. "I have to go away too."

"Again?" Maryna's eyes filled with tears.

"Again. This time I might have to go fight."

"I can fight." Devyn's chubby face was serious.

"He can," Maryna said. "He can almost beat me with his toy sword and he's very strong."

"That's good. Someday you'll get a chance, I'm sure. But in the meantime, I need both of you to take care of things here for me."

"I will watch over the boys," Maryna said.

"What about me?" Devyn pouted. Kendryk knew he hated it when Maryna bossed him.

"Will you look after the horses?" Kendryk asked. "I will have to leave some behind. You can visit them every day, all right?"

Devyn nodded happily.

Kendryk sighed and kissed each of them on the tops of their fluffy heads. "I love you. I'll be back soon."

Tears prickled against his eyelids as the children clung to him, but he screwed his eyes shut. He helped the nurse tuck them in, then took her into the nearby kitchen to give her more instructions. "If you need anything, or have any problems, send for Edric Maximus."

"How long will the princess be away?" she asked. "It's not my place, but I can't bear to see Your Grace looking so unhappy. It's not right."

"A lot of things are not right. I don't know how long the princess will be gone. But no matter what happens, I want the children to see her as often as possible."

The nurse nodded, tears in her eyes. She'd been Kendryk's nurse, and when he was a little boy, he'd never hesitated to run to her when hurt or upset. He would have loved to cry into her shoulder right now, but he wasn't that little boy anymore. He still loved her though, and pulled her close, surprising her, and kissed her forehead.

"Take care of them for me," he said, then turned and left the room before he lost all control.

He made his way back downstairs, doing his best to pull himself together. He still had a few letters to write. To his surprise, when he got back to his study, Landrus was waiting for him.

"I hope I'm not intruding. They said you'd be back down here soon."

"Not at all." Kendryk was pleased to see the only person he could talk to right now. "I was putting the children to bed." He sat down behind his desk. "It's impossible to make them understand any of this, even the half-truth we're telling everyone. All they know is that they're being left behind."

"It's difficult. But I'm sure you are doing the right thing. Was the princess very upset?"

"Yes. I couldn't meet her eyes and she said little, which is unusual for her. Surprisingly, she went without protesting more."

"I'm sure she sees the wisdom in it. It will be easier for you to heal without her close by, and the sooner you heal, the sooner she might find forgiveness."

"That word. I don't know if I can. Ever."

"Perhaps not. Though it would be unlike you. Still, it needs time. You will miss her, and there's no question she is very contrite. As awful as her deed was, Orland's was worse. He took advantage of her situation. She's been unhappy for some time, and I'm at least partly to blame."

"How can you be responsible for that?"

"I took so much of your time and often advised you against what she did. She felt neglected. Once that's happened, it's easy for someone like Orland to move in. Even the most virtuous woman, when unhappy in that way, can be susceptible."

"So it's my fault. For neglecting her and for trusting Orland."

"In part. There's blame enough to go around. We all made mistakes and none of us behaved exactly as we should. The gods will forgive us for that and will help us be stronger in the future. Please don't stop praying because of this."

Kendryk gave a short laugh. "That's exactly what I've done. But you're right. I have to make all of this worth it somehow and it's the gods who matter now."

After Landrus had gone, he went to the chapel to pray. It felt good to ask for help since he couldn't think of any solutions on his own. He had to believe the gods heard him, forgave him, and would show him the path which had long ago disappeared from his sight.

BRAEDEN

Braeden was still grinning and shaking his head by the time he reached his tent. Romantic advice from the prince was never worth much. Novitny always courted the worst harridans, and never kept them for more than a month before the crockery flew, or worse. The last one had tried to use his saber on him.

Things were in a flurry inside his tent. Janna knelt over a trunk, pulling out items of clothing. She'd already handed some of them to Gergo while telling him how they should be cleaned. She'd wanted to be helpful, so Braeden told her she could organize inside the tent. He had a tendency to throw things that weren't weapons or armor into piles and forget about them.

Gergo grumbled under his breath while brushing a doublet.

"You must brush much harder if you want it to look good." Janna had more authority in her voice than he'd ever heard. She looked up as he entered. "Oh, there you are, sir." He still couldn't get her to call him by his first name in front of anyone else. "I didn't even call my own husband by his first name," she had confided.

"What did you call him?" Braeden wondered.

"Why, Master Kronek."

"He didn't mind?"

"He never told me to call him anything else."

"It seems rather formal, for a married couple."

"It was strange at first," she admitted.

Watching her face glowing from exertion, he thought it was a real shame that a sweet little thing like her had been wasted on such a troublemaker. If Dimir hadn't gone rebel, she might still be living in Kaleva, happy and comfortable with her children. He told himself that finding someone nice for her to marry was the right thing, even though it made him feel bad.

"What's in there?" He came over and knelt next to her. It was a chest he'd had with him for a long time, but never opened. Probably because it contained nothing useful.

"Some rather fine clothes. All in black, worked in silver thread, very handsome. They look foreign. Did you get them somewhere far away?"

Braeden picked up a silk shirt. "In Zastwar long ago, when the old emperor arranged the last truce. They called us to Melampis to escort him and I needed fine clothes for a banquet so I bought them there."

"It seems you haven't used them in quite a while." Janna picked up something that looked like hose and regarded it with a frown. "The moths and the damp have been at it. We can rescue most of it if you ever need banqueting clothes again."

"As it turns out, I do, and I must ask you something. Out with you," he growled at Gergo, who seemed happy to escape.

Janna turned toward him with a worried expression. He always wondered what she feared he might do.

He told her about the empress's invitation, and her large eyes grew even wider. "Oh dear," she said. "What will I wear?"

Braeden laughed. "We'll find you something. I'm sure Senta can help. And thanks to your organizing, I don't have to worry about it."

She looked him over with an appraising eye and he reddened. "I don't mean to be rude sir—I mean Braeden—but are you sure those clothes still fit?"

That made him laugh. It was a good question. He was in excellent condition for his age, but it was true he was no longer as trim as he had been in his youth. "I'll try them on, all right?" He grinned at her and she smiled back.

"Can we do it now, so I can alter them right away?"

Braeden took the doublet from Janna. It had a rather foreign cut to it, being much longer than was typical here and flaring out at the hem. He peeled off the plain doublet he wore and put the fine one on over his shirt.

Janna walked around him, tugged at a few places, and said. "Can you button it?"

He could. It was a little tight around the waist.

She did something at the back. "I can let out a seam here. It won't need much. So when is this banquet?" He noticed the strain in her voice and realized she had been trying to stay calm.

"Four nights from now." He turned to face her. "Janna." He took both her hands in his. "There is nothing you need worry about. We'll use your maiden name and the story we talked about and the empress won't have the slightest suspicion. No one will." Her hands were trembling, so he held them tighter.

"I don't understand why I'm invited," she said in a small voice. "It seems odd that a well, a camp follower ..." It seemed to cost her a great deal to say those words. "Would be invited to dine with the empress."

"It is strange, but not for the reason you think. Come here." He kept one hand in his and pulled her to his cot and they both sat down on the edge. "I have an odd relationship with the empress and she's curious about the woman in my life."

"That does seem unusual."

"Its a long story," Braeden said, and told her all of it, starting with Daciana Tomescu.

"She threw you in the dungeon because of her?" Janna put her face in her hands. "How dreadful."

"It wasn't that bad. Boring, damp, awful food, but only for a few weeks."

"I'm so sorry about what I said."

"What you said?" He didn't follow.

"What I said about you working for the empress and what kind of person that made you. It was wrong of me when I knew nothing about you and had no right to say anything."

"Janna, stop it. You were right to be upset about what was going on in Marjatya, especially after what you'd been through. And there was no way you could have known. Since then, the empress has always seemed curious about me, maybe because so few tangle with Tomescu and survive it."

"So she's just curious. Perhaps a little jealous?" There was a hint of a smile, so he knew she was teasing him.

"I doubt that. She flirted with me, but mostly because she liked making me squirm. Her manner is unnerving—you'll see that. She's invited the other high officers to bring their wives, and since she heard that I had someone, she asked that I bring you too. Oh, and one more thing Janna."

She looked at him, her eyes clear and unafraid again.

"I don't want you calling yourself a camp follower."

"But that's what everyone thinks I am."

"What they think doesn't matter. Everyone who knows you knows that you're not that sort of woman. If you were, you wouldn't have your own little corner over there, with a curtain, would you?" He nodded toward her cot.

"I suppose not. I just had some experiences with those kinds of women and swore I would never become one."

"I know the type you're talking of, and it's not possible. You don't have to worry about that, all right?"

"All right. Now take the doublet off so I can let it out. I'll see Senta later about getting a dress."

It was nice, being taken care of like this. And he liked the idea of approaching Teodora with Janna on his arm.

GWYNNETH

It was a relief to be on the boat even though she didn't want to be there. The captain offered her his quarters, and the cabin was minuscule, but at least it was hers. Gwynneth sat on the edge of the little cot and gave herself over to tears. That Kendryk hadn't said goodbye and never once looked at her was unimaginable. It was as though she didn't know him.

Perhaps he felt he no longer knew her either. She stopped sniffling for a moment. As terrible as she felt, it must be so much worse for him, and she wasn't there to comfort him. Couldn't comfort him. But he'd put on a brave face for the children, at least for as long as he remained at Birkenhof. She had to find a way back, but it would be better if he weren't there when she arrived.

After wiping her face, she opened the door and called for Avaron, lodged with Linette in a tiny compartment next to hers. "Find some water please. I wish to wash up."

Avaron scurried off, but the boat's movement caught her, almost throwing her off her feet. After that, she went more carefully. Gwynneth pulled her hair down and tried to run a comb through it. She had brought only plain dresses since she had no intention of appearing in the Norovaean court. How she would manage that remained to be seen.

After washing up and getting her hair arranged with her maid's help, Gwynneth decided to brave going aboveboard. Her first order of business was to fix her location. Then she needed to learn Kendryk's plans.

The boat was winding its way downstream to where the river met the Northern sea at Kaltental. The banks of the river rose high on both sides, vineyards and orchards covering them in steep terraces. A ruined castle lay straight ahead, a picturesque town at its base. She turned to a guardsman standing nearby. "What is that town?" she asked.

He looked shocked. She wondered if he had orders not to speak to her. She waited while he stood before her, looking awkward.

"Rudelsstadt," a voice came from behind her. It was Merton.

She turned to him. "Thank you. We haven't gone far, then." That was good, considering she still had no plan.

Merton nodded at the other guard and he went his way, scowling at Gwynneth.

"Have you ordered them not to speak to me?" she asked.

"Oh, no." He laughed. "I'm sure he's just intimidated."

Gwynneth frowned. "He didn't act intimidated."

Merton looked uncomfortable.

"You can be honest with me, Captain. I wasn't expecting friendship, but I do require respect for my position."

"You are right. I apologize, Your Grace. I will speak with the men. Many have known the prince since they were boys together, and this is difficult for them."

It had been too much to hope that everyone didn't know what had happened. "That's understandable. I only wish they realized that I am as interested in Prince Kendryk's well-being as they are."

"I don't doubt you." Merton had a plain, pleasant face that seemed incapable of guile. "But others won't agree."

She flinched, realizing she likely deserved this. But she wasn't here to wallow in self-pity. "I wondered if Prince Kendryk told you what his plans were. I wish to write to him."

"I don't suppose there's any harm in telling you. He's leaving tomorrow to join Count Faris and his army, wherever they might be. According to the last dispatch, they were making good time through Brandana."

"I see. How will a messenger find him?"

"We will send a courier from Kaltental when we are ready to take ship. He knows where to look."

"Can you include a message from me?"

"Of course. Will you and your ladies join us on deck for dinner?"

Considering the reception she'd just had, Gwynneth said, "No, I'll have them bring a tray to my cabin. I'd prefer it if they stayed with me."

For the first time that day, she smiled. Finally, she had information she could use.

JANNA

By late afternoon, Senta had descended upon her. She drove a cart while Adela and Cara rode in back holding a dress. It belonged to one of Adela's grander neighbors who had been presented at court a few years ago. She was a little bigger than Janna, but Senta had already made the adjustments.

"It's lovely." Janna gasped as they laid it out on Braeden's cot. The skirt was of heavy green silk, embroidered with a dark green and a darker orange. The bodice laced up the front, with white puffed sleeves, and it took Cara several minutes to fasten the many hooks in the back. Janna had already had a bath, washed her hair and let it dry. It had gotten most of its shine back and even a bit of curl.

She let the others fuss over her while she tried to stay calm. Senta alone knew of her problems with the empress, but even she seemed excited. "Now sit. We'll do your hair."

"It's so pretty," Adela said. "You should leave it down, with just a ribbon or two."

"Not fancy enough for court," Cara said. "Up in front, down in back. That will be simple enough."

There was combing and twisting while Adela pulled her hair away from her face and wound it into a pretty knot with green ribbons. Senta transformed the rest into long, wavy curls with a hot iron. When Cara at last held a mirror up in front of her, Janna gasped. She had never looked so fine.

Dimir always preferred modest dresses and simple hair, so she'd never worn such a low neckline. The tops of her breasts were clearly visible. She gulped. "Isn't this rather low-cut?"

"Not at all." Cara knew all about the latest fashions. "In fact, it's too modest to be the latest. Still, a demure style suits you."

It seemed Cara had a very different idea of what demure was, but Janna couldn't deny that the overall effect was pleasing. She couldn't have looked less like a Kaleva housewife. She also couldn't have looked less like the typical soldier's woman, for which she was grateful. Instead, she looked rather like she belonged in a sturdy Marjatyan manor house with a minor noble for a husband.

They had finished when Braeden came in. "Well then, let's see what you've done," he said to Senta, who turned Janna around.

What she saw in his eyes surprised and gratified her. Until this moment, he'd always looked at her with the slightly exasperated affection reserved for little sisters.

"You look very beautiful." A flush rose over his face. "All the other fellows will be jealous."

Janna blushed, but Senta agreed. "Yes, and it will be your job to keep them away from her so she's not frightened. You know how these court dandies can be."

"They'll stay away from her all right." Braeden got a dangerous glint in his eye.

Janna smiled. "You're looking rather fine yourself, sir." He'd already dressed, probably in Novitny's tent. She wondered when they had arranged all of this. It warmed her through to know that so many people were helping make this easy for her.

It was true, Braeden looked splendid. The long black doublet fit perfectly after she'd altered it and it went over puffed black breeches that ended in tall black boots shinier than she'd ever seen him wear. His beard was neatly trimmed and even his wild hair had been tamed to resemble a lion's mane.

Senta looked back and forth between the two of them. "You will be the best-looking couple there."

"And the most exotic," Adela added. "It's said the empress likes seeing foreign costume to remind her of the reach of her domains."

"Happy to oblige," Braeden said, with a wink at Janna.

Senta caught it. "Come girls." She herded her daughters out of the tent. "It's time we were off. I'll come by tomorrow to pick up the dress," she told Janna.

Janna ran to hug her before she left. "Thank you so much. I don't know what I would have done without you."

"Have a wonderful time." Senta kissed her cheek. "And don't worry about a thing. Braeden will take care of you."

There was a long silence once they were alone. The shadows were lengthening so it would soon be time to go although the palace was only a short walk away.

"I almost forgot." Braeden reached into a pocket somewhere in his capacious breeches. "I got you a little something to wear tonight." He pulled out a slim wooden box and opened it.

In it lay a delicate gold chain with a translucent orange gem hanging from it. "Is it amber?" Janna asked. She'd heard of it, but never seen it.

"Yes. Here." He handed her the box. Inside the orange drop was a tiny leaf, fallen centuries ago and perfectly preserved.

Janna felt tears start to her eyes. "It's the loveliest thing I've ever seen."

"At least one of 'em, eh? Here, let's put it on. Lift your hair."

She pulled her hair off her neck and he laid the chain around her and fastened the clasp, then turned her around to face him.

"Perfect." He picked up the little mirror where Cara had left it. As wonderful as she'd looked before, now the effect was even better. Her face was a little flushed, and the amber pendant matched the dress's embroidery.

"I love it," she said. "Thank you, although you didn't have to."

"Stop that. I wanted to. You've been such a great help. The least I can do is get you a pretty bauble every now and again."

Janna opened her mouth to thank him again, but he stopped her. "We had better go. Everyone needs to be there before the empress arrives." He opened the tent flap and followed Janna out.

A few other highly ranked officers and their wives were making their way toward the palace, but Janna felt none looked as interesting as she and Braeden did.

Braeden gave her his arm and she put both hands around it and clung to him. He smiled down at her as they entered the palace grounds. Janna felt it was pointless to pretend nonchalance to such grandeur. She looked around, delighted. Wide walkways passed between elaborately sculpted flower beds, all in various shades of red and white. Someone had tended them carefully through the siege.

At the end of one walkway, Braeden stopped her. "Look at that." He pointed toward the city. The view was spectacular. Arnfels Castle stood at the base of the towering mountains, but still high above the multi-colored domes and spires of the city. The setting sun bathed it in a golden glow, catching the gold tips of the temple spires and their green rooftops.

"It looks like something out of a fairytale," Janna said.

"Just wait until you see the palace."

They joined the stream of finely dressed people entering the Arden. Janna tried hard not to stare, for once inside, there was a riot of color and jewelry. Janna saw right away that her dress was far from revealing, compared to those who were likely wearing the latest from Galladium. She wondered how they kept their bosoms from popping out altogether.

She clung tight to Braeden's arm as they entered a magnificent reception gallery.

GWYNNETH

Though it was difficult to get used to being on a ship again, Gwynneth slept soundly. She'd made her plan and was sure it would work. The next morning, she went on deck again. It was cool and foggy, and the boat steered around rocky outcroppings. The channel here was narrow and shipwrecks littered the river bed.

Gwynneth found Merton. "Would you mind walking with me? This deck is rather slippery."

Merton gave her his arm. Until she received his reaction, she wanted no one else overhearing.

Once they were out of earshot of everyone, Gwynneth said, "I received some disturbing news, and never told the prince. I fear my letter may reach him too late to do anything about it."

Merton frowned. "Are you at liberty to tell me? Perhaps I can help somehow."

"Not if you're with me. I'm sure you're aware of how the Duke of Emberg feels about Edric Maximus?"

"Not friendly."

"It's worse than that. I have a source in his palace who overheard a most extraordinary conversation between the duke and his son. Once Kendryk has gone to meet Count Faris, they plan to ride to Heidenhof, arrest Edric Maximus and take him to the empress."

Merton went white. "He wouldn't dare! That's treason."

"It is. I wasn't so concerned because I knew that as long as I was at Birkenhof, I could see the maximus properly guarded. I'm usually able to intimidate the duke myself."

"But you're not there," Merton said. "And he'll learn that soon enough."

"Yes. And since I never had a chance to tell the prince, he won't have left enough guards, or even warning it might happen."

"We must do something and soon." Gwynneth hadn't been wrong in guessing at Merton's devotion to Landrus. "But how? Our orders are to take you straight to the Norovaean court."

"But that was because Prince Kendryk wasn't aware of this danger. I doubt very much he would have provided me such a large escort if he had known."

"Why did you not tell him before you left?"

"He wouldn't allow me to speak," Gwynneth whispered, allowing tears to fill her eyes. "And I couldn't think straight, I was in complete despair at making such a terrible mistake." She let the tears spill over and run down her cheeks.

"Your Grace." Merton reacted the way most men did to tears. Anything to make them stop. "I didn't wish to distress you. It doesn't matter does it? What matters is that Edric Maximus is alone and unguarded. We'll come up with something."

"I already have." Gwynneth wiped her eyes. "Though I fear it will mean you disobeying your orders. I will of course take full responsibility for that."

"Why don't you tell me your plan, and then we'll see," Merton said, a little calmer now.

"It will require at least half of your men." Kendryk had sent an escort of fifty.

"I can get half, maybe more, if need be."

Gwynneth told him her idea, and he listened carefully. Afterward he looked a long time at the passing vineyards.

"You're right, Princess," he said. "It's the only way to ensure his safety."

"Can you get anyone else to help?"

"I'm sure I can. Most of the men here helped guard Edric Maximus when he was a prisoner and regard him as a friend today. We all of us realize he's shown us the true way to venerate the gods."

"I'm glad." Gwynneth smiled, feeling triumphant. At times, Landrus's easy likability bothered her, but this wasn't one of them.

At first, Avaron and Linette were upset they would not be visiting the famous court of Andres Roussay, the Sea King. But Gwynneth convinced them this was an even greater adventure.

The riverboat would dock in Kaltental the next morning, but it would be a day or two before the next ship sailed for Norovaea. In the meantime, they would stay in a quiet inn near the port.

Merton assured Gwynneth that most of the men were eager to join in on her plan. They might have found her character questionable, but if there was the least talk of harm coming to their beloved Landrus, they seemed inclined to overlook the direst of sins. To Gwynneth's relief, no one had bothered to question her more deeply. She had no sources at the Emberg court and she doubted Duke Evard would bother Landrus now he had the power of the office of maximus behind him.

What worried her was that Evard would take his considerable militia to join Teodora as soon as Kendryk left Terragand. She did not intend to allow that.

They reached the riverside docks of Kaltental by mid-morning. There was great confusion as they disembarked, but she spotted the boy Merton dispatched to a nearby stable as she came down the gangplank. Her ladies and maid were behind with her baggage. A few of the guards would accompany them to the inn and discover no princess when they arrived. Merton had arranged it so everyone with knowledge of the plan went with Gwynneth.

Once out of sight of the boat, Merton motioned to her. "Your Grace, the stable is nearby." She hurried after him through the dirty narrow streets.

There were almost forty guards with them and they hired all the horses from that stable and the one next to it. Merton inspected them with care. Most looked fit. They would have to make the journey with all speed. Merton picked a fine three-year-old for Gwynneth. He was large and spirited, but she was sure she could manage him. It would give her something to occupy her mind.

It took only a few minutes for everyone to mount their horses, but Gwynneth was anxious that their absence would be discovered too soon. "How many did you leave behind?" she asked Merton.

"Less than fifteen. Enough to bring your ladies back to safety, but not enough to stop us, even if they try."

"You won't let them, will you?" Gwynneth asked, looking over her shoulder as they rode down the narrow street to the city's eastern gate

"Of course not. But I doubt they'll find us. They're not mounted, and I left none of the smartest behind. It will take them hours to figure out what's happened. Unless one of your ladies says something."

"I've sworn them to silence. It's true Avaron can't stop talking and Linette is a silly goose, but I've convinced them how important it is that they play their part."

"I trust they'll do well."

Gwynneth breathed a sigh of relief once they reached the open gate and left the city. It was cooler up here, near the sea, but the morning mists had burned off and the sun shone bright. It would aid them to have clear weather and dry roads. She offered a prayer to Vica for guidance and to Ercos to give her and her horse speed and strength. It felt good to have Merton beside her. He was a comforting presence and reliable. She would have to make sure Kendryk wouldn't be too angry with him. What was one more bit of trouble for herself?

JANNA

They stood in the crowded reception hall, the sounds and sights overwhelming. Knowing the empress herself was so close, Janna's heart pounded alarmingly and she found it hard to breathe. She was sure Senta had laced her corset too tightly.

"Here we wait for the empress," Braeden whispered, looking down at her and giving her hand a squeeze. "There's nothing to worry about. I can do all the talking if you like."

Already speechless, Janna nodded.

The chatter died down and everyone lined up along both sides of the enormous room. A tall double door opened and Teodora Inferrara entered. She wore an embroidered deep red silk dress, with a stiff collar of black and gold lace that towered high over her head. Her hair was elaborately dressed with diamonds and gold ribbons.

Janna tried to put her terror aside and just look. Teodora was beautiful in an imposing way; tall and strong-featured. Even in her finery, Janna felt a drab little mouse next to her, but stood up a little straighter all the same.

The empress made her way down the room, greeting people here and there. The rest bowed or curtsied as she passed. Janna had been practicing hers for days so she wouldn't embarrass Braeden.

As she had feared, Teodora stopped in front of Braeden. "Commander Terris," she said. "It's good to see you. And this must be your, hmm, wife, is it?"

Janna's cheeks burned.

Braeden didn't flinch. "Your Highness, this is Janna Beran, of Moralta." He made it sound like she was a fine lady, without addressing the wife question, for which she was grateful.

"You may rise, sweetheart," Teodora said, and Janna realized she was speaking to her. She'd remained awkwardly sunken in her curtsy. She made herself gaze into the empress's eyes. They were large and brown, but not warm, sparkling with aggression and intelligence. Janna forced herself not to look away.

Teodora regarded her, appraising. "Lovely. You surprise me Terris. I hadn't expected you to manage such a pretty young thing." She looked around, acknowledging the general laughter. Braeden's face was set in a pleasant and highly unnatural smile. Janna suppressed the sudden urge to laugh.

When Teodora had moved on, Janna almost collapsed against Braeden.

He squeezed her hand again. "See? That wasn't so bad now, was it?"

"No, though it seems she was trying to embarrass both of us."

"She was. It's her way. She likes making people squirm."

"Is that all? Do I have to talk to her again?"

"I think not. She might address you at dinner though I doubt we'll be close enough to speak with her. With any luck."

They weren't quite that lucky. Janna nearly panicked when she realized she and Braeden wouldn't be seated together. He was several places up the table, between two stunning women, one of whom he already seemed to know rather well.

Janna found herself between an ancient Olvisyan duke and a dashing Maladene officer. Her Olvisyan was rudimentary and her Maladene nonexistent, but the Maladene carried on in heavily accented Olvisyan, not bothered that she couldn't understand either language, and ogling her bosom all the while.

She shot Braeden a worried glance from time to time, and he often caught her eye with a reassuring smile. The beautiful blonde he already knew also gave Janna a friendly smile when Braeden pointed her out. Janna remembered Franca mentioning that Braeden liked buxom, vivacious blondes, not timid, scrawny brunettes. She told herself she had no right to be jealous.

Servants in ornate liveries brought out one course after another and kept refilling numerous crystal goblets with wines of varying shades. Janna was already sick from nerves and couldn't identify most of the food. The Maladene officer tried to explain at length, but she didn't understand him, so she picked at her plate and tried not to drink too much wine.

She was just within earshot of the empress. For the first part of the meal, Teodora conversed with an ugly yet attractive Maladene in an elaborate uniform. Janna guessed this was General Barela, whom Braeden admired very much. It seemed the empress also admired him a great deal. Prince Novitny sat on her other side, but didn't seem keen to engage her in conversation.

Somewhere around the seventh or eighth course, the empress turned her attention to the rest of the table. She sent some joking barbs toward a dour-looking old woman and a thin, pale aristocrat, then focused on Braeden.

"So Terris," Teodora said, taking a sip of wine. "You must tell me more about how you met this pretty girl of yours."

"It was in Moralta," Braeden said.

Everyone waited for more, but he stayed silent. Many eyes turned to Janna, and she hoped she didn't look as bright red as she felt. The room was too warm, and she was certain she had had too much wine.

"Obviously," the empress said, to more laughter. "But where in Moralta did you meet her? Did she offer you hospitality in Kaleva, or were you quartered in her family's house in some god-forsaken town?"

"We met in Nitrany." Braeden was as cool as could be. "She thought it was time to see the world."

"So you rescued her from a life of boredom?" Titters all around.

"Yes, I did."

"You are a most difficult man, Terris." The empress laughed, though her eyes sparked dangerously. "Here we want the details of your romantic life and you give us nothing."

"Begging your pardon Your Highness, but those things are rather personal," Braeden said, boldly, judging by way the blonde covered a gasp.

"You are quite right." The empress turned to Janna. "I'm sure you never thought such a rough-looking fellow could be so discreet, did you?"

Janna raised her chin and hoped her voice carried. "I've always known Commander Terris to be a gentleman, Your Highness."

"Well said." Teodora looked none too pleased. "I can see you two are well-matched in wit," she added. This was clearly not a compliment.

Janna pasted a smile on her lips and kept it there until Teodora's attention moved to another unfortunate soul. When she dared, she looked at Braeden again. He was quick to catch her eye, and she gave him what she hoped was a reassuring smile.

The empress worked the table, bullying some far worse, and Janna realized with relief that she wasn't the only target. Teodora was unpleasant to everyone, except perhaps, General Barela.

KENDRYK

Much as he hated leaving the children, it was a relief to get away from the palace. Kendryk wondered if he could ever gaze upon it with pleasure again. Fortunately, there was much to occupy his mind. As he rode north, hoping to find Faris and his army, messages from the south caught up to him. His Aunt Gallena Sebesta, Princess of Oltena wrote that Marjatyan marauders were ravaging her borderlands. They had come through Arcius, where Princess Zelenka was a firm supporter of the empress, but that had not spared her, either.

"Everyone is certain the raiders are led by Daciana Tomescu, the empress's wolf," Princess Gallena wrote. "I have called up the militia to protect the populace, but they are not equipped to counter anyone so ruthless. Please send help as soon as you can. While I will do everything in my power to aid you against the empress, I cannot do much alone. I've tried to rouse Benda and Martinek to action, but they do nothing but wring their hands and prevaricate." Among the states of southern Kronland, Kendryk held out the greatest hope for help from Princess Martinek of Podoska since she constantly engaged in disputes with the empire.

"There are troubling rumors of goings-on at Birkenhof and I can only hope they are rumors spread by the empress's friends to cause you grief. What I am more sure of is that Arian Orland is operating in these parts. We have not seen him, but many have reported a great force of cavalry looking to engage Daciana Tomescu. I doubt she will be so obliging."

Kendryk frowned and put down the letter. He had hoped Arian would leave Kronland altogether. Something needed to be done about Tomescu, but he'd prefer Orland stayed out of it. He would consult with Faris when he found him. The last dispatches showed that he was marching across Brandana at speed. Princess Bensen had so far declined to offer military aid but was more than happy to let his army march across her land. Knowing Faris, they would pay good coin for everything and cause no trouble.

Kendryk found Faris at the border.

"Your Grace," Faris said, surprised. "I expected you'd be on the Sanovan border right now."

"I was." Kendryk dreaded the coming conversation. He joined the head of the column heading back into Terragand, and told Faris everything that had happened.

"You must send for Orland at once," Faris said. "We cannot do this without him."

"It's too late."

"No, it's not. If he's in Oltena, as your aunt thinks, he can be back at Birkenhof by the time we arrive."

Kendryk shook his head. "I can't do it. If I see him right now, I might try to kill him."

Faris sighed. "I understand how upset you must be. And yet, the situation is dire. You must put your personal feelings aside."

"I can't," Kendryk whispered. "I'm very sorry."

"But at the least, you can call back the princess. Birkenhof should not be left empty."

"It's not empty," Kendryk said dully. He couldn't think of Birkenhof as home without Gwynneth there. "The children and all the servants are there and Edric Maximus will keep an eye on them."

"That's not what I mean. Someone needs to govern there with both of us gone. Life continues. The princess could manage most tasks."

"I can't bear to look at her either, I'm afraid." They rode in silence for a while. "I've made a horrible mess of things, haven't I?" Kendryk asked.

"You? You've done nothing wrong. I have to confess I'm amazed at the princess, but the fact remains she is at fault here. And Orland's part is inexcusable. It's unfortunate you banished him, but understandable."

"Perhaps the princess will be able to get help from her father."

Faris frowned. "There has been much news from Norovaea. It seems King Andres is ill, and the court is in an uproar."

"I knew he was ill but didn't know how seriously."

"It's serious enough to start a power struggle."

"I thought Prince Arryk would inherit. What's to struggle over?"

"The prince is impetuous, and he's picked a fight with Count Classen, his father's chief adviser. Classen wants to hold onto power as long as he can while the prince tries to wrest it from him."

"That will give Gwynneth something to do. She's always liked sorting out those types of situations."

"True, she might do well there. From an objective standpoint, I can't help feeling she would be a far better ruler than Arryk."

"She would be," Kendryk said. "But she'll be a help to Arryk now, though it will be a hard time for her. She was close to her father."

He shouldn't feel sorry for her. But he did anyway.

JANNA

Even though Janna tried to drink little or no wine with each toast, there were too many. Before tonight, she'd never had anything stronger than beer or ale and worried she might be drunk. After Teodora rose and left the room, Janna stood up carefully. The room spun, then straightened out while she held on to the back of her chair. The Maladene officer smoothly caught her by the arm and walked her back to Braeden, chuckling under his breath. Janna was sure he was laughing at her.

Braeden met them halfway around the table, the blonde still with him. He introduced her as Brytta Prosnitz, the empress's personal secretary.

The Maladene officer's attention shifted in an instant. Brytta was exquisite in a way Janna never could be. Naturally, all the men stared at her. But Braeden didn't. He was looking at Janna.

Back in the fragrant night air of the gardens, they both drew deep breaths at the same time. "See," Braeden said. "That wasn't so bad."

"It wasn't. It was awkward and embarrassing, but also interesting. And I wasn't frightened like I thought I would be."

"You were quite a success. Everyone complimented your beauty and your ability to reply to the empress without breaking down in tears."

"She makes people cry?"

"Often," he said cheerfully, slipping his arm around her waist as they strolled through the gardens. Moonlight glinted off the tops of the temples and from the bulk of the Arnfels, a few lights burned.

Janna leaned into him. She was sure she'd had too much wine. "Then it wasn't as bad as it could have been."

"And it's over now, isn't it? Teodora hasn't a clue who you are, and now she's had her fun at our expense, she doesn't care."

"I was so frightened before, but I'm not anymore. And I don't think it's because I've had too much to drink."

Braeden kept her close as they entered the camp. Torches lit their path. "You've faced a lot worse than her and survived. There's nothing to be afraid of."

"It's you," Janna said, as they entered his tent. "It's because of you I feel safe. You didn't let her bully me. You shocked everyone with how bold you were. I hope it doesn't cause trouble for you."

"It won't. She's used to me speaking my mind. That's what she expected."

"Thank you all the same." They faced each other in the middle of the tent. She suddenly felt awkward. Even worse, she remembered something else. "I'm afraid I'll need your help to get out of this dress."

That seemed to stop the awkwardness. "That's easy enough." Braeden turned her around. "Hook and eye?"

She nodded.

First, he took the necklace off and put it back into the box. "We'll get you a little trunk for your things."

"I don't have any things." Her only possessions in the world were two cast-off dresses.

"That will change soon enough." Braeden unfastened the hooks on the dress while Janna held it up in front. She wondered when he'd become so practiced in undoing dresses. "You'll need a few new dresses and warmer things before winter comes. I'll have Senta take you shopping while we're still in Atlona."

"I can't ..." Janna began.

He turned her around, her dress now unfastened. "Janna, stop it. I want to, all right? I like having you here and taking care of you, that's all."

She nodded, not knowing what else to say, still holding the dress up in front.

He brushed her cheek with his hand, a strange look in his eyes. "Now off to bed," he said, giving her a gentle shove toward her curtained-off corner.

"Good night," she whispered, before turning away.

Her heart pounded in her head as she lay down, trying to calm her breathing. More than anything, she wanted to climb into bed with him. The realization had been there for a while, but for the first time she let herself think it openly. What did that make her? Wasn't that just what all of those disreputable women did; climb into bed with the first man who gave them a pretty trinket?

She was sure if she went to him right now, he wouldn't turn her away. But what would happen beyond that? She didn't know if she was ready to be with a man again, although she was almost certain she could be happy with Braeden. She wondered if she could make him happy as well. Her mind wouldn't stop turning in circles, but finally she heard his even breathing, and she fell asleep, matching it.

GWYNNETH

The horses traveled well, but the land road took a long circuit away from the river, meaning they had to travel far to the west before reaching Duke Evard's lands. In sight of Emberg Castle at last, they camped in the woods and laid plans.

By now, the men had a much different view of Gwynneth. That she was traveling and sleeping rough without a complaint or even a servant to help her seemed to impress them. And she was doing this to rescue Landrus, someone they all adored.

As they sat around the fire after an appalling supper of dry biscuit and even dryer meat, Gwynneth asked everyone to gather around. "Our best chance is to catch Count Balduin at the hunt. He goes out every morning."

"What does he hunt, Your Grace?" someone asked.

Gwynneth shrugged. "Anything that moves. For someone who does it so often, he's not much good at it, so the game at Emberg survives. But the trees are riddled with lead." That brought a laugh. "Now, Balduin is not an intelligent man, but he will resist and he is strong. He usually hunts with a small escort of a groom, a beater, and one or two friends. I think none of them will offer much resistance."

"Dogs?" A man asked.

"A few. Our greatest worry is that they will sound the alarm too soon."

"What if we throw them some meat?" someone else asked.

"Good idea. I hope it tastes better to them than it does to us. If the dogs are nearby, throw them meat while the rest move on Balduin. Try to see that no one is harmed. Use the blunt ends of your pistols or swords. Balduin must be kept as uninjured as possible. I want him strong and healthy for an extended stay in the dungeons."

That brought a small cheer and shouts of, "Our princess is a right trooper."

Gwynneth smiled. "It's not done yet. Captain Merton will have specific instructions for each of you. I'll stay out of the way, but will be ready to ride to Birkenfels at speed. We make straight for the castle, put Balduin in the dungeon and lock the place up after I go. I'll handle the duke."

"He won't hurt you, will he?" Merton asked.

"He wouldn't dare. Not with his precious boy in the castle at our mercy. It helps that he thinks I'm capable of any atrocity. I will also see that Edric Maximus is well-guarded, though once I've dealt with the duke, we'll have no more worries from that quarter."

Rolled up in her cloak on the mossy ground, Gwynneth found it hard to sleep. The long ride had been exhausting, but she was exhilarated at what lay ahead.

The morning dawned cool and foggy, perfect for their plan. Gwynneth stayed near the road with a few men who had reluctantly volunteered to attend her. She wanted to be left alone, but Merton wouldn't allow it. In the distance, hounds bayed, then Merton and his party disappeared into the foggy woods.

Her horse stamped and snorted. One of the men lit a pipe. No one felt like talking. There were a few gunshots, some shouting, then there was silence again. Gwynneth wasn't sure if she could bear it. At last, Merton came crashing through the trees on his big horse. "We have him, Your Grace," he said, grinning. A few more horses, then she saw Balduin, riding his own horse, his hands tied to the pommel.

"Good morning cousin," she said.

"Don't speak to me, you whore," he burst out.

A guard backhanded him across the mouth. "You don't speak to your princess like that." Blood streamed from Balduin's mouth and Gwynneth smiled.

"Gag him," she said. "I've heard enough of his stupidity in the past few years."

Someone tied a rag into his mouth which also stopped the bleeding.

Now the horses had to prove their worth. They could lose no time getting to Birkenfels. If the duke found out soon, he could send a party large enough to stop them.

"What did you do with the others?" Gwynneth asked.

"Tied them up and left them in the forest. We turned their horses loose, so they'll be found, but hopefully not for a few hours."

"Good. I want no one raising the alarm too soon."

In less than two hours, they were at the river, clattering across the bridge as Birkenfels rose above them. Gwynneth rode into the castle with them and waited until they had locked Balduin into a cell. Merton arranged guards at all important entrances, then followed Gwynneth down to the gate.

"Raise the drawbridge," she said. "I'll deal with the duke and when he realizes he can't get to you, I'll relieve you with those I can spare from the palace." She turned to face him before mounting her horse. "I can't thank you enough. What you have done today may turn the tide for Prince Kendryk. He might be angry at first, but I'll see it's directed at me."

"Not necessary, Your Grace." Merton bowed. "It was your plan and well done. I would be happy to take any credit I can."

"I will not forget this." She pressed his hand, then rode for the palace.

She surprised everyone when she galloped into the courtyard, dirty, alone, and on a strange horse. She handed him off to a groom, then ran inside, calling for a maid. Catrin was likely on a boat sailing up the river from Kaltental. She found a young chambermaid who had helped dress her a few times. "Bring up hot water," she said. "There won't be time for a bath, but I must clean up. Can you dress hair?"

"Some simple things, Your Grace," the girl stammered, frightened and delighted at the same time.

"Simple is perfect. Now help me out of this filthy dress."

She had washed and dressed when a servant announced the duke's arrival. "I'll meet him in the entry." She had no intention of making this a long interview.

The duke stood at the foot of the stairs as she came to the top. "I knew you were behind this," he shouted. "I always knew you were no good. First you betray your husband, and then you abduct my son. I'll have you killed for this."

"You can't," Gwynneth said, gliding down the stairs and coming to a stop halfway down. "The guards at the castle will cut Balduin's throat the moment they hear that any harm has come to me, to the children, to Kendryk, or to Edric Maximus."

"Whore!" the duke spat.

Gwynneth raised an eyebrow. "You're not in a position to call me names, Uncle."

The duke ground his teeth.

She went on. "If you take your troops anywhere outside Terragand, your son dies. Is that clear?"

The duke looked startled. She'd been right, then. "How did you? I mean, what makes you think ...?"

"Oh never mind how I know. Though it seems I was right to take precautions. As long as you behave yourself and follow Kendryk's orders, as you are supposed to, no harm will come to him."

"My son will die in those cells." Balduin seemed to be his one soft spot.

"He's being kept in the best of them and will receive excellent care," Gwynneth said. "It's in all of our interests to keep him alive. Don't you agree?"

The duke's look was murderous, but there was nothing he could do. He stomped back down the hallway and out the front door.

KENDRYK

Kendryk hoped the weather held a few weeks more. It was the golden autumn, and Terragand was at its loveliest. Gold and orange trees stood against the dark of the evergreens and the grape harvest had started in the vineyards they marched past. And having so many thousands of men behind him made Kendryk feel better.

But there was a hollowness that was new; it differed from the sharp pain that came years ago with the news of his brother's death and being forced to leave Benet and Prince Gauvain in Galladium. At the time, his eleven-year-old self had thought he would die of grief. On the long journey back to Terragand, he had kept his face stern all day, but soaked his bedroll with tears every night.

Kendryk had always expected more grief in his life, at some point. He had worried about losing Landrus, and realized that death would part him from Gwynneth, in a far distant future. That Gwynneth might betray him had been beyond imagining. Perhaps it was worse because no one would talk about it even though everyone seemed to know what had happened.

The army paused its march at the crossroads into Aquianus, and Kendryk called for his officers. He was sure of his course, but wanted those with real military experience to have their say. Someone set up a table in a field and Kendryk sat down with Faris at his right, a map spread out before them. "I had thought to go straight south, through Terragand. That's what Teodora suspects, but it's by far the fastest way."

"How's the road through Aquianus?" asked DeGroot, a weathered veteran from the western islands of Zeelund. "Are they friendly?"

"The road is good though narrow as it cuts through some hilly country here." Kendryk pointed at the map. "Prince Fabrey is friendly enough. He won't offer help, but won't try to stop us either."

"It would take an extra two or three days at the rate we're moving," DeGroot said. "I doubt we can afford that."

"I doubt it too," Kendryk said. "So we'll march through Terragand. We won't surprise Teodora, but there will be many of us. Let's move on." He rose from his chair and the others stood. Suddenly, DeGroot lurched forward and vomited right onto the map. Another officer caught him before he fell and lowered him back into a chair.

Kendryk started toward him, but Faris pushed him back. "Best to stay clear until it's certain what it is, Your Grace," he said.

Kendryk looked at DeGroot, now slumped back in the chair and gasping for breath. Sweat bathed his yellowing face. Someone opened his collar to help him breathe, and then they saw the telltale red rash on his chest. If Kendryk had thought he couldn't feel any worse, he was wrong.

"Stand back," Faris said. Everyone else seemed on the verge of panic, so Kendryk composed his features as well as he could. It hadn't escaped him that DeGroot had been less than three feet away from him across the table. He might already be infected. It was on the mind of every person there, but Faris acted like it was nothing more than a head cold. "Send for the stretcher bearers and alert the doctors. They'll send people who can help."

Kendryk swallowed hard and pulled Faris aside. "But they'll be exposed," he said as softly as he could without whispering.

"They've already been exposed." Faris stepped away to let the implication sink in.

Plague.

And this was not the first case seen in camp. Kendryk prayed to the Mother that this had started in the past day or two. If the cases were few enough, the spread of the disease might still be stopped.

He wasn't sure if it was good or bad that the medical staff was so well-prepared. Two strong men came with a stretcher, their faces covered in linen masks. They picked the burly DeGroot up as if he weighed less than a child and laid him on the stretcher.

"Is it all right to handle him with bare hands?" Kendryk asked.

One voice came back, muffled by the mask. "We won't get it from touching him but we don't want him breathing on us."

"I see." Kendryk wondered how close he had to be to the man for his breath to travel that way. He felt sick, but it was most likely fear. The symptoms took a few days to show themselves. For a moment, everyone stood around, waiting for an order from Kendryk.

"Let's stay here a while longer," he said. "I need to assess the situation." He would have preferred to grab Faris by the throat and shake him. He wondered when he'd become so violent. "Count Faris, might I have a word in private?"

He turned his back on all of them and walked down the road, away from everyone.

Faris caught up to him. "I'm sorry Your Grace. There were a few scattered cases, and I didn't want to add to your burden."

"This is my burden whether I'm aware of it or not," Kendryk said through clenched teeth. "How am I supposed to make reasonable decisions when I don't know that I'm in danger of losing my army to plague?"

"You're right. I apologize."

Kendryk took a deep breath. "How long have you known about this?"

"A few days before we met you, just over a week ago, was when I heard of the first case. In the meantime we've heard of the plague found on the ships arriving in Zeelund from Cesiano. A few of these troops came off those ships."

"Someone must tell me the precise number of cases. We're not leaving this place until I know. I also want to speak to the doctor in charge of these patients as soon as possible."

"That's not advisable."

Kendryk wheeled on him. "Why not? We've already been exposed. What difference does it make?"

"Please Your Grace, don't be unreasonable. You didn't get that close to DeGroot, and neither did I. You mustn't take the chance."

"Find a way I can speak to the doctor. I'll just have to keep my distance and I suppose it won't be a confidential conversation. Not that it matters, since I always seem to be the last to learn anything of importance anyway."

"I'll arrange a meeting as soon as possible."

"Arrange it at once," Kendryk said. "Right now."

Faris nodded and walked off quickly. He wasn't used to Kendryk being a tyrant. Maybe it was time to change that. Not being a tyrant hadn't helped his cause so far.

Kendryk followed Faris, his mind whirling. He didn't know what he would do if he found out the worst. He couldn't camp here and wait for everyone to die. And yet, if they marched on, they risked spreading it to every person they encountered on the road and in the towns. By the time Kendryk faced Teodora, half his army and his country might be sick and dying.

BRAEDEN

The morning after the banquet, the Sanova Hussars received orders to invade Terragand. Prince Novitny called Braeden and the rest of his captains to the command tent. "Count Ensden will be here in a few days, most like," he said. "He and Barela will combine their forces, and march on Terragand from the south. They expect to meet resistance from Princess Sebesta in Oltena, but also expect to overcome it quickly. The defenses of Terragand itself are another matter, and we can be sure that Kendryk will meet them with a sizable force of his own.

"The empress's agents in Zeelund report that Count Faris put together infantry and artillery of at least twenty thousand veterans, while Arian Orland has another ten thousand cavalry. There have been strange rumors about Orland, but Kendryk might have planted them to create confusion. We can expect a good fight no matter what.

"We won't be part of that big army. General Barela thinks that our best chance lays in outflanking Kendryk and the empress agrees." Novitny allowed himself a smirk. "We will travel at speed through Moralta, into Sanova and attack Terragand from the east, bearing down on Kendryk's base at Birkenhof. We'll take what we need for the next week and let the wagons catch up. If you want to take your women and children, be sure they're in good condition for riding."

As they left the tent, Reno said to Braeden, "I'm sure Senta will want to stay here. She doesn't want to leave Adela's baby yet and needs to find Cara a husband before she gets herself into trouble. Janna can stay with them if you want her to."

"Not sure I want her to."

"Oh-ho." Reno punched his arm. "You've made progress, then?"

"Of a sort. She's still shy, and I don't want to frighten her any more than I already have. But if I leave her with your wife, she'll be married to someone else by the time this war is over."

"You're probably right. Senta has her heart set on matching up the two of you, but if you leave her behind, she'll think you've lost interest."

Braeden stopped in front of his tent. "I'll ask her right now."

"Ask me what?" Janna was just inside, mending by the light of the open flap.

"We leave for Terragand in a few days, on a real campaign. This will be different from Marjatya. The baggage train will be days behind and we'll bring only those who can keep up on horseback."

Braeden saw he had taken her off guard, so he sat down on the edge of his cot and waited until he caught her gaze and held it. "You'll have Zoltan, but it will be hard riding; thirty leagues a day or more, up the eastern border of Kronland. If you don't want to go, Senta is staying here and can put you up at her daughter's house. No doubt she'll find you a husband before long." He tried to say that part with a laugh, but failed.

Janna put her work into her lap and took a deep breath. "I'll come, but only if you want me to."

He felt he should make everything clear. "If it's the empress you're worried about, I don't think you need to be."

"I'm not. After last night, I'm not afraid of her anymore."

"Good. You shouldn't be. You don't mind a rough road? We'll be a few days without the tent. It'll come on the baggage train, but in the meantime you'll be rolled up in your cloak on the ground."

"I've done that often enough. And too many times without the cloak."

"All right then," he said, trying not to look as happy as he felt. "You'll want to pack things up soon, but first, I wanted to say ..." He stopped and chewed on the inside of his cheek.

He could tell she was as nervous as he was. "You could just come with the baggage. It'd be easier. But to tell the truth, I like having you close by."

She flushed, though she kept her lovely eyes on his.

"And I don't much like the idea of Senta marrying you off to someone else. Which she would."

"I know." A smile reached her lips. "Though she's had great hopes for you from the moment she first saw me, I think."

"I'm sure she did." Braeden smiled back, relieved. "I like you very much, but I understand if you're not ready for whatever comes next."

"I like you too. I don't know if I'm ready, either. But I want to go with you and see what happens."

He stood. "I'll leave you to it then," and he left in a bigger hurry than he meant to.

GWYNNETH

"He's here now, Your Grace," the footman said. It was strange, not having her ladies around her, but Gwynneth enjoyed the quiet. They would be back soon enough, full of excited chatter about their adventure.

"I'll see him in the prince's study." She stood up and smoothed her skirts. She hoped the trappings of authority might help, though she doubted it.

When she entered the room, Landrus was still standing. He was likely to make this interview as uncomfortable as possible.

"Please be seated, Maximus." She walked around Kendryk's desk to sit in his chair. "This might take a while."

Landrus took a seat on the edge of a leather chair. "I would ask what you mean by all of this, but it's pointless. It's clear you will do whatever you wish."

She felt indignation rising, but pushed it back down. She gained nothing by losing her temper. "I have good reason."

"I'm sure you think you do." He'd clenched his teeth and there was a sharp line between his eyes. She'd never seen him so angry. "Several guardsmen told me your so-called concerns about the Duke of Emberg and I doubt my safety was the reason behind your rash action."

"It was, in part. You are dear to Kendryk and I doubt he could go on if something happened to you. And you can't deny it was a possibility that the duke might try something with no one resident at Birkenhof."

"I could have dealt with him," Landrus said, his jaw still tight. "You forget, I have armed men at my disposal now."

"I know. I would rather not take chances with your valuable person, all the same." She turned a blinding, false smile on him. She wondered if he might lose his temper. That would be something to witness. "I do have another motive. Knowing the duke as I do, I realized he could convince himself that the right and patriotic thing would be to join Teodora's forces. I cannot allow that to happen and holding Balduin hostage will ensure that it doesn't."

"Evard's militia wouldn't turn the tide," Landrus scoffed. He seemed less tense, but his voice was still much louder than it normally was in conversation.

"No. But while the duke might not fight for Kendryk with enthusiasm, his troops will. And we need them here in Terragand." She leaned forward. "Birkenhof is unguarded right now and I'm sure the empress will hear of it, from the duke if from no one else. I am sure she will send a force ahead to strike at us before Kendryk can reach her."

That seemed to shake him. "You think so? How would that help her?"

"She would get the same benefit as I do from holding Balduin. If she gets her claws into me or you, or Holy Mother forbid, one of the children, she can force Kendryk to stop everything. We must be strong enough here to hold them off until he can engage her directly. From what I've heard of the force Count Faris has assembled, they are excellent on the battlefield, but such troops are of little use scattered all over the countryside. Under no circumstances must Kendryk break up his army. Without Orland's cavalry, he can't afford it."

"It seems you've thought of everything," Landrus said, his tone still unpleasant.

"I've tried to. I'm hoping to receive more information soon because I'd like to be more sure of what we're facing. My greatest fear is Teodora sending the Sanova Hussars against us in force. They survived the siege of Atlona with few casualties. You remember those fearsome-looking brutes surrounding the empress in Isenwald? Now picture seven thousand of them, or more."

" Duke Evard's force can't stand against that."

"You're right," Gwynneth said. "And if I find they're coming, I'll take other measures. I'm having the castle provisioned to survive a long siege. If the hussars come our way, all of us must take refuge there until Kendryk can relieve us."

"I suppose you expect me to join you," Landrus said with a sour look.

"I do. With any luck we won't be there long so we won't have to spend too much time together."

"That would be a relief."

"There is no need to be rude." She held her temper with some effort. "I'm doing this for Kendryk, not for you."

"He won't be pleased when he hears of what you've done."

"He'll be angry I'm sure. But I'd prefer he didn't find out until it's necessary. I trust you haven't sent a message to him yet?"

"I was waiting until I had spoken to you."

"Good. Please do not send one now."

"What happens if I do?"

"I will stop any messengers leaving Heidenhof and shoot down any pigeons. It is important that Kendryk stay at the head of his army and not leave at such a critical time. It would be bad for morale."

"Not as bad as being forced to exile his most powerful ally."

She would not allow him to goad her. "No." She kept her tone even. "But that's done, though I would undo it if I could, and not for the reason you think. What's important now is to not make the situation worse. And Kendryk coming back here right now would be worse. Surely you can see that."

"Yes," Landrus said, grudgingly.

"I understand your feelings about me and I don't blame you for them. But you have done your part, and the rest is between me and Kendryk. Is that clear?" She put authority in her voice.

Landrus sat up straighter. "Clear enough. What you're doing is sensible, but please involve me as little as possible. It would be best if we didn't have to work together unless it's necessary."

"You're right," Gwynneth said, with more emphasis than was polite. "If need arises, I'll send for you." She stood, indicating the end of the interview.

By the time Gwynneth returned to the library, a messenger waited. Hope sprang into her chest, and she wondered if there was a letter from Kendryk. But it subsided as she realized he didn't yet know she had returned to Birkenhof.

Gwynneth opened the worn, dirty message pouch and pulled out a letter addressed to her, but written in an unfamiliar scrawl. She scanned the page down to the signature and seal, then nearly fell into her chair. It was from Arian Orland. The message came from Moralta several days ago, and he was making his way south, into Marjatya.

"I beg your forgiveness, my darling, though I have no right to call you so. I realize I have caused you a great deal of pain," he wrote.

"It's late for that now, isn't it?" Gwynneth muttered to herself and kept reading.

He went on in that vein for a while, then mentioned how terrible he felt about betraying Kendryk, who had shown him only trust and friendship. Late for that, too, Gwynneth thought.

Being apart from her made him realize that he truly loved her and this had not just been a carnal episode.

Gwynneth snorted.

He realized that they could never be together, but wanted to make amends, help in some way. How he proposed to do that from Marjatya was anyone's guess. He added a few garbled words about joining up with Andor Korma and raising a new army, but she couldn't imagine how that would help Kendryk. She didn't know what the purpose of the letter was, besides a request for absolution she was unlikely to give.

A more romantic soul might have thought several smears at the bottom of the page were tears, although knowing Arian, Gwynneth thought it more likely that they were mud. She threw the letter down on her desk and paced along the windows. The day had become warm and sultry, with dark clouds building overhead. There would be a storm.

The tears came suddenly. She had hoped the worst of the guilt and despair had passed, but it seemed not. Relieved that she was alone, she gave herself over to them completely for the first time. She sank into a heap on the carpet and cried. Thunder crashed, sheets of rain pounded the windows and she cried harder. The rain had decreased to occasional drops and the lowering sun was breaking through the clouds when she stopped at last.

She picked herself up, walked back to her desk and sat down. The letter she wrote was short. *"Everything between us is over. If you wish to redeem yourself, do it for Kendryk and not for me. You must face the empress and win. If you ever cared for either one of us, see you stop her before she enters Terragand."* She addressed it to Count Orland, anywhere in Marjatya and told the footman to take it to the messenger.

JANNA

It was strange seeing Moralta like this. Before the war, she almost never left Kaleva, and then only for a half-day excursion when the weather was fine, or to go sledding on a hill nearby. Here on the border with Kronland, the country was rugged and wild since most towns of any size were further east. The weather remained pleasant though the nights were cool.

Janna enjoyed traveling this way, at the back of the column, but not in the midst of the enormous baggage train. Zoltan was happy to be on campaign again and Janna found herself comfortable with him; she could even jump down without help and spring back into the saddle as well as Franca.

She still felt that Franca did not quite approve of her and understood why. At first she had thought it was simple jealousy, but Franca didn't seem to have any romantic feelings toward Braeden. She looked up to him a great deal, but was protective as well, seeing Janna as a silly baggage who might take advantage of him, or worse, break his heart. Janna hoped she would do neither.

Few women had come, except for some officer's wives of the tougher sort, veterans of many campaigns who no longer had small children. There were also two newlyweds, just married in Atlona. They had it the worst, away from home for the first time, saddle-sore and sleeping on the ground every night. Compared to them, Janna was more like the hardened veterans. She liked the idea.

Moralta was quiet, the rebellion largely subdued. The hussars worried about attacks from inside Kronland, but they followed the border of Podoska, ruled by the fierce Princess Martinek, without incident. Janna wondered if anyone knew they were coming.

Now that she no longer feared Teodora, her mind seemed clearer. She still found it impossible to talk about the children to anyone, but she could think about them without being overcome by grief and horror. In fact, she sometimes sensed that Anton was still alive. She didn't know how or where, but something inside her was certain, and that comforted her. Tough and resourceful as he was, she was sure he'd make the best of any situation he found himself in.

That night, they made camp well inside the borders of Sanova. The few women joined the men around the cook fires and the atmosphere was easy and companionable. Someone with an accordion started a song and before long, someone else was dancing. After helping clean the cooking things in a nearby stream, Janna came back and sat down next to Braeden. She laughed as Prince Novitny grabbed someone's wife and launched into a Sanovan peasant dance.

"You laughed," Braeden said.

"I did, didn't I?" She turned and smiled at him.

"I'm glad. I thought this would be difficult for you. So many leagues a day and living like we are."

"It's luxurious compared to what things were like after Kaleva. And for the first time in months, I feel a little better. Almost like I'm on holiday."

"Some holiday." Braeden grinned. "And I apologize for the prince's dancing."

"It's funny."

"It's not meant to be," he said, but he smiled all the same. He glanced up at the sky, clear and blanketed with stars. "It will be colder tonight. I'll get one of the extra blankets. Hope you don't mind sharing."

He said it lightly, but Janna caught the heat in his voice. Since leaving Atlona, they'd been sleeping side-by-side on the ground every night, each of them wrapped up in a warm cloak by a banked fire. They'd get even closer tonight.

GWYNNETH

It was as Gwynneth had feared. Teodora was sending the Sanova Hussars ahead to attack Birkenhof. Her source was reliable, and already in Moralta when sending the message.

She prepared for the worst. At least the harvest had been good and money was flowing into the treasury. She had worked on lists of supplies needed for the castle so piles of long-lasting and preserved foods and fuel were already filling its spacious cellars.

The next step was moving anything of value from the palace. It was impossible to take everything, since every piece of furniture, every rug, every tapestry was valuable, if not priceless. But she could take smaller items, all the family treasure and all of her considerable jewelry. She packed plenty of warm, plain clothes for herself and the children, and in several sizes, in case they grew in the months there.

Then she wrote a message to Landrus, telling him to be ready to move into the castle. She asked that he send a wagon with anything larger and heavier ahead and she would have it put in his old rooms.

By now, Avaron and Linette had returned and considered themselves seasoned campaigners, so they had become more useful than ever. Linette even volunteered to ride to Heidenhof herself to deliver Gwynneth's message.

"Help him decide what to bring and escort it back," Gwynneth said. "He likes you and is more likely to do as you ask than if it comes as an order from me."

"I believe I can manage him," Linette said, then trotted down the long avenue at a smart pace.

She returned late, glowing with success, a small cart hitched to her horse. "All of his finished works are in there. I'll see they are brought to the castle tomorrow. He was not happy about it, but I persuaded him to join us there whenever you send the word. I told him you had everything in hand and we'd likely never have to go there."

"Good." Gwynneth smiled at her. "You've done well. If the worst happens and we are all forced to live together up there, you can be my liaison."

She hadn't taken Linette to be a religious sort, so she was surprise to find her curled up in the drawing room after supper, reading a lengthy Landrus tract on the Life and Work of Ercos.

"Is it interesting?" Gwynneth asked.

"Marvelous. I never knew about any of this. I do wish you would also read it, Your Grace."

Gwynneth did her best to conceal her amusement at her flightiest lady-in-waiting turned missionary. Perhaps if it came to a siege, and she was overcome by boredom she'd be forced to become a Landrus acolyte herself, just to find reading materials.

The next morning, she went to visit Balduin. Gwynneth wrinkled her nose and pulled her cloak closer. It was cold in the dungeon and it smelled bad. She had expected that, but it was still unpleasant. She didn't have to go far, since she kept Balduin on the highest level, in one of the nearest cells.

As she approached it, the guard banged on the bars. "On your feet. The princess is here to see you."

There was some rustling and grumbling and then her prisoner stood at the bars, blinking in the sudden torchlight.

She smiled at him. "How are you doing? Not too uncomfortable, I hope?"

He muttered something rude, then turned his back.

"Hey." The guard poked him through the bars with a sheathed sword.

"It's all right. I wanted to make sure he was alive and well so I can reassure his father."

"He'll kill you on sight." Balduin snarled and lunged at the bars.

Gwynneth took one step back. "No, he won't. We've already spoken and he won't lay a hand on me. It's touching really, how much he loves you. He'll do anything to keep you unharmed. You should be pleased."

It worked. Balduin's face took on a kind of glow. She knew he cared for nothing in the world so much as to please Evard.

"I may bring him here to prove that you're in good condition. If I do, you will speak only when spoken to. If you make a scene, you will spend the rest of your days in a far more unpleasant cell, in which case those days will be very short. Is that understood?"

Balduin narrowed his eyes and huffed, but nodded.

"Good." She turned and went back down the corridor. The duke would be here before too long in response to her message. She liked having him at her beck and call.

KENDRYK

Kendryk longed for Landrus with his cool and calm faith that would tell him to pray and trust in the gods. He longed for Gwynneth, and her practical, optimistic advice. She, more than anyone, would assess the situation and make the best of it. But by now she was in her father's court, immersing herself in the intrigue.

At least he had done that right. Across the water Gwynneth would be safe from the plague. He tried very hard not to worry about the children and thanked the gods for Birkenhof's current isolation.

But his concern right now was his army. Kendryk made his way back through the troops, who parted before him. He wondered how many of them were already infected, but reckoned it would be best to show no fear. So he smiled at all he passed, several times asking directions to the hospital wagons.

These sat in a field at a distance from the rest of the baggage train. A few men were putting up a tent since it was easier for the doctors to work if they had space and light. Kendryk walked up to it without hesitating. "Can someone tell me where I might find the chief doctor?"

"She'll be at the head cart, talking to that count fellow." The man doffed his cap, uncertain as to Kendryk's identity.

Kendryk saw Faris talking to a short, sturdy woman in white. She turned as he joined them. "Your Grace should put on one of these," she said without preamble, handing Kendryk a linen mask to tie over his mouth and nose. "It's not foolproof, but better than nothing."

Faris was tying his on.

"You needn't come," Kendryk said. "In fact, I want you to return to camp. I'll confer with the doctor and send for you later." He turned back to the doctor and heard Faris leave after a moment's hesitation. "What's your name?"

"Etta Darstel." Her voice was as weary as her face. "I'm glad you've come. I have ideas for treatment, but the orders must come from you."

"Tell me." Kendryk tied on his mask. "But first I want to see the patients."

"Are you sure?" Doctor Darstel fastened on her mask as well. "A few are far gone. In most cases, the sickness takes only five days, from first symptoms to death."

Kendryk shuddered. "I'd like to see." That was a lie. He would have given anything to be anywhere else right now. If Teodora had been standing in front of him, he would have surrendered to her without hesitation to spare himself this.

The doctor led him to the wagon that held the three worst cases. Kendryk had to bite his tongue until it bled to keep from whimpering like a child. Just three days of this sickness and they were no more than yellow skin hanging from their bones, with black splotches covering their bodies. These were beyond all help, the doctor told him, though a fair minority seemed to survive by never getting quite that sick.

The less severe cases were all being taken into the tent. "The fresh air seems to do them good," the doctor said. "And it helps to get a break from the jolting of the wagon."

Kendryk nodded, feeling hopeful. There seemed to be less than twenty cases of the plague itself. A few remaining patients in the wagons had other illnesses or wounds.

As they walked back to the front he asked, "How can we stop this?"

Doctor Darstel sighed. "It's too late. If we'd been able to quarantine the first few cases, we might have had a chance."

"Why wasn't that done?" Kendryk kept his voice gentle, knowing it was not her fault.

"No one would give the order. It was several days before you arrived and everyone seemed to think it best to wait."

Kendryk shook his head. Everyone included Faris, but also DeGroot, who now lay unconscious in the tent. Kendryk made a point of looking for him. He wondered if Faris had planned to let him know before arriving at Birkenhof with a plague-ridden army.

"Can we still quarantine?" he asked. "Several of us were exposed just now. What if we stayed apart for a few days until symptoms appear, or not?"

"If you can spare the time, it might be worth trying." Her tone was sympathetic. She understood how desperately he needed a solution. "But by now, so many have been exposed, there's no point."

"I understand. All right then. How can I help you? I can't stop the whole army if a quarantine won't work, but I can give you more help and find a better place for you to set up a hospital. We can send any new cases back to you."

Her face lit up. "That would be helpful. In this fine weather, the tent works well, but this might go on for weeks or months. A roof over our heads would be welcome."

"I'll find one." He might have to turf a lord out of his manor house, but Kendryk didn't care.

He took off his mask. "Thank you for showing me everything and for your honest opinion. I'll find accommodation and send you further instruction."

Kendryk walked back to the front of the column, trying to remember who lived near here. By the time he'd reached Faris, who looked at him warily, he knew. "I have a job for you," Kendryk said. "I know Baron Torsten has a nice solid house of some size not far from here. Tell him we need to borrow it for a time. He must move out by morning, I'm afraid. Give him gold if he complains."

Faris stared at him. "Your Grace, I don't understand."

"It's simple. We need a hospital. With proper care, many can survive this plague. We also need a place we can send new patients. The Torsten house should be big enough. I don't want sick soldiers traveling across the countryside, spreading disease everywhere."

"The baron won't like it."

"I don't care. I don't like it either, but something has to be done since it's too late to do what's easier and more effective." He let the implicit accusation linger.

Faris hesitated, then turned away. Kendryk hoped he wouldn't hear any more about it. He had been too kind all these years, with everyone around him thinking they could do as they pleased.

While he waited for Faris's return, he walked to a stand of trees and sank down on the grass in the shade. He needed to pray, and this was the only place he could. A great fir towered over him, large and comforting, as he had always thought of the Father. He was beginning to understand what Landrus had been trying to teach him. He could kill himself trying to do his best, but he had to trust he was on the path the gods had ordained for him. And if that path was wrong, it was too late to change now.

JANNA

When it was time to sleep, Janna curled up in near the fire. Husbands and wives often put their cloaks together and took advantage of the closeness, judging by the noises. By now it was no use denying she wanted the same, but Janna still couldn't get over the embarrassing lack of privacy.

Braeden seemed to have no such worry as he spread the heavy wool blanket over her and lay down next to her while pulling it up over himself. "You'll have to come closer for this to work." He slid his arm under her shoulders as she scooted nearer. "I have a draft going up my backside."

She giggled and left her head pillowed on his arm. He used his free arm to pull the blanket most of the way over their heads. It got warmer fast.

"This reminds me of sleeping with my sisters," Janna said.

"That's not quite what I had in mind," Braeden said, with a laugh.

"No, no, that's not what I meant. When I was little, I shared a bed with two of my sisters. We'd pull the covers over our heads so we could talk without disturbing the others. Otherwise, this is very different." It was, and lovely. She had never even slept like this with her own husband.

"Tell me about your sisters. How many do you have?"

"Four, all of them older."

"That's a lot of girls in one house."

"Oh, yes. My poor father. He tried to marry us off as fast as he could."

"Surely not you, the baby?"

"Me most of all. By the time I was sixteen, my oldest sister was a widow with two little ones and living with us. The second oldest and her husband still lived there too, while they saved money to buy their own house. It was crowded, to say the least."

"So they foisted you off on an old troublemaker."

"It wasn't like that. Dimir was a good match. He had money, a good reputation, a nice house, and he was kind. Back then no one expected he would get involved in radical politics. Still, I didn't want to do it until I met the children. I fell in love with them right away ..." She trailed off, and a tear slid down her nose.

They were silent for a moment, but she knew he was still awake because his fingers stroked her hair. Tears had run into her mouth, so to distract herself she asked, "Why don't you tell me how you met the prince?"

"It's not a nice story."

"Will you tell me anyway? I want to know." She put her hand against his cheek.

After a long silence, he sighed then spoke. "I was eight years old, living on the eastern coast of Anglana. My father was a fisherman, and I had two sisters, one older, one younger. My mother worked mending nets, so we ran wild most of the time. One day raiders came, probably from Estenor. My father never even made it to shore. Once they'd killed all the men, they started in on the rest of us."

Janna stopped a sob from rising in her throat. "Oh gods." She stroked his cheek with her finger.

"They killed my little sister and then my mother after they—well, you know what happens as well as anyone."

"In front of you?" She couldn't stop the tears now.

"Yes."

"How did you bear it?"

"Because I had to. What else was I going to do? They carried me and my older sister off to their ships, though I never saw her again, either."

Now Janna cried, in great gulping sobs. Braeden kept stroking her hair, then wiped her eyes with the corner of the blanket.

When she could speak again, she said, "It's too dreadful. You would have been younger than my Anton. He's almost ten, and oh gods, he saw all of that too. But you survived and did all right."

"I did. There's no need to cry over it now. It was almost thirty years ago and I never think about it. Your boy will be all right too."

Janna loved him for his calm assumption that Anton lived, and in that moment she knew her heart was safe. The past still haunted her, but more than anyone, Braeden had helped her realize that her life wasn't over and she might be happy again. She moved closer, wrapping her arm around his waist and resting her cheek on his chest, feeling his solid bulk protecting her from everything bad. "Now tell me the rest."

Braeden wrapped both arms around her. "The raiders sold me to the Novitny estate, which has a huge salt mine. It makes them richer than the Sanovan queen. I never saw the inside of it, and it's a good thing. I found out later the slaves lasted less than a year, the children maybe six months."

"Oh, how could they?"

"They don't anymore. At least not like that. It was a terrible waste of money, especially when slaves became scarce and more expensive. So, they were bringing me off the ship with all the others, and the prince and his father were down at the docks. The prince spotted me and decided he wanted me for a pet. He was a stubborn bugger even then and wouldn't let his father alone until he'd told the overseer to let me go."

"How wonderful."

"Terrifying more like. I didn't understand a word they said. The prince's father looked like a barbarian king and even as a little boy the prince himself looked as fierce as he does today. I thought they would have me for dinner, or worse."

"Oh dear." Janna pictured a small Prince Novitny, braided beard and all. "But they didn't."

"No. The little prince had no brothers or sisters and needed a playmate. I figured it out soon enough and then we were always together. They educated me right alongside him though neither of us learned much; we were more interested in riding horses and playing with swords."

"That I can imagine. How very fortunate you were. Unfortunate at first but then something good happened after all."

She sensed, rather than saw him nod.

"That's how I feel," she whispered. "Unfortunate because of all of those terrible things that happened since spring, but fortunate now." Before the tears came again, she tucked her head under his chin and fell asleep to the rhythm of his heartbeat.

GWYNNETH

After the foulness of the dungeon, it was a relief to step back into the crisp autumn air. Gwynneth crossed the castle's little courtyard, enjoying the view of the bright blue sky. She was meeting Duke Evard here because she could force him to leave his men outside the walls. That would be far more difficult at the palace.

She went into the little library that Landrus had used during his earlier stay. All of his things would be brought here later in the day.

"He's here, Your Grace," Merton said. In spite of Landrus's public dislike of her, Merton remained her stout supporter, all while never giving up his hero worship of the maximus. Gwynneth admired his flexibility.

"Send him to me." She took a seat behind the heavy old desk, the window at her back.

The duke swept in, stomping up the stairs. "I must protest my men being detained."

"They're not being detained, Uncle. I simply don't want them all crowding in here. It's a lovely day and they can enjoy it until you return."

"You have some nerve, sending for me like this," the duke huffed.

"It's a friendly request from one family member to another."

"Family doesn't kidnap each other."

"Depends on the family." Gwynneth smiled. "I think we are still well-behaved compared to say the Inferraras, or the Martinek clan." Over the past centuries, members of those families had an alarming tendency to die under suspicious and sometimes violent circumstances. Most recently, it had been the mentally feeble but otherwise healthy emperor who died of an unexplained fever overnight, with Teodora conveniently available for coronation the following day.

She continued. "I invited you here because I have news that concerns all of us and I will need your help."

"It's not like I can refuse, is it?" the duke grumbled.

"True. But on to the news. I have received word that the empress is unleashing the Sanova Hussars upon us. They are traveling through Moralta at speed and plan to overrun our eastern border. I'm sure they hope to take Birkenhof and outflank Kendryk before he can meet her in battle."

The duke sat up straighter. "You are sure of this?"

Gwynneth nodded. "I have reliable sources at the Atlona court and one amongst the hussars themselves. Kendryk is making his way south, but all the same, we must do what we can to stop them ourselves. He cannot fight on two fronts."

"I agree with you," the duke said, to Gwynneth's surprise. He adored all things military and had forgotten for the moment that he wanted nothing to do with her or her plans.

"Your forces will need to face the hussars. I'm sure they will make short work of our border defenses. I also expect they'll make short work of your troops, but if we're clever about it, we may slow them down while minimizing your casualties."

"My troops are well-trained," Evard protested. "I know they can meet the hussars in the field."

"I'm sure you have done well with them." Gwynneth was feeling charitable at the moment. "But they are a force of at least seven thousand and you cannot field over three. That needn't be a disadvantage if we make the most of the terrain and our knowledge of the country."

She unrolled a map laying at her elbow. "They will come through the Garsten Gap, right here." She pointed, and the duke leaned forward, clearly interested against his will. "You could post musketeers all along here to pick them off as they come through. At its narrowest, they'll be able to ride no more than two abreast. It will be key to surprise them, but I'm sure you can manage that."

"But if we hold them off there, they will go south," the duke said, now engrossed. "At some point, they will meet with Teodora's army if she comes up through Oltena."

"Yes, they will. But it will give us a reprieve here, and if Kendryk is quick enough, he will meet Teodora before the hussars can join her. That will give him a much better chance."

Evard suddenly seemed to remember the situation. "That's all well for you, but I don't see how it benefits me."

"Simple. Balduin remains alive and well."

"How can I be sure you haven't already killed him or he isn't dying of a fever?"

"Let's pay him a short visit so you can see for yourself. I told him to expect you." The eager, hopeful look that flashed across the duke's dour features was almost touching. Gwynneth had been right in assuming Balduin was his softest spot.

Leading the way, she allowed the duke to master himself on the way down, if he needed to. Guards flanked her and there were more when they reached the dungeon.

It was a short interview.

"Are you well?" the duke asked.

Balduin's expression was pitiful. "Father," he gasped.

Gwynneth hardened her heart.

"Tell me how you are," Evard demanded, his angry mask back in place.

"I'm well enough," Balduin said. "When can you get me out of here?"

"Remember what we spoke of," Gwynneth warned.

"All in good time," the duke said, calmer now. She was sure he was already devoting his thoughts to the coming campaign, now he knew his son was safe. "When all of this is over, I'm sure we'll be able to come to an accommodation. Don't you agree, Princess?"

"Absolutely," Gwynneth said. "I have no wish to keep you here any longer than is necessary. Now, Uncle, if you're satisfied that all is well, it's time to go. There is much to be done."

The duke nodded at Balduin, then turned away. He would never show his feelings. No wonder Balduin was such an idiot.

The duke was silent until they were back in the courtyard. "We will resolve this, Princess." His old manner had returned full-bore. "Of that you can be sure."

"I am. In the meantime, you will be on your way east by dusk tomorrow. I'll expect your best efforts."

"I always give my best effort," the duke sniffed, before turning to the gate.

Once everyone else had gone to bed, Gwynneth sat down at her desk, alone in the library. She had saved the most important task for last. A shudder went over her when she pictured Kendryk at the head of an army facing one even greater. He would not stay back since he would never ask his soldiers to do what he was unwilling to. She pushed the thoughts of him dead and wounded out of her mind. She could not lessen the danger by worrying about it. Far better to distract the Sanova Hussars and get Arian Orland's help.

It was hard to begin the letter. Since he thought her well away in Norovaea, she started with why she had come back. She gave no names of those who had helped her, only saying they had done it out of loyalty to him and to Landrus.

"I could not risk your uncle taking matters into his own hands. I have taken measures to assure the safety of Edric Maximus." She detailed her plan to make Evard hold off the hussars, and Kendryk's need to be speedy. *"If you can meet Teodora before the hussars reach her, you will have a much better chance at success."* She didn't mention her hope that Arian Orland would help. Then came the hard part.

"You were very upset the last time we spoke, and I understand if you still are. But I do not know when we will next see each other and I cannot bear the idea of dreadful things happening to either one of us without some clarity. I beg your forgiveness, make no excuses for my behavior and understand if you find it unforgivable. I will love you no less and will always work tirelessly to help you in any way I can.

"Do not fear for Birkenhof, the children or the maximus. I have made provision for siege and everyone here will be safe. Do not worry about us and think only about facing Teodora. No matter what happens, I love you more than anything. The children send their love and miss you terribly."

That was enough. She copied the message into the private cipher she and Kendryk used. Though she didn't mean to be melodramatic by covering her writing with tears, a few dropped at the bottom anyway, smearing her signature. She sealed it, then sent a sleepy servant to take it to the messenger who would ride out at dawn. Now all she could do was wait.

BRAEDEN

The Sanova Hussars were deep into Terragand now. They had crossed the border with little trouble. There had been a challenge from a castle near the main road, but the small force had fled when they saw the thousands of hussars bearing down upon them. At this rate, they would be upon Birkenhof by the next evening. Unfortunately, the terrain wasn't so agreeable.

Novitny sent for Braeden as they approached a range of low, but steep hills. "There's a road through that gap." He pointed straight ahead. "It's just a few leagues to the other side, but it's a good spot for an ambush."

"If anyone's there," Braeden said. "Isn't Prince Kendryk further west? Aside from the few at the border, it seems everyone is with him."

"Until now. But we're nearing his home. I doubt he'd take any chances, and that's the perfect place for a small force to trap a larger one. It would take less than a regiment of musket to cause us all kinds of trouble."

"A few of us can take a look." Braeden didn't mind a bit of scouting. "If we run into trouble, we'll come back. If we get through all right, we'll send a message back and make sure no one comes in from the other side. How many should I take?"

"A few hundred. Enough to make it look like we're all coming in. I want you in full armor with all weapons loaded. You might well have a fight on your hands."

Braeden rode back to where Gergo led the horse carrying his armor and extra weapons. "Gather up five banners," he told Miro. "We ride into that gap in an hour."

Janna was nearby and came to help Gergo get everything down from the packhorse.

"Will it be very dangerous?" she asked, frowning. "That forest looks so deep and dark." Even though many of the leaves were falling, the evergreens grew close together here, forming a wall broken only by the road leading into it.

"Might be," Braeden said, while she helped him get his mail shirt over his head. She was much stronger than she had been just a month before. "That's why a few of us are going ahead while the rest of you wait here. We'll find out what's what and report back."

"Why do you have to be the one to go?" Janna looked worried.

"I'm always the one to go." He'd never thought of that before but it was true.

"That doesn't seem fair. Everyone should bear equal risk, don't you think?"

"That's not how it works," he said, while Gergo buckled on his cuirass and Janna held the pauldrons ready for him. "Besides, for something like this, better I go, than someone with a family, eh?"

"Yes, but ..." She chewed on her lip, while he realized what he'd said.

He grinned at her. "Seems things are different now, and I'm not used to it yet."

Her face brightened.

"Still, I volunteered, and I'll go. Don't worry. It always turns out."

"I'll pray to the Mother to protect you." She helped with the pauldrons while Trisa loaded his pistols and made sure the powder in his horn was dry. He doubted he'd have time to reload, but it was best to be prepared.

Before he mounted Kazmir, he took Janna's small hand in his gauntleted one. "If all goes well, I'll see you on the other side in a few hours. If not, I'll be back soon." He smiled and squeezed her hand until she smiled back.

Weighed down as he was, he needed two men to boost him onto Kazmir. He grinned down at Janna one more time and kept smiling as he joined the rest of them on the road. He'd had women before, but none of them ever felt anything like a family. This was different, and he didn't dislike it. Now he had to make sure he didn't get picked off by a musket so he could enjoy the feeling for a while.

He explained to the officers what they might expect once they got into the woods. "The road likely cuts through rock. There'll be trees and brush on top of the rocks, a good hiding place for muskets. Keep your eyes and ears open and shoot at anything that moves. Visors up for now." When they were down, it was hard to see and hear, and peripheral vision was nonexistent.

Braeden took his place at the head of the column. Franca and Miro flanked him. They never failed to volunteer for expeditions like these. They squabbled as usual, but Braeden shushed them as they entered the woods. "No point in letting them know how far away we are," though he suspected anyone inside would know already.

The populace so far had been docile, but he was sure they had been watching the hussars all along the road. A surprise attack on Birkenhof was unlikely though it could still be a success.

The woods muffled all sound as they entered. A cool breeze had been blowing, but it was still amongst the trees. The horse's hooves clomped on the hard-packed dirt of the road and there was an occasional clank of armor, but the deep quiet swallowed up even those sounds. The trees were tall and wide, probably hundreds of years old.

Braeden was alert, and once they entered a defile between limestone cliffs twenty feet high, he slowed down and pulled out both pistols, pulling the firing mechanism back. Others did the same.

He had strung his troop out so they would not all be in one place, but if there was to be an ambush, it would be after most of them had entered the gap. He was right. The report of a musket rang out and there was a loud ping as the ball bounced off someone's armor.

"Fire only if you see them," Braeden shouted, though he didn't know if anyone heard. A dozen reports followed the first and somewhere behind him a horse went down. He glimpsed movement above him in the trees and fired without aiming. Either he or someone else got lucky because a body crashed through the brush and thudded onto the road in front of him.

Braeden glanced at it. The light armor of the musketeer covered the blue and silver colors of Bernotas. Thank Ercos for Novitny's good instincts.

Considering the tremendous disadvantage of the hussar's position, they were faring well. But Braeden wasn't taking any chances. Bernotas had thousands of muskets and they might all be in the trees above and ahead. "Fall back," he shouted, reloading as Kazmir turned. The horse understood orders better than most humans.

The hussars peeled away, two at a time to follow him, firing as they went. He was glad that most were still upright. Even the horse that had gone down was standing again. Perhaps it had stumbled in the confusion.

Word had been passed to the back, so by the time Braeden reached the second rank, at least half his force was back out of the limestone gap. He caught flashes of blue in the trees, but they didn't follow the hussars out of the woods.

As soon as they were clear, Braeden stopped by the side of the road and counted the rest as they passed. Everyone was accounted for. One young ensign had a bloody leg, and two horses had minor wounds, but for all the bullets and smoke, they had done well. And now they knew what lay ahead.

Braeden cantered back through the ranks to reach Novitny.

"Just as I thought," the prince said. "Any idea how many?"

"Several hundred at least. We didn't get far into the gap, so if they're ranged all along it, there might be a lot more."

"Bernotas?"

"Without a doubt. Don't know about the prince himself, but they all wore his colors. We got a few and saw them through the trees."

"Regulars then, interesting. The boy may be in a hard spot, but we shouldn't underestimate him. Let's go sit down and decide what's next."

Novitny spread out a map across a hastily erected table. "We could fight our way through, I'm sure, but it would cost us time, and at least a few troopers and horses. It's not worth it. Rather than go through the gap, we can go around. It will take an extra day or two, but from there we'll still be only a day's march from Birkenhof."

"We'll lose the element of surprise," Reno said.

"We've lost it already," Novitny replied. "If we head south and take this road," he pointed at one that looped around the mountain range they faced, "We might meet our baggage train before the end of the day."

That seemed agreeable since everyone had tired of sleeping on the ground and eating terrible rations. And tired of the lack of privacy, Braeden noted to himself.

"We might also meet the empress," Novitny said. "She, Ensden and Barela are making good time and have reached southern Terragand. It seems they met no resistance to the south."

"Not even from Princess Sebesta?" Everyone assumed Prince Kendryk's aunt would do what she could to slow the empress.

"At least nothing that couldn't be dealt with quickly. All in agreement?"

All were. They stood up and prepared to go.

Braeden found Janna and Gergo rubbing down Kazmir.

Janna gave a small cry when she saw him and dropped the brush. "You're hurt," she said, and ran to him.

"No, I'm not." He held onto her all the same.

"There's blood all over your face." She wiped her hand against his face. It came away red.

"Well, I'll be. Must have been a rock or a bit of metal. No harm done."

"You're all right then?" She made no move to pull away.

"Of course I'm all right. Nothing to worry about at all."

She collapsed against his cuirass for a moment and when she pulled back she said, "The noise was dreadful in there and it went on for ages. I was sure that all of you were dead though no one else was too worried."

"It's always a noisy business. Now help me out of this armor will you? We're heading south. With any luck, we'll eat real food tonight and maybe even sleep in a real tent."

"I'd like that," she said, smiling.

KENDRYK

"It's impossible." Kendryk jumped up and nearly overturned the little table functioning as a field desk. He kept reading, feeling more incredulous as he continued. "Send for Count Faris," he said without looking up, and the adjutant disappeared.

Faris was there in minutes. "What's happened Your Grace?" his face was weary and concerned. "More bad news?"

"I'm not sure." Kendryk sat back down and read the pertinent parts to Faris, who smiled when he had finished.

"Your wife is an extraordinary woman, you must admit." He chuckled. "Though the news of the Sanova Hussars is worrying, she has done you a good turn."

"By kidnapping my cousin?" He had no affection for Balduin, but didn't like the idea of anyone in his family in the castle dungeon.

Faris shrugged. "In doing so she has ensured your uncle's cooperation, however reluctant. It's without question better than the alternative."

"I suppose so." Kendryk put down the letter. "I'm glad she's taking measures to keep herself and the children safe. It's unbearable to imagine what might have happened had the Sanovans come upon them unawares and unguarded." A cold chill crept over his spine. "She also says that Edric Maximus will join them in the castle, should the need arise."

"That's interesting," Faris said, implying that Gwynneth had no reason to be helpful to Landrus, and he had none to be cooperative. "And not a bad thing. It's imperative he not fall into imperial hands."

"I agree. But now what do we do? This is completely unexpected."

"Will your uncle be able to withstand the hussars?"

"I doubt it. Even if he tries, he's outnumbered and his troops aren't trained to deal with a force of that quality."

"Will he surrender without putting up a fight and risk losing his son?"

"Probably not. Gwynneth says he has real feeling toward Balduin and won't risk harm coming to him. According to her, he thinks her capable of any monstrosity."

"Is she?"

"No," Kendryk said without hesitation. "She would never kill a hostage. I'm sure of it. But it doesn't hurt if my uncle believes she will. But the fact remains that even if he does his best, he won't be able to do more than delay the hussars."

"That might be enough."

"Enough for what?"

"For us to get back in time. The hussars are still a few days away. We are only three days march from Birkenhof. We can get there and hold off the hussars before Teodora arrives."

"She'll be there soon. We've been much too slow." He'd had little hope that his aunt could slow Teodora's progress, but Princess Gallena had surrendered even faster than expected after Ensden's troops overran one of her towns and slaughtered all of its inhabitants.

"We have to find the best advantage we can. Much can happen in a few days."

"Yes, and the hussars might break through at the same time that Teodora reaches us."

"Do you think she can?"

"If she leaves her baggage behind, which she may as well at this point. She can easily live off the land for a few days."

"We must slow her down," Faris said.

They were silent for a few moments. It was impossible to split the force. Plague had diminished their number by over a third and soldiers were still falling ill. Tired and heartsick as he was, Kendryk sometimes wished he would get sick, so it would all be over within days.

"I have an idea," Kendryk said at last. "Although I hate it."

"We have to entertain every possibility."

"If Teodora is traveling ahead of her baggage, maybe we can slow her down. If she can't live off the land, she must wait for supplies, won't she?"

"I suppose she would. What are you proposing?"

"We burn it." Kendryk was barely able to force the words through his throat. "We burn everything between here and Birkenhof."

Kendryk saw Faris's face blanch, but continued. "We have enough time to get everyone into fortified towns, or castles. The harvest is over and there should be enough time to get everything inside a safe place. Once that's done, we burn the rest of it."

"Teodora will consider it a desperate measure," Faris said.

"It *is* a desperate measure." Kendryk put his head in his hands. When he looked up again he said, "I care little for appearances at this point. If Teodora assumes she has the advantage of me, let her. It's far worse than she thinks it is anyway."

At this point he saw no way to pull a victory out of this, barring a miracle. And there was no miracle he could imagine short of the gods themselves striking Teodora down where she stood.

"Then we must make the best of it," Faris said. "I agree that we can slow her down by removing possible food sources. Beyond that, we should take advantage of what time we gain by choosing the best position we can."

"I can think of one, but I don't want to bring them so close to Birkenfels."

"That doesn't matter. Birkenfels won't fall. The Roussays will send help before they allow Princess Gwynneth to be captured."

"They've seemed not to mind so far." Kendryk tried to keep the bitterness out of his voice. He hadn't wanted the help at first, but now there was nothing he needed more.

"Things are in disarray there as you know. They might still change, and soon. I say we fall back in good order and do as you say for the countryside. It's only a small part of Terragand and will recover soon enough. We can cross the river, blow the bridges and take positions on those hills beyond it. We should have time to place the guns where they can do the most good."

"If I had known I would lose so many soldiers, I would have ordered more guns."

"You still need soldiers to fire them."

"True enough. I'll send Gwynneth a message telling her to prepare for the worst and watch for our coming. Give the order to march in two hours' time."

Kendryk was careful not to reveal too much of his plan even in a cipher. He simply told Gwynneth that he appreciated what she had done and he would see her soon. In the meantime, she was to continue getting everything of value into the castle, including Landrus.

That completed, he handed the message to a fast courier and made his own preparations. The head of his column reached the first town in less than an hour. Starnheim was a large town with a sturdy wall. It would not withstand prolonged cannon fire, but he hoped Teodora wouldn't take the time to besiege it.

The burgomaster met with him at once. The old man with immense white side whiskers was nearly beside himself with nerves upon meeting Kendryk. When he explained what they had planned, the man paled. "Those poor people," he said. "They will lose everything."

"Not everything. They have the rest of the day to get everything they can inside the walls. Please open any warehouses and cellars with extra space. My men are already spreading the word in the farms and villages. Their homes will have to be rebuilt. I'll do what I can to help."

He had little money left with him, but it was best to give it away now, while he could. The burgomaster seemed an honest sort, so Kendryk sent for a small chest of coin to be delivered to the town treasury before they left.

On the way out of town, they met a trickle of people going in. Kendryk forced himself to stop in front of a man holding the hand of a little girl and carrying a large bundle on his back.

He jumped down from his horse. "I am very sorry about this, my good man," Kendryk said. "I realize it's little comfort, but I appreciate your sacrifice and will do what I can to help when this is over."

The man bowed and when he rose, his eyes were shining. "It is no hardship to do this for you, Your Grace. We are with you, all of us. With you and with Edric Maximus. We know you stand for the truth against the forces of evil and the gods require us to stand with you."

Kendryk couldn't speak, but pressed the man's hand and tousled the little girl's curly head. As he passed through the village and on to the farms outside, the mood was the same. Everyone wanted him to shake their hands and kiss their children. He dismounted and walked much of the way, taking the time to talk to everyone who wished it. It was the least he could do, considering what they were sacrificing.

At one of the last farmsteads, the young couple there insisted that he stay for a hurried meal before they packed up and drove their livestock into town. When he arose, Kendryk left his last gold coin on their table.

It was time to get back on his horse, but he felt so heavy he almost needed to ask for help. This was unbearable, but he had to bear it anyway.

As they plodded northward, Kendryk tried to picture his reunion with Gwynneth. He still couldn't think of seeing her and Arian without feeling intense agony. But that was not how he wanted to leave her. If he'd had a few months, he would have taken them and be sure of himself before forgiving her. But there was no time. What mattered now were not those weeks of betrayal and anger but the years of happiness they'd had. He'd give anything—his kingdom, his life, his soul—to have that joy again, even for a few moments.

BRAEDEN

The hussars met their baggage train about an hour before it was time to make camp. Because of the confusion and many happy reunions, Prince Novitny ordered camp made in the first decent spot. On this side of the mountains, the land was flat and there was plenty of water, so that was easy enough.

Braeden located his wagons and told Gergo to leave out Janna's corner. "The lady is moving in permanently," he said, feeling a warm glow. "Oh, and you can find another place to bunk for the night, can't you?" She'd have to get used to the lack of privacy, but maybe not just yet.

Janna wasn't far behind, and quick to oversee the arrangements. She saw her little cot and the curtain left in the wagon, but Braeden caught her eye and shook his head. He hoped she didn't mind and judging by her blush and smile, she didn't.

Now the sun couldn't go down soon enough. Cook fires had long been going, roasting real meat and the wagon-mounted ovens disgorged hundreds of loaves of hot, fresh bread. There would be a feast of sorts to celebrate everyone surviving the day and getting back together with friends and family.

Braeden was glad to see Janna and Franca laughing together over something, and the two of them sat down on either side of him. "My two favorite girls." He grinned. "Glad to see you're getting a bit to eat." Both had bread trenchers piled high with steaming meat and vegetables.

"I'm so hungry I don't care what kind of meat this is." Janna sighed before digging in.

"Even horse?" Franca asked, a gleam in her eye.

"Except for horse. I used to not care, but now I think of poor old Zoltan or darling Kazmir, and I just couldn't."

"Darling Kazmir?" Franca snorted and rolled her eyes. "Don't ever let him hear you call him that."

Braeden was happier than he had been in a long time. It had been a good few days, riding across peaceful countryside and cuddled up with Janna during the cool nights. He'd had a good tussle with real soldiers this morning and looked forward to a pretty girl in his bed very soon. And not just any pretty girl. He looked sideways at Janna and she caught his eye, blushing again.

Janna helped clean up after the meal, but Braeden didn't go far so he wouldn't lose track of her in the crowds milling around the fires. She seemed surprised to see him, when she came back up from the nearby creek, wiping her hands on her apron. "You didn't have to wait for me."

"I wanted to." He reached down and took one of her hands, still damp and cold from the water. "Did you want to sit by the fire with the others for a bit, or ..." He suddenly felt as shy as a boy.

"Let's go back to the tent." She squeezed his hand. "Before Gergo comes back."

"He won't tonight," Braeden said. "I told him to bunk down elsewhere."

"You turfed the poor boy out?"

"I did. He'll be all right. He's been courting a laundress much too slowly. Perhaps she'll take pity on him tonight so he can speed things up."

"You're very efficient." Janna laughed, still holding his hand and falling in beside him. Everyone else was by the fires or taking care of the horses, so it was dark between the tents.

Braeden took advantage of the darkness to stop, grab Janna around the waist and pull her close so he could finally kiss her. They were both laughing when they pulled apart and gasping for air.

"I liked that," Janna said. "No one has ever kissed me like that. Can we do it again?"

After that, they were in a hurry to find the tent. Gergo had left a lamp burning, and Braeden tied the flap off tight. No visitors tonight. "I hoped you didn't mind that I ..." He nodded toward his cot.

"Oh, not at all." Her cheeks were bright red, which suited her terribly well. "After the last few weeks, I would have hated to sleep apart from you again."

"Me too. Do you need help with your dress?"

She obligingly unbuttoned his shirt while he unlaced her bodice. They'd left Atlona in such a hurry, he never had gotten her anything nicer.

It was chilly in the tent, so they were quick to crawl under the covers, which were even colder at first. They didn't stay cold for long.

Afterward, she lay curled up against his side, with his arm around her while his other hand stroked the side of her face.

"That was nice," she said after a while.

"It was."

"I'm very relieved, you know."

"You are? Why?"

"I thought for a while you didn't want me, that you might never want me. Because of what happened."

"Oh, I don't care about that at all," Braeden said. "Those things happen all the time. I thought you might never want me because of that though."

"I just needed some time, but now I'm ready." She leaned in to kiss him, long and soft.

Much later, they were both very sleepy, when he thought of something. "I'll marry you as soon as I can," he said.

That seemed to rouse her. "Oh, you don't have to." She smiled at him. "I understand you aren't the type and I don't want you to do it if you aren't."

"Who told you I wasn't the type?" Braeden frowned.

"Everyone. Well, everyone except Senta who was sure you were just waiting for the right woman."

"Turns out Senta is right, as usual."

GWYNNETH

Gwynneth walked to the outer gate alone. She had filled the castle's cellars and stores to bursting and everyone who needed to be inside was safe. All but one.

He came alone, peeling off from the column that had marched across the bridge. When he saw her, he jumped off his horse and ran to her. She pulled him into her arms and held him for a long time. When they broke apart, she gasped at the sight of him. He was pale and gaunt, his face covered in soot. His eyes, still that beautiful blue she had always loved, were weary and bloodshot. He was still her Kendryk but not quite the same one who'd sent her away several weeks ago.

She felt tears well up and pushed them down with an enormous effort. She had to be strong for him now. It wouldn't be much longer. "Can you come inside?"

He nodded and picked up the horse's reins. It had been standing patiently behind him.

"How long?"

"Until morning. Count Faris is setting up our guns and what troops are left on the two hills behind the palace."

She took his arm, and they walked inside the castle walls. Behind them, the gate clanged shut. They were taking no chances now. "How far away is Teodora?"

"Close. You might see her fires tonight. Faris will blow the bridge when everyone has crossed over and burn the village." His tone was as flat and casual as if he had been discussing plans for a hunting party. But then, he'd seen a fair number of bridges blown and villages burned these past few days.

She wanted to beg him to stay with them in the castle, but she was sure it would do no good.

By now they had wound their way up into the castle courtyard. Someone came and took the horse. Kendryk looked around at the supplies stacked against the walls. "You're a marvel." He turned to her. "I'm so glad you came back. Forgive me for sending you away. I was out of my head ..."

"Shh ... we'll talk later. Now you must visit the children before their bedtime, and I'm sure you'll want to see Edric Maximus."

"So he came? I'm glad."

They climbed the winding stone stairs to the makeshift nursery in the sunniest room of the tower. She hoped it was also the safest. She rocked the baby and held back her tears while the older two flung themselves at him. They had always loved him the most; it wasn't fair they should lose him.

A wild thought flashed through her head. What if she could detain him here while she took his place in the field? Right now she would put her head on the block in front of Teodora if it would save him. But she knew him and even if she managed it, he would never forgive her. And that was worse than anything. Even worse than losing him.

So she somehow held back her tears, swallowed down the knot in her throat and ignored the painful one in her middle while she watched him play with the children.

As the sky darkened, Kendryk's smile fled. "Give me the baby." Little Andres had long been asleep in Gwynneth's arms. Kendryk kissed him on the forehead, then handed him to the nurse to put to bed.

He turned to Devyn and knelt to look him in the eye. "I have to go again and might not be back for a while. Can you be good and do whatever Mama tells you to?"

Devyn nodded and yawned. Kendryk smiled and pulled him close, then kissed him before handing him to Gwynneth.

She turned to put him to bed herself because she didn't think she could bear to watch him say goodbye to Maryna. She was old enough to understand that something was wrong and now she clung crying to Kendryk's neck.

"Don't go don't go," she sobbed. "I'm so afraid Papa. I will never see you again if you go."

"You will." Kendryk held her close, stroking her back. Gwynneth stared at them appalled, but his eyes met hers and they were clear and resolute. "You will, I promise. I'm not sure how long it will be. But you will." Kendryk kissed her one more time, wiped the tears from her face, and rose to leave.

Gwynneth grabbed at his hand once they were outside the door. "I can't bear it."

"You can." His voice was different now. Something about being with the children had helped him. "I'll go visit Landrus now for a little while. Can you get me a bath and something to eat? Then I'm yours for the rest of the night."

She made her way to her chambers. Smoke stung her nostrils, and she leaned out one of her windows. Flames mingled with smoke came from the village below. According to Kendryk's instructions, she had evacuated it yesterday. She'd brought the blacksmith, the baker, their children, and a few elderly seamstresses and laundresses into the castle, sending everyone else to Runewald.

Gwynneth ordered supper and a bath, then waited for Kendryk. He wasn't gone long.

"Can you help me with this?" He struggled with the buckles of the rusty cuirass he still wore.

Gwynneth got it off him, wrinkling her nose at the sight of the dirty, sweat-caked shirt beneath.

Once undressed, Kendryk slid into the still-steaming tub. "Oh, this is marvelous. Can you believe it's been weeks since I've had a bath?"

"I can." Gwynneth picked up his shirt with one finger and tossed it into the fire. "A military encampment must have a marvelous scent."

"You have no idea." Kendryk scrubbed at his blackened arms. "Though you get used to it after a while. I didn't realize how awful I must look and smell until I saw you standing there, all clean and pretty."

Gwynneth knelt down next to the tub to wash his hair, just as she'd always done.

"Did you have a good visit with Edric Maximus?" she asked, more to distract herself from how thin he looked than because she cared.

"It wasn't happy. But I'm glad we spoke and I'm glad he's safe. I owe that to you. If you hadn't done all of that, he'd be a captive of the Sanova Hussars right now."

"That man has a lot to answer for," Gwynneth said, scrubbing at Kendryk's neck harder than necessary.

"So do we, darling. I hope the two of you can learn to be friends."

"Hmph. It's all I can do to be civil."

"I understand. Now get me out of here. I'm starving, and not just for food."

They rushed through supper, and Gwynneth was just as anxious as he was to crawl into bed and feel his skin against hers at last. There'd been a time

406

when she thought it would never happen again and she nearly cried, relieved that he still wanted her.

She had feared that the cold, formal Kendryk who'd sent her away would return today, caring only about the children and Landrus. She didn't know why he had changed back to the man who loved her, but there was one more thing.

Gwynneth sighed, sat up and took a deep breath. "I didn't want to bring this up, but it's very important. I understand if you can't or won't, but I have to ask ..."

"Yes." Kendryk leaned up on one elbow and pulled her back down to him. "The answer is yes."

"How did you know what I would ask?"

"Because I know it matters to you. So yes, I forgive you."

"Just like that?" She couldn't stop the tears now.

"Exactly like that." He pulled her closer, and she cried into his shoulder. "Darling, it's all right. It's over now. You made a mistake. I've made mistakes too; far worse in the scheme of things."

"No you haven't. Tomorrow might go very differently if Arian Orland were here."

"Probably not. They'd all have plague too."

"Oh, I hadn't thought of that. I rather like the idea." She smiled. "What a shame; he could have died a horrible death. If we were really lucky, Schurtz would have caught it too."

"That's awful," Kendryk said, but he was smiling, too. "Now come here, we have better things to do."

JANNA

First there was lamplight, then Gergo clanking about, gathering up Braeden's armor. Janna opened one eye and saw Braeden looking at her. "You're awake already," she said, opening both eyes and smiling.

"Seems it's time to go, damn the empress."

She yawned. "I'd almost forgotten about the war."

"So did I." He grinned and stroked her hair. "At least for a while." He pulled her close for a kiss, then sat up. "Novitny sent a message after we changed directions and Teodora is so close, he's already got a reply. She's marching straight up the road to Birkenhof and we will meet her there."

Janna sat up too, careful to hold the bedclothes against her, though they were alone again, at least for a moment. "Prince Kendryk won't try to stop her first?"

"Probably not." Braeden stood up and reached for his clothes. "Once he's beyond the river he can take the high ground so his guns can pummel us as we come up."

Janna shuddered. "Does he have many guns?"

"No one knows." Braeden seemed far too unconcerned for her liking. "I suppose we'll find out when we get there."

Janna got up too, retrieving her dress from a pile on the floor. By the time she had it on, Braeden had dressed. She walked around the cot and into his arms. "I don't know if I can get used to this," she murmured against his chest.

"What, this?" He squeezed her a little tighter. "I can."

"No, this is good." She smiled up at him. "I mean, I don't know if I can ever not worry about you. Most of the other women are so casual about it. They're so used to their men being in danger. I think I'll always worry."

"They know it does no good. But they all carry on at first, like you did yesterday."

"I did not carry on. You have no idea how much I restrained myself."

His bright eyes twinkled down at her. "If you say so. I don't mind. It's nice to be fussed over; doesn't happen too often."

"Well, get used to it. I'll fuss over you all the time, although I'll try not to carry on too much, as you put it. I don't want to embarrass you."

"Oh, you don't. Besides, it makes the others jealous, having a pretty young thing weeping all over you."

"I'll try not to weep all over you at least." Janna smiled again and turned her face up for a long kiss. "I smell breakfast; let's go."

They left the tent hand in hand and found porridge and coffee ready at the nearest fire. It seemed they were late, judging by the disapproving look on Gergo's face. Janna gulped down some food standing up, kissed Braeden one more time, and then ran to the tent to help pack everything.

Their wagons were among the last to go, although a few were slower. The families with small children had the hardest time. Janna helped with the last one. A young woman with three children was struggling to pack all the bedding in while holding a baby on one hip and dragging a toddler clinging to her leg.

"Thank you." She smiled at Janna, when she took the blankets, folded them, stuffed them in the back of the wagon and snatched a little boy before he could crawl underneath it. "I could manage well enough with two, but three is too many."

"Three must be very difficult. I should think two would be more than enough." Janna wondered with mingled hope and dread how long it would be before she had little ones again. She helped the young woman into the wagon, then handed up the two children.

"I haven't seen you before," the woman said. "Do you want to ride with us for a while?"

"All right," Janna said, jumping in as the impatient drover whipped the oxen into motion. "I need to find my horse, but I think he's somewhere with the spares."

"So you were one of those who went ahead."

"Yes. It was very exciting. I'm Janna by the way."

"I'm Nisa. My husband is Yvan Retter, in the Parzin banner. Which one's yours?"

"Terris, though he's not quite my husband." To her surprise, it didn't make her uncomfortable to say so.

"Oh, the commander. You've done well then. Good man and fierce fighter. And don't worry about the husband bit. Yvan didn't marry me till I was huge with this one." She held up the baby. "The main thing is that he takes care of you. And happy as you look, he does that well enough."

"He does." Janna smiled. "Better than anyone."

The morning passed pleasantly as Janna chatted with Nisa. She didn't bother looking for Zoltan until they stopped for a quick meal. It took a while since she saw many people she knew as she walked along the baggage train.

She found Zoltan about halfway up the column, on a line with spare mounts and found someone to help her with the saddle. She didn't see Braeden, but he was probably at the front of the column. "Let him eat a little grass," the groom said. "Once we reach the crossroads there won't be any more."

Janna wondered what he meant, but it soon became clear. As the army moved onto the main Terragand road, the world changed. There were no more pretty farms and villages among harvested fields and meadows with tall yellow and green grass. The ground was black, and nothing but smoking ruin stood in every direction. Even the trees had been burned.

Janna looked around her, appalled. "What happened to all the people?" she asked the older woman riding next to her.

"In the walled towns and castles. Seems they all swore to Prince Kendryk and his priest they wouldn't give the empress or her horses a single bite in their lands. They did it all willingly for their prince, it's said. Too bad it's all for nothing. Now that the empress has met up with the hussars and our supplies, there's enough food to last everyone to the prince's front door."

"This Prince Kendryk must be quite something," Janna said, picturing a younger version of Braeden wearing a crown.

"Oh, he is."

"You've seen him?"

"In Isenwald. He passed through the streets every day on his way to and from the temple. The men called him the savior of Kronland while the girls swooned."

"He's very handsome then?"

"In that way that young girls like. Pretty face, eyes the color of the sea. On the small side."

Nothing at all like Braeden then. "Why would he destroy his land because of a priest?"

The woman shrugged. "Hard to say. Maybe these princes get bored when things are too easy for them and make trouble where there is none." She looked around at the scorched ground. "And then their people suffer. As usual."

GWYNNETH

Though they didn't sleep, morning came all too soon. Several hours before dawn, Kendryk sat up and said, "It's time."

Gwynneth didn't protest. It wouldn't do any good and would make him feel worse. All that mattered was giving him the strength to do what he needed to.

"You remembered my good armor?"

She nodded. He'd asked her to bring it from the palace, so he wouldn't take the field in the old, rusty pieces he'd been wearing.

"Help me put it on, then."

It already lay in a pile in the tiny chamber that was now her dressing room. A sleepy Catrin brought a lamp and Gwynneth sent her for food.

"I don't think I can eat," Kendryk said.

"Then take something along. Perhaps you'll have time later."

"All right. Thank you for taking such good care of me, darling."

She swallowed hard and said nothing, just helped him get dressed. Once Catrin brought bread, sausage and cheese in a bundle, they were alone again.

Gwynneth was struggling with the buckles of the fabulous silver cuirass with its blue inlay when he said, "I need you to do one more thing for me, and you must promise to do it before I tell you what it is."

"That doesn't sound good." She looked around her for the next piece.

"Do you promise, Gwynneth?" He looked at her, pale and intent. "Please; it's the most important thing of all."

"Oh all right." She yanked at a strap. "What horrible thing do you want me to do?"

"It might not come to it. Maybe we'll win, or get away, or there'll be a miracle."

412

"Does His Holiness expect a miracle?" she asked, her tone nastier than she intended.

"No, he doesn't. And that's not the point. The point is this—if the worst happens, and I'm captured."

"That's not the worst."

"It is. If I'm dead, Teodora can't use me as a bargaining chip, can she?"

"Don't say things like that." Gwynneth strapped on his vambraces.

"It's the truth. But if the worst happens, and I'm taken alive, you must promise me you will not surrender the castle."

"All right. I won't surrender the castle."

"There's more." Kendryk stopped her and held her by both arms. "If she offers me in exchange for Maryna as a hostage, or for Landrus, you must refuse."

"I can do it for our daughter. I don't know if I can do it for that man."

"You can. And you must. It's the only thing that matters now. If I lose to-day—and I expect I shall—there's still a chance it will not have been in vain if Landrus survives."

"He seems irrelevant at this point."

"He's not. You don't believe him darling, and I don't blame you. But you must understand something. These past few awful days, when I was asking my subjects to sacrifice everything for my folly, every single one I saw did it gladly. Do you know why?"

"Because they love you."

"No, because they love Landrus and they believe his teachings. They will give up everything so he can go on. Please don't dishonor their sacrifice."

"But what about your sacrifice?" There was that awful feeing in her mid-dle again. Something was winding her so tight she would soon be squeezed into nothing.

"In the eyes of the gods, it's no better or worse than theirs. We all have to do our part."

She kept working in silence. When she finished, she said, "And I suppose that's mine now. To keep your precious preacher safe no matter what horrible things Teodora does to you."

"It is. I don't think Teodora will be too horrible. Sure, she'll throw me in her dungeon and make me uncomfortable, but the rest of Kronland won't stand for me being treated like a common criminal."

"They seem to stand for it well enough right now."

"It's different."

"If you say so." She didn't want to argue anymore.

He stood before her, shining in his bright armor, the perfect prince of her dreams. "Promise me, Gwynneth," he said, his eyes with that same intense look they'd had when he'd asked for her hand.

"I promise."

"Say it. Please. I need to hear you say it."

"I promise I will not surrender the castle, or Maryna or that bastard Landrus, no matter what Teodora does to you."

"Thank you. Now come here." He pulled her close against his armor and she prayed it would protect him. Then he kissed her. "I love you very much. Now come, I need to get to my army before daybreak."

Unable to speak, she picked up his helmet and carried it down to the courtyard for him. His horse stood ready. "Don't you have any weapons?" she asked.

"Faris has them all. Everything is ready for me." He kissed her one last time, then climbed into the saddle and she handed him the helmet.

"You look wonderful." She no longer cared that the tears ran down her face. "They'll die for you. I'd die for you."

"Please don't." He smiled down at her. "Now, after I'm gone, bar the gate and raise the drawbridge and don't let it back down again until your brother comes."

She nodded.

One last smile, then the horse clattered across the cobbles, through the inner gate and disappeared. She ran back up the stairs, but it was still too dark to see him on the road. She knew the direction he'd take and looked that way until she was sure he had reached Faris and the rest. Feeling almost too heavy to move, she trudged across the room to another window. The light of thousands of torches flickered above a thin layer of fog in the distance. They were coming.

BRAEDEN

Kazmir picked his way through the fog and Braeden tipped his head back as far as he could. The pointed towers of Birkenfels emerged from the mist. Judging by the angle, the castle perched high on a cliff over the river, well out of reach.

"She's up there somewhere, that princess with the golden hair." Miro sighed. "Ercos willing, we'll make her a widow before sundown. Do you reckon she's looking down on us?"

"If she is, she can't see through the fog." Braeden peered ahead and saw nothing but a few feet of road. "Stop worrying about the princess and worry we'll stumble onto her husband before Novitny and the rest come up. Though come to think of it, I'm sure she'd be happy to have your ugly mug on a spike over her gate."

"One look at me and that princess will forget all about that stupid prince of hers. It's your scruffy head she'd stick up there while I stick her ..."

"There they are. Thanks the gods." Braeden spotted more hussars emerging from the fog. Since Prince Kendryk had blown the bridge, everyone had to ford the river downstream. By the time the hussars crossed, the fog was so thick Braeden had lost track of all but his own banner.

"Glad you're here, Terris." Prince Novitny's drooping mustache was white with frost. "Was worried you'd gone the wrong way. Would be a shame to miss all the fun now it's finally come to it."

"It would," Braeden said. "Running the other way in the mountains didn't sit well with me." Kazmir snorted in agreement.

By now all the hussars coming up from the river had fallen into formation on the road leading away from the castle. Braeden spared one more glance for Princess Gwynneth barricaded up there and Novitny followed his gaze. "They won't get any help from there. At least I hope not."

"There can't be more than a skeleton garrison."

"It's not the garrison that worries me. It's that girl's father. Don't you think it's strange that there hasn't been a peep from King Andres? It's not like him to be quiet at a time like this. I wouldn't be too surprised if he's got ships sailing up this river."

"That would be inconvenient." Braeden thought of Janna, still far away on the other side. They'd left the baggage train well-guarded, but if they should be unlucky enough to reach the river when an enemy force arrived...

"It's unlikely, though," the prince went on. "General Ensden has given word we're to mind our rear. He's posted scouts at least twenty leagues down-river so we should have plenty of warning if any ships come."

"Good." It felt strange to have someone else to worry about, but it was nice, too.

As they reached open country beyond the river valley, the imperial right flank came into view. Pale sunlight caught thousands of spear-tips as enormous squares of pike and musket moved into place. Solid and slow-moving, the squares were easily outflanked, but Prince Kendryk didn't have enough cavalry to be a threat. Arian Orland's ten thousand horse were nowhere to be seen. Maybe the rumors were true.

Braeden took his place at the head of his banner on Novitny's right flank. A slight breeze blew in a faint, smoky scent. They were upwind of the burned village and the troops had received strict orders not to set fire to anything else. Rumor was that the empress had her eye on taking Birkenhof palace for her own use while she mopped up here in Kronland.

"Dura!" Braeden snapped and Franca materialized instantly. "Do you smell the smoke?"

"Yes sir."

"I want you to find out where it's coming from and who started the fire."

She saluted and galloped off.

He turned to Miro, riding at his elbow. "How far are we from the line?"

"Not far. Imperial messengers sent word that the empress is drawn up in front of those two hills. Bernotas should be straight across. When we run into a little creek, we're there."

"Good enough." The horses walked slowly across grass already trampled by thousands of feet.

Franca galloped up a moment later in a spray of mud. "It's the palace, sir."

"Vica's tits!" Braeden swore. "Everyone got that order a dozen times."

"Sir, Prince Kendryk burnt it himself. It was already on fire when our scouts got here."

"Can it be put out?"

"Not a chance. It was all in flames by the time I got there. One fellow thought he'd get in for some plunder and is in a bad state. I told his comrades they should put him out of his misery."

"Go tell Novitny. We'll let the empress hear it from someone else."

Miro snickered as Franca galloped off again. "That'll put Her Highness in a rage."

"She's been in a rage since she was born. Just as well it was Bernotas did this since she wants to kill him anyway."

Braeden pulled Kazmir to a stop as he stepped into a small stream. The fog against the hills in front of them hadn't lifted, and it was hard to tell what was directly ahead. To his right he could see the front ranks of the empress's personal troops. Over here the fog had burned off, and the sun shone bright.

Teodora wore a full suit of gold plate armor and rode a magnificent white courser. A deep red cloak fell from her shoulders. She wore no helmet and her heavy black hair hung loose to her waist, lifting like a flag in the breeze.

"Now that's a sight to behold," Miro said, frankly appreciative.

"She's still an evil bitch. I hate fighting for her."

"Rather fight for the loser?"

"He wouldn't be losing if we were over there. In fact, if Orland were here, it'd be a different story."

"Wonder why he's not. Thought he and Prince Kendryk were like brothers."

"Theological differences." Franca rode up between them.

Miro rolled his eyes.

"Do you reckon?" Braeden wondered. "Arian Orland doesn't strike me as someone who cares much about religion."

"But Prince Kendryk does," Franca said. "And he's even thicker with that Landrus fellow. One word of disagreement with the priest and you'd be out on your ear. Anyway, I delivered your message and Novitny had a good laugh. Said you should be ready to go soon and watch out for guns on that hill. With any luck we'll crush the right flank straightaway and swoop down on the prince himself. Oh there he is!" A sudden breeze had cleared away the mist clinging to the hills.

Braeden followed Franca's gaze. Prince Kendryk was right in front of them, conferring with one of his officers. With his glittering silver armor and a blue plume rising high from his helmet, he'd make a good target, even in the smoke and confusion of battle. He looked quite cool, sitting his horse with the same easy grace that had first impressed Braeden. If he was bothered because he'd just burned his ancestral home and sent his young family into that mousetrap of a castle, he didn't show it.

"Oh, he's lovely." Franca sighed. "I hope I'm not the one to kill him. I don't think I could bear it."

KENDRYK

"It's done," Kendryk said, as he joined Count Faris and the rest. His battle charger was waiting for him, so he checked his weapons and mounted. As he left the burning palace, he had already heard the splash of troops fording the river. They would be here soon.

"I don't understand." Faris shook his head. "There was no need to destroy Birkenhof. If the empress occupies it, I'm sure she would leave it unharmed."

"I don't want her to occupy it," Kendryk said through clenched teeth. He felt if he relaxed a single muscle he might collapse into a thousand pieces.

He didn't tell Faris the real truth, which was that he felt compelled to punish himself. It didn't seem right he'd asked his people to destroy their own homes while his still stood.

And even if he survived this and came back someday, it would never be the same. Though he was glad of his reconciliation with Gwynneth, his marriage would never be what it had once been. If he ever saw his children again they would be older and the little ones might not remember him. If he ever was to have a home again, he'd rebuild it from the ground up, on some other, impossibly distant day.

Once mounted, he and Faris rode to the front of the lines. There was a heavy fog but Kendryk wanted to be ready, in case the enemy stumbled upon them accidentally. That at least might give them an early advantage though he doubted any of Teodora's commanders would be inexperienced enough to let that happen. "Take as many troops as you can through the gap behind us when we're overrun," he told Faris.

"Let's not talk of retreat."

"I don't want you to sacrifice yourself needlessly."

"So you can?" Faris was the closest to angry Kendryk had ever seen him. "It's all very well they'll write poetry about your heroism but you being dead won't help the rest of us."

"I'm not sacrificing myself. If we can regroup and fight again, I'm all for that. I want you to know that if something happens to me, you should salvage what you can."

"I'll keep fighting. You needn't worry about that." Faris's jaw was set, his gray eyes resolute.

"Thank you," Kendryk said, then looked forward. The mist lifted, and he saw them now. As he had expected, Teodora held the middle with Ensden's veterans. That meant Barela would be on her right, and Novitny on her left. Kendryk rode toward his right. His best and most experienced troops were here; pike accustomed to repelling heavy cavalry.

He hadn't seen his uncle, but Faris had sent him to hold the left. He would have preferred to have the professionals face Barela, but he didn't have enough to put them in both places and make a difference.

Kendryk spotted Colonel DeGroot, who had survived the plague in fairly good condition, though he still looked somewhat yellow about the gills. "How do they look?" he asked.

"Good, Your Grace. I've got them swinging the pike around like a lot of lubbers. Put on a good show for Novitny."

"Ah yes." Kendryk looked ahead. The Sanovans had come up, their black standards fluttering over a sea of wings. At least DeGroot had experience in fending off cavalry, so he might hold on long enough. But long enough for what? There was no rescue coming, no reinforcement.

He nodded to DeGroot and cantered back to the center. The imperial troops kept coming. "How many do you reckon?' he asked Faris.

"At least thirty thousand."

Kendryk swallowed hard against a sudden surge of nausea. He had less than fifteen thousand, and those included Evard's green militia. It had done well enough in the Garsten Gap, but was at a disadvantage right here. Best to just get it over with.

He nodded at Faris, who gave the signal. Guns on the hill behind him fired all at once. The balls landed in Ensden's third rank, but the group was so vast, there was barely a ripple. The imperial guns replied at once. Kendryk winced as cannonballs shrieked overhead. They landed in the middle of the troops behind him. He closed his ears to the ungodly sounds and pulled down his visor. Time to advance before any more damage was done.

His guns fired again. Their crews were well-drilled and experienced. He just needed three times as many. Shot whistled around him now and the noise rose. He saw only straight ahead through the slits in his helmet, and smoke billowed everywhere. He spurred his horse on and drew both pistols. Glimpsing the imperial standard, he wondered if Teodora was near. His only hope of turning the tide was to find her and fire before she did.

BRAEDEN

Braeden turned his attention to the enemy troops. They looked impressive. The backbone of Prince Kendryk's force stood across from them in alternating blocks of pike and musket in the Zeelund style.

Braeden eyed the pikemen. It looked like their pikes might be longer than the hussar lances, but if the soldiers weren't used to that length, their maneuvers would be clumsy. He was more worried about the placement of the muskets.

"Send word to the captains," he told Franca and Miro. "We'll move double-time with close ranks. The muskets will be quick on the first round. I want them overrun before they can get off a second one." Now he could see the clumsy movements of the pikemen. "Tell them not to worry about the pike."

Franca returned and took her place on his left, fidgety and bright-eyed. Smoke and flame burst from Prince Kendryk's guns on the hillside, but all the shells landed well to Braeden's right.

The imperial guns replied, and the shells landed somewhere in the back of Prince Kendryk's ranks. The imperial center moved forward, the black and red Inferrara standards fluttering boldly, in front of endless ranks of shining pike and helm.

His way was clear. He looked back for the last time. The Sanova Hussars stood ready, the rising breeze rustling through their black wings and the black banners fluttering from their lances. Kazmir snorted and pawed at the mud.

"Forward!" Braeden shouted and spurred Kazmir into a gallop. The pike swung into formation, but Braeden waited for musket fire. The sound of the wings rushing in his ears made it hard to hear anything else. Straight ahead he noticed a young musketeer, his eyes wide as he raised his weapon. A puff of smoke came from the barrel. Braeden's lance slid into forward position as

Kazmir bore down on the bristling hedge of pike. Franca was no longer at his side and Kazmir veered away when the pike didn't budge.

Braeden pulled Kazmir around. "Regroup!" he called to Reno, at the head of the second rank, which hadn't yet reached the line. With lances down, no one was prepared to shoot. In the meantime, the musketeers might have time to reload.

Braeden threw his lance down and pulled out both pistols. Miro was beside him. "Dura?" Braeden asked.

"Her horse went down." Miro's voice shook a little, and he swallowed. "I don't know what happened to her, sir."

Braeden swore under his breath, but he had no time to look for Franca. The pike were advancing in good order so the clumsy maneuvers had clearly been a ruse. Novitny should have been too experienced to fall for it though Braeden had been no better. "It's time we stopped underestimating Prince Kendryk," he said to Miro. "Get word to Novitny that everyone keep their eyes open for Arian Orland, on our flank in particular. The way things are going, he's likely to give us trouble when we least need it."

He turned to the rest of his banner as Miro galloped off. "One more time." He urged Kazmir into a canter and raised his pistols. "We go around the pike and take down the musketeers."

That worked well enough, and just in time, too. Just past the first rank, Braeden pulled out his saber and spotted a flash of red braid. Franca was using her dead horse's body as a shield, but she was nearly surrounded. Fortunately, the musketeers near her hadn't finished reloading when Braeden arrived.

He used his left hand to pull out his arquebus while slashing his way through with the saber in his right. Kazmir charged ahead like normal. "Dura," he shouted as he came up behind her. In the blink of an eye she was on Kazmir's back and pulled out Braeden's hammer.

The two of them cut through reloading musketeers like butter and suddenly were on the pike's flank. "Now we roll them up," Braeden said under his breath. The ranks were much thinner than they'd looked at first. A second rank of muskets couldn't get off a shot before the hussars were upon them. Once Braeden saw their backs, he circled around so Franca could get another mount.

Even though it looked promising, Braeden didn't want to take any chances. He grabbed an enemy pike by the collar and dragged her back. "Where's Arian Orland?" he asked.

Her eyes had been large and terrified, but she laughed. "Who knows? He's been banished from Terragand."

Braeden dropped her. "Why?"

She shrugged. "Rumor is he got too familiar with Princess Gwynneth and the prince sent him packing."

After the other stories he'd heard about Orland, that seemed plausible. Braeden hoped it was true. He handed the woman off to an ensign who was already rounding up prisoners and got back into the fight. He couldn't see what was happening on the rest of the field because of all the smoke, but the hussars were deep into Prince Kendryk's right flank. With any luck, they'd be on the prince himself before long.

KENDRYK

Kendryk noticed vague shapes ahead of him and fired. One of them went down. He shoved his pistols back into their holsters and drew a second pair. This got him right into a sleeve of musketeers, who were busy reloading. He set to with his saber, unsure if anyone had followed him. If he was lucky, someone would get a good shot off at him right now. No one did, although bullets whistled all around him and clanged off of his armor.

He slashed blindly with his saber, and a few times felt he'd caught someone or something. A horse screamed, and the ground rose to meet him. Instinctively, he flung himself clear and struggled back to his feet. His horse lay on its side thrashing and then stopped. Kendryk held his saber and looked around. The fight had somehow gone around him. Sweat poured down his face and then a horse snorted in his ear.

"There you are, Your Grace," said someone whose name he couldn't recall. "I brought you another mount."

"Right, thank you." Kendryk swung into the saddle, gratified to discover more loaded pistols. His men were right behind him and had cut a small swath into the enemy line. That wasn't always helpful. The imperial troops were in the deep Maladene formations, staggered to catch their opponents in crossfire. A step in any direction would put Kendryk in its path. Unable to see, he chose a direction and went.

A slight breeze lifted the smoke a little and Kendryk noticed that his small contingent was even deeper into the enemy ranks. He saw no point in falling back now. If he'd had a larger force they might have regrouped and tried another frontal assault, but he didn't know what was behind him. By now, it might be Teodora.

All of these thoughts took little time. Kendryk spurred his horse again, toward the side of a square where the pike faced forward. He got to them before they swung around to meet him and crumpled that corner of the square before the muskets came to their aid. He still had a few soldiers behind him. His saber came out again, and he waded further into the square. This wouldn't end well, but he didn't expect it to anyway.

There was still firing and shouting, so he must still have had troops fighting on his side. Who they were and where, he didn't know, he just kept slashing at anyone who stood in front of him. Many went down, and soon the enemy surrounded him. But now they formed a wide circle around him and he could reach none of them. He tried a pistol, but he must already have fired it, even though he didn't remember doing so. He knew he should reload, but didn't quite remember how.

It was hard to say what the enemy was doing. They weren't retreating, but they weren't coming at him, either. Then the troops before him parted and Teodora was in front of him on a white horse. Kendryk cursed himself for his empty pistols, but pulled his saber out again. Maybe if he was fast enough ...

Teodora laughed. That made him angry, so he put the spurs to his exhausted mount and raised his saber as he drew near. Teodora laughed again and raised a pistol. He was close enough now that a ball might pierce his armor, but she didn't aim at him. He heard the report, saw the smoke and then his horse went down. Unprepared this time, he fell with it. His head bounced off the ground, and light exploded in his head.

The pain was immediate and overwhelming and his sight went black. His vision came and went for a few more seconds, and he tried to make sense of what was happening around him. The horse had landed on his right leg, still trapped in the stirrup. He pushed at the horse's body, trying to get the pressure off his leg, but it was impossible. He bit his lip until it bled. Every motion was excruciating. He lay back on the ground, trying to catch his breath and opened his visor. That helped a little.

Armor clanked near his head and Teodora's laugh was very close now. He clenched his teeth against the pain. He refused to cry out in front of her. There was another clank of armor and suddenly the pressure was off. It felt better for a split second, but then the pain came back in a bigger wave and he moaned in spite of himself.

"Oh, poor darling," Teodora said. "That looks terrible. Take him."

Kendryk blinked and lifted his head. He saw his leg. The armor over it was red and a white bone stuck out from the side. Someone picked him up under the arms and he lost consciousness.

JANNA

Riding by herself was too nerve-wracking, so Janna found Nisa Retter's wagon and joined her until they reached Birkenfels. The slow-moving train was a good ten leagues behind the fighting forces. "I'm glad we won't be close to the battle." Janna shuddered.

"It's better that way." Nisa agreed. "I didn't use to mind so much, but once I had children I worried whenever the fighting came close. No one's ever overrun our camp, but you hear the most dreadful stories."

It was evening by the time they reached the valley leading down to the river. The wagon came to a halt and Nisa jumped down and let the two older children run about in the trampled grass. "It looks like our lot made camp here last night. We can set up here."

Janna said her goodbyes, wishing she were as calm as Nisa, who seemed altogether unworried about her husband's safety. She found Braeden's wagons a good distance up the line and Gergo was already setting the tent up with the help of a few other servants.

She saw the towers of Birkenfels from here and wondered if the battle was over. No one else seemed concerned, so she bit her tongue and concentrated on unpacking.

Restless, Janna left the tent with piles of blankets lying around and the bed unmade. Once she knew Braeden was safe, it would be easier to get her work done. She left the hussar encampment and found herself among Maladene women and children, also setting up tents and chattering in their musical, unfamiliar tongue.

She kept walking until she stood above the river. The castle's towers soared over it, golden and undamaged in the late afternoon sunlight. Smoke still rose from the blackened ruins of the village at its base and heaps of stone stood where the bridge had been.

From here, she gazed across the river to the battlefield. The rising breeze carried the faint cries of the wounded all the way to where Janna stood. Among piles of dead horses and humans, rose the standards of Inferrara, Barela and Novitny. They had won.

Tired musketeers trudged up from the river, heading toward camp. "How are you crossing?" Janna asked one young woman.

"Ford a half-league that way." She nodded her head in the direction she'd come. "Slow going, getting everyone back across along with the wounded."

"Are there many wounded?" Janna could tell the woman didn't want to talk. She looked uninjured but her expression was blank and her face covered in soot and dirt and streaked with what might have been sweat or blood, or both.

The musketeer barked a short laugh. "Only on their side. I don't reckon we have more than a few hundred casualties. It was a right slaughter."

"Thank you." Janna stepped out of her way, relieved. If it had gone well then perhaps Braeden was all right. She should get back to their camp. By now, the road coming up from the river was crowded, the paths between tents clogged with soldiers.

Janna side-stepped several wagons full of wounded, and one that looked as though it carried bodies. She looked away. She felt terrible for the wounded, many of whom would die before morning, but she was terrified that she might spot Braeden, or anyone else she knew among them.

She heard horses crossing the field to her right, but it was too dark to identify them. When she got back to Novitny's camp, most of the hussars had returned. Janna ran to their tent, her heart in her mouth.

She ran into Kazmir first, being led off by a horseboy. He looked well, and bad-tempered as usual, though he nodded his beautiful head at Janna as she passed him.

Braeden was inside the tent, Gergo helping him take off his armor. "There you are. Gergo said you'd run off all of a sudden."

Janna threw herself into his arms though he was dirty and bloody. "I'm sorry. I just couldn't bear waiting around here so I went closer to the river to find out what happened. We won, didn't we?"

Braeden shooed Gergo out of the tent and pulled Janna close. "Yes, we won. Prince Kendryk put up a better fight than we expected, but we beat him all the same. Count Faris might have slipped away with a few hundred troops, but the rest are dead, wounded, prisoner or fled."

"Did you kill the prince?"

Braeden shook his head. "No. Teodora shot his horse out from under him herself. Crushed his leg. She's taken him prisoner, but word is he might not live through the night, he's in such a bad way. Princess Gwynneth holds the castle and perhaps she'll surrender it in exchange for her husband if he makes it."

Janna shuddered. "How dreadful. If I were the princess, and you were the prince, I would have already given up the castle to have you back."

Braeden held her tight. "I know you would. But there's nothing you need to worry about now. The enemy's defeated, the war is over, and we're headed back to Atlona with the empress. Maybe we'll find a house and live like civilized folk for a while. Never wanted to try that before, but I want to try it with you."

Janna thought her heart might burst with joy. She kissed him and smiled. "I'd like to try it too."

GWYNNETH

It was dark now, and the lights of thousands of cook fires flickered to life. Gwynneth wondered what they'd done with all the bodies. They hadn't had many casualties; the bodies would belong to Kendryk's soldiers, some of them people she knew. At the edge of the parapet she let the paper in her hand fall over the side. That was her answer.

"Your Grace?" she started at Linette's voice. "Supper is served in the great hall."

"Go away," Gwynneth said, and waited until Linette's steps retreated down the stairs. The idea of supper was obscene after a day like today. She realized she hadn't eaten at all. Once Kendryk had left her before sunrise, the idea of food never crossed her mind. She was glad someone else was caring for the children, or they would have gone hungry too.

She looked back toward the fires. The empress's message said there were fifteen thousand soldiers out there. It seemed an excessive amount, considering she had only fifty armed men inside the castle. Perhaps Teodora worried that Arian Orland would try to break her out. Gwynneth laughed under her breath. That would be awkward though she didn't suppose she could refuse help from any quarter.

She walked to the other corner and looked up the river. Real help would come from here. She wondered how many ships Arryk would bring. Had he sailed yet? He probably hadn't received her most recent message. The only reason he wasn't here right now was because of her father, she was sure of it.

There were footsteps again, the clank of something on the stone, then someone coming up behind her.

"I told you to go away," she said through clenched teeth.

"I'm sorry Your Grace." It was Landrus. "It's very important that I speak with you before you send a reply to the empress."

Gwynneth turned toward him. It was dark now, but the moon had risen, bathing the tower in silvery light. "Why? There's nothing to discuss."

"I disagree." The maximus looked as tired as she felt. "But first, you should eat something." He nodded toward a tray he'd set on a nearby step. "Linette wouldn't let me come up here unless I brought you food."

"The time has passed for you to tell me what I should and shouldn't do." She wanted to be angry, but couldn't muster up the emotion.

"I apologize, Your Grace. That was never my intent."

"You still did it enthusiastically."

He sighed. "As ever, I sought to protect your husband."

"Between the two of us, we've done a fine job, haven't we?" she snapped.

"I don't blame you for being angry with me. Please hear me out." He walked around so she had to face him. "You haven't told me what the empress's terms were, but I can guess. If you turn me over to her, will she return Kendryk to you?"

"Kendryk is dead. She is bluffing."

"Kendryk is not dead. I'm sure of it."

"Oh you are?" Gwynneth laughed. "Are you sure of this the same way you are sure of everything else? Because the gods spoke to you?"

"They don't speak to me directly, but in this case, I am certain that your husband is alive."

"I don't believe you. You've been wrong about everything. After today, I doubt very much that Kendryk is the ruler from your prophecy. And this battle? If it was the great one at the end, well, the forces of evil won and we're still here."

"This was not that battle. As to Kendryk being that ruler, the Scrolls never said that his path to the battle would be straight."

"So you conveniently left out the part about all he must suffer first? That was kind of you."

"If I had known all of this would happen, I would never have asked for his help." There was a quiver in his voice. Unbelievable.

Gwynneth stole a sideways glance and saw what might have been the glitter of a tear in the corner of his eye. He hadn't shown emotion like this when facing his own execution.

She took a deep breath. "All right. I believe you. But that changes nothing. Whether Kendryk is alive or dead, I will not turn you over to the empress. I promised him I wouldn't, and I swore in the sight of the gods I would never break another vow to him. As long as I hold this castle, you'll be safe, whether you like it or not."

"Very well then; I won't fault you for abiding by his wishes." Landrus looked up the river. "How long will you be able to hold out?"

"A long time. We laid in supplies to last at least a year, and I had planned for more people. Rations will be dull, but we won't starve. Besides, my brother will be here before long. He'll bring more than enough troops to defeat Ensden."

"And now Your Grace, won't you take some rest? I understand if you don't wish to eat, but everyone here is looking to you to lead us through the coming weeks."

"I feel like I should punish myself," Gwynneth said softly, but he heard her.

"That won't do anyone any good; Kendryk least of all."

"It's my fault all of this has happened."

"Hardly. I bear an equal share of the blame."

"If I hadn't encouraged Kendryk, you would have died months ago and already be forgotten. Everything here would have gone on as usual, just the way Kendryk wanted it to."

"It's not that simple." His voice was very soft. "The gods have ordained all of this and you were just one of their instruments."

"I won't be a tool of the gods." She wanted to stamp her foot, but was too tired. "What kind of gods would do this, anyway? Kendryk has only ever been a good man; devout and kind to everyone. He deserves a reward, not to lie bleeding and in chains, at the mercy of that horrid woman."

She was unprepared for the tears when they came. Sobs shook her body, and her legs wobbled. She nearly fell, but he caught her and sat her gently on a step. Then he stood nearby, looking up the river. To her relief, he didn't try to comfort her. This was humiliating enough.

Finally, the sobs subsided. She wiped her eyes on her skirt and looked up. "So what happens if I turn you over to the empress? Besides your death, obviously."

He turned toward her and leaned against the stone parapet. "If I die, it's possible that the changes I've started will continue. There are many more teaching the truth now than when I began. That's why I asked you to give me to the empress. My death won't make much difference, but Kendryk's life will."

"I won't do it." She wanted Kendryk back; nothing else. She felt like cursing him for forcing her to do the opposite.

"Very well then, but might we call a truce between us? The next weeks will be difficult, and it will do us no good to be at odds. I can't make you trust in the gods, but I can pray that they will give you strength and comfort. Perhaps you don't believe me, but I care about Kendryk a great deal, and he loves you more than anything. For that reason alone, I would do everything I can to be of help to you."

"I believe you, strangely enough." She tried and failed to smile. "I won't deny that I'm tempted to give you to Teodora, and I would, if I hadn't promised Kendryk. But if I do, he will never trust me again. This is my last chance."

EPILOGUE

ANTON

The scout came to a stop in front of the commander's tent. He leapt off the horse and tossed the reins to Anton who had just come back from feeding the other horses. Anton caught them and stayed close. Something had happened.

He fished in his pockets and pulled out the last of the gnarled apples he'd found along the road. While the horse crunched happily he moved closer to the tent. He'd caught the word "empress" from inside.

"You're sure it's her?" Count Orland asked.

"They're flying the imperial standards, sir."

"How far?"

"Ten leagues, dead ahead."

There was some loud swearing and Orland burst out of the tent. Anton had no time to escape. "You, boy," he said, "Let someone else take care of that horse and find Colonel Schurtz. I need him here right away."

"Yes sir." Anton flung the reins at another boy who had sidled up and ran for Schurtz's tent. He slowed down at the sound of female laughter from inside, but steeled himself to open the flap anyway. If he had to choose between an angry Ossian Schurtz or an angry Arian Orland, he'd choose Schurtz, ugly as that was.

Schurtz had a girl on his knee, a tankard in one hand, and a fistful of her dress in another. "What do you want?" he snarled.

"Count Orland needs you to attend him right away." Anton looked away from the girl, whose dress was falling off her shoulders.

"What does he want at this hour?"

"No idea sir, but he says it's urgent."

"Bah." Schurtz slammed down the tankard and stood. The girl squeaked as he dumped her on the floor. "You." He poked her with his foot. "You stay right here. I'll be back." She nodded and crab-walked into a corner, her skirt tangled around her ankles.

Anton backed out of the tent as Schurtz barreled through the entrance and followed him at a safe distance. By the time he positioned himself behind Orland's tent, hoping no one noticed him, they had started talking.

"Is it over then?" Schurtz asked.

"Seems so," Orland replied. "Though we're not quite sure what happened. I'll ask around the villages later, but first, we need to get out of Teodora's way. The scout didn't see what was behind her."

"Might be her whole damned army," Schurtz growled.

"Might be. But if not, we may have an opportunity here."

Anton's heart beat loudly in his head. He couldn't believe Orland was talking about taking on the empress. He'd thought it might take years before that happened.

"So now what?"

"We disappear. I doubt she knows we're here, and it's better if she doesn't find out. Let's head into the Osterwald. It should give us good cover while we find out what we're up against. I want to move out right now. She's probably made camp for the night, but I don't want to take any chances. We can be at the edge of the woods by morning. Send riders ahead to scout out likely camps."

Thousands of horses had to be saddled and thousands more readied to move. As part of an army of grooms and horseboys that kept Orland's Cuirassiers in fighting order, Anton spent the rest of the night in a fever of activity. Knowing the empress was so close was a dream come true and the whole reason he'd joined Orland in the first place.

Things had been all right with the Marjatyans who'd captured him though he quickly lost track of the men who had killed his mother. But when word came that Count Orland was nearby, he decided to escape. Korma had been defeated, and it might be years before he'd be ready to take Teodora on again. Orland was ready now though Anton didn't understand why he wasn't in Terragand fighting her.

When Anton heard that Orland was returning to Kronland, he slipped out of the Marjatyan camp one night and hid in the woods until morning. In broad daylight, while Orland's camp broke up, Anton strolled in, found the horses and prepared them to go. With so many people about, no one noticed he didn't belong. Two days later, one boy asked, "Aren't you new here?"

Anton shrugged, said, "Somewhat," and went back to his work. No one paid him but they fed him regularly and he always found a place to sleep rolled up in a saddle blanket somewhere under a wagon.

Once they'd reached the Osterwald, a great, dark forest that stretched east for untold leagues, they set up camps along the creeks that ran through it. Few people lived here, but Orland had sent out scouts to the surrounding villages to gather news.

Gerd, one of the younger grooms, had the good fortune to hold Orland's horse while he debriefed a messenger. "There was a great battle at Birkenfels." Gerd relished his moment, with all the younger boys clustered before him. "The empress trounced Bernotas five days ago. She shot the young prince herself after he'd killed at least a hundred Maladene pikemen with his bare hands. Now she's taking him back to Atlona, where she'll cut off his head in front of everyone."

"She will not," one boy said.

"She will so," Anton said. "She hanged my own father, and he wasn't nearly as bad a rebel as this prince."

That attracted some interest and Gerd cleared his throat loudly. "Kronek can tell you about his stupid father some other time. The point is, the count is thinking about attacking the empress and rescuing the prince."

The boys murmured their approval at this. Anton twisted his hands together. He wondered how he might join the fight. "When will we attack?" he asked.

"Don't know. The count has sent out more scouts to find out what we're up against. I suspect he'll know tomorrow."

Anton spent half the night contriving a way to be near Orland as much as possible so he could be the first to learn his plans. The count had ridden out early in the morning to take a closer look at the empress's force himself and would be gone for a few hours. Anton scanned the direction he'd gone, hoping to see him return.

In the early afternoon a small cluster of horsemen thundered into camp, Orland at their head. Anton ran toward him and had the good luck to catch Orland's reins when he jumped off his horse. Another officer came up from somewhere else, probably waiting for orders. "Do we attack sir?" he asked.

"No." Orland shook his head. "Not this time."

Anton's heart fell. "Why not, sir?" It came out before he realized it.

There was a long pause as Orland wheeled around to see who had spoken. Anton prepared for a beating, but resolved not to cringe.

"Why do you care?" Orland was laughing, though that wasn't always a good sign.

"Because I want to kill the empress. The sooner the better."

"Fierce little bugger, aren't you?" Orland looked around at the other officers standing nearby and they all laughed.

Anton stood his ground, pushing out his jaw.

Orland came a little closer, so he loomed over Anton. "So, why do you want to kill the empress?"

"Because she killed my parents and my sister."

Orland grinned. "That's as good a reason as any, but we won't attack for a while. Teodora's got every last one of the Sanova Hussars with her. You've heard of them, haven't you?"

Anton nodded, then asked. "Are there too many of them?"

"Too many for us," Orland said. "Our ten thousand to their seven thousand."

"So we have a lot more." Anton didn't understand.

"Not enough. They win when they're outnumbered four to one. No one's ever beaten them."

"You could be first," Anton suggested.

"Oh, I'd like that very much," Orland said, "But this force isn't at that level yet. Perhaps we will be one day."

"Can you hurry?" Anton asked, since things were going so well.

Orland threw his head back and laughed. "I like you boy. Eager to get to killing, are you?"

"I want to be a soldier so I can kill the empress and those hussars too."

"Well, maybe you will be." Orland looked down at him and Anton stared straight back. "Do your job and if you live, you'll get a chance to learn how to fight, I'm sure."

Anton hardly believed his good fortune. He couldn't wait to tell the other boys. "When?" he asked.

"Soon." Orland laughed again and ruffled Anton's hair with a gauntleted hand. "There'll be more than enough fighting to go around."

THANK YOU FOR READING RISE OF THE STORM!

Please don't forget to give this book a quick review on Amazon. Even just a two-word, "Liked it" or even better, "Loved it" review helps so much. Positive or negative, I am grateful for all feedback from my read-ers.

.

The story continues in Valley of the Shadow. Keep reading to sample the first few chapters

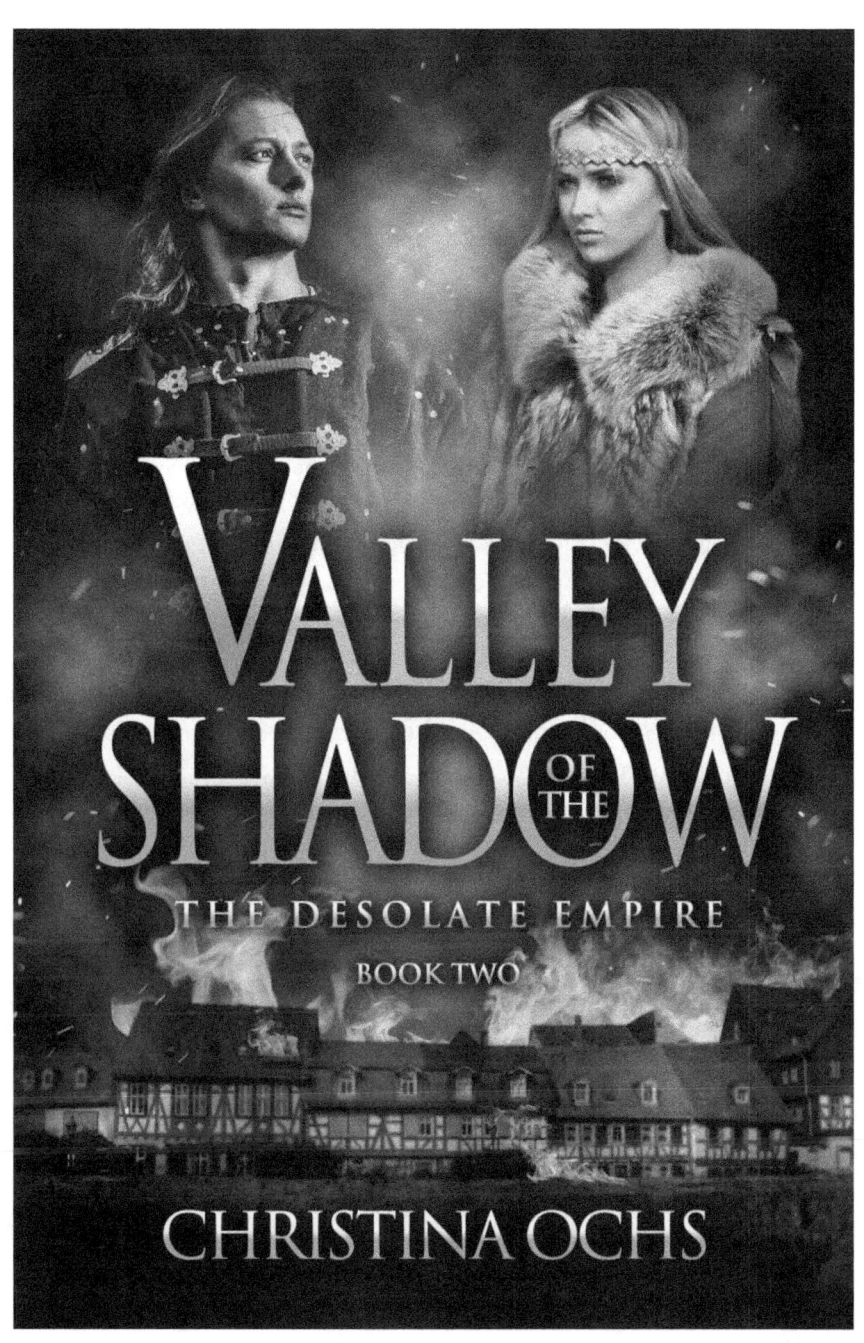

VALLEY SHADOW OF THE

THE DESOLATE EMPIRE

BOOK TWO

CHRISTINA OCHS

KENDRYK

Somewhere, someone was moaning. First the sound seemed distant, but it came ever closer, finally waking him. He opened his eyes with difficulty, feeling as though weights hung from his lids. Then the pain hit him in a wave, and he bit his lip to keep from crying out. The wave crested and receded just enough for him to tell it was coming from his right leg. Something about that leg niggled at his consciousness, but he couldn't call it forth.

Another wave hit and he cried out before he could stop himself. It was only when the jostling stopped that he realized he'd been moving all along. Light flooded over him, burning his eyes, and through a squint, he saw a face swim into view. It was a woman's, small, pointed and mouse-like, with something like a hat on top of it. Kendryk tried to open his eyes further, but the light was still too bright.

A cool hand touched his forehead and a sharp voice said, "The fever is strong. Send a message that we must stop or he will die."

Kendryk wondered who was dying. He heard a sound of protest, and the sharp voice replied, "Do it. I'll deal with her myself if need be." When the next wave hit, he realized he'd been holding his breath, and a whimper broke out against his will. He felt the cool hand again. "Can you speak?"

After a moment he realized she was talking to him. "I think so," he croaked through gritted teeth, his throat dry.

"Good," she said. "I will give you something for the pain. It won't make it go away altogether, but will help for a time." A spoon materialized above his face and a liquid slid between his parched lips, cooling his throat as it went down.

"Thirsty," he croaked again.

"I know," she said. "But first you need more of this."

He didn't ask what it was, just parted his lips again. The pain returned, but was muted already. He knew what she had given him, but wasn't able to remember its name. He found he didn't care.

With the pain receding to the edge of his consciousness, he tried to get his bearings. He looked up at dirty white canvas, stretched over ribs of light wood. He wondered if he was in a tent, then remembered the motion. No, a wagon. Why would he be in a wagon? He must be hurt and someone was taking him to safety. But safety from what?

He thought hard but didn't find an answer. He decided he might as well ask. "Who are you?" he croaked. The woman was doing something to his leg.

"Sybila," she said. "I'm a physician."

That was good. "Do you work for me?"

"No," she shook her head. "I do not. I'm so sorry."

He didn't understand why she would be and attempted a smile. "It's all right. Who do you work for?"

"Oh dear. You don't remember what happened, do you?"

Kendryk carefully shook his head. He wondered if rocks were rolling around where his brain should be.

"Hmm." She frowned. "I don't wish to upset you because it might kill you."

"You'd better tell me anyway." He tried to smile again though foreboding niggled at him.

"I suppose I should. I'm personal physician to Empress Teodora, and you are her prisoner."

Kendryk felt a vague shock. He tried to remember what had happened, but couldn't. "How?"

"You fought in a terrible battle," she said. "Your horse fell on you and your right leg is broken in two places."

"That's what hurts, then."

"Yes. I'm afraid I had to set it rather violently, at which point you passed out. You didn't wake up again until just now. I worried I'd killed you."

Kendryk's brain tried and failed to make a connection. "What does this have to do with the empress?"

Sybila sighed. "After you were wounded, the empress made you her prisoner. She is taking you to Atlona, where I imagine you will stay for some time." She paused. "If you live."

"So, I might not live?" When he said it, it didn't sound so terrible.

"I don't know," Sybila said. "The broken leg is healing well enough. But the wound around it got dirty and now you have a terrible fever."

"That might kill me." The idea didn't bother him overmuch.

"Yes, it might. It doesn't help that you've been bouncing in this cart for the last six days. I can't take care of you properly."

"Six days? Where are we?"

"Somewhere in Lantura. I've asked that we stop for a day at least, though her highness won't like it. But I'm sure she's eager to keep you alive, so maybe she'll agree."

Kendryk remembered something. "No, she wants to kill me."

Sybila laughed. "Oh, she does. But she has other reasons for keeping you alive and those will win out, I hope."

Kendryk couldn't remember what those reasons were, although he was certain he knew at one time. He was exhausted and had figured out little except who and where he was. He had no recollection of battles or horses or anything else of the sort. His teeth chattered.

Sybila pulled a blanket up to his chin. "I realize you're hot, but it's freezing outside and I don't want you taking a a chill. Try to sleep, and I'll be back soon. Her highness may wish to see you, so try not to be upset if she appears. If you like, I'll tell her you aren't able to speak yet."

Kendryk agreed, though he wasn't sure why. He was suddenly very drowsy, and the light faded as his eyes fell shut.

ARRYK

Arryk read the letter on horseback, then stuffed it into his pocket after dismounting. "The king must see this," he muttered to himself. He entered the palace from the stable-yard, then took the main staircase two at a time, heedless of the mud he left on the Zastwar carpet.

Arryk passed the guards standing at the doors to the king's personal wing as if they weren't there. He knew they had orders to stop him, but they'd never dare. The long corridor was quiet, but more guards stood before the bedchamber. Two doctors conversed in hushed tones at a small table in the corner just outside.

"Is the king alone?" Arryk asked without slowing down.

"The duke is with him," one doctor said. "He asked not to be disturbed."

"Of course." Arryk gave the guards a friendly nod as he pushed the door open. He practiced swordplay with them several times a week. They wouldn't stop him either.

There was sudden darkness inside the bedchamber. Arryk wrinkled his nose at the stuffy air, redolent of illness and ointments, letting his eyes adjust to the gloom. A single small lamp burned in the corner, far from the bed on which the king lay.

Norvel Classen rose from a chair. Immensely fat, he blocked the already meager light. "The king needs to rest," he said sharply, adding, "Your Grace," just a second too late.

"I know," Arryk said. "You should leave him alone so he can."

Classen opened his mouth to reply, but stopped.

"This won't take long." Arryk waved the letter and looked for a seat. He found a plain wooden chair and pulled it up to the bed while Classen stood, a disapproving frown creasing his broad forehead.

"Father," Arryk said, "I have more news about Gwynneth."

The king was awake, but seemed barely aware of Arryk. He turned his head slightly and his eyelids fluttered. Arryk took that as permission to go ahead. "Terragand is a disaster." He placed the letter on top of the brocade coverlet. "Empress Teodora has defeated Kendryk and taken him prisoner."

"That's the end of it then," Classen said, sounding rather too satisfied.

"Hardly," Arryk said. "Ruso Faris escaped with a remnant of his infantry and is headed for Zeelund. Arian Orland is also at large with his cavalry intact. But best of all, our Gwynneth still holds Birkenfels."

"That's excellent news," Classen said, although Arryk was looking at the king. "She can trade the castle for her husband's life."

"She will not. My sister is made of better stuff than that. She will hold Birkenfels until I can relieve her. Surely you'll give me permission to sail to Kronland now?" He looked at his father intently, but the king's face was slack and unresponsive. The doctors had said that the attack had taken his speech, but Arryk wondered if Classen had put the story about to keep others away. "Father?" Arryk asked again.

"You should not trouble his highness with this sort of news. It's upsetting." Classen glowered at Arryk.

"It's important." Arryk felt heat rising up his neck, but did his best to stay calm. "Gwynneth is his daughter, and the honor of our family and our country is at stake. What will everyone think if we abandon her? It's a sign of weakness."

"The princess created her own problems and is capable of solving them her-self. We will of course welcome her here should the empress exile her along with the prince."

"That is unacceptable." Arryk curbed his temper with some effort. "I refuse to see my sister humiliated in that way. It's time we intervened."

"We cannot intervene now," Classen said. "The empress is far stronger than she was a few months ago. I'm sure she'll meet any attempt to relieve the prin-cess with considerable force."

"Perhaps. But we are more than a match for the empress."

Classen made a huffing noise that might have been contemptuous. "I doubt it very much. I understand Prince Kendryk could match her numbers and yet she defeated him in a matter of hours."

"This latest dispatch says he lost half his army after being struck by plague."

"All the same, Teodora's force is impressive and experienced. Our troops are green and poorly trained."

Since Arryk was responsible for training, he took this as an obvious slur. "Mind your words Classen. You understand little of these matters."

Classen seemed unintimidated. Arryk was not eager for his father to die, but he looked forward to the day he could send the duke to a well-deserved, prema-ture retirement.

"My soldiers may be inexperienced, but they are full of fire. They would give everything to save Princess Gwynneth." He made a note to himself to drill them more diligently. The hunting season had been excellent, and he had neglected his military duties as he often did this time of year.

"It doesn't matter," Classen said. "I too am fond of Princess Gwynneth, but she no longer belongs to Norovaea. This is an imperial affair and we cannot interfere."

"Of course she belongs to Norovaea. If something should happen to me, she will become queen. It's impossible that she lose this fight. I won't allow it."

"It appears you must." Classen looked down at the king's still form. "The king cannot authorize any kind of action."

"You can act for him." Arryk didn't try hiding his impatience. "You do it every day."

"Oh, I can carry on with administrative tasks, but I cannot approve of military action against a foreign power on his behalf. I'm afraid you and the princess must wait until the king recovers."

"He won't." Arryk looked down at his father once more, then stood. "We both know that. We also both know that I will be king when he dies. And when I'm king, we shall sail for Kronland at once. We should do it now, before it's too late. It would have been better if we had helped Kendryk sooner, but we can still do something."

"I don't agree," Classen said. "And as long as your father draws breath, you must do what he orders. He trusted me to let me rule on his behalf, and I will continue to do so. I'm sorry you are not satisfied."

Arryk walked to the door and paused before opening it. "I'm also sorry, but I'm afraid I can't accept your answer. You'll hear from me again." He let the door fall shut behind him with a bang. Classen was far too arrogant. No matter how sick the king was, a royal family member, and not some jumped-up clerk should make the big decisions. Arryk would talk to his brother.

BRAEDEN

"Sir, we're making camp just beyond the crossroads," Trisa said.

"Isn't it early?" Braeden asked. With the days so short they rarely stopped before dark.

Trisa shrugged. "I suppose so. Don't know much except the order came down from the empress herself and Papa wanted me to tell you." Trisa was eager to become a page, though Reno and Braeden both agreed she could start by delivering messages. Braeden thought a twelve-year-old girl was still too young to take into combat.

"All right, we'll come in as soon as I round everyone up."

Braeden had headed up a scouting party since there had been rumors of other cavalry in the area. So far, they had seen nothing, but the land was hilly and wooded, and it was easy for a smaller force to stay hidden. But now, with night falling and snow swirling on the wind, he was happy to stop. By the time he returned, servants would have put his tent up and Janna would have made it warm and comfortable. It was nice to have someone waiting for him.

"Might I stay with you, sir?" Trisa asked.

"Sure." Braeden knew he should send her straight back, but they'd all be on their way in a few minutes.

Braeden told Miro to round everyone up, and an instant later, heard pistol fire. He couldn't see where it came from but it was close. "Form up," he shouted, wheeling Kazmir around to get in front of the others and pulling a pistol from its holster. Then he paused, holding his breath.

More shots followed a few seconds later, whizzing past his head, but not hit-ting anyone. They were lucky it was already so dark and that they weren't on the road where they might have made easier targets. The dark also meant they should be able to spot muzzle fire if the enemy was close by.

"That way," Trisa said in his ear.

"What did you see?" Braeden asked.

"Flames, little ones, over there near that house."

"Get behind me," Braeden told Trisa, then had Miro bring everyone else up. "Head toward the house and fire at anything that moves."

They moved slowly toward the tall farmhouse, nothing but a shadow against the increasing snow. Braeden didn't want to give the others time to reload, but he didn't want to charge into an ambush either. When the next crack came, he was ready. He saw the flash and fired straight at it, and so did several others. There was a scream in front of him, abruptly cut off, and the thump of a body onto the ground behind him. He hoped it wasn't Trisa, but couldn't look back right now. He kept moving forward and pulled out his other pistol. In the dark there'd be no reloading. But that was also true for the enemy.

He advanced on the house, pistol raised. There was a rustling, the jangling of a harness and he resisted the urge to fire in that direction. Instead, he spurred Kazmir on and came upon them as they were getting away. A few of their num-ber were hurt and trying to scramble onto their horses. It seemed their pistols were spent, since Braeden heard, rather than saw, swords being drawn. He fired at a shadowy shape in front of him and it fell. He drew his saber and Kazmir rushed forward.

Now they had them on the run, but Braeden's blade caught one unfortunate fellow across the shoulder. His armor might have stopped the worst of it, but he was already hurt and slid to the ground under the force of the blow. The rest were getting away. "Hold!" Braeden shouted. It was too dark and he didn't want to risk the horses slipping into a hole in the snow.

He paused until he was sure they were gone and asked for someone to light a torch. He dismounted to look at the fallen man. His horse had run off with the others and his breath came in harsh wheezes. Braeden knelt next to him and held up the light. "Who are you with?" he asked.

The young fellow gasped for air, though Braeden reckoned he might be put-ting on a show. "Tell me," he said, shaking him by an injured shoulder. The man moaned, turned his head away, and died.

Braeden looked him over. Cavalry, as expected, with the fine armor of a cuirassier. It had been his bad luck he'd been shot in the side, in a small area the armor didn't cover.

Braeden stood. "This is one of Arian Orland's cuirassiers. No other enemy force is this well-equipped. I don't know what he's doing here, but we'd best get back and warn the camp."

They helped one slightly injured hussar onto his horse and hurried back to camp.

Braeden went straight to Prince Novitny, who stamped around in front of a small fire, while he shouted at servants to hurry setting up his tent. The fire snapped and hissed as the wind blew snow across the flames. It was a terrible night to be out.

"I'll tell the empress," the prince said, "but we can't afford the distraction. Orland's force is large enough it won't be easy to beat. And this snow will make it hard to find fodder for the horses. We have to keep moving."

"I reckon Orland thinks he'll rescue Prince Kendryk," Braeden said, pulling off his wet gloves so he could warm his hands over the fire.

"Maybe. Or he'll try to take on Ensden up at the castle."

"Either way, we need to stop him."

"Don't get me wrong, I'd like to. But our mission is to get the empress and the prince to Atlona with no mishaps. We have to defend, not attack. Double the guard tonight," Novitny said. "Set another perimeter so we have plenty of warning if he tries anything. I'll go talk to her highness right now. Be ready to move out in the morning just in case."

GWYNNETH

There was a puff of smoke from the guns and a second later, a tremendous crash. A few chips of rock flew, but the tower held.

Gwynneth forced herself to stand up straight. "Everyone into the cellars," she said. She had hurried into the courtyard from the library after the first bar-rage. Most of the castle's population had joined her, but she had to get them inside. Another crash followed, a few people screamed, but everyone made for the stairs. She stood outside and counted as everyone went below. Just a few missing.

She looked around for Merton, pounding down the stairs from the wall, fol-lowing the rest of the guard. "Where is Edric Maximus?" she asked.

"Still in his study, I'm sure," he said.

"Get everyone else below and keep them there. I'll find the Maximus."

"Your Grace, it's not safe."

"I'm sure it sounds worse than it is. These walls will hold well enough."

"But the flying rock. You could be hurt."

"Maybe. But I can't risk the Maximus. Please, go below so I don't have to worry. I'll bring him."

Gwynneth turned away, ignoring Merton's protests, and ran across the courtyard, praying she could get indoors before the guns fired again. She was running up the spiral stairs when the next blast hit. She kept going. If Edric was foolish enough to stay in his study something might fly through his win-dow and hit him. He wasn't that foolish.

He stood outside the study door, at the head of the stairs.

"You must come below," she said.

"Won't it be over soon?"

"Probably not. They needed three days to haul the guns across the river. I imagine they'll blast away until they run out of ammunition."

"That's very inconvenient."

"I'm sorry if it interferes with your work, but you must come down. Bring what you can." She didn't give a fig about his work, but he was useless to her dead.

He pointed to a folio tucked under his arm.

"Good," she said. "Then come." A blast hitting the walls just outside drowned out her words. It was gratifying to see Edric flinch. That took some doing.

"They won't break through, will they?" he asked as he followed her down the stairs.

"I doubt it. The weakest spot is at the gate, but they haven't found an angle that can reach it. So now they're trying the other side."

They paused at the foot of the stairs, and waited for the next round. "So he's trying to batter the wall down," Edric said.

"Yes, he's trying. But he won't succeed. He's got to do something, of course. I'm sure Teodora is furious that I'm not cooperating, and she needs me to sur-render before I can get help. At best, he might hope to intimidate me into sur-rendering."

"I find that hard to believe," Edric said.

"You know me that well at least." And it was true. Much as Edric had hurt and angered her in the past, he was one of the only people who knew what she'd done. So he understood better than anyone why she had to atone for it now.

There was a quiet space. "Now." Gwynneth gathered up her skirts and ran across the courtyard. Merton waited at the heavy door and opened it just wide enough for them to slip inside. Everyone had crowded into storerooms at the foot of the stairs. They weren't comfortable, but better than the dungeons.

Gwynneth had planned for this and stocked the cellars with food that could be eaten cold, barrels of water, and plenty of heavy blankets. Hopefully they wouldn't stay here long. At the rate he was firing, Ensden would run out of shot before morning.

"I don't suppose he can keep this up for long." Merton looked pale.

"No, he can't," Gwynneth said. "It's a good show, but completely useless for him. Best of all, he'll be out of shot and powder when my brother comes."

"You seem very certain of your brother," Edric said. "I wonder he's not here yet."

"There've been complications." Gwynneth was still unwilling to believe that her own father hadn't come to her rescue at once. "But I'm certain Arryk is on his way by now."

"I hope so," Merton said. "Even if they can't break down the walls, they might break down our nerve."

"I should think not," Gwynneth said. "And please keep your misgivings to yourself. It's up to us to set a good example to those who aren't as strong. There will be no talk of surrender. Anyone who does so will find themselves keeping Count Balduin company in the dungeon very shortly." Gwynneth wished she could find a use for Kendryk's unpleasant, unfortunate cousin, but for the time being, he was just another mouth to feed.

"Of course." Merton was still a bit pale around the gills. "I apologize, Your Grace."

"See it doesn't happen again." Gwynneth kept her tone stern. She hated be-ing hard on him, but Merton was a stout as they came and she wanted him to help keep up everyone else's spirits. She didn't want to do it alone, though she would if she had to.

With the great door shut, it was much quieter in the cellar. After a while, people talked softly, and Maryna led a group of children into a corner to play a game. Gwynneth sat on a pile of blankets and tried hard to keep her thoughts from Kendryk. Whenever she thought of him, she felt her resolve weakening. Even if he hadn't been hurt, she didn't want to imagine what Te-odora might do to him.

She glanced across the room at Edric Maximus, talking with some of the sol-diers. It would be so easy to send a messenger to Count Ensden, surren-dering Edric and the castle in return for Kendryk's life and safe passage to Norovaea for all of them. It would be over and Teodora wouldn't be able to hurt any of them again.

Gwynneth hardly dared admit it, but she wondered if Arryk would ever come. Winter was setting in now and crossing the sea would be difficult. And by spring it would be too late. She thought she'd stored enough food to last a year, but the cook had quietly shown her meat already rotting and weevils in the flour. They would starve by spring.

But she had promised Kendryk. And worse than thinking about him suf-fering was picturing the disappointment in his eyes when she told him she hadn't been able to keep her promise. She had seen it once and couldn't bear remember-ing it even now. It wouldn't happen again.

TEODORA

Teodora paced the length of her tent while Sybila stood calmly at the brazier, warming her hands. The sharp wind of a winter storm made the canvas walls snap and and icy air crept into every gap. But Teodora was warm.

Maybe because she was angry. It was bad enough that her doctor had more or less ordered her to stop her entire army in the middle of nowhere, but she also had the nerve to give Teodora instructions on how she ought to handle her captive.

"He's slipping in and out of consciousness," Sybila said, "but you can visit him for a short time."

"Good," Teodora said. "I'll try not to be too horrible."

"Your Highness, with respect—" Sybila began.

Teodora knew her well enough to expect that she wouldn't want to hear Sybila's next words. "What?" she asked, impatient.

"I realize you are feeling triumphant, and rightfully so. But the prince is still near death. If you upset him too much he might succumb to the fever within hours."

"Yes, I understand," Teodora grumbled. "A dead prince does me no good at the moment. I hope I can kill him later, if his wife refuses to cooperate."

Teodora wondered if there was a way to force Gwynneth to surrender the castle and the priest, but still kill Kendryk after that. Her victory would then be complete.

In the meantime though, it was time to pay Kendryk a visit. Outside, Teodora

452

wrapped her heavy fur cloak close against the biting cold. Once she entered the hospital tent, it was warm again.

A light flickered near Kendryk's head, and she sat on a stool someone hurriedly pulled up for her. He looked quite white and she would have thought he was dead if she hadn't seen the slightest movement of the blanket over his chest. She stared at him until his eyes fluttered, then stayed open. The first thing she spotted in them was fear, but then he smiled.

She smiled back. "It's lovely to see you, darling."

Kendryk nodded pleasantly, though she was sure she was the last person he wanted to see. But it was true he'd always had good manners and too much com-posure for her liking.

"You look dreadful." She pretended concern, putting a hand on his forehead. Sybila hadn't been wrong about the fever. He was burning up.

"Oh dear, you're in terrible shape." She pulled back the blanket, picked up one of his limp hands and put it in hers. "I don't want you to die. Do you understand?"

Kendryk nodded again, though his eyes were so glazed over she doubted he comprehended anything.

"I can't stay here, and I can't leave you here either. Arian Orland's been sniffing about and I can't give him a chance to rescue you." She had hoped to finish off Orland, but he'd disappeared and Prince Novitny was adamant about getting her and her prisoner to Atlona first. It was maddening, but she knew he was right. After nearly losing her capital earlier in the year, putting her base at risk was unacceptable. Bad enough she'd had to leave it this long to take care of Kendryk.

It hadn't escaped her that Kendryk winced when she said Orland's name.

"You'd like that wouldn't you? He didn't help you when you needed him, but he could redeem himself now. Well, I won't allow it." Her words were angry, but she felt happy. She kept holding his hand. "I have good news I wanted to share with you. Not only are you completely defeated, but the Marjatyans won't trouble me anymore. They will need years to recover from what I've done to them."

Kendryk smiled pleasantly, his stare still blank. He'd probably forgotten who the Marjatyans were, even though their rebellion against her must have been his greatest hope. According to Sybila, he'd awakened without knowing who he, or

Teodora, was. It rankled that he had no recollection of her marvelous victory, but with any luck those unhappy memories would return as he recovered.

"And now that I have you, sweetheart, I'll get the rest of Kronland to behave too. Terragand is practically mine." She paused and frowned, thinking of Prin-cess Gwynneth still in her way. "I suppose you're wondering what's to become of you."

Kendryk nodded politely, though he seemed uninterested. No matter. That would change soon enough.

"You will be my guest," she said. "You won't be comfortable, but I won't give you the worst cell in the Arnfels either. If your wife behaves, you might not spend the rest of your miserable life there. I'd like to make an example of you, but my advisers tell me I might cause more rebellion if I had you beheaded. It would give me immense satisfaction, but I must be practical."

Kendryk appeared far too unconcerned at the prospect of beheading.

She smiled at him bracingly. "Now I'm ordering you, as your sovereign, to stay alive. You are no good to me dead. Is that understood?" She gave his hand a squeeze for emphasis, then dropped it and left him.

JANNA

The wind changed direction, blowing sleet into Janna's face. She pulled the hood of her cloak farther forward, but then she couldn't see. Not that she needed to. Zoltan, the old warhorse, obeyed instructions perfectly and failing those, just followed the horse in front of him. Janna fell asleep in the saddle more than once, to awaken with a start and see she was still moving at the same pace in her same position in the column.

But when the wave of nausea came on, Janna barely had time to leap from Zoltan, and vomit into the frozen grass at the roadside.

"I hope it's not plague," she moaned.

"How long have you felt this way?" Nisa was already next to her. She'd been riding in a wagon alongside.

"It came on just now." Janna stood up, a little shaky.

Nisa laid a cold hand on her forehead. "You're not feverish. I doubt it's plague, though I have an idea of what it might be." She smiled.

Janna remembered and shuddered.

"When did you last have your courses?" Nisa asked, practical as always.

"I don't know." Now she considered it, well over a month. "I thought it was the stress of being on campaign."

"That rarely includes being sick the way you are," Nisa said, with a meaningful look.

"Oh." Janna looked for Zoltan, who stood waiting for her nearby. "Are you sure?"

Nisa shrugged." It seems natural."

"I suppose it is. Should I tell him?"

"Right away. He'll be thrilled."

Janna mounted Zoltan, wincing as she did so, and looked down at Nisa."Will he? Some men aren't happy about it."

"Pfft. Those men don't want a future with their women. Yours does." Nisa smiled over her shoulder as she climbed back into her wagon.

"I think so," Janna said. "I hope so."

"Are you sure?" Braeden asked when she told him after making camp that evening.

"I seem to have the symptoms," Janna said. "Nisa believes it, and she would know."

Braeden pulled her into his arms once they'd entered the tent. "It's never happened to me before. I never wanted it, to be honest."

"But it's all right now?" Janna looked into his face anxiously even though he was grinning.

"More than all right. It's a surprise, but I love the idea of being a father, hav-ing a child with you. Do you suppose it'll grow up to be a hussar?"

She smiled up at him. "I don't see why not. Although I'd wish for more peaceful times, and work."

"You're right," Braeden said. "Peaceful would be better."

"He could still be a splendid horseman," Janna teased.

"Oh, I'm hoping for a girl. It's hard to keep 'em interested once they turn fourteen, but every now and then you get one like Franca. Wouldn't that be something?"

"A girl." Janna was laughing now. "She'll have to be very different from me."

"You're turning into a splendid horsewoman yourself." Braeden started un-doing her dress.

"Adequate perhaps. And that only because Zoltan is splendid."

"Was," Braeden said, sliding her dress down and lifting the hem of her shift. "He's rather old at this point. Like me."

"You're not old. What are you doing?"

"Seeing if anything's there yet." They both looked at her middle. It didn't look like she'd gained any weight.

"I suppose it's still early for me to get fat."

"I can't wait." Braeden picked her up and laid her on the cot. "You'll be very pretty when you're fat."

"Not too fat I hope. Zoltan will complain."

"He won't." Braeden lay down next to her, and put his hand on her stom-ach. "He's used to carrying someone my size, with armor."

"True." She turned toward him. "I'm glad you're happy about it."

"I am. Mostly."

"Mostly?" She wondered what the catch was.

"Completely. But I'm worried, too. Being pregnant and having a baby while we're at war could be dangerous for you."

"Isn't the war over?"

"Who knows? The empress is in a strong position, but things change quickly. Just think of how promising Prince Kendryk's affairs looked a few months ago."

Janna shivered and pulled the covers over both of them. "You're right of course. But there are a lot of other pregnant women about and many who've already had children. If they can do it, so can I." Though she'd never say so, she didn't look forward to being sick every day while it was so cold and unpleasant on the road. Even inside the tent, she never felt warm until she'd been snuggled up to Braeden under the fur robes for hours.

"You're much finer than they are," Braeden said, stroking her hair. "More delicate. You belong in a nice house, with a doctor close at hand, where it's warm and dry with plenty to eat. A winter campaign is always miserable."

"We'll be in Atlona for the winter, won't we?"

"Depends." He smiled again. "We can get married there. Maybe you can wear that dress again. If you don't get too fat in the meantime."

"The empress dress?" Janna poked his chest playfully. Both of them remem-bered the night of Janna's debut at the palace with some fondness. "But we don't have to get married if you don't want to. I never thought I'd say this, but I don't care about that."

"I do," Braeden said, looking earnest. "You're a respectable woman and you're having my child. I want everyone to know you belong to me."

"I like belonging to you," Janna whispered, and blew out the lamp.

ANTON

"They're coming," Anton said. "But I get Orland's horse."

"You're welcome to it," Gerd said. "You'd be smart to stay out of the way and let someone more experienced handle him."

Anton shrugged. He wasn't afraid of Count Orland. Not too much, at least. He'd seen him beat a boy with the butt of his pistol for putting on the wrong harness, and the boy still couldn't eat anything but porridge. Couldn't talk, ei-ther. But Anton was smarter than that, so he didn't worry.

Snow had fallen in light flurries all day, and now it was almost dark. Serv-ants were building fires and setting up tents, but Orland and his officers remained mounted, discussing something. After sneaking out of the forest where they'd been hiding from the empress, they were approaching the be-sieged castle and the count seemed preoccupied.

For all he liked to talk about women, he clammed up the moment someone mentioned Princess Gwynneth, and made the others shut up too. The other boys said she was very beautiful, so Anton thought the count would want to talk about her more. Maybe he wouldn't, because he was such great friends with her husband. Anton was disappointed that they hadn't been able to res-cue Prince Kendryk. He didn't see why they couldn't fight those Sanova Hussars. When he was a grown man, and a cavalry trooper himself, he'd find a way to beat them.

Anton edged closer. Part of being smart meant paying attention so you knew what was about to happen before it happened. When the count was ready to

dismount, Anton would be there the second he was needed; not a moment too soon or too late.

"It makes no sense," Commander Schurtz was saying. "The King of No-rovaea's own daughter. If he lets the empress capture her, he will look like a fool who can't take care of his family. Bad enough he let the empress have the prince."

Orland shrugged. "Word is that King Andres is ill, but Prince Arryk sur-prises me. I thought he'd be here by now, king or no."

"We'll have to act without him," someone else said.

Anton darted forward as Orland dismounted, tossing the reins in Anton's di-rection without looking at him.

"If we can," Orland said. "I want to count Ensden's troops, and see how well entrenched they are. I'm not sure what Faris is doing in Zeelund. He's a re-sourceful fellow, but I doubt he'll find the money to rebuild his army."

"Maybe he'll borrow it, like the rest of us." Schurtz laughed.

Anton moved as slowly as he dared while holding Cid who had his nose in Anton's pocket, looking for treats. The officers hadn't noticed him yet and he wanted to hear more.

"Can't imagine those Zeelund bankers extending him much credit," Or-land said. "They used to turn their noses up at me."

"But not anymore, eh?"

"Oh, I have collateral now," Orland said, and they laughed.

Anton didn't know what collateral was, and why it was funny. Then the talk turned to some woman Count Orland knew in Zeelund, and then to the count's wife. Anton didn't quite understand what they said, but turned red all the same. He didn't see why these men were so interested in something bor-ing like women when they had such splendid horses and armor and could fight just about anyone they wanted to.

Anton liked taking care of Cid, Orland's enormous, bad-tempered black stal-lion. There wasn't much competition for tending him. Anton knew how to handle him, though. So far, he hadn't met a horse he couldn't handle.

Anton got Cid ready early the next morning, but then Orland and his scouts went ahead and there would be no news until they returned. Everyone else camped at a safe distance from the castle, on the other side of the hills that sur-rounded it. They were very near Ensden's army, but the freezing weather meant everyone kept to themselves. It was much too cold to pick a fight.

Snow covered the ground, but underneath it, everything had been burned. They'd had to range far to find fodder for the horses. Anton nearly killed himself running around getting hay and oats from the wagons parked throughout the camp, but at least that kept him warm.

Orland returned by early afternoon. Anton could see on his face that he was angry, so he stood back. The count leapt off of Cid, and threw his helmet on the ground, letting fly a string of curse words that Anton hadn't heard before. Which was saying something. The clang of metal on the frozen ground made Cid shy, but Anton was right there to grab him.

Schurtz dismounted as well. "It's not impossible," he said.

"Not impossible," Orland replied, "But almost. Ensden knows what he's about and is dug in as well as any I've ever seen. We could ride right over them and they wouldn't budge. And those guns will make mincemeat of us before we get that close."

"What will it take?" another officer asked.

"Another ten thousand at least," Orland replied.

"That many?"

"Well, perhaps a few less. But we need overwhelming numbers against that position. Foot and horse. And artillery. As many guns as we can get."

"Where do we get 'em?" Schurtz asked.

"I'd hoped for Norovaea, but I won't wait for them any longer. Tomorrow, we march west. Our best hope now is to recruit whatever friendlies we can from the rest of Kronland. With any luck, Faris will come through sooner rather than later. I'm sick of dealing with this scorched earth. There should be plenty of food to the west, and if they don't give it up cheap, plenty of plunder as well."

Anton liked the sound of that, and smiled as he led Cid away.

GET YOUR COPY OF VALLEY OF THE SHADOW AT
AMAZON.COM

CAST OF CHARACTERS

Kronland

Kendryk II Bernotas, Prince of Terragand
Gwynneth Roussay, Princess of Norovaea and Terragand, Kendryk's wife.
    Their children: Maryna, Devyn, Andres
     Kendryk's father: Edwyn V Bernotas (deceased)
     Kendryk's brother: Lukan III Bernotas (deceased)
     Kendryk's mother: Rikarda Sebesta, Duchess of Bonnenruck

Evard Bernotas, Duke of Terragand-Emberg, Kendryk's uncle His son,
Balduin, Count of Holstein
Rheda Bernotas, Princess of Helvundala, Kendryk's aunt. Married to Bronson
Falk, Prince of Helvundala

Andres V Roussay, King of Norovaea, Gwynneth's father
    His son, Arryk Roussay, heir to the throne

Ruso Faris, Count of Bryda, chief adviser to Kendryk
Julia Maxima, religious leader of Terragand
Edric Landrus, Priest of the Runewald temple

Avaron Dancey, Countess of Winsebach- lady-in-waiting to Princess
Gwynneth
Linette Trevin- Baroness of Kralfeld, a lady-in-waiting to Princess Gwynneth
Edson- a male servant at Birkenhof
Halvor- Gwynneth's secretary
Merton- a member of Kendryk's household guard
Etta Darstel- a doctor with Kendryk's army
Catrin, Gwynneth's maid

Aidan Orland, Duke of Kaltental-Terragand
Arian Orland, Count of Hornfels, son of Aidan
Ossian Schurtz- mercenary officer in the employ of Arian Orland

Flavia Maxima- religious leader in Isenwald
Octavius Maximus- religious leader in Helvundala

The Kronland Rulers

Eldrid Benda, Prince of Lantura
Floreta Bensen, Princess of Brandana
Ossian Dahlby, Prince of Ummarvik
Dristan Fabrey, Prince of Aquianus
Bronson Falk, Prince of Helvundala
Viviane Kasbirk, Princess of Isenwald
Keylinda Marthaler, Princess of Fromenberg
Edyta Martinek, Princess of Podoska
Herryk Peloso, Prince of Tirilis
Gallena Sebesta- Princess of Oltena and Kendryk's aunt
Alarys Zelenka, Princess of Arcius

Moralta

Braeden Terris, mercenary commander with the Sanova Hussars
Vluda Novitny, Prince of Galeva, commander of the Sanova Hussars
Reno Torresia- a captain in the Sanova Hussars, his wife Senta and their
daughters Adela, Cara and Trisa
Miro Blavic- a lieutenant of the Sanova Hussars
Franca Dura- a Sanova Hussar
Gergo- servant to Braeden
Kazmir- Braeden Terris's horse
Karil Andarosz- a Marjatyan hostage
Zoltan, a retired warhorse
Zluba, headwoman of Moraltan town of Martiz, her son, Jonni

Daciana Tomescu- guerilla commander and friend of Teodora

Dimir Kronek- a Kaleva merchant and rebel
Janna Beran Kronek- Dimir's wife
Anton Kronek, son of Dimir, stepson of Janna
Anyezka Kronek, daughter of Dimir, stepdaughter of Janna

Dimir's country relatives:
Bora, Disla,
Dusek, Irina and Seko
Ivor, Greta and Franz Kalina, refugees from Kaleva
Maya, inn-keeper at the Sanova crossroads
Betha- an old farm woman, her son Havil, his wife Gerda and their daughter Petra

Olvisya

Teodora Inferrara, Empress of Olvisya, Queen of Moralta and Marjatya
Raynard Ahrend, Count of Marsbach, Prince of Olvisya, consort to Teodora
Their children: Elektra, Berenika and Rudofo

Livilla Maxima, religious leader in Olvisya
Ahbert Solteszy , Duke of Halavo, Head of the Imperial Council and Teodora's closest political adviser
Brytta Prosnytz- secretary and lady in waiting to Teodora
Kypris Arseo- ambassador to Zastwar
Demario Barela- Maladene general working for Teodora
Niklas Ensden, Count of Herzbirg, Teodora's primary military commander
Andor Korma- Marjatyan rebel leader

Other countries and kingdoms

Gauvain Brevard, King of Galladium and childhood friend of Kendryk
Acon Benet (deceased), theologian, Kendryk's mentor in Galladium
Natalya Maxima, religious leader in Galladium
Beatryz Inferrara- Queen of Maladena, cousin to Teodora
Ottylia Sikora- Queen of Sanova and married to Atinos Inferrara, Teodora's brother
Imperata Vittoriana- head of The Faith in Forli

The Holy Family

Osgan, the father god
Saira, the mother goddess

Vica, the sister goddess
Ercos, the son god

ABOUT THE AUTHOR

Christina Ochs is the author of historical fantasy novels Rise of the Storm and Valley of the Shadow. Her first series, The Desolate Empire, is based upon the events of the Protestant Reformation and the Thirty Years War (1618-48). Many of her characters are also based on historical figures.

With a bachelor's degree in History and an MBA, Christina uses her writing to indulge her passion for reading and research. Publishing as an indie author provides an outlet for her entrepreneurial side and she is an avid supporter of fellow authors, both independent and traditionally published.

Christina lives in a semi truck full time, traveling the United States with her truck driver husband and two cats, Phoenix and Nashville.

You can learn more about her at her blog: http://christinaochs.com or follow her on twitter @therollinwriter

www.ingramcontent.com/pod-product-compliance
Lightning Source LLC
Chambersburg PA
CBHW051328020726
47502CB00010B/177